THE BRONZE SWORD CYCLES

Book I

HAG OF THE HILLS

J.T.T. RYDER

Old World Heroism

First paperback edition February 2022
Book design by Nada Orlic

ISBN 978-82-692791-1-5 (paperback)
ISBN 978-82-692791-2-2 (ebook)
ISBN 978-82-692791-0-8 (hardcover)

Published by Old World Heroism, ENK (Norge)
www.oldworldheroism.com

CONTENTS

FOREWORD

This work takes place on the island of Skye, in the Hebrides, which are the islands along the northwest coast of Scotland. The era this book takes place in is circa 200 B.C., in what we call the Iron Age of Britain, or Le Tène period (400-200 B.C.). I have left the exact year the story takes place open for interpretation. As an archaeologist that specializes in the period I am writing in, I must stress that this is a work of fiction, even if I strived to be as historically accurate as possible while still maintaining an artistic license.

Everywhere in this book is an actual geographical location, and places that I have been to personally. Whether or not everything is geographically accurate as told by the narrator is up to the reader to decide. The placenames used in this series are based on modern Gaelic placenames. In short, on the isle of Skye, the oldest placenames are Old Norse in origin, as a result of Scandinavian-speakers (Vikings, if you will) colonizing the islands from the 9th century A.D. onwards. As a result, there are very few Celtic placenames that predate the 9th century A.D. on the island. I have chosen to use generic or common placenames in modern Scottish Gaelic, and did my best to avoid Scandinavian-derived placenames.

PLACENAMES

ALBU – Gaelic name for Scotland but sometimes for both Scotland and England.

ASHAIG – this is a modern placename on Skye, and probably means the ferry crossing in Scottish Gaelic.

ASHMORE – this is a modern placename in Scotland that means "the big waterfall" in Scottish Gaelic.

BLACK HEADLAND, THE – I will leave this somewhat ambiguous, but somewhere between Suiginish and Heast.

BRIDE'S ISLES – the Hebrides.

ERIN/HIBERNIA – old/poetic names for Ireland, in Irish and Latin respectively.

ETRURIA – what is now modern Tuscany, which, at times, expanded throughout a good portion of the rest of Italy.

HALOGOLAND – Hordaland, historic *fylke* of Norway. This placename in early medieval sources refers to Hålagoland, the traditional name for North Norway, but the inhabitants of 200 B.C. Skye do not know that.

ITALIA – the Italian peninsula.

LONG ISLAND/ISLE – the Outer Hebrides, or the Western Isles, the islands to the west of Skye.

MONA – an archaic name for the isle of Anglesey, Wales.

TAMAN – proto-Celtic word for the ground, or the earth.

TORRIN – Scottish Gaelic placename that means the hillocks.

SCYTHIA – the Eurasian steppes, more or less.

SEAL STRAITS – the Kyleakin, or passage to the mainland. I nicknamed it *Seal Straits* because the area today is known for a population of seals that often follow the tiny ferry that crosses it.

SKYE – the island of. The modern name for the island, though the word Skye itself is likely ancient, pre-dating the Norse incursions and probably the Celtic language itself. It is first attested as *Scetis* by ancient Greek sources.

SLIGHAN (pronounced Slig-a-shean) – this is a Gaelic word that is often used to designate shelly places. There are many places named Slighan in the Hebrides. The actual Slighan Hill in the story is *Beinn Na Callieach* – the hill of the crone, or rather, the hill of the goddess of winter in Scotland and Ireland.

SOME NON-ENGLISH WORDS

BANAGHAISGEICH (pronounced *bag-an-achais-eick*) – this is a Scottish Gaelic word for a mythological woman warrior, akin to an Amazon.

CAITH SIDHE AND CU SIDHE – Scottish Gaelic words for 'cat fairy' and 'dog fairy', respectively. See *sidhe* below.

DOMINE – vocative form of 'master' in classical Latin.

DUN (pronounced *doon*) – modern Scottish Gaelic generic for 'fort'.

KELPIE – a spirit horse of folklore from Britain and Ireland that would appear in rivers or streams and entice humans to ride them, and subsequently ride down into the water and drown their riders.

LEANDROS/LEANDRES – nominative forms of 'lion man' and 'lion men' in ancient Greek.

MORGEN – a sea-woman that would lure men to their deaths in British folklore.

PUELLA – vocative/nominative form of 'girl' in classical Latin.

PUER – vocative/nominative form of 'boy' in classical Latin.

SERVI – vocative form of 'slave' in classical Latin.

SIDHE – (pronounced shee). Scottish Gaelic word, also *sìth* and *sithean*. *Sidhe* is a synonym of fairy/fay/fey/faye in English. I avoided the word fairy due to connotations of minuscule girls with butterfly wings. The sidhe from folklore encompass many different types of beings, from the abovementioned minuscule girls with butterfly wings, to giants, to dwarf-like creatures, to deities.

TÍR NA NÓG – Irish for 'land of the young', somewhere in the Otherworld, or the afterlife in Celtic mythology, or perhaps separate from it.

"…I heard something, the Badb from the corpses:
'ill the stuff of a hero that is under the feet of a phantom.'"

—from *Táin bó Cuailnge* (the cattle raid of Cooley)

PROLOGUE

Let the god of wordsmithing drape me with his cloak and light our night with his inspiration. I will tell you, my dearest Luceo, the tale of how I came to sit next to you at this fire, far from our homeland, after the so-called queen Slighan and her Hillmen tore it asunder. May you always recount my words at anyone's beckoning. You are a budding bard, and your skill will wilt if your attention wanes.

A bronze sword strapped to my side, my feet caked in wet sand, the cold air on my warm face. I rode the world that day, down the strand against the Hillmen, and many crumpled before me. Even if you were to betray me, dearest Luceo, and wrought a lie from this tale, none could deny I struck true with my sword and spear that day.

In the span between Lughnasa and Samhain I had been a different man. In the grey tomb, I buried my soiled clothes, and the darkness of the tomb birthed a new man on a young day, out of the clothes and bronze and glory of my long dead ancestor.

My name is Vidav, but it had not always been so. Let it be known to all that one must rip himself from himself to form anew. Even still, as the new man walks, parts of the old one shadows him. Past features of him remain in me, just like the features of my father live on in my face, even if he is dead.

I bear bronze, a new soul, and both a gift and a curse. The latter is the ability to see the *sidhe* – the beings from Otherworld that often lurk in ours. This has brought both misery and glory upon me, ever since the hag had lured me into the hills.

Now I shall tell you how I first scaled the Slighan Hill, and why I would ever agree to the conditions the hag had offered me. I do not regret my choice. It has brought me men, a sword to kill my enemies, and honour back to my name. To attain that honour, I waded through briars of torment, deceit, and anguish. I saw what no mortal man should ever see, and all the gods above and below, and the sidhe that inhabit every glade, glen and grove, and every malign sidhe that inhabits every wind, snow and bog, could not have inflicted worse upon me. Yet I trudge on, through this thorny path, and I will free Skye from this foreign tyranny.

Now I shall start from the beginning, my dear Luceo, before I had killed myself.

CHAPTER I

Come to the Slighan Hill...

Slighan Hill loomed over the land. She drew all eyes onto her gargantuan form. She stood as a shadow in the sky, a silhouette of red no matter how far one may stray from her, ever-present on her side of the island of Skye. Skye is my home, and even if I long for its long summer days of hunting seal and stag and fishing for salmon, I still take solace in that I am now away from that hill.

The inhabitants of the moors, headlands and bays that surround her dwelled in her shadow. We drank from the streams that came down from her like breastmilk, and edged close to her during the summer when we milked our cattle, yet we all heard the tales and steered clear from the Slighan Hill. The hag of the hills haunts there, and she will eat you up.

I never knew anyone who surmounted her. It was possible; she was not too steep, and covered in a clutter of boulders that could be climbed. No one except a lad named Brennus ever scaled the boulders, and they say the hag ate him up, too.

'That strange rock's visible today – I've heard the vates say she was a princess from far away – maybe Halogoland. Turned to stone because she missed her home so much. Those vates discern the will of the gods from the flights of birds and patterns of entrails and suchlike, so I don't know if their word can be trusted on this history,' said my bronze-skinned neighbour. His sheep brayed around him. He stood with my other neighbours on a hillock, next to a cart packed with fleeces.

I approached them. I carried a bucket of flounder, freshly caught from the coast. I eyed a fleece in the cart. The breeze ruffled it.

The other man scratched his grizzled face with his horned crook. 'Why, I once heard a bard say – you know, bards remember all histories and suchlike – that she was a queen of the giants. Giants ruled Skye, and they and their queen waged war against man. But our ancestors invaded Skye, fought against the giants and won, then drove them into the sea. The gods punished the giant queen – turned her flesh into stone, like a caterpillar in its cocoon, and like the caterpillar, she will emerge from her cocoon as something new.'

I set the bucket of fish down and eyed the hill. Parents raise their children around here on these legends. I heard them around the hearth in my home late at night from relatives and neighbours. The legends made me shudder or ponder but I always yearned for those nights; cockles and crab and ale and mirthful tales. I yearned to hear them again, even though I had heard them all, and knew now most of them were wrong.

'You know,' said the bronze-skinned man, 'the druids – keepers of all law both man and god – say that when that stone falls down, and shatters, the giants will return from the sea, and wage war against man.'

'Fish for the fleece?' I asked.

The man leaned on his crook. 'Aye. You're going to need a fleece. Best have Auneé line your jacket with it. Winter's going to be cold this year. The vates say it's because of the way the geese are flocking, the salmon swimming, and bucks locking antlers.'

I thanked them, emptied the bucket into one of theirs, took the fleece and was on my way back home. I crossed the red moors, my bare feet passed through a cold stream, and then when my neighbours faded behind the hillock, the voice returned.

Come to the Slighan Hill…

The voice. That crackling, strained, near-whisper that has haunted me since the day I reached nine Samhains. It always comes on a clear, blue day, when one could watch the eagles dive, and when the sun sets the heather alight in gold, and the clouds pass over and send giants of shadows across the distant, treeless moors. That is when the voice passes through me.

'Badb! Macha! Fea!' I prayed the three names of the Morrigan, goddess of death and battle. The clouds had parted for the sun which cast a shadow over me. Slighan's shadow. I stood far away from the mountain, yet still in her shadow.

Everyone on Skye always stood in her shadow.

At the time, I lived the life of a Skye freeman, though my family is of warrior blood. I woke before dawn, went to the shore, and there I collected bait, driftwood, shellfish, fished, and then I came home and fed the pigs.

I oversaw the slaves who worked in the wheat field and garden. I visited neighbours and traded. There were tasks to do, such as fixing a bedpost here, slaughtering a sick piglet there, or cutting peat for the hearth.

After supper, we would dance and play music, throw stones, fence with wooden swords, ride our horses, and in the summer, trek up to the common grazelands to find the neighbouring girls. We often went to Dun Ashaig, the ramparted fort near the bay. The druids, vates, and bards lived there. We carried our wares there to trade, and we often met foreign merchants who told us news of the world. It was a good, tedious life; since we lived so far from the centre of our realm of Taman, those seeking to take land, power, and women rarely bothered us.

I went to Lugus' cave where my forebears smithed since they arrived on Skye. My brother Fennigus, the middle of our line, often worked hard in Lugus' cave. He was in there now, and as I trudged up the red moorland, I heard the echoing dings of the hammer. It was named after Lugus, god of crafts, the patron of our family, and the first father of our lineage.

The cave lit the dark day red-yellow. My brother Fennigus, blackened, shirtless, sweaty, swung the hammer in the smoky cave. I approached. He squinted his eyes as the hot iron yellowed. He turned, lifted the iron with his tongs, and sank the iron into a pile of coal. I watched on. He placed the blade back onto the anvil and struck again.

The world knew our father as both ironsmith and warrior. He adventured around the world until he died somewhere in a place called Scythia. It was not uncommon for foreigners who visit our island to have known him. Father only visited the island a handful of times since we live on the western edge of the world, and each time, he taught me something I have never forgotten.

Fennigus, smudged with coal, shirtless and beaded in sweat, banged the glowing iron. He stood taller than I, with dark blond hair, and his muscles corded as he worked. He slid the iron blade off the anvil and stuck it into the vat of water again, where it sizzled. The air was smoky, the ground ashy, and one of our slaves idled near the grazing horse nearby.

'We're going on a cattle raid,' he said, without looking at me. He placed the iron back on the anvil and hammered at it. The ringing pounded in my ears. 'You should come.'

'Bodvoc would kill me,' I said. Bodvoc was our eldest brother, and he acted much like a father towards me. He was much older, and he had a foreign wife. He permitted me to be neither ironsmith nor warrior. He contended that I ought to wed the neighbour girl and inherit the land.

'You need to find your balls,' Fennigus said, wiping black sweat from his brow as he hammered. 'We stand in Lugus' cave – come on, we are descended from him. You cannot fight and you cannot smith, what sort of son of Lugus are you? We're warriors, but Bodvoc made you into his slave.'

I longed for the cattle raid. It was the way of our people – we have farming season and raiding season. We farm and eat in the farming season, and then we're starving in the raiding season, so we go and take the cattle from someone else to feed ourselves – and then they starve. Often all winter we raid each other's farms, and steal cattle and then they come and steal it back, then we get angry and steal it back again and this lasts all winter. The raids had been infrequent lately, though, since the druids at Dun Ashaig made peace with our neighbouring clans. But Fennigus and his boys still went raiding.

'Did the druids approve of the last raid?' I asked.

'The druids have been acting weird lately. They're not letting us fight, not even the enemy clans.'

'Auneé doesn't like druids,' I said. Auneé was Bodvoc's wife. She was skilled in the healing arts, and had a distrust of druids.

'No one likes them. They claim to discern the will of the gods, but it's the vates that do the real work. Anyway, something is going on. Rumour has it that the head druid, you know, Ambicatos, with the dark-eyed daughter – the one with the big tits – has been attracting some strange visitors to Dun Ashaig. They have a suitor for her, but her father won't wed her. I don't know what's going on, but once they came around, the druids have been forbidding fighting against other clans, enemies or otherwise. But that Skeane boy – you remember the little mouse – pissed me off, so we'll steal a cow or two. We're off tomorrow. Coming?'

'He's not,' said a voice from behind us. It was Bodvoc. He had salty dark hair and an old man's gizzard neck. He had stubby arms and legs but broad shoulders and a back so strong you could haul three full bags of grain on his shoulders and he'd ask for another. He was huffing after he had trudged up the moorland to the cave. A hairless slave accompanied him, shirtless, with a woollen collar around his neck.

'Stupid business, this raiding is.' he said between heaves, leaning over to catch his breath, he continued, 'we get raided – then what? No boys of ours left to fight. All lame, maimed or dead. Useless.'

He straightened himself, sucked in a long breath and walked through the thick ash of the smithy. 'You're not doing it right,' he said to Fennigus.

Fennigus brandished the bright yellow blade that sparked. He dipped it into the vat of water, and the hiss filled the cave. He lifted it out, took it in his brown gloved hand and whacked the spearhead against a rootless tree stump next to his bare feet.

He had been working on a spearhead for days. Father had shown him the secret of iron last time he was here. Back then, Fennigus was just twelve and I nine, and only on the winter solstice, when the sun winked across the broadside of Lugus' cave, could Fennigus learn to smelt iron. I had not been present at the ritual, but a friend of Fennigus', Sego, spied on them and watched the whole thing. He said they both donned wolf masks so that their faces became the faces of wolves and they howled all throughout the night.

Fennigus' muscles contorted as he hammered away at the spearhead.

'It's too hot. You're too rough with it,' Bodvoc said, and snatched away the tongs from Fennigus and hammered it himself. Fennigus funnelled air into the forge, the flames stretched upward, and Bodvoc stuck the spearhead into the burning coal. Father entrusted us to Bodvoc, and Bodvoc ought to be listened to. We should have both respected that more, since he had a lot to teach us, and he was a good and just foster father.

I spotted the cairn in the distance. The weather on Skye, compared to other lands I've visited since my youth, was awful, with rain and fog and seldom can one see far away. Even mountains were obscured for days or weeks and travellers often never realized that they are even there at all. On this day, the weather had been clear for some days, which was all together unusual, and I don't think any of us had a good feeling about it. On this day, the cairn stood stark against the moors. I walked down the hillock to the cart and fumbled with the yoke.

The cairn looked as if it had struck into the sky from its burial mound, green-white bump against the black mountains, the Cuillins, behind it. Our people bury our dead in the sky; we place them on platforms or in trees and the birds pick them clean so they may leave the world for the next in haste. In the olden days, we buried heroes in great mounds, covered in stones, at roadsides, or waterways, harbours, or passes, so that all travellers may know their silent heroism. This cairn here, at the trackway, was upon such a mound. What sort of hero deserved a burial as that?

Bodvoc had followed me down, shirtless and sweaty, and he grabbed the yoke and lectured me about how to tie a new one to replace the one that had frayed. I had little attention to pay him as I thought about the cairn. It must have been a grand man under the cairn, who had left such an impact on this world that his followers heaped earth upon his body.

I bet father has a mound somewhere in Scythia. The Scythians love to erect mounds. When a Scythian lord dies, his men and horses are all killed with him and the whole company is propped up upon the mound in a grim assembly until the children of the Morrigan satisfy their palates. My father must have had such a funeral.

Bodvoc's meaty knuckles cuffed me on the head.

'I'm sorry, Bodvoc, I promise I'll pay attention.'

Bodvoc turned his sweaty, hairy back to me and marched back up the hillock to the smithy. I followed and eyed the long scar on his shoulder.

I ventured back to the darkness of the overturned boulder, where the ground became ash-softened and glowing iron lit the way. A skull was pegged to the back of the wall of the boulder by an iron nail, and I knew him as a nameless ancestor of ours. I started to sweat, and took my tunic off.

Bodvoc held Fennigus' sword now, his squinted eyes checking every detail. He stroked his greying moustache. Fennigus' sword came from the sidhe, so to say. When a young man turns thirteen Samhains, he must go and find a sword. I don't know where the swords come from, since it's a secret kept by the sword-armed boys, but I've heard they come from bogs or lochs or old tombs, gifted by the sidhe of those places. Bodvoc and Auneé forbade us from partaking in this ritual, even though it is our birthright, but Fennigus snuck out one night and returned in the morning with an iron sword. Sometimes, the boys bring back bronze swords, though those are probably ill luck, cursed weapons from a bygone before men knew the magic of iron.

'Not bad. I would take it into battle,' said Bodvoc as he hefted the blade, 'I always thought of myself with this in my hand. Another stuck in my chest. Used to think that was the death. Now I'll be happy to die in my bed, when I am no longer useful for our world of Taman.'

For a moment, I imagined him wielding our clan's war-kit: a bare chest covered in a green cloak, green-yellow check trousers, face painted blue in woad, and a reddened sword in hand.

I had many thoughts and questions, but I dared not ask.

'Bodvoc, why'd you put down that sword and take up a sickle?' Fennigus asked. 'Our father was a warrior. His father was a warrior. We are descendants of Lugus of All Crafts. Why don't we honour him with the greatest craft of man, the craft of war?'

Bodvoc sighed. 'All young men crave a death in battle, especially when it's in our blood, like us. Will you die in battle? Maybe a festering wound. Maybe starve to death. Maybe drown. Captured. Sold into slavery. It's not all gold and glory.'

The hot blood in my veins turned cold. I ignored Bodvoc's words. Something within me told me that I desired more than this life of cows, pigs, and the neighbour girl. Something told me that glory flowed through my veins, dormant, patient yet eager like a bear just waking from winter. I had to say something, perhaps, to stir Bodvoc's spirit.

'But father lived that life. He didn't die at sea, he was never a slave, he didn't starve, and he died in battle,' I said.

'That life is not yours. That Cloda girl isn't so bad. She comes with as much land as the crow flies.'

He placed the sword down on a bench, walked over to the other side of the cave, picked up a whetstone, and picked up the sword again. He nodded to Fennigus as a command to watch him, and whetted the edges of the blade.

'Nothing wrong with this life. I've given you food, and shelter, and work that is the salt of the good Danu. The land is yours after I'm dead. You are a free man, and answer just to the druids, and the gods. Most men do not have this choice.'

The whetting stopped, and Fennigus handed me both the whetstone and the sword. I attempted to sharpen the dull side of the blade.

'Father travelled the world. He made a name for himself. He is known after death. I am sure his grave is glorious, like the mounds and cairns we see all over Bride's islands,' I said.

'You didn't pay attention, did you? Far too hard – look, like this.' Bodvoc said, and pulled both objects out of my hands, and whetted the sword. 'No idea how he died. We've heard second-hand accounts. He died in battle, so what? Would have been better if he were here now. Could teach you lads a thing or two about sharpening a blade.'

Bodvoc raised the sword and stooped over, then hacked at a log near his feet.

'Decent blade, but the tang is rusty. A rusty tang means a broken sword,' he said to Fennigus. 'But a good sword. Probably will have to sell it to pay off your blood debt.'

Fennigus grunted as he shovelled some hay onto the pile of coal. Bodvoc handed him his sword the correct way that is pommel first, and left down the hillock. 'Beware the hag of the hills,' he said, an adage I had always thought scared children to come back home before dark and to stay away from the deep mountains.

When Bodvoc's cart disappeared in the meld of the red moors, Fennigus spoke. 'The spearhead is finished. I'll attach it to an ash-pole and then it's yours.'

'For what?' I asked.

'The raid,' Fennigus said.

'Who are you raiding?' I asked.

Fennigus grinned at that. His eyes perked like a wildcat's ears when they hear their prey nearby.

'The Ashmore clan. You know, we slaughtered the bull last night that I had captured last season. That bastard son of the clan, Skeane, grabbed for the thigh when it was rightfully mine. You know what that means – it's a fight, a fight to the death. I drew my sword but the druids came and stopped it, and called for peace.'

'The Ashmore lad? But they're our neighbours, and we're in debt to them. How can you?'

'To the crows with the Ashmore,' he said, and spat, then poured the vat of clay on the forge's fire. It hissed and I turned from the smoke. 'I'll pay off our clan's debt when I shove my sword up Skeane's arse.'

'I can't do it, Fennigus,' I said. 'The druids will hang us if Bodvoc doesn't first.'

'Fennigus?' a voice chirped from below. A girl's voice, a sweet voice that sounded as endearing to me as the chime of birds in the morning. It was Cloda, the neighbour girl. I thought it strange to see her now, since the women go up to the hills with the animals to milk them at this time of day.

When I heard her voice, it soothed me. She had a fringed, fluttering brown cloak over her white wool dress. She was walking up the hillock barefoot. She possessed wide, shapely hips that swayed, as curved as corbels.

Her father and Bodvoc had already worked out the deal for me to wed her. Next Beltane, after the whelping of the last foal, I will present Cloda with a horsehair rope I had made myself, and then I will tie it into a lariat, catch her and drag her back to my house. Then the men in her family shall contend this, through chasing, wrestling, and some light fisticuffs with the men in my family. Her attendants will dress her in yellow and green to symbolize fertility and maidenhood. After we win the skirmish, I will put her on my horse and ride her to Dun Ashaig. There the druid will wed us in the name of Bride, our goddess of our marriage and the hearth, and our two lands will be joined as one.

It was Bodvoc's dream, and the only reason I had never snuck out at night and snatched a sword from a tomb was that I had Cloda promised to me.

'Cloda, hello – what are you doing down from the commons so early?'

'Brennus – I've come to tell you – oh, Fennigus is here. Hello, Fennigus!'

Fennigus took a whetstone to the spearhead. Scrapes filled Lugus' cave, sandstone on iron. Sweat dripped stripes down his soot-covered half-naked body.

'This whetstone has been in my family since Cúchulainn walked Skye to find Sgàthach,' he said, as Cloda edged closer.

'Really?' She edged closer to him, ankle-deep in the soot.

'Cloda, what did you have to tell me?' I asked.

'Yeah,' Fennigus said. 'On his way to the mountains to train with the amazon queen, and goddess of Skye, Sgàthach, Cúchulainn was challenged by a young Ashaiger man, eager to prove his worth to the Hibernian. He struck high, Cúchulainn struck low, and Cúchulainn's sword chopped his cock clean off! When Cúchulainn returned from the mountains, he met the Ashaiger mourning on the road that his wife will never love him again. Cúchulainn gave the whetstone to the Ashaiger, to use instead of a cock.'

Fennigus set the spearhead down, picked up the whetstone and put it between his legs and wagged it at Cloda. She laughed, red in the face.

'Why are you back so early from the pasture?' I asked again.

'Oh, no, how could I forget! Auneé sent me – both of you need to go down the trackway! And bring some charcoal!'

I grabbed a clump of charcoal from the ground, turned heel and started down the hill. 'Come on Fennigus,' I said.

'I'm not going anywhere – I'm busy,' he said. 'But you go and then tell me what she wants. Beware the hag of the hills,' Fennigus said, and then said to Cloda, 'you're not allowed to have a dress on in here.'

I stopped.

'That's not true,' Cloda laughed.

'Yeah, it's true. Look, both Brenn and I have no shirts on. You have to take yours off.'

'My dad would kill me!' she said.

'He's not going to find out, right, Brenn?'

I looked on, aghast.

'You can't do that,' I said to her.

'I can't?' she asked, and her voice perked.

'No,' I said, somehow finding my balls as Fennigus suggested before. 'I'm your future husband, and I say you can't.'

'You're my future husband, not my husband now, Brennus, son of Biturix!' she said, and stuck her tongue out at me. She pulled the cloak from herself and revealed her long, elegant neck, her slim and narrow shoulders that just accented her wide hips. I knew I had been summoned by Auneé and it sounded urgent, especially since the women shouldn't be down in the lowlands this early in the year, but I failed to budge.

Now, dearest Luceo, when you relay this to the men of the south, who take godly pride in their naked bodies, and who know that we up in the north do, too, and when we bathe there is little division between men and women, and that I have seen Cloda naked before, though only a glimpse for it is wrong to stare at women during our baths. Now Fennigus simply wanted to see her tits.

Her dress had two straps over the shoulder pinned by bone pins, and she unpinned the straps loose and the dress flapped over her belt. She stood in the darkened rock shelter now and she looked shadow-like, yet the flow of her body and her bare hills mystified me. I nearly snatched my tunic off the ground and draped her in it, and then a great warmth fell over my face. What I would have done to both her and Fennigus, if I had found my balls, I will not relay now, but there I walked off, marched down the hillock and to the dung of the trackway.

I headed down the trackway toward where Cloda said Auneé would be. The trackway was two carts wide and nothing but mud and puddles. It stank of shit and piss and soon my feet became encrusted in it. The animals must have returned early this year. A much-needed numbness overcame me, until a dog yapping and loping over the hill and down the trackway came toward me.

It was Lappie, our black and white sheep dog. She sprang into my arms and her coarse fur ruffled against my arms, and her dry tongue licked me across the lips. I had not seen her either since Beltane. She darted off and I followed up over the hill, and there at the base of the hill down in the valley, a company of men all stood around, dressed in white robes and I knew it was the druids of Dun Ashaig. In the centre of them, a girl lay prone on her back. An oxcart stood idled near a stream.

Auneé was stooped over the prone girl. Auneé's white-streaked blond hair danced over her brown shawl. She said something in her foreign tongue, repeated the phrase nine times, and rubbed red powder over the girl's bare white leg.

Auneé looked up at me. 'Where's the charcoal?'

I handed it to her. She rubbed a chunk of it across a red wound on the girl's leg.

Nine druids encircled us. They all were older men, over fifty Samhains, greying or grey, bearded, dressed in pure white robes and they walked on raised wooden shoes so the trackway would not blemish the purity of their vestments. They all carried shepherd's crooks, and the highest druids carry gilded crooks like curved sunbeams.

The men of the south know our druids well, and they despise them because our druids are smarter than their druids. All men are dumb animals compared to the intellect of our druids. They study for twenty years on the isle of Mann in the arcane arts. They master healing, poetry, warfare, theology, astronomy, philosophy, math, law. They divined the will of the gods and all they said must be followed.

Auneé looked up at me again with her big green eyes. They looked desperate. 'I need your spit,' she said, her accent bleeding through, palm bared.

I spat in her hand.

The wounded girl's teeth clattered and Auneé held her hand as she applied the salve of charcoal and my spit to her wound. Auneé, armed with a bronze needle, sewed the wound shut.

The girl was Myrnna, the brunette daughter of the chief druid. Her big brown eyes welled with tears. She wore a green dress and a brown shawl, and her gold armrings and earrings glittered. I had known Myrnna by her long, wavy, brown hair. Our clan had been blessed chiefly with blond and red hair, and nearly all of Skye displayed this trait, except for a few clans down in the southeast who were said to have been the descendants of the island's original inhabitants. Myrnna had both dark hair and eyes and many speculated that the druid's wife had cuckolded him with a foreign merchant.

'I wasn't chasing butterflies,' Myrnna said. Our eyes met and she looked away.

'Myrnna was chasing butterflies, and she was bitten by a snake,' said one of the druids. 'May Cernunnos crush all snakes in his mighty fist.'

I thought that explanation odd. Chasing butterflies? That was child's play, and Myrnna was a woman, and she studied for a few years at the druid's academy far south on Mona. The druids rarely permit women to join their ranks, but the daughters of the druids are sometimes allowed to become druidesses, but Myrnna left the academy and returned to Skye around Lughnasa.

'There was a raid reported on the cattle up over at Cuidrach,' a druid with a long white beard said. 'And another raid over at the glen in Ashmore. We're taking everyone down from the pastures immediately. There are some rumours of boats of strangers being sighted around the coasts. All men are to arm themselves and watch their beasts. Be on guard. And you lads best not raid other clans.'

Boats of strangers? Foreign raiders? On our island?

Auneé beckoned Lappie. The dog cantered over, delved down in front of Myrnna's leg and started to lick it.

'Nodens, Nodens, Nodens…' the nine druids chanted all around me. Nodens is the god of healing, hunting, dogs, and the sea.

Lappie stopped licking, the druids stopped chanting, and Auneé helped Myrnna to her feet. She stumbled and brushed her wavy hair off her wet face.

Auneé helped her into the oxcart, the druids piled in, and they disappeared down the glen toward Dun Ashaig.

'They will claim my work as theirs as they always do, but I couldn't leave the lass like that,' she said.

'Are they hiding something?' I asked.

Auneé paused for a moment. 'I don't know, but that was no snakebite. The druids hide things from us for our own safety, I think.'

'Wouldn't they tell you since you were a druidess?' I asked her.

She laughed. 'Oh no, no! I did visit the druid's isle, but I did not like it there. It is too formal, and Druidry is too strict. I may be a healer, but I am not a druidess. But remember my dear, I am not of your kind, the kind others call *Celts*, I am from a different land, so I cannot practice Druidry.'

I noticed her wide face, snubbed nose and her greenish eyes, flecked in brown. She could almost pass for a local, but the trace of her accent branded her as foreign.

She looked into my eyes, puffed her cheeks and bit her lip. 'Bodvoc told me that you want to raid like Fennigus. Why?' She put a hand on my shoulder. Lappie, ever jealous, nudged my hand. I petted her while Auneé spoke. 'Why do you hate the life we've given you? Why do you want to go and get yourself killed in a raid?'

'I want to travel the world like my father, and fight, and have a band of brothers to call my own that fight at my side.'

'To travel around like your father, and you know, my husband, too,' she said, placing a hand on my shoulder. 'Do you know how I met Bodvoc?

'I had not seen fifteen summers when they came to my village. They killed everyone – all the men and boys. They burned down our home. They took our cattle and anything of gold and silver. They took the women and children. Your brother – my husband…,' she said, taking a sob, and tears forming in her eyes.

'And he took me as his wife, and every day I hated him. I was taken all the way to Skye, so far from home. I had never even seen the ocean before, and now I was living on an island, surrounded by it. But as the months went by,' she said, sucking in a sob, and stiffening her body. Lappie dove at her feet and whimpered.

'That day when the donkey kicked him, he was in such terrible pain and I thought he would die. I wept and realized that if he died, I would miss him, and I knew I felt love for him. He became gentle after I healed him. I realized I had no home but Skye, to suckle from the breasts of Sgàthach, and no family but yours, and no clan but Ashaig.'

I could hear the accent in her voice strengthen. I stared at my sister-in-law, my foster mother, the one who cooked my porridge every morning and my stew every night, who weaved my wool, who brought me milk, who tended Bride's fire, and who had been so mistreated by my own brother. Now we embraced and she wet my shoulder with her tears. Lappie cuddled against us.

Auneé pulled away from me and stroked Lappie's head. 'I just wanted you to know that because that is what warriors do. They travel to other lands, and they hurt people. Not just in battle, but they make widows, they make orphans, and they take widows and orphans as theirs,' she said, and grabbed my hand. 'And I don't want that to happen to you. You're a good lad. You want excitement and adventure, but you don't understand that you could be killed!' Her eyes teared up again. 'You could be killed, and Fennigus could be killed, and when Bodvoc drinks himself to death, who will take care of lonely old me?'

My eyes drifted away and down the rolling red moors. There the cairn stood, between the trackway and black mountains, and its stony crown aimed at the stony crown of the Slighan Hill.

'But Skye is covered in cairns of great men,' I said. 'I want to be one of those great men. I'm a descendant of Lugus, and it is my right to be so.'

'We have a girl for you,' Auneé said.

'And every day, must I be reminded of the cairn on our land, that marks where it ends, where my brave ancestor lies, while I spend my life tending animals and fishing?'

'Brave ancestor?' Auneé said, and she too looked at the cairn down in the valley. Her parted blond hair danced at her shoulders.

'You assume too much, my dear Brenn. Long before Cúchulainn came to Skye, a goddess resided on Slighan – *the hag of the hills*, as we know her. She was the goddess of lambs, the patroness of sheep, and warden of spring. She was deposed by Slighan, a serpent-queen, who cast her down from the mountain on the spot where the cairn stands. That is where her children, little folk, built her mound.'

'Not a warrior, or a king?'

'A hag, Brenn. And that is why no one tends to the cairn – see how some stones have already fallen over? The hag does not fight against time. She believes she should age, and her grave should age, too. So, her stones fall, and her mound shrinks, and sheep graze on it. But she stares up at the mountain – Slighan – just the same, awaiting the day for her to reclaim her throne as the warden of spring. Now I must go back home and tell Bodvoc I am back so early! Go fetch Fennigus and come home.'

She walked down the trackway. I pet Lappie until Auneé whistled for her, and they left.

Crows cawed in the distance. Their caws cut me, slow and jagged, like freshly-broken flint. It reminded me of the fate of those who did not receive glory in life. I looked in the direction of the grim cries.

The boughs of a willow tree hung low over the loch. A hoodie crow landed on the slumped head of a figure that swung in the wind. The willow tree there was the hanging tree, where the dead were left out to the Morrigan. Bones were littered around the trunk and on the reedy shores of the nearby loch, strewn about until foxes or dogs gnawed the remains into dust.

The black-feathered children of the Morrigan feasted upon them to bring them to the Otherworld. They were buried in the sky, the chief druid Ambicatos proclaimed at the funeral I had watched of a young cousin being placed in such a hanging cemetery. I can still remember the putrid stench of the tree when I went near it almost ten years ago.

Father's grave must be different. It makes one ponder the deeds of the man that lies below. I must visit his grave someday. But can I? The sheep need to be guarded, the ling need to be fished, the kelp needs collecting, the cows need to be milked, and Cloda must be married so that Bodvoc can have his large farm.

Fennigus would have loved it, too. Fennigus would have a similar grave, if the gods favour him to flourish into a renowned warrior and to carve his name across Europa as our father did.

Our father was Biturix the adventurer. Biturix the ironsmith. Biturix the warrior. Biturix the commander. Biturix the conqueror.

My brother already fancied himself as Fennigus the cattle raider. Fennigus the fighter. Fennigus the bold.

And I, Brennus, the herder. Brennus the peat cutter. Brennus the yoke maker. Brennus the fisherman.

I took one last look at the hanging tree near the loch. The water mirrored its slumped branches. The hoodie crows had been routed by ravens that now bowed to feast.

Perhaps I would be laid to rest there, my neck dislodged by a noose, my body swaying in the wind, my shoulders clasped by black talons. I looked to the east and saw Slighan Hill.

On this side of the mountain, a mundane life of driving cattle from one moor to the next remained. On the other side, glory and the ecstasy of battle lay at Ashmore, the land of the Ashmore clan.

I hiked up my trousers and tied them tight. I'm going on a cattle raid.

CHAPTER II

We sit at the hearth, bellies full of pork, lips wet with beer, willing women in our beds. My dearest Luceo, tomorrow, we ride to battle, to test our strength, skill, and will against our enemies, to dare the gods to strike us dead. If we live, we feast; if we die, we die in glory. What more can a man want? Oh yes, I haven't always had such a life. I command men, I raid, I slay, yet once I could barely hold a spear. I knew nothing of warcraft. I knew little of the mores of combat even in my own tradition, since Bodvoc had sheltered me from it.

I found Lugus' cave smouldering and smoky, but no one inside but the sidhe that guide our hands when we smith. I did find the spearhead nailed to an ashwood shaft. Trees are rare on Skye, and good trees suitable for lumber even rarer, so to have ashwood was remarkable. Fennigus had taken it in a raid and now he had assembled the spear for me.

They were all gone, though. I heard hooves galloping off in the distance and I assumed the horses bore Fennigus and his lads. I ran to Slough, the old horse, a former feral that father had broken in when I was just thirteen Samhains. At thirteen, us boys of the warrior blood are given a horse to be raised with us. I must care for him until one of us departs. The gods bless the luckiest man and horse with death together in battle, side by side, man-blood and horse-blood mingling. Most men and horses, however, do not die at the same time, and I fear that Slough will die before my time. He was old, with rusty joints and a greyed snout. At the end of his life, I must sacrifice him to Epona, goddess of horses and riders, for our unending bond.

Now I rode Slough into battle, spear in hand, bareback. I rode for an hour down the valley of the red moors. A sea eagle swooped down somewhere in the heather. I thought of Tartarus, the god of the sky. I thought of the crows and ravens I had seen at Morrigan's feast, and I knew the day belonged to her.

An ill omen, dark as death on a sunny day.

Slough reared and kicked up mud in the trackway as I halted. I was late and I had no idea how to wield a spear except the pointy end sticks in the enemy. I had no shield, sword, or knife. The Morrigan cackled in my mind. I imagined her wings wrapped around my shoulders, holding them there, unable to act as the enemy struck me down. Badb, goddess of fear, an aspect of the Morrigan, seemed to creep into my chest.

More hooves raced down the trackway, now toward me. They came from the direction I rode in, and I feared it had been the victorious enemy, riding to Dun Ashaig to reap vengeance upon us all. Or perhaps it was Fennigus and the boys? Either way, I backed Slough from the trackway and into the brush. The bracken and heather scratched my legs through my trousers as I awaited who came.

Blue hedgehog-headed spirits descended the trackway upon roan horses. No, they had been painted blue in woad. Their hair was spiked by beeswax and their long moustaches riffled in the wind. They were equipped with shields also painted blue, and had spears strapped to their backs. The first amongst them had a sword that bounced in a scabbard at his side. They rode hard and they rode past me. The woad, arms, and horses told me they were men with riches. They were unfamiliar to me.

I raced down the trackway, toward Dun Ashmore, to the Ashmore clan, to bring them steed and iron. Today belongs to Tartarus, this glorious blue day.

The smoke billowed from the houses of the Ashmore clan over the pine trees in the distance. It guided me in navigating Slough through the boggy moorland. The peaty water felt good on my bare feet since the sun blazed hot. The closer I drew, the deeper fear set in. My legs shook, and Slough shook, too, as if he sensed my fear.

A dog bayed from beyond the trees. The pines were dense, and I could not see through them, but metal clanged. I rushed Slough around the forest, smelled the sea water in the distance. Then I found an open span, a sward where a circle of men had formed in front of a house raised on a knoll. Two men faced off with spears and shields ready.

Now men were running, jumping, falling. Horses neighed and kicked. Unleashed dogs ran through the crowd. Rocks rained down from the sky behind me. Slough bucked, throwing me off. I thudded to the ground. My poor horse collapsed upon the sward broadside. The dogs barked and snapped. My ears rang and I tasted copper.

Two men vied with spears. Dogs leapt around the battlefield. A sword sheared through the shoulder of a young man and four dogs leapt clear over him.

I grasped for the spear near Slough's wheeling body. The horse clambered to his hooves and more slings slung stones from the boughs of the trees behind me. Slough wheeled again and neighed ghastly.

I climbed to my feet as I witnessed two hounds on the heels of a rider. They nipped at the flanks of the horse until one grabbed the rider by the ankle and yanked him to the ground. The dogs tore the man asunder. A warrior wrestled against another, emerged victoriously and then a spear from a third man plunged into his belly. His guts spilled out. A dog tore at his intestine, the red rope wrapped around its snout. The smell of blood and shit and piss enveloped all. Shouts, cries, neighs, barks, clangs and hooves reigned.

A horse ran along with me and halted. A hand yanked me to my feet. I followed the arm. Fennigus! Behind him, two men stabbed at three with spears and a fourth flanked them with a revving knife. The sun illuminated Fennigus' hair gold, his face and iron sword reddened.

Fennigus kicked the horse into a trot as I climbed up, but I had failed to fasten myself. Men rode in front of and behind us and I reckoned them Fennigus' lads. We rounded the pine forest through the bogs. Dogs barked and crows cawed from the trees. I felt myself slipping off my horse, foreseeing myself torn to death by the dogs and then eaten by the crows.

Fennigus glanced at me when I finally slid off, crashed into a bog, and found myself submerged. I pulled myself out of the bog, spitting the green water out, sheets of it coming down from my sleeves. I groped around for the spear as I feared the dogs would come. Fennigus had left me behind and none of his boys stopped, and I understood why. There was no time to save me. The raid had ended in disaster and now the enemy pursued us like a hunter pursues wounded quarry.

The dogs came charging. Snarling and nuzzles painted red and black as if they had just eaten burnt meat. They were big mastiffs, and in moments I'd be maimed. Behind the dogs came shouts of men on horseback, brandishing spears to stick me. Children trailed behind them, armed with slings.

I turned and faced them. I could not outrun them, not in this bog, not in this bramble, not when I possess just two legs and my pursuer, four. I thought of Cúchulainn, the hero of my people, who's corpse had stood to face his enemies. I stood there, facing my enemies, in the shadow of the Cuillins mountains, where Cúchulainn trained with the goddess of Skye, Sgàthach. The slavering dogs drew near, the spears of the riders glinted in the sun, and the children approached striking range. I took a breath, and laughed that the day belonged to the Morrigan indeed.

A horse ran behind me. I turned, and someone whisked me upon a horse. I hauled myself on, and this time I wrapped my arms around the waist of the rider. Fennigus had come back, his horse wheeled, and stones plopped into the bog just behind us as we dashed away.

'This time hold on, you idiot,' he said.

I looked back. The dogs were splashing through the bog still, but none of the enemies pursued us. We circled the forest and now we were back on the trackway and away from the enemy.

'You idiot,' Fennigus said, and he bit into me with his insult so hard I wished a dog had bitten me instead. 'We decided to settle it man versus man. Me versus the Ashmore bastard. We were in the middle of a duel and then you show up and they must have thought you were there to ambush them. We lost two men.'

'And Slough!' I shouted, nearly losing my grip on Fennigus. I reset myself on the horse and I grimaced. He had died miserably, hailed by bullets, at least one broken leg – the dogs were probably eating him alive now. I began to cry, but Fennigus shushed me and I quenched my tears. *I cannot act unmanly around him now*, I thought.

'And you lost the spear. Precious ash and iron, and all the time I spent on it, lost,' he said. Fennigus had spent weeks of his life working on it, he had infused it with the power of the sidhe channelling the posterity granted to us by our first ancestor, the god Lugus, and I had just dropped it somewhere in a bog.

'This wasn't a raid, but it resembles one now, don't you think?' Fennigus asked me coldly, and for the first time, I feared him. I didn't know why, but I feared him now. I knew he had wrath in him and I worried that he'd direct the wrath at me. But something deeper also lurked, a burning coldness that terrified me as much as the Slighan Hill.

'Two dead on our side, at least one more wounded – three dead on their side, methinks. It wasn't a raid, but it ended like a raid, except we have nothing for it. The druids will treat it like a raid.'

There were dozens of fresh footprints on the trackway, no hoofprints or cartwheels ruts, but just footprints, dozens of them heading toward our farm and Dun Ashaig. I forgot about them when Fennigus spoke.

'They will charge us with banditry, and we will face death or banishment.'

The druids wield the law of the land, as the warrior wields war, and the bard wields the fate of men. The druids alone can try a man. Some druids are judges, others lawyers, and only druids are called upon as jurors. The druids had just warned me about raiding, and now we just raided a blood-bonded clan.

We rode on in silence down the well-trodden, muddy trackway, through the red and purple moors. The raid ended in failure, but the day was far from over.

I had gone home that day twice.

I encroached upon my land gingerly, like an enemy scout. I had not wanted to see Bodvoc but wished to see Auneé. The judgment of the druids loomed, and I feared their judgment. Even if they had pardoned me since I had not attacked anyone, Fennigus had, and if they convicted Fennigus, I do not think I could live with the guilt. I just wanted to find Auneé and bury my face in her bosom and cry over Slough and draw upon her wisdom of what to tell the druids at court. Usually, we would have to pay a blood fine – a terrible garnish of our wealth, it could be a calf or a sow or grain and we'd be much poorer off for a year or more. But now it was different, because the druids had forbidden us.

When I arrived, I saw my cousin Vasenus with the whip over the slaves in the barley field. The sow rooted around her pen, other slaves stacked blocks of peat, and the donkey brayed at a fleeing pheasant. I passed the byre, where we all shit to gather dung. I passed the tunnels that run deep into the hillock where we brew beer, store cheese, and give offerings to good Danu. I passed the altar in the holly grove to Bride. I went down the stone path to our house, set on its stone foundation, its wattle-daub walls painted white, its chimney billowing smoke that was the eternal flame of Bride. I smelled that Auneé had dinner ready, and Lappie barked from beyond the door that had a cartwheel nailed to it, Taranis' charm to ward off ill sidhe. Dinner beckoned my muddy belly.

Caked in peat and mud – I was free of blood, but not of bog water.

We *Celts*, as you and I both are called by the Greeks, Luceo, have certain customs. One custom is to never enter our own home dirty, or any home, for that matter. Certain customs must be followed no matter what. We must never approach a man on the left unless we itch for a fight, we allow the foremost warrior to have the top cut of meat, and we don't hump each other's wives. These are the three rules that one must follow to avoid death, but even then, there are many rules that one must obey, for good luck and good manners. Covered in peat water and mud, and I may have even shit myself when I had fallen off Slough, I could not return home unwashed. I went to the river Linne.

Rivers cleanse. Man enters the water to become anew, cleaning himself of the grime of the past and presenting himself for the future. Rivers are the milk from the breasts of Danu, they trickle down and they nurture us, yet they still kill us when we fall into them and the hags that live in their depths drown us, or the kelpies lure us in and whisk us away to the Otherworld. I went down to wash my clothes.

I crossed the rocky riverbank and spotted the dense willow tree on the other side. I stripped, washed myself, then I washed my clothes, and hung them over a boulder near the bank to dry. My hand began to tremble. I had been numb, and hungry, somehow more concerned with eating delicious dinner Auneé had cooked than the repercussions of the cattle raid. Men had died, men had been wounded, and Slough was dead. We faced banishment or death if convicted. Yet I could feel nothing, just a knowing that I had made a mistake, and that there was nothing I could do.

Knee-deep in the river Linne, the frigid water cleaned my filthy loins. If the druids spare me, I decided to forgo my adventuring. Cloda was enough, and I could forget my lust for the warrior's life if I could wake up to her face and tits every morning. Father's life would have been ideal, but the gods have decided upon a different path for me.

A strange noise arose from somewhere yonder. Behind the willow's arbour, I saw two figures moving. I waded across the river, careful to give thanks to the river, and approached the willow, parting the branches, and there my dream was crushed.

Moans, grunts, and a hard thwap. Fennigus' bare arse greeted me as he thrust into a girl, as naked as our goddess of fertility Damara. The girl had clasped herself to the trunk of the tree, her bare breasts scraping the bark. Her wide hips and her tangle of blond hair told me it was Cloda.

Fennigus turned his head to me, eyebrows raised, still thrusting hard, face flushed. 'What is it?' he asked, with a heavy breath.

I found no words. My brother had Cloda spit like a suckling piglet. My mouth dropped agape. There was a plunging wet sound and Cloda kept mewing and it all smelled funny. It all looked, sounded, and smelled sour to me.

'Come on,' he said, between breaths. 'It doesn't matter anymore. The druids will hang us at twilight.'

I turned to leave. Where to leave to, I did not know. We could not just flee from the island. The druids have eyes all over Alba and we would be snitched on and hunted down and brought to their judgment in chains if need be. There was no escape from the judging of the gods.

'I'm heading home,' I said.

'Then go,' said Fennigus, still thrusting. Cloda had quieted her moans, but she did not cease.

I waded across the riverbank to retrieve my clothes, Cloda screaming loud now, and there, sitting on my tunic, found a cat.

We had wildcats that came to our farm to beg for milk. We fed them milk on Samhain to convince them to chase the spirits of the dead away from our house, but they could be a nuisance if they killed our fowl. We could not kill them, though, that was forbidden, and we'd jinx ourselves if we did. The same wildcat haunted our farm, normally. I did not recognize this one.

The wildcat was black with big, green eyes that stared into mine. It licked its lips and switched its tail. It started up the heathery hillock behind it.

I retrieved my clothes, still wet, threw them on anyway and approached the wildcat. It never ceased its stare with its big, lustrous, too green eyes. The black cat sat upon the hillcrest now, on a boulder in the sunlight, a silhouette against the stony peak of the Slighan Hill far behind it.

Come to the Slighan Hill…

I looked behind me and saw and heard nothing but the rustling of the arbour of the willow beyond the river. Words came to me every so often, to startle my soul, to sully my sanity, to threaten to drive me into the mercy of death. Sometimes, men hear voices and it is because malevolent sidhe have driven them mad. Or perhaps, the malevolent sidhe speak to them.

Malevolent sidhe. The cat never ceased its stare, and I thought for a moment that the voice had come from it. I stared back into those wondrous green eyes of the cat. A wisp of breeze fluttered over the waist-high red heather, and the sun had risen high. The cat switched its tail back and forth, and just for a fleeting glimpse, I saw a white spot on its chest. I shuddered but felt intrigued.

Have the sidhe been speaking to me? They sometimes communicate to men, and some of our heroes have been blessed by the aid of the sidhe. I could not help but think that the voice that enticed me belonged to such a being. I was, after all, descended from Lugus, and descended from greatness, and glory flowed through my veins.

Come to the Slighan Hill…

'Badb! Macha! Fea! I will!'

I started toward the cat. It trotted over the ridgeline. I followed and found it waiting on the slope. It switched its tail after a brief gaze into my eyes, and trotted through the heather. I followed it until I noticed the hills had grown around me. I passed a ruined stone house, and then finally, ended up in the red-purple highlands that were the foothills around Slighan. She loomed over me as the cat led me deeper into her shadow.

CHAPTER III

At thirteen Samhains, when the gods sprinkle boys with the first signs of manhood, the son of Lugus must be cast out into the wilderness. Far away from the warmth of Bride, he must contend with the wilds, brave the weather, and untangle himself from the mesh of the sidhe. He then returns with a sword that had been gifted to him from the white hands of the Otherworld, from a bog or a loch or a tomb of an ancestor. The sword to which his name is attached, his deeds echoing with the clash of the blade, intertwines its soul with his, until they depart from one another and both must perish from this world together. Sometimes, a goddess gives a weapon to her chosen warrior, a champion, her utmost and foremost man, forsworn to her and her interests on Taman.

While I followed the cat into the foothills of Slighan, the rocky, craggy, red hills, I had realized I was myself unarmed.

Now I ventured deep and high into the foothills. Sheep were strewn in the distance like ripened dandelions. I turned and looked back and saw my home, billows of smoke always twisting from its chimney. I saw the ocean, vast and rolling. Ships rolled from the horizon. Ships with sails, at least six of them. Greeks?

Come to the Slighan Hill.

It was that voice, a crisp, raspy whisper that entered my head and beckoned me to the hill. I am of warrior blood and a descendent of Lugus. Why would a goddess mislead me?

The hag of the hills. I shivered to that thought. In truth, I knew the hag of the hills was beckoning me there. Who else could it be? She stalks the hills and eats children alive.

Or perhaps she grants them swords?

The moorland stretched out around me. The heather reached waist high, I struggled to keep the cat's bushy tail in my sight, and I sloshed through a bog, all the while the sun beat down on my head. Red moorland, indiscrete, nondescript moorland stretched for spans. The sun left me battered, thirsty and dizzy. Usually, we get sweeps of rain that thrash us from the west in bursts of rage; truly, the west wind loves our island. Yet we had not had rain in days and the wind was nearly still.

The cat climbed higher, and I followed it. I trudged up the narrow ridgeline, upward toward the Slighan Hill. Her grey crown of stones grew larger, the sun beat down harder, and on a neighbouring hill, a goat darted away. Slighan's cairn came into view, three men high, twenty men abreast wide, round and capped in a monstrosity of stone. It was still far away, yet I shivered at its form.

The cat vanished in the heather long ago, and I thirsted. I must have walked for an hour. When I reached the false summit of Slighan, I came upon a terrace. I spotted a spring that ebbed and flowed from a boulder.

I kneeled at the dirt-brown spring and put my hands in its gritty water. I heard a meow behind me.

The cat meowed again, its tail switching, its green eyes glowing. It sat among a ring of mushrooms. Auneé always said rings of mushrooms were where the wee folk have their moots. One ought not besmirch it or else little folk will damn our luck. The wildcat had just sat right in the middle of it, without regard for the little folk at all, and now its eyes looked different – not the pale green eyes cats tend to possess, but a deep, wet-grass green.

I turned back to the spring. I cupped my hands and I lapped up the water from them.

Then a dread hit me like a gale. Badb crept up my chest, gnawing and rending around inside me.

Wet hands to my face, I bellowed as the gruesome feeling overtook me. Something horrid had cast a nightshade over me, and Badb grew bolder and fatter and she ripped at my courage with her talons. If only I could have run back down the ridge all the way down the mountain and back to Auneé and Lappie.

It stood behind me, that which had possessed the creaking whisper that had haunted me for years. I gazed down at the spring. What strangeness this spring was, seeming to come out from the boulder, and it ebbed and flowed like the tide. I wanted to get away and never feel that ghastly feeling again. I moved little. It was as if a giant had grabbed me up and never would let me down again.

I found myself unable to move. It drew near.

'Lugus!' I screamed and imagined his wheel revolving around me, as Auneé had told me to do when I feared malign sidhe while I slept as a child.

A snicker came from behind me. A taunting little snicker.

'Lugus is not here, dear.'

I had heard a granny's voice.

'Young man, you drank from my spring without permission.'

The terror that threatened to enclose me withered away. My hands ceased to shake, my lip halted its tremble, and I turned to look at her.

There stood a tiny old lady knee-deep in the heather. She looked decrepit, so much so that she would crumble into dust if I sneezed on her. She had a pointy chin that aimed at her hooked nose, droopy lips, and her right eye opened by just a slit while the other one bulged. Her bony, spotted hand grasped a gnarled cane and the other hung limp at her side. Tufts of white hair divided by bald spots ruffled as she nodded at me. She wore a ragged red robe, its tattered hem tentacle-like as it danced at her ankles in the breeze. A toothless grin engulfed her face, stretching her loose skin.

'Won't you come inside, my dear? Share bread with this crone! It's been too long since I've had an uninvited guest. My road is not the one that is often travelled.'

There had been no house there, and how could there have been? Who would have lived up there? No one would have dared to live on the Slighan Hill.

As if the land had changed shape, a gentle grove rustled in the breeze behind me. The sun illuminated it in a golden lustre. Periwinkle engulfed it like a great green beard and beyond that there sat a hut, nestled in the ground as if partially burrowed. An unkempt lawn surrounded it, and its wooden walls looked dilapidated and mouldy. Its roof arched and smoke signalled a chimney near the centre. The house was rectangular. I thought that queer, as all houses here were round. We built them round because the wind blows so strong and the shape allows our structures to stand longer. I knew other people in other lands built their houses egg-shaped, but I had never seen one before.

'Your face is so red,' she said, and she grinned a toothless grin. 'Come inside, and take refuge from Belenus. He's turned you bright today!' she said as she spun on her heel and wobbled through the golden grove.

I followed. I had to accept the invitation. It would have been insulting to Epona, our goddess of travellers, to turn down an invitation to dinner. It was something you must do, unless you had a good excuse, and I had no excuses. I had also drunk from her well, so I had owed her company.

Could I have turned back then and there? I always ask myself that question, perhaps daily, Luceo. Every day, I am reminded of my choice, and my foolish venture into the Slighan Hills. In the back of my mind, I knew who I had met, and I did not care. I was, after all, destined for the greatness that runs through my veins. I owed it to the bones of my ancestors to claim my sword and wage war in the way my line of men has, all the way back to Lugus. If the druids were to hang me on the morrow, I would greet my death more eagerly if I had been granted my sword. There was no other route for me but to that strange, rectangular, periwinkle-engulfed hut.

'Epona smiles upon you today, so you need food and water,' she said. Those words cut me, they invoked Badb in my chest, it was if she had heard my thought.

'Neither of them smile upon this crone,' she rambled on. We approached her door, and she opened it and it creaked on its pegs.

'Don't mind him, he doesn't bite,' she said and gestured toward the ground.

An elderly, solemn, pure white dog rested on the porch, jaw flat on the ground, eyes closed, its belly raising and falling slowly.

I stepped over the dog and into the musty interior.

'Be a dear and close the door.'

I turned to close the door and gasped. The dog's fur burned red like blazing fire. I closed the door, my hand trembling against the raw pinewood.

My dear Luceo. I am unsure if your audience will ever believe the tale from here on, but this is the truth. By the gods above and gods below, by sword at my side and by the grassy mound of my father. What I say is the truth, or at least, what my eyes have seen. I will say this, dear Luceo. Even if what I say is untruthful, or embellished by you, or by the next bard who retells my tale even taller, or if fanciful legends about me grow and obscure the original structure, like vines obscure a stump, then I can say that the original structure still stands true. Its roots of honour, still in the ground. The arbour of valour is still in the sky, and the sap within runs gloriously, just as the blood in me runs red.

I sat down at the lopsided table on one of nine stools. She gave me a wooden cup of cold water and I drank. A faded bearskin bed was nestled along the windowless wall, a cauldron hung from a wooden firedog over the hearth, and an altar stood at the other end of the house topped by curious headless figurines of voluptuous women. I had never seen anything like those figurines before. When I looked at them, the air staled and I found myself breathless. Something about them unnerved me, as if I had considered something I could never understand.

The crone stirred at the cauldron with a wooden spoon. I had not yet realized it, but I would then come to realize I smelled nothing from the cooking stew. Despite retrieving my manners from the depths of stark, Badb-fear, I smiled, and noticed the wooden bowls set for each of the stools.

'This is a lovely house, but pardon me,' I asked. 'What is your name?'

'Uman!' she said, shouting out the little square window. 'Bring me the blackthorn! Oh, how could I forget?'

Blackthorn. We never ate blackthorn berries, even though they were tasty, and not poisonous. They brought ill luck, at least.

A squirrel scuttled through the open window and ran down the wall and leaped up on the crone's robe and shot up to her shoulder. It carried a sprig of blackthorn with frosty berries in its buck teeth.

'Thank you, dear,' she said, pinching the squirrel's ear tufts.

Squirrels are red and have white underbellies, yet this squirrel was pure red, without a white underbelly.

The crone dropped the blackthorn sprig into the now bubbling cauldron. I watched her toil, and she asked me to hand her my bowl. I did so, and she asked me to fill the rest of the bowls. I thought it strange because there were only two of us. I set the table regardless of the missing guests.

'Oh, dear me!' she said, bent over the cauldron, her hunch exposed from top of her robe. She approached me, and extended a shaky, fragile hand.

'I am Calli,' she said.

'I am Brennus, son of Biturix,' I said, grasping her hand. It felt cold. Very cold. So cold it burned.

She let go and implored me to eat, and I ate. The stew was tasty, lots of herbs and vegetables, and I only realized that it had no odour. I smelled nothing but the stale mustiness of the hut. There were cabbages and carrots and onions and yet I smelled no aroma from the soup right under my nostrils.

Calli's face smiled so wide that her wrinkled face resembled a walnut shell.

'Brennus, what a strong name! You were named after a heroic man!'

'My nine-time grandfather rode with him, from Skye to Rome,' I said.

'And your mother's side,' said the crone, seated at the table opposite me. She put her elbows on the table and it hobbled to and fro. 'Your mother's side is from Hibernia.'

I nodded.

'So, what are you, then?' She asked.

I had no answer. I had never really thought about who I was. I was a member of the Ashaiger clan, the son of Biturix, and descendant of Lugus. That's all I knew and I didn't think more of it.

'Allow me to fix your table,' I said. It was customary to give a small service to your host after an exchange of food. 'I should be going, it will be dark soon, and my family will be cross with me if I am late.'

My dear Luceo, I knew I was going nowhere. I was just being polite. I knew who sat before me, and I knew I would leave with something from her. It was, after all, my birthright, as I had assumed, and as I had known at the time.

'The table is fine, dear. It hobbles! It is the shaky one, as I am. We hobble and wobble and then we never fall because we are the shaky ones!'

'Then, there must be some task I can do in return for this delicious dinner,' I said, still eating. 'Anything that you desire, gracious host.'

'Anything I desire? What if, my dear Brennus, or should I say Brenn,' she said, watching me take another sip of the soup. 'My desire is to give you what you desire? You desire much in this life, my dear. I know it. I can feel it. It stirs in you like a whirlpool, burns in you like hot coal, twists in you like the wind. I know. You wish to live up to the deeds of your father!'

'I can give you what you want, my dear.'

Her eyes vexed me. Two abysses. That dreadful feeling, unsurmountable, the phantasm presence that stalked behind me as I drank from the spring before I met the old woman. The invisible thing at which dogs barked at in the night, which sent sheep braying across the moors, which piqued the interest of wildcats when they stare idly at the nothing on the wall. That was what sat across from me, its eyes on me, cold, pallid hands folded neatly, now with a red sunburst behind her head.

'It's you!' was all I could manage. The red glow behind her head flittered, as red as the sunset.

I gripped the edge of the table as my body trembled, my bare feet rumbling against the hard dirt floor.

'Badb – Macha – Fea!' The sunburst behind her head glowed deeper. 'You're the hag of hills!'

'Maybe so,' she said, nonchalantly. 'But I am the solution to your troubles, my dear. I am a giver, and a receiver. I can give you what you want, for a price. My dear, you have little choice but to accept my offer. It is either you accept my gift, or you will receive death.'

She was after all, right. Fennigus, the boys and I had committed a grave crime. We faced a trial that would result in death or banishment. I figured we would receive death, since men had died and we were warned not to raid anymore just hours beforehand. Even if we were pardoned, somehow, what more was there left for me? Fennigus had humped my girl. There was nothing to do but to accept the offer of the hag of the hills.

'Then I accept,' I said, and held out my hand for the sword.

'I knew you would,' she said, and took my hand in her bony, cold grasp. She opened her mouth to display a set of jagged, red teeth, like rusty iron daggers. 'And just in time for the guests!'

Beware the hag of the hills.

She'll eat you alive…

I ripped my hand from her, and bolted up off the stool. I pointed a finger at her, somehow finding my courage, and I shouted.

'Evil! I don't accept!'

'You have already,' she said, her grin wider and her teeth sharper and the sunburst behind her brighter.

My mouth parted as if to scream. Stark, screaming Badb clawed at me and I nearly pissed myself. Then I saw two childlike hands place a bowl of soup in front of me.

I looked down and saw a bearded, human-like thing in a brown conical hat, a green tunic and curled shoes. He took a bow, and sat on the stool to my right. He started slurping his soup, shredded carrots stuck in his white beard.

'The sidhe have joined us,' said the hag.

The sidhe linger around us all the time. They inhabit every tree, boulder, waterfall, stream, hillock. They live in the water and the wind and the fire and in the soil and the sky. They have their own world, the sidhe-world, where they mostly dwell, but they also dwell in Otherworld where us mortals go when we die. They inhabit the mounds of our forebears, the cairns of our ancestors, and the hearths of our homes. Some help us around the house while we sleep, others kill us while we sleep, some strike us dead in the fields, yet others aid us in the fields. Some haunt the moors and they pull you into their homes. Some inhabit the river in the forms of white horses that lure you onto their backs and race through the water until you drown. Others wear the skins of seals and some are beautiful women that when men fall in love with them, they are taken down to sidhe-land and there they live happily forever, except the man can never return from there. They are all around us and enliven every facet of our being. Some are cats, some are dogs, some are birds, some are fish, and some are gods, chief of all, our goddess Bride is the sidhe-queen.

Now the sidhe sat in the empty stools. Three squat men in green conical hats with beards over misshapen faces stared at me. A woman clad in a white dress, straight blond hair that caressed her bosom and warm owl-like blue-eyes met my eyes, then giggled and turned away. She was beautiful, probably more so than any human woman I have ever seen, and I steered my eyes from her since I knew if I gazed too long, I'd fall in love and want to follow her to the sidhe-land in the ocean, where I'd drown. Then there was a handsome man, with a strong chin, and chin-length blond hair. He seemed too large to be seated there, or seated in the hut, for it was as if he had been larger than the hut, but when I looked at him, everything around him grew larger. I took my eyes off him like the rest, and kept them on my refilled bowl of soup.

'The soup! The damned soup!' I shouted. All the guests glared at me at once. I was an impolite guest, and they disapproved.

'Not the soup, deary,' the hag said.

'You drank from the sidhe spring, didn't Auneé tell you to never drink from a brown spring in the mountains? And to beware of the hag of the hills?' she said, as she held her spotty, bony hand to her mouth and giggled.

I stuttered, stammered, and swallowed.

'These are sidhe?'

Very few claim to have seen the sidhe, and even fewer have believable tales. The sidhe are the unseen, those that move after we have left, they who speak lower while we speak high, and they who churn our fate in their own little ways. Now I sat among seven of them eating, as the guests of the hag of the hills.

'Indeed, they are the sidhe, now take a seat, my dear. It is rude to stand up while others sit,' she said.

My trembling hand snatched the now trembling stool and I placed it and sat down, still, knees buckled, slow-moving, trembling hands gripping the brash edge of the wooden table.

I quenched Badb's fear in my chest. I needed answers. I kept my eyes off the sidhe for they scared me, and though the hag was not much better to look at, her hunched posture and calm demeanour somehow endeared her to me.

'What have you done to me?'

'There are many worlds, my dear. You live in your world, and the sidhe live in theirs. Some of those in your world can feel the sidhe. They can feel them like they can feel the wind, they cannot see but they can feel. Now a few of them can hear the sidhe, and even fewer can see them, and even fewer can see them when they want to, and just a wee amount can speak to them. But now you can do all, because I have given that power to you.

'I can walk both your world and theirs. I am a sidhe-walker, and now so are you, since you have drunk from my spring!'

I roused in my seat.

'You've spoken to me! You have been for years! It is you!'

She flashed a grin of jagged red.

'You are right. I have been speaking to you since you began to desire a different life than what was destined for you, and I did lead you there. There in the boggy ground, you sealed your fate in blood. Fate has two choices, but there is a third way. I will weave you a new fate because you burn for the life of the warrior. Your choice now is to follow my path or you will die.'

I flinched. My eyes met her stretchy face. I worried for the fate of my soul, now bound to such a hag. Sickness overcame me, Badb chewing up all my insides with her long, doubt-inducing fangs. Should I be seeing the sidhe? Should mortal men walk Taman wielding such a power? What will come of all of this? Death, perhaps, is an easier solution.

My hair touched the soup in my bowl. I now pined for my old life. Right then, we would have been eating dinner and hunted out to the moors. Instead, I dine with the hag of the hills and her sidhe guests. I missed my old life, missed it dearly, my life right before I had blundered and ruined the raid and sullied my name forever.

Sullied my name forever. No. There was a chance.

'Are you choosing death, my dear?' she asked. I looked up. The sunburst behind her head returned.

'No,' I said, finding my courage in the face of her jagged, red shark-teeth. 'Give me what I want.'

'I will, my dear,' she said. 'I will give you the life you desire for a price.'

'What is the price?' I asked.

'The sidhe will guide you. They will guide your path, and that path of yours will be the warrior's path. You will know all the pride and the pain, the death and honour, all the blood and battle, and the gold, and glory, and girls. That is what you want. Now go home and face the druids with comfort in knowing they shall not grant you death – go on the new thread we spin for you. Go home, I am sure Bodvoc is worried!'

Peril lingered, I ought to listen to her, I thought, before she changes her mind and just strikes me dead then and there.

I stood up, took a bow, and thanked the guests for their company. I turned to leave and the hag spoke.

'And my dear,' said the hag, and now her eyes glowed red.

'Beware the hag of the hills!'

Laughter erupted all around me. I looked and all the guests laughed, the three odd little men, the enchantress, and that giant of a man, all of them laughed heartily and deep and at me. The hag the foremost belted a shrieking laughter.

I opened the door and closed it behind me. The white, overweight dog pulled himself halfway up, and lazily laid back down, grunting on his way like a tired grandfather. I stepped over him. He had red ears.

Cu sidhe, I thought. A sidhe dog that men see before they die.

My legs carried me away, pacing through the golden grove. I found myself back on the scree path and then I wondered: did I die? Did the witch that haunts the fields when the sun is at its peak strike me dead? Did I never return from the raid, and this was all some nightmare of death?

The grove shimmered golden in the setting sun. The grass swayed in the wind near the apple tree, and I took solace in the serene sight, until I turned and saw the hag's hut missing. I saw a rocky outcrop of a steep hill and nothing more.

A quartet of shadows had been cast upon the golden grove, and I looked up at the hill above me and there four giant figures tottered betwixt the tall rock stacks. They were men, thrice the size of humans, with long lanky legs, scraggly black hair tasselled over loose skin, and garnished in nothing but tattered loincloths. They carried something gargantuan on their shoulders, and before they passed from my sight, I saw that they carried the hag's hut on their shoulders like a litter. A chill jolted down my spine, and a raven cawed from the heights of the tallest tree in the grove.

I found my legs and fled, passing the mountain spring from which I drank before, and started down the scree pass to the valley below.

Scraps of wool on the path wrapped around twigs like ghosts in the wind evidenced that it was a shepherd's path, and it must lead out of the mountains. I headed westward to get back to my pasture. They all must have been worried sick about me, perhaps more than they were angry at me for the misdeed of the morning, and more worried than anxious about the outcome of the judgment of the druids.

I left the Slighan Hill, with a heart excited that there was truth in the hag's claim, that I did not face death at the hands of the druids' trial – and that the life destined for me had now been granted to me.

For a price...

Dozens of feet were shuffling down the scree path below me. Throngs of men marched from the east down the pass.

I hid behind a boulder. It had been split in half as if by some great strike. I crouched down behind it, hidden like a lynx watching a hare. There was nothing normal about dozens of men in these hills. I spied a copious number of men. They had spears, sticking up from the crowd of them like beanstalks. When the men hiked up the path that ascended the hill toward me, I studied their equipment. They wore wooden armour, clamped together by leather thongs, and painted yellow and green. They were garnished in bones hanging from their ears and around their necks, and feathers fluttered from their grey flint spearpoints. Some had stone maces, polished black, others wielded flint daggers knapped so sharp and smooth that they gleamed in the sun. A steady drumbeat heralded their march and I knew they marched for war.

They all possessed dark hair, almost colourless in the sun. They were like Myrnna, brunettes. They must have been foreigners, there in the Slighan Hills, marching toward Dun Ashaig. But where was their iron? All men of the world use iron for weapons. Lugus had granted us that knowledge, and we no longer had much use for bronze or stone tools or weapons. I had never seen such weapons before, save the stone ax head or mace head that popped out of the ground when we ploughed the fields back home. We reckoned those to be the weapons of the sidhe. And where did they get the wooden armour? We never wore armour, we thought only cowards needed armour. We guarded ourselves with our swords and shields and the bodies good Danu bestowed upon us at birth.

Could these be sidhe? Armed sidhe? Are they just foreigners?

I remained hidden. The dark-clad company passed and melded into the moors. The drumbeat rat-a-tatted from the far distance.

Home. I must head home.

Go home…

CHAPTER IV

I fled out of the hills. I raced across the untamed moorland. I jumped over the earthwork that separated my farm from the next, evaded a bog and found myself near the trackway.

A horseman galloped down the trackway. He recognized me. It was Vasenus, my cousin, who lived with us, and had been up in the foothills hunting. He was a simple lad with an innocent chubby face. He loved trapping and took great pride in his collection of fox skins. His father once purchased for him the services of a Greek whore and he didn't know what to do with her, so he's been on the receiving end of many jokes from his brothers. We grew up together, and we hunted and fished and farmed together.

His face was scrounged, his eyes daft, and he rode his horse hard toward me.

'Brenn! We're under attack!' He shouted.

That brunette, dark-clad, flint-wielding company. It must be.

'Where did they come from?' I asked as Vasenus slowed his horse down in front of me, the musk of the horse deep and its hooves kicking up mud all over me.

'They came from the hills!'

And from that moment on, we called them *Hillmen*, misnomer or not.

I vaulted up the horse and gripped onto Vasenus' waist and he fled down the trackway, toward our pasture.

Bodvoc. Auneé. Fennigus. I thought of them all while Badb crept up my chest. I hoped Fennigus was home. I knew he would fight valiantly and kill thrice as many men before they killed him. The horrid visage of the hag and her sidhe guests and the dog all white with red ears all piled upon me.

Vasenus spoke, and I straightened my back.

'I saw them fighting with the Kualhan boys... their house was on fire! There were so many of them! They shot arrows at me! I saw more of them coming out of the hills, and then I saw more running down the trackway, moving some clan women and children and cattle!'

'A cattle raid?' I asked, but Vasenus did not answer.

'Cattle raiders, from where?'

Vasenus shook his head.

'The Long Island?' I asked, but did not know. The Long Island were the islands across the Minch, the sea, but the men there were like us and probably distant relatives. We lived on Skye, and all these islands are part of the Hebrides. The islands were all named after Bride, and we were all kin around her fire, her islands like seats around her warmth. The men of the Long Isle were indebted to us, to fight for us when we light our roofs on fire, as beacons to beckon them over, and we them, if either of our people faced a foreign threat.

We passed the cairn. It was devoid of sheep and its stones had tumbled even more than the last time I had seen it. Our wooden byre came into view, and beyond it I could see the shade of our house, smoke billowing from its chimney. It was not on fire. Perhaps there was still hope.

We must fight, I thought. It is what my father would have wanted. Vasenus was younger than myself and he was no warrior, as he was from the simple yeomen of my mother's side, but he was still kin. What would my father have done? What would the warrior buried under the cairn have done? What would Fennigus?

'Let me off,' I said, 'go and find your family and slaves, arm them all with whatever you can. I'm going to run home and get Bodvoc and Fennigus and the slaves and we're going to meet back here, and defend our home together!'

Vasenus looked back at me, his chubby face flustered, mouth agape. He nodded, the horse slowed then stopped, and I jumped off as he sped toward the byre.

He neared the byre. He shouted out suddenly, a shout sudden, loud and violent that the horse fled.

Vasenus flew off the horse, fell on his shoulder, scrambled to his feet and flung the wooden doors open. He fell to the floor and I saw him huddled against a body lying on its back amid other bodies all lying in a pool of blood and viscera, like lilies in a pond.

'Pappa! Wake up, pappa! Get up, pappa, please!'

Tears began to well in my eyes. That was my great uncle.

'Bodvoc! Auneé! Fennigus!'

I bolted across the darkening pasture. The setting sun streaked the sky red and now overcast.

No one responded to me.

Vasenus screamed behind me in the distance. 'They're all dead!'

I shouted the names of some of our slaves. No response.

'Lappie! Lappie! Come here girl, come here!' I shouted so hard my throat clenched. Lappie did not come trotting toward me, tongue lolled and tail wagging like she always did.

I saw neither her nor the slaves.

The roundhouse was in sight and my heart raced, my breaths heavy. The pigsty was bare. The horse was gone, so was the donkey, and the ducks.

'Fennigus! Fennigus, where are you? Bodvoc! Auneé! Lappie! Somebody!'

The pasture was barren. I came to the shed to find it ransacked. I rushed down the stone pathway toward my house.

'Auneé! Auneé! Answer me, please! Lappie! Lappie! Come here, girl!'

No response. When I reached the portico of my home, I knew why there was no response.

Three bodies lay outside my home, scattered around the entrance, and there were more bodies lying inside. The light was too low to tell who they were.

I stood, heart-pounding, breath sapped, eyes twitching. The grass had drunk so much blood that it squished under my bare feet.

I drew closer, fist clenched, weary that *they* may still be lurking.

Our door had been battered into splinters. Lugus' wheel had been smashed beneath it. Blood hung heavy in the air. Three men lay dead inside. One had a broken spear that stuck up from him like a banner. Another had his chest slashed open. The third had his forearm torn asunder, veins hanging out.

Right behind the doorway, Bodvoc laid stiff on his back, an iron sword planted in his ribcage. Next to him laid Lappie, splayed out, her white fur stained red, her bloodied snout in an eternal snarl with a chunk of flesh in her fangs. Surrounding them laid four of the slaves, two with bludgeoned heads, one with his viscera spilled out, and another shot in the head with an arrow.

My brother, the slaves and Lappie had given the Hillmen a fight. They felled three of the enemy before their defeat.

I stood still and silent and stared at the corpses. A thundercloud of crows flew over my home, pealing wingbeats, and raining caws. This shook me out of my surprise and now I fell by my eldest brother's side.

Bodvoc had been struck in the jaw by something that crushed it. It disfigured his handsome face into a gory mess of shattered bone and broken teeth. I shut his eyelids over his glassy eyes.

My dear Luceo. You are from Hibernia and I from Alba, but we both share the same mores. We both know that a man should die not too early or too late. A man who dies early never reaches his potential, while a man who dies late will become a mockery of himself. Bodvoc, in a mess of blood and gore, held a manliness that impressed me. He stood at the house entrance like a stalwart watchman and only allowed the enemies over his dead body.

Bodvoc, my brother, you died not a moment too early or a moment too soon.

I kneeled beside Lappie. My eyes welled up because I knew I would never wake up to her bad dog breath again. I quenched those tears.

Lappie was centred in the entryway and had separated her pack from the enemies. She looked more vicious in death than she ever had in life. Dogs protect our homes in life, and protect them from malign spirits in death. Now she would lay here, frozen in her time, a ward against all malign sidhe that would ever dare venture to my home.

I kneeled beside each slave and closed their eyes. They died in yoke, but their loyalty and bravery allowed them to die as free men.

The enemies all had dark hair and strange dark clothing. They looked like the men from the hills. They had no weapons with them now and I assume their comrades had taken them. By the fact that they had left their corpses in my house, their comrades must have acted in haste. Kill all the men and take all the women, children, and animals.

I shouted for Fennigus and Auneé. I vaulted up the ladder to the loft and saw only bloody footprints. Downstairs, the hearth still blazed, but the peat had not been fed into it for some time. I raced outside. I checked the slave's quarters, the paddock, the long underground shaft where we stored our dairy and brewed beer, and the barn where we shat. I did not find anyone – Auneé, Fennigus, any of my other family members, or the remaining slaves.

Invaders. They had come and ravaged our land, and who knew who was still alive? I thought, *I must head to Dun Ashaig. Maybe, just maybe the druids have mustered a defence. There was no time to bury the bodies of my brother, dog, or the slaves. I must go now, I told myself. I will get Vasenus and we will revenge upon my enemies.*

I returned home. I placed my foot on my brother's shoulder, and tried to draw the sword out from his chest. It was the iron sword that he had sharpened just yesterday. I moaned. It was horrible. His body pulled up with my sword and slid off. The blade shimmied from his ribs. My brother's body slopped down on the hard dirt floor in a thud.

The blade was smeared in blood. I approached our altar in the rear of the house, head bowed, where my great-great-great grandfather rested in the form of his grinning skull. I smeared Bodvoc's blood on his bony cheeks and prayed for his valour to visit me. I left him and returned to Bodvoc, and placed him in the position of the unborn with his hands in front of him. Now I saw he had a swordbelt and scabbard. He had been prepared for the fight, at least. I took the belt and scabbard and fitted them around me. I also took his shoes and to my surprise, they fit fine.

'Thank you for the gifts, brother. We will kill our enemies together now.'

I left home, stroked Lappie's bloody neck and left her to guard the entry. I had no time to bury them. Bodvoc, Lappie and the slaves ought to have a mound on our property so that when all pass down the trackway they know that the dead there had done great deeds. If I am to survive long enough, I shall build them just that.

I searched the pasture again, fearing I may have missed bodies lying in the heather in the low light of dusk. Auneé and Fennigus were still missing and I found neither them nor anyone else. I returned to the byre to find Vasenus.

'Come on, Vasenus! We're going to Dun Ashaig!' I called out and retrieved the horse he had ridden on. A sickening, consistent creaking noise interrupted the silence that juxtaposed the slain bodies in the byre.

There, a shadow swayed to and fro inside the structure. When I drew nearer, I saw a belt hanging from a bowing ceiling plank, wrapped around the limp neck of Vasenus.

Perhaps it was a good idea. Don't give the enemy the satisfaction of killing you. No, I will kill at least one Hillman before they kill me. I will honour the death of Bodvoc by iron.

Horsed, I galloped down toward trackway Dun Ashaig in the last dark blue light of the day. The full moon already shined bright. I unsheathed the crimson-splattered iron sword and painted my face red with it. I raised the sword to the moon, and swore to Epona, who rides her silver horse to lighten the darkest night.

The gloomy moors encroached on both my flanks as I rode down the dark trackway. A flock of geese flew overhead, a horde of black silhouettes in the dark blue sky. It was an omen, of course, but I remain ignorant in that craft. The moon lightened the trackway into a slithering white snake through a sea of dark moorland, nondescript, harrowing in its indistinction. I hated how I could not tell one bush from the next, or what type of tree lurked out in the valley, and above all Slighan still loomed, a dark knuckle. I knew the hag lurked out there somewhere. She had left the mountains in her hut carried out on the backs of four giants, and after that came the Hillmen with their queer weapons and armour that killed my family and forever robbed me of the life I had.

I can give you the life you want…

For a price.

She'll eat you alive.

Was this the price? The crisp autumn wind reminded me of the dry blood on my face. Was this blood the price of this life? Had the pact I sealed with the hag brewed this evil?

I couldn't fathom it. I had no time. There is little time when revenge beckons.

That poor horse rode hard. When the trackway veered off into the open moorland between the hills and sea, the full moon illuminated scores of men across the moors.

Black silhouettes like scores of minnows swarmed across the moorlands. They had fires that glowed red in pockets like fireflies. I could hardly make out individuals, just clusters of shadows. Some crept around the fires like moths to lights, and they strolled horseless. Above them, on the promontory, Dun Ashaig sat.

Dun Ashaig had been built in the dim days of our ancestors, by Vitellius, the first ancestor of mine to reach these shores. He and his men invaded the island, defeated the inhabitants and drove them deep into the hills. They constructed the fort and the enemy counterattacked and besieged it. Vitellius and the men held out for nine days and nights, and on the tenth day, Vitellius rode down from its great trackway and they all rolled over the enemy in tidal waves. They drove the enemy into the ocean and feasted all night on Dun Ashaig.

Now, Dun Ashaig was the centre of our clan. It had a cluster of houses where craftsmen produce, a grove to Cernunnos that the god himself is said to walk through, and the druids reside there. We went there for our four seasonal festivals, weddings, funerals. Our druids met foreign dignitaries there, and much commerce occurs. It was still a fort, and indeed, stone ramparts fortified it, and Vitellius' grinning skull hung from the centre of its entryway to guard against all ill spirits.

The Hillmen had besieged it.

The poor horse I had ridden so hard now became a target. I turned the horse around, hopped off, and slapped its rear hard with the flat of my blade to send it away down the trackway.

I waited in the dark off the trackway in the heather. The moon which had lit my way and showed me the hundreds of enemies in the fields around Dun Ashaig might have given me away, so I waited for clouds to obscure it so I could reach Dun Ashaig unnoticed. It was besieged, but I knew of a hidden way inside, a cavern with a tight mouth that I could squeeze through and climb up the well. Perhaps the Hillmen had discovered this, but it was my only shot at getting inside Dun Ashaig. I had not the foggiest idea what to do besides that, but I could not leave my homeland while the Hillmen still dirtied it.

Night passed and only grew brighter. Now some blue-red omen spangled the sky and all the stars shone. We hardly ever had cloudless nights like this, especially around this time of the year, and I shuddered at the omen. It must be the Morrigan, the queen of the night, warning us of our fate. Bright in the darkness, that is, glory in death.

Slinking through the shadows, sword in hand, I crouched and crawled and started toward the Crow's Nest. A scream caused me to jump and I dived to my feet, sword in the air. The thing growled now, deep and intense and I found myself faced off with a badger. A relief, yet the badger growled, and I worried since badgers lobby great offensives against humans, but I growled back until it slunk away. A small victory.

In the Crow's Nest, I crept until the forest dwindled into a copse that sat atop a hill, and from there I scanned the moorland again, and followed dozens of black figures heading toward the landing-place. That is where the

Greeks used to beach their boats with their wine and olives and fabulous beasts. They had a lion once, miserable in its cage yet prideful and ferocious even in its bonds, and I loved that. I had fond memories of waiting at the landing-place with my father, where we would see him off to his next journey. Sometimes, we would get word that father would soon return, so we would wait there after we finished our daily tasks and eat raw cockles we had collected from the mudflats nearby. Sometimes he would come and sometimes he wouldn't. Then that day when we thought he would come, but he did not arrive. The Greek merchant told us he had died, and suddenly the cockles tasted so sour, and I hated the brine breeze and the fester of baby seagull cries that cut into me and made me jealous because they had parents and I didn't. That day stung me, but I got over it, and still always had fond memories of the landing-place.

The black figures carried torches, and I saw their dark features in the red glow. Balls of fire hurled seaward. The torches landed on the boats moored there. Flame engulfed them, and soon the sheds and storage houses too, and the entire harbour burned.

Above it all, Dun Ashaig sat, lustred in the moonlight, a white egg sitting on a black litter. Shadows roamed near it, billowy shades of black in the hundreds, assembled around it while other packs patrolled. *I must avoid them all*, I thought.

That tight little mouth. They must have missed it, and had no reason to squeeze into it. There was an underground spring where Dun Ashaig got its water to bless us on Beltane.

I crawled through the wild moors, clambered under logs, skirted around boulders, and pushed through tangles of briar that left scars on me I still have today, for I dared not cease my stealth. I feared bogs and badgers and of course, the sidhe, who live underground and pull men through hare holes so that they never return. All the while on my mind was that little chink in the armour of Dun Ashaig, that tight little mouth I must squeeze through. I had been exploring with Fennigus when we were just boys, and he dared me to squeeze through it and I did, and discovered the well. There I would join the besieged, pledge my sword to my gods, and die for my people.

The hillfort approached me, lit like a beacon, billows of smoke pouring from the roofs of its steepled houses. On the distant swards of the trackway, twixt the great fort and I, the shadows had morphed into men. They were all bare-chested or wood-adorned, crowded in clusters around the hillfort and the surrounding fields. Whatever houses outside the fort that had been farms were now smouldering ruins. The houses on the hillfort seemed intact. Though the hillfort was quiet, I knew there must be a considerable defence there.

I edged toward the moorlands, with the scent of burnt wood stinking the air, ready to scream if startled, but instead of growling like the badger, I would lobby a great offensive with Bodvoc's sword.

The Hillmen had congregated in a great circle in the middle of the moors around a wagon. A figure stood on the wagon and must have been giving a speech, but I could hear it clearly. The Hillmen were distracted. *Now was my chance*, I thought. I then ran across the moors, hopping and jumping and skirting around boulders, taking refuge in ditches, and soon reached the earthen walls of the hillfort.

The smoky air caused me to choke. I crept along toward the cavern.

I heard some odd noise. A juddering, right by my ear. Something moved swiftly up and down near my head. The butt of an arrow, stuck in the earthen wall right next to my head. I spotted someone forty paces away, bow in hand, fletching an arrow.

I darted away, another arrow hissed through the air and checked off the rockface of the wall. I ran, grunting about the coward with a bow, then I slammed right into a Hillman. We both fell and I shot back up, the Hillman also got up, black flint blade lit by the moonbeam. He smelled like pork and had surprise in his big brown eyes. He wore just dark trousers and grey winnigas, and his chest had been painted in odd white shapes. Flint-ax poised, he lunged at me.

Retreating, I dove on my belly. Another arrow stuck in the earthen wall, just above my shoulder. I rolled to my feet and ran outward toward the bowman.

Shouts came in some language. It was not *Celtic* and didn't sound Greek, either. I had no idea what it was, but the axman behind me shouted hard, probably for his comrades.

My father's voice came to me. When I was a boy, he had told me if a bowman ever fired arrows at me, the only hope lies in running in a manner without a pattern, and closing in on the bowman. I zigzagged across the sward, thankful it had been well kept so I could find proper footing, and the bowman notched another arrow. I shot a look behind me at the axman. The bow fired. I dove out of the way, landing hard on my chest so hard that the impact winded me. I had hoped to see that the arrow had plunged into the axman. I tried to align my body with his and goad the bowman into killing his comrade. The arrow missed, but hit the earthen wall a pace from the axman, causing him to shout in his language.

The bowman shouted back and looked furious, and I swore I had heard something in *Celtic*, a swear word that would make a mother blush. They weren't taking me seriously, but soon they would regret that.

Now was my chance, I thought. I snatched a rock off the ground and pivoted, poised to toss it at the axman. The axman tottered backwards and I pivoted again and struck the bowman with the rock. He stumbled and now I ran toward the axman. I never knew if I had injured or killed the bowman, but I had at least distracted him, and I am still proud of that throw to this day.

My sword sung in the air as I ran toward the Hillman. All of me raged for revenge, my hand hot, my sight reddened. The crushed face of Bodvoc, a fiery image, his blood hot on my face. I wanted to kill the axman, I wanted to kill him dead, but Badb pounded in my chest. He had that sharp stone ax and he did not shirk at my charge. I raised my sword to strike and he stepped around me, flanking me.

The Hillman gave chase as I fled around the curved earthen wall of the hillfort, but I outran him. I still had to squeeze through the hole, and that would take a few moments, enough time for the Hillman to strike me as I did. I had to subdue him, but I dared not try in battle. Badb took me, and it is still in deep shame I say this, but that Brennus is dead now.

I climbed upon a rock outcrop. The Hillman pursued, failed to see me, and I fell upon him. I struck him on the head with a piece of rock and we fell. I bashed his head with the rock, again and again, his mouth agape. His warm hands grabbed my face and his hot breath was on my stomach as I bashed his head again, and again, his mass of brown hair tangled in blood and stuck on the rough edge of the rock. I bashed the piece of rock on his head until it crumbled into pebbles across his bleeding face. I had dropped my sword clumsily, so I snatched it off the ground and I drove it into his chest shouting *Bodvoc!* as I did.

My taste for revenge was teased, not satisfied, but merely teased, and I wanted more Hillman blood. I thought I ought to return to the sward to find that bowman so he may join his comrade. The axman whined on the ground, his bare chest shimmying up and down my bloodied blade. I couldn't get the sword out, and I had to place my foot on his shoulder and press down while pulling, just like with Bodvoc. It took too long and I feared the bowman would come back. He did, but with his friends.

'Badb!'

Five of them came hard down the sward on foot, flint-tipped spears grey in the moonlight, and two bowmen fanned out with loaded bows.

'Lugus!' I cried out, and I ran hard toward them. I came closer and closer and then the first javelin was hurled. It landed several paces away, and then the arrows fired down at me.

'Lugus!' I cried out again. I dove on my belly and covered my head. No arrows hit me, but they all stuck in the ground around me as if one had unfurled a hedgehog. I rolled to my feet and ran.

The crevice! There it was, just above the ground. The spearmen came closer and soon they would stick me and arrows would pierce me and I'd have as many spikes sticking in me as hedgehogs have spikes sticking out.

There was no way to get through the crevice without getting hit. It was simply too small, and I was too big, and by the time I squeezed through, they'd snatch me out of it by my ankles like a carrot by its leaves from the ground, if they didn't simply pin my feet to the ground with their spears.

I had to do something else. The spearmen came first. The words of my father came into my mind. There came their spears, sharp flint, grey as the moon. I held Bodvoc's sword firm and thought I'd stand and die like a man.

Nothing is unconquerable. Even our gods can die.

Father had once shown me how to fight spearmen. One must close the distance between them, and he must place his body between their blades and their bodies. The close distance renders their spears near useless and now one's blade will strike while they cannot.

The spear came at me and I ran. I swung my sword at the spear and a clank rang as blade hit blade, I shoved it down to the ground and held it there. My foe tried to pull his spear back and my arms tensed as his pressure clashed against mine, my hand keeping his spearpoint down, his spearpoint holding me in place. The bowmen had fanned out and could not hit me. One shouted and they all dropped their bows and drew daggers from their scabbards and they moved closer. The spearmen too all rushed in, from all sides.

The cold flint came for me, three spears and then the two bowmen and their daggers. I charged – a feint – forcing my foe to increase the pressure, and then I released my sword and sidestepped. He staggered and the spear fell from his hands. The other spears jabbed at me. I ran, feeling a cold rasp against my bare back. I dove at the crevice, crashing on the ground, my sword clanked against the rubble, and then I squeezed in. The crevice ripped the skin from my chest as I shimmied, and slid, scurried, scuttled, cried for Lugus, and finally squeezed through. I pulled one leg in but then I felt something grab my foot, but I yanked it back in and then the spears struck the rubble under the crevice. I jumped up, dove back down, and snatched my sword through from among the bare feet of the Hillmen.

As I leapt from the entrance, a spear had been stuck through to stab me. I climbed upon rock and sat there staring at the dark crevice at an angle away from the Hillmen's spears. They shouted at me, grunted, cursed, and jammed their spears through.

After I caught my breath, I laughed. I laughed hard and loud, enough for them to hear.

They lingered outside as I calmed myself, bloody sword across my lap. It was too dark to see in here, but I knew there was a well. I heard the water tinkling behind me.

I gingerly walked upstream through the black cavern, feeling my way. I sheathed Bodvoc's sword, and groped for the well, placing my wet warm hands on its damp cold stones, and climbed up. I heard nothing but an ever-present echo. My face went through a spiderweb. A light flickered, and hushed noises came from above. I also heard an ambient, dull roar of a crowd. I found the edges of the well and pulled myself out.

I nearly shat myself when spears were upon me, iron ones now. The spears lowered when someone yelled 'It's Brennus!'. I found myself amid hundreds of Skye's inhabitants. They all looked confused. I had popped out like a hunted hare, sweaty, filthy, dreary eyed, teary eyed, bruised, sunburned, scraped, scratched, huffing and puffing, leaves and twigs matted in red clots in my hair. My trousers were tattered. Pebbles dribbling down my face like raindrops. A spider crawled along my shoulders.

I raised Bodvoc's bloody sword. 'I killed one! Bring me some beer!'

That is what I would have said, if it had been Vidav that climbed up the well, and not Brennus. What I did and said shall not be repeated here, for it is shameful. Brennus is shamed, and there is no reason to shame him further.

CHAPTER V

Truth is, my dear Luceo, that I am of two minds when I think of Dun Ashaig. Before I made my entry through its well, Dun Ashaig occupied my wonder. There the druids discerned the will of the gods. There we feasted on holidays. There we drove the cattle through the fire to protect them from evil that they can catch in the mountains. It was where we solved legal matters, or traded with foreigners.

For nine days, the Hillmen besieged Dun Ashaig, and I enjoyed it. Yes, enjoyed. We faced death, but I enjoyed it. Those nine days were the hope of the smith. When he works his iron, and he follows the procedure right, honouring Lugus with his craft for nine days, but on the tenth day, all goes wrong and he has wrought a nightmare, a misshapen thing that should not be. That was the tenth day on Dun Ashaig.

But I will start from the first.

They brought me into one of the tents that housed the sick and wounded, who laid strewn about like harvested wheat. The nurses there tended to my scrapes and fetched me water. I listened to the wind rattle the thatch while I asked for my missing Fennigus and Auneé and a few of my younger cousins I had not seen in the byre. Only Fennigus was here.

I found Fennigus sitting with the boys around a fire. His eyes lit up and we embraced. I wanted to keep holding but he shoved me away, then gestured for me to sit down. I sat on the log and among his six friends, on the windy plateau of the Dun Ashaig among the roundhouses, they told me what happened to our ravaged homeland.

An invasion had occurred while I was up in the Slighan Hills. Boats had landed all over the island, dragged upon its beaches and slipways, and men poured out like ants from a disturbed anthill.

They were called *Hillmen* because the survivors here, including myself, first spotted them coming out of the hills, though they had come from the ocean, but Hillmen was their first moniker and no one cared that it was a misnomer. They had swarmed over the island, as quick as a surf, and devoured all they could like crabs devouring dead fish. There were thousands of them, and they were mostly armed with flint weapons, or some, it had been reported, with quartz, or jadestone, hornstone, greenstone, bloodstone, or with clubs. Nonetheless, they did not use iron or even bronze. The chiefs among them wore wooden armour as I had observed, latched together with thongs. What was the queerest was that they all had black hair like ravens. Even men like the Greeks who normally possess dark hair have the occasional redhead or blond among them, but not these Hillmen. They stood out in deep contrast to our clans, since we were all blonds and redheads. The only brunette I knew was Myrnna, and now men whispered rumours about her having a connection to the Hillmen because she shared their hair colour.

With their strange weapons and armour they waged war against us, or rather, cold murder. They killed whatever man they found, and then took the women, children, the slaves, and animals, though they hated horses as they hated iron. They did not wage war as we did. We *Celts*, as the men of the south note, make a spectacle of it. We dress in woad and spike our hair in beeswax and charge in nude. We dance with our swords and dance on our horses and dance in our chariot cars. We shout insults and blow our carnyx and then we dance some more. When we do fight, we tend to duel, man versus man, for we seek to honour the gods by conquering another man, and there is no honour in killing two-on-one.

Yet the Hillmen had no such honour. They warred when they had to and they did war well, but they sought to kill us. They sought to remove us, the men that is, from Taman, a task that must be done like how the crops must be harvested before winter. They stalked the countryside and murdered whatever man got in their path.

We had no idea what they wanted, we of warrior, farmer or slave blood. Lots of folks suspected the druids knew something that they refused to tell us, perhaps out of fear, or to save their own hides. All the druids were here, as well as the vates and bards, and we found it suspicious that not one of them was left at the mercy of the Hillmen.

I sat with Fennigus and his boys – six of them, all clansmen who were around Fennigus' age. I recognized some of them from the failed raid, but that hardly mattered now.

'Maybe it's lucky for us, our trial is postponed,' Fennigus said with a grin. 'We'll die freemen, and in battle, Brenn. It's what we always wanted. It was father's fate and now it's ours.'

'And Bodvoc,' I said. I had been quiet, just listening to them speak, for they had a lot to say and I was afraid to tell them about my encounter with Calli in the hills. But I told them my story now and how I ended up among them.

'What a man!' Fennigus shouted, as he stood up and raised a finger toward the sky, 'I never thought the old man had it in him! Three, you say?'

'Lappie also killed one.'

'Ha! I never knew that bitch had a fighting bone in her body. By the gods, tonight, we drink to their deaths! Then they drink to ours in the Otherworld!'

The Otherworld is the realm opposite of this one, the land of the dead. I didn't know if men and dogs drank there, but I did know it is where you rest among your ancestors. Fennigus had funny thoughts sometimes, but such a thought is more inspiring than just sleeping.

A fat druid with a flat nose and a shaggy beard, dressed in his golden embroidered white robe and bearing his hazel-bough staff, emerged from the night and told us to drink tonight and that we would sleep in tomorrow before training. So we all drank ourselves stupid and one of Fennigus' boys, Tascio, vomited, while Fennigus and another boy whom the gods had blessed with both height and broad shoulders tried to sneak to where there were some pretty girls quartered on the other side of the promontory, but the boys were far too drunk and they both slept in the muddy trackway. I slept in an unfurnished tent with the boys, all haphazard and with the pungent stench of beer and vomit, I drifted asleep for possibly an hour and then a horn blew.

Pain shot through my head. A raspy voice ordered me up to my feet, and we all clambered up and it felt as slowly as plants grow. My head throbbed and my stomach quivered and my ears rang, then rang again when the horn blared again. An undertow of groans accompanied it, the seven of us coming to our senses. The fat, flat-nosed druid with the shaggy beard stood in the doorway before dawn. The promise to sleep in had been a lie, and he hectored us out with his hazel bough staff.

We went outside. Fennigus was up, running in place. He was dusty from his rest in the trackway. He was still drunk, but he looked ready for war and his fire heated the other men around him. They all woke up, and I too stuck my shoulders back. We were all ready.

'I'm Cammios,' said the druid, 'every single one of you will be dead soon. Does that scare you? Cúchulainn said 'It matters not to me if I die tomorrow or next year, if men remember my deeds!' So now all of you now must honour his memory by your warcraft. You will be warriors, and the Hillmen will know our iron!'

It had not been the best speech, but it roused us enough to wake us up to soberness. Cúchulainn was our hero, there was none else before him except for the gods, but the gods were distant and Cúchulainn had walked our lands. He had trained with the *Banaghaisgeich*, an amazon in civilized men's tongues, in the Black Mountains – the Cuillins, named after our heroic Cúchulainn. Those were the mountains just beyond the Slighan Hills, and he may as well have been a clansman. All men listen when his name is spoken, and all men listen when we hear his words, and there is no easier way to rouse a man to war than to speak of his deeds.

We followed Cammios into the great trackway where we drive the cows in a circle during the winter. It encircled the grove sacred to Cernunnos, our god of the hunt, forest, and kingly sovereignty. We met a hundred other men ranging in ages from fourteen to fifty, I reckoned, perhaps some younger and older. They marched us around the trackway once, then made us run, and kept making us run. Sometimes they took us into the grove to toss stones around or grip the boughs of the ash trees there and pull ourselves up until we couldn't pull any longer. We were told to pull ourselves up more if we wanted beer that night, so we did and then didn't receive anything that night but milk and stale bread.

The next morning, they armed us with short spears that could be thrusted or thrown. We had also been given shields, oblong ones that ran from knee to shoulder, edged with rawhide, and held with a clenched fist in the centre behind the iron boss.

The plateau had been loaded with eager aspiring warriors, and not enough druids to train us, so the druids appointed lieutenants who had battle experience, and they appointed Fennigus as my lieutenant.

We had a small group of nine of us armed with our short spears tipped with small wooden blocks so that we would not stab each other. Two in our group were Fennigus' boys, and the rest some neighbours from the neighbour clans, including one I remembered seeing at the botched raid. His name was Varatus, and he had a long nose and sunken eyes and a skinny, long neck that would beg a sword to swing toward it. I hated him the moment I saw him, and he hated me, too. That bad blood had been washed away when the Hillmen washed over our island, at least I thought that at the time. He befouled me with a look so foul that I wondered if he hexed me.

We stood with our short-spears and our shields in the trackway. Sweat poured down from me on that balmy day before I had hardly moved. Women, children, and the druids all wandered about outside the fence of the trackway, watching us, surely praying to the gods that this new crop of warriors would somehow grant them victory over the Hillmen.

Despite the seething hatred from Varatus, the impending death waiting just beyond Dun Ashaig's tall walls, and the worry that I would disappoint Fennigus, I felt happy. Yes, my dear Luceo, happy. I had finally gotten what I wanted. Holding ashwood in one hand and the iron in the other, I had realized I received the life I wanted.

For a price...

Fennigus faced us all. He strutted up, stripped to the waist, sun glistening on his sweaty chest and his sword that he poised at us, his shield at ease.

'Rules for the game,' he said, 'first to hit wins. Who's first?'

Varatus charged in first, hopping through the mud and closing the distance with Fennigus. He jabbed his spear toward Fennigus' head. Fennigus raised his shield, sidestepped, and stabbed Varatus' exposed belly.

Varatus struck again, ignoring the rules of the game, and Fennigus blocked, pivoted, parried another of Varatus' blows. Fennigus then drove the shield edge-first into his jaw. Varatus stumbled, the shield fell from his hand, and he fell to his knees. Two boys pulled him up to his feet, the knees of his yellow trousers stained brown. He was bleeding from the mouth and the boys hauled him and tossed him on his arse at the fence. He never messed with Fennigus again.

'You see, boys, what he did wrong was,' Fennigus said, 'is that he assumed power means most in combat. Finesse is what matters the most: the ability to work around the attacks of your opponent, to cut him where he is exposed, to dance around his blows. Cractacus, come,' he gestured to one of his boys. Cractacus was wiry with a weak chin and a fat nose, ruddy face, and jovial eyes. He had a black scab on his face from the botched raid on Varatus' clan. He looked like he was always on the verge of laughter, and now was no different, toothy smile and approaching Fennigus.

'Cractacus is more experienced. Show them how it's done.'

My mind wandered now. I had wished Fennigus would have called on me to display the proper way of combat. If only Bodvoc had allowed me to train! But now Bodvoc was gone, and I had his sword at my side, and as if his ghost had come back to slap me upside the head, I heard his words.

Pay attention!

Now that Varatus had been dispatched, the real fight began. Fennigus had his spear over his head and held his shield outward. Cractacus mimicked Fennigus' stance. They both leaned forward as they moved toward one another, one foot straight and the other poised. Fennigus must have trained Cractacus, for they moved much like one another.

Like a badger, Fennigus snapped forward, his front foot stomping the baked mud of the trackway, his spear struck. Cractacus lifted his shield up and blocked, and Fennigus feinted – and I felt pride because I had feinted against the Hillman – and struck. Cractacus jumped back and they both lowered their weapons. The fight had lasted just moments.

'One or two hits, and then you leave. The longer you linger, the better chance your enemy will kill you.'

We trained in that manner in the hot sun. Fennigus and Cractacus fought, and then we fought amongst each other. We learned to keep our feet in the right places. We learned how to block and how to dodge and how to counter. We learned to use the shield as a weapon. We learned how to use our weapon as a shield. We learned to expose the enemy by forcing him to expose himself.

I learned. But learning and doing are two different things. I will admit now, my dear Luceo, that I simply could not keep up. My feet always faced the wrong way. I always leaned backward instead of forward, throwing myself off balance. My strikes were predictable, and I received deep bruises from all the times I missed with my shield. Now I am a formidable opponent, and men dread to face me in single combat, but then I dreaded facing anyone in single combat. Each day went much like this, we trained and fought all day and at night, we were given ale and meat and we drank. Each day I tried, and never gave up.

'Brenn is struggling,' Fennigus said to Cractacus, while the two shared a cup of ale by the fire one night. They had no idea I was nearby. 'He tries, but he just can't do it.'

I went to bed that night without my ale, just gazing up at the stars outside my sleeping hut.

The next day, after more training, we readied for the nightly feast. It had been a typical day of failure for me, and I grew frustrated until I realized that it was day nine, and on the tenth day, we would die. That is, tomorrow.

All day long, the Hillmen outside the fort pounded on drums in one big *dumpth*. They never stopped *dumpthing* until we would stop them. Each strike reminded me of how close we were to the end, and now at the end of the day, when the sun streaked the sky red, where the sidhe were most active, when magic was most potent, and when our dead ancestors visit the living for a while, we stood in the trackway after the final day of training. We warriors all idled around in clusters of circles. We were all weary, except for Fennigus, who had spent much of the day beating us all silly. The druid Cammios brought us two girls dressed in drab brown tunics. He hauled them toward us like he drove cows. He stepped behind them and yelled.

'You see these?' he asked. We nodded.

'No, you don't see these. Now, see these!'

He yanked their dresses down to the waist to expose their perky breasts. The two blond girls looked like sisters. They both blushed and covered themselves. I couldn't believe my eyes, fixated upon those pointy breasts.

'Each warrior gets a girl tonight,' Cammios said. But we're uneven, so one warrior will have to go without a woman. We're going to have a tournament now – all will watch it. Whoever wins gets the first pick for a woman, and the second a second pick, and so on, but the last will get none, and will have to chaff the wheat from their own cocks instead.'

We don't swear feeble oaths, my dear Luceo. An oath is a bond between man and the gods, the mediator between us. When we die, all that is left of us is our deeds and our honour, and a man's word is tied to honour. I then swore an oath, silently, holding the blade to my forehead, that I would not be the last in line for a woman. No one heard me except for myself, but it bound me just the same as if I had shouted it to the scores of warriors on the trackway. I would not die before tasting the sweet fruit of woman, not when those perky breasts were burned in my eyes.

Cammios hauled the girls away, and we stood awestruck. It was as if one had just dangled a steak in front of caged wolves. We all turned to one another in the dimming twilight, our spears and shields raised.

Fennigus approached me across the muddy span of trackway. It had been beaten muddier by our feet in the last few days, and the brown had crept up his green-yellow check trousers. He came to me with a nondescript face. He pointed his spear at me.

'You and me first.'

His hungry eyes called for my defeat, I feared, but I knew that if I shirked from him then he would despise me even more. The gods hate cowardice.

I aimed my spear at him in response. All eyes were on us. The night seemed to darken by the second and soon the druids would light the torches. The Hillmen outside the moors beat on their drums as they had been doing all day, and the beats hit me in the chest.

We closed in slowly.

'I fucked Cloda, Brenn.'

I looked on, agape.

'I fucked her real hard, Brenn. She screamed so loud. Isn't that something? If we ever find her, you're going to wed her, and she'll always remember how hard I fucked her when she fucks you.'

In an instant, my spear was upon him. I slapped and slammed at him and pivoted to and fro. He countered my every move. I had not charged in wildly like he had expected me to, since I knew I must defeat him. His spear scraped across my belly, the scraping wood cooled my anger, and I stopped because that meant I lost.

Fennigus grinned at me and gave me a gentle slap on the cheek. He moved on to the next fight.

Then I lost again, and again, and again, and I dare not say how many times I had lost. I was not a natural at fighting like some of the other boys were. Then at the end, when Cammios came and told us that we soon would stop and tally our wins and losses, Varatus challenged me.

Varatus smiled. He was covered in mud and had a black eye, and a deep scar on his lip from when his tooth snagged into it after Fennigus reamed him with the shield. He came to me from across the trackway, the hogs oinked from the pen behind him.

A horn blared. Cammios had blown it.

'Last fight!'

Now was the time to keep my oath. I shuddered to think what would happen to me if I had not fulfilled it, but then I knew I could not let Varatus beat me.

I learned a lot those nine days of training in Dun Ashaig, especially from Fennigus.

'I fucked your mother,' I said.

'The Hillmen have her,' Varatus said and snorted, and I thought he had just quenched a sob, and I smelled that weakness.

'Too bad! Then she got fucked,' I said, and grinned and I heard the grumbles of the crowd around us. No one liked that.

It was crude. I do regret having said that, despite him being scum. Few people deserved such an insult, and it was especially ill to speak of the dead with such a regard, but I wanted my woman tonight and this was the last fight.

Varatus rushed me. He was upon me with the brunt of all his anger, his spear down at my face. I flung my shield around me, and he kept smashing into it. I jabbed at his hip and he blocked – or rather, slammed his shield down onto my blade. I jumped back and he jumped forward and then I stabbed, and he parried, and thrusted his shield toward mine. Our shields met and I could sense the anger bridling in him, his eyes wide, drool hanging from his lip. I hopped back, remembering to always keep a distance from the enemy, and he hopped forward. This time I blocked a strike toward my leg and then I manoeuvred away from his spear, my spear struck at his shoulder, a straight thrust, and he twisted to block it. I vaulted back, he vaulted forward, and I feinted a strike to his thigh, his shield moved down and then I struck with my spear at his long neck.

I hit him hard. Hard enough for him to wince and drop his weapons and fall on the ground and hold his neck with both hands.

We tallied up our wins to the druid. I had just one win, but there was one who had not won at all, an older man with a wooden shaft for a leg. Cammios had not announced the winner, but after the counting was done, we were all rounded up and sent off to the tables for the feast.

The druids drove the pigs toward the dais in the middle of the tables. All the men were seated here, and the druids, vates and bards all stood around the dais. The chief druid was absent, I had seen neither him nor his daughter. They were holed up in their house on the hillock in the corner of the hillfort and guarded by blue-painted spearmen.

The pigs on the dais were slaughtered one by one, their squeals rang throughout the night and their blood remained pungent in the air. They had gurgling, mournful, humanlike squeals and for a moment, I could almost feel the scrape of a flint dagger opening me up that way.

I drank ale, we all did, as I sat at the table with Fennigus and his boys. They were all bragging about their wins that day, and I think we all knew Fennigus would have the first pick for women.

Ale cup in hand, with a dog sniffing at my feet, I sat there among the warriors. Fennigus chattered with his men, who all bragged about their victories, examined their defeats, and compared their warcraft. They acted as if death did not await us tomorrow, and somehow it mattered if they improved their craft.

'You really beat that Varatus kid,' Fennigus said, 'you beat him good, Brenn, right in that long neck of his. Wish your spear were sharp. You got him riled up like how I got you riled up. Good.' He said, and took a gulp of ale.

I sat content. Just for a moment, for the gods did not leave me long in peace, but for that moment, I sat among them. I was a warrior, and now I drank my ale and awaited my pork, and there were rumours we'd slaughter the cows in the morning before we set out upon the Hillmen, and fight, and die in front of Dun Ashaig. It was an honour to achieve just that with my brother, with my silent oath fulfilled.

Sego came along, the skinny lad, a little spy that discovers everything and never gets caught. He sat down at our table and we leaned in to hear his latest news.

'Seems like the druids had some visitors,' he said in a low voice. 'Emissaries from the Hillmen. I didn't catch all of it, but they were negotiating about Myrnna. The chief druid, Ambicatos, looked miserable. I couldn't really hear what they were saying well, but they couldn't reach a deal.'

Before we could ask for more, a horn blew.

Cammios summoned all of us in front of the dais. The druids led out scores of women. They were all either unwed, widows or suspected widows, and all dressed in white robes. The only unmarried women not present were the daughters of the priest class.

'Camulus blesses the warrior with the fruits of Damara,' Cammios cried aloud, raising his hands into the air, his ivy-wrapped birch bough in one hand, hand-scythe in the other.

'The three greatest warriors will have the three most beautiful women, by the decree of the gods themselves. Let each of you not pass through the sharp stone of the enemies tomorrow without first gorging on the three delights of this mortal realm: fighting, feasting, and women! Fennigus – Rocatos – Vosenios, come hither!'

Fennigus rose from his stool, and we all applauded. Vosenios came up next from our table, he was one of Fennigus' boys with big arms, a strong chin and a foul mouth. Then came Rocatos, the chief druid's youngest son. His sons had all become druids except for Rocatos, who was a warrior. He was the handsomest, an innocent face behind a fierce moustache.

Three women were presented to them on the dais. All three were young, and one had such a beautiful smile enriched by her chubby cheeks that I swooned. I wanted them, all three of them, then and there.

Someday, I would have first pick.

Fennigus chose the one with the chubby cheeks – she just had the dearest smile – and one would kill to wake up next to her bright face in the morning.

Rocatos picked one with a shapely arse and lovely thin eyebrows, and Vosenios took the last, a busty girl with red blustery locks. They all faced one another.

Fennigus' girl grasped the string he had for a belt and unravelled it, loosening his pants which fell to his ankles. The girls did the same to Rocatos and Vosenios. The girls had left them skyclad and now shrieking erupted from the mass of girls on the dais. They erupted into a cacophony of shrieks. Fennigus grabbed his girl and threw her over his shoulder and ran off the dais. The druids scurried away as the mob of men rushed the dais, grabbing whichever woman that they could. The women were shrieking and laughing and some even bared their breasts.

I ran among them, eager to grab a girl. Lads and lasses ran off into the bushes in droves. I darted my head about, eager to grab ahold of one, but then a voice called my name from deeper in the grove.

Following the voice, I found Myrnna seated on a knoll in the grove, combing her hair like a mermaid on a sea-rock. She had two seastacks of men standing at her flanks, blue ghosts in the dark light, two warriors in woad. They had bleached spiked hair and wild thick moustaches twirled with beeswax. Their presence and their spears at hand told me that I had been summoned. I knew warriors employed by the chief druid could not speak, so he sent her to fetch me, but he knew better than to send her out alone among young drunken men who know they will die in the morning.

'Please, come with me,' Myrnna said, stood up, and she and the warriors walked through the grove. I followed, stumbling in buffoonery, aware of the owl hooting a tree.

The chief druid's house sat on the hill in the southeast corner of the hillfort. Its coned thatched roof peeked above the wooden ramparts. A certain calm hung in the air from this side of the Dun, save for the war-drums beating from beyond, constant and rampant like the honking of so many geese.

Myrnna beckoned me from the entrance. The two warriors guarded the house, spear in hands, like two blue gnarled trunks carved into figures in a dark grove. One sucked a snort in as I passed. He could smell the ale on me, I am sure.

The interior resembled my home, though it was smaller, with two floors and a curtain obscured the upper floor. Myrnna informed me that I could not so much as peek up there, let alone see what is up there. That is for the druids alone.

Every three paces, a spear was leaned against the wall with a shield at its base. Each shield was painted green and adorned in a white and green check pattern, the adornment of Clan Ashaig. In the centre, at a round oak table, sat the chief druid, Ambicatos. He possessed a mighty white beard, an equally white robe cinched together by a bronze brooch of a bow, and a gold torc around his neck, the two ends morphing into snakes with ruby eyes. He had his birch staff across his lap. He gazed into nothing, twirled his moustache, and hardly noticed me. Then his eyes met mine, and he motioned for me to sit down.

I sat across from him. Myrnna stood opposite us, hands folded over her lap. Her face was puffy and red. In the corner, seated on a stool, a blond woman in a green dress had her face buried in her hands. I could tell by her hair that she was Aine, the wife of the chief druid. Auneé had pointed her out to me once at the market.

'What is your name, my guest?' Ambicatos asked, his voice groggy, his demeanor tired.

'Brennus, sir, son of Biturix.'

He slapped his hand on the table. His back straightened and he had a surprised smile.

'You're Biturix's boy? Well, that explains a lot!'

'You knew my father?' I asked.

'Yes! He taught me the secret of smithing, back when I was a lad. His knowledge was invaluable to me, and I would not have come as far in Druidry had I not had the ability to forge,' he said and smiled. 'I would love to share stories with you about your father, but we just don't have the time for that. We have little time for anything. Myrnna – food and drink!'

Myrnna came over and poured us ale from a pot, and placed a bowl of blueberries on the table between us. I didn't want more beer or ale and I wasn't hungry but the druid commanded me to eat and drink, and one never turns down the requests of their host.

'Tell me, son, exactly how you made it here alive.'

I relayed how I crept through the moorland on my belly, outsmarted the bowman, jumped the Hillman and bashed his head in, faced a troop of spearmen and crawled through the crevice and up the well. Ambicatos kept eye contact, nodding in approval, slapping blueberries into his mouth that reddened his beard.

'You're a bit drunk,' said Ambicatos, picking a blueberry that had fallen into the expanse of his white beard.

'I apologize, druid,' I said, 'I didn't know I'd be here tonight.'

He grinned. 'I'm sure you'd rather be spending your last night on Danu's green land with a lass,' he said with his eyebrows raised, then gestured toward his wife, 'I'm sorry – that was crass.'

Truth is, my dear Luceo, that my eyes wandered to Myrnna. Myrnna had wide hips, a stern jaw and shiny, brown, alluring eyes. She had brown hair, thick and wavy as kelp that danced at her lithe back when she moved.

'Let me get to the point,' Ambicatos continued, slapping his hand on the table again, 'I'm sure you know our ancestors practised human sacrifice, in their days of ignorance. But the druid order of Mona forbade it, except for in times of extreme circumstances. This is one of those times. The council decreed that we must sacrifice our most beautiful maiden, and our most powerful warrior. We had to vote on who fits the criteria of each. And we did. One maiden and one warrior will be sacrificed at dawn. A horse died today, seemingly for no reason, and the vates interpret that we've done something to make Epona angry, and that's why the men came out of the hills, to punish us. We're going to sacrifice our most beautiful maiden and our most brilliant warrior to her.'

He paused. Aine led out a sob, and then another, until Myrnna ran over and hugged her and they both sobbed. They sobbed until their voices raised into a loud hum.

Ambicatos leaned back in his chair, his eyes closed, head bobbing. His shaking hand wrapped around his cup and he drank. He looked me in the eyes.

'The druids will judge who is the most beautiful and the most brilliant. For the maiden, they have chosen Myrnna.'

Aine sobbed hard. Myrnna and Aine hummed and keened. We sat and listened to the keen for a while. For how long I do not remember, but it both saddened and sobered me. Still, to this day, when the gods have reminded me of my mortality, by taking someone dear to me or another misfortune, I remember the daughter and mother keening in the chief druid's house, and my heart keens with them.

'The reason why they voted for her was because she's a brunette and brown eyed. Most of our clan is fair haired and eyed. The Hillmen aren't. No one's outright said it, but they're all thinking it. The Vates think she's a bad omen and she's damned our luck, and the druids probably suspect a connection.

'Well now there's where you come in. We all know about the well, but I didn't know it would be possible for anyone to squeeze through to the outside. Could say, someone like myself fit through?'

'I barely can,' I said.

He slammed his hand on the table.

'Badb! All the women and children should escape, but the more we send out, the bigger the risk. We already tried sending some men to climb down the walls, but the Hillmen just shot them – Badb curse this full moon!'

'It is my duty as chief druid to hold up the will of the druid council. I am a druid. I have set out on this path and never have I strayed. Never until now. I want my daughter to live, and I would rather face the wrath of the gods than watch my daughter die.'

The two women sobbed until they hummed.

'I'm pardoning her tomorrow. I have the authority to do so, but someone will have to take her place. Is it fair? No. Someone must die so that she may live, but she is my daughter, and that's what I will do for her, and little is fair in our unfair world. The druids won't like it, but we are all going to die tomorrow anyway.

'And that's it, isn't it? I pardon Myrnna – she dies anyway. We don't know what the Hillmen have been doing with our women and children, but we assume they're being sold off as slaves, or something else equally cruel. I don't know,' he said, his speech slurred, and he took another sip of ale. 'We've decided on a plan. Tomorrow, we hold our sacrifices and feast, and then we set forth against the Hillmen. It will be something for the bards to sing about – if there were any bards to witness it – we are all doomed men, but we will kill as many of them as we can. We are the corpse of Cúchulainn facing his enemies upright. The women and children are to commit suicide. That will include Myrnna, even if I pardon her. But we have a different fate for her, and for you.

'You're going back down the well with my daughter and you're sneaking out together. You will get her to Dun Torrin.'

Dun Torrin was a fortress on an island, nestled in an inland loch, a day away southwest. There foreigners from an order of horse riders from the Cat people of Alba had come and never left. No one liked them but there was little we could do about it.

'Does Dun Torrin still stand?' I asked.

'Aye,' he said, eating more blueberries. 'It stands, for now. Perhaps it will still be up by the time you get there. Take refuge there. I don't know if they'll want something in compensation for their... hospitality... but you better not give their chief, that cur Fenn Beg Corm, my one and only daughter,' he said as he snorted.

'We're in an unsteady peace with Fenn Beg Corm. If there's one thing I learned from my time as chief druid, it is not to antagonize someone stronger than you. And Fenn Beg Corm is stronger. I just hope they're strong enough to withstand an assault from the Hillmen.

'What I'm doing will send the druids into anger, and cause my people to distrust me. But they are right to. I'm playing favourites, and allowing Myrnna to escape just because she's my daughter. It is unfair, and perhaps unjust.'

Ambicatos looked at his daughter and wife.

'Please, mother, come with us!' Myrnna pleaded, and started sobbing. Aine held her.

'Oh, Myrnna, my baby, I can't. I promised the gods I would never leave the side of your father. I must die here with him.'

They both sobbed, and delved back into a keen.

The chief druid looked at me, biting his upper lip.

'If Cúchulainn were here,' I said, 'he'd smite them all!'

He raised his cup, I raised mine, and we drank.

'But he isn't here, and we are left to stumble in his wake.'

'But why me?' I asked. To be honest, my dear Luceo, at that moment, I wished nothing more than to die alongside my brother Fennigus. Now, fate had sent me sneaking across the moors again, away from combat. I say fate, because I knew that this was not a request from the chief druid, but a command, and one never disobeys a druid, the bridge between our world and the gods.

'You got in here, didn't you? Listen, son, you're of good breed. You're not of the priesthood, but you're your father's son. Like him, you're crafty, and resourceful. That's important for what I need you to do. My daughter is going to need someone with those capabilities if she's going to get to Dun Torrin safely.'

I found myself grinning, and Ambicatos scowled at me for it, but he had compared me to my father. For the first time in my life, after spending nineteen Samhains hearing about his deeds, someone has compared me to my father. The burden no longer daunted me, but gilded me in pride.

'I accept,' I said, but a hint of Badb-fear crept through me.

'Now this is no small task. Torrin is normally a day journey on foot. It may take you longer. Perhaps you can get a boat but the Hillmen are on the locks like waterskeeters on ponds. Both of you will have three days' worth of food. Anything beyond that and you're going to have to forage. I don't know how Skye looks now, with these Hillmen. I don't know. But I know I am giving you no small task. But I must ask something of you first.

'My daughter will be entrusted to you. You will be her guardian, until death or until she gets married. I will go over the stipulations of this arrangement. Don't think I don't have anything to settle with you about your degenerate behaviour – you did raid kin – but we will ignore that incident, since we figured you would all die tomorrow anyway. But now you have been given a chance to not face trial. I don't know if you will make it to Dun Torrin, or if Dun Torrin is still there. But your chance at life comes with ramifications, and the burden of my daughter is just that.'

I stiffened my back. I had many questions. What did he know about the Hillmen? But I could not speak, he was speaking, and I sat and listened and never got to ask anything.

'Myrnna, pay full attention and prepare to recite,' said Ambicatos. Myrnna lifted her head and ceased crying.

'Brennus, son of Biturix, you are hereby the guardian of my daughter Myrnna. She is under your authority. You have full custody over her, but you are bound to certain conditions. My daughter must stay a maiden; that is, you may neither sell her as a harlot, nor sell her into sexual slavery. She cannot fornicate under any conditions, except if she is married. You will protect her chastity with your life. In case of rape, it is your duty to seek death for the rapist. Bastard children will go to the birds.

'She is not to be made a servant. And you must treat her with respect. You may not lay a hand on her. You must kill any man that does so to protect her honour.

'You must seek her wellbeing until you are relieved of it, whenever that time comes. The only way you are relieved of this authority over Myrnna is through her marriage. You do have a role in choosing the man that she marries – however! – she must agree to the marriage as well. You are expected to protect her from unsuitable suitors and use your judgment, and you have the power to override her decision. But she still must agree with the husband that you have chosen.'

Ambicatos took another sip from his cup.

'The other way out is if you die. I imagine you no longer have any next-of-kin?'

'Just my brother, Fennigus, who is here. My eldest brother, and my cousins, were all killed by the Hillmen. Some missing, too, but I assume they are dead.'

'Have I been clear? Do you understand everything that has been said? Do you have any questions?'

'I understand,' I said. I had many questions, yet I found no words to say. He had compared me to my father, and that was all I needed.

'Good. Aine, bring me the brooch.'

Aine raised her head from her palms. 'He hasn't a cloak to attach it to.'

'Then bring him a cloak.'

Aine opened a chest, and approached me, then wrapped a green-yellow check wool cloak around my neck, holding the brooch.

'That brooch, Brennus, son of Biturix, is the oath between us. Now swear an oath that you will be faithful to it, and that you may never break it, only the marriage of my daughter or death relieves you. Swear it to Camulus – you have a sword, don't you?'

I nodded.

'Then swear it on your sword. Aine – have someone fetch it.'

We waited for a while, in silence. A warrior fetched me my sword, and now I knew I had been privileged, since no man could wield weapons in the abode of the priesthood.

'Sharpen it, Camulus will not accept an oath on a dull sword – bring him a whetstone!'

I brought the whetstone to the blade and soon rasping filled the house. Ambicatos shook his head. 'By good Danu, lad, not against the grain!'

He got up and came behind me, grabbed both my wrists and motioned the right way to do it. I smelled the ale about him.

I sharpened the sword. My face reddened. I asked if it were sharp enough, Ambicatos nodded. He instructed me to stand up and place one hand on hilt and the other on blade.

'I swear to Camulus that I will never break my oath.'

'When Myrnna is married, break the brooch and bury it in the ground for Camulus.'

'I will.'

'Then we are oathbound!'

Aine clipped the wet brooch together across my bare collar.

'You may cease,' said Ambicatos to Myrnna.

'Did you know, Brenn,' Ambicatos said, taking another chomp of blueberries, 'that my daughter remembered everything from this meeting? She is able to repeat everything I said, word for word. She will demonstrate. Myrnna!'

Myrnna began repeating everything her father had said during the official oath, starting from the beginning.

She remembered everything – the pitch, the tone, every stutter, aspiration, pause and breath.

'Amazing, isn't it? Myrnna trained to be a druidess, but she stopped her education. Did you know that in far distant lands, men can draw sounds? They call it 'writing', and their secretaries draw everything they say on clay tablets, or goatskin, or chiselling the words in stone. But it comes with a price! The so-called literate men have poor memories! If their clay tablets were destroyed, or if parchment no longer were made, nothing would be remembered. Yet nothing can destroy the spoken word. The written word as they call it sullies the memory. The druids forbid writing, except for a small group that does claim to chisel words in stone; a secret – but don't tell anyone I said that.

'Now I have given you a hefty burden, lad. You will do your duty to your people by fulfilling your oath – and we know what awaits oath breakers in the afterlife. Now I'm giving Myrnna an iron bar, and I'll give you three to carry. Trade them wisely. She will conceal her gold and her jet pearls, and wear an undyed dress, so that she appears poorer than she is.'

I suspected Myrnna's brown hair would cause her to stand out even if she wore grey rags.

'Brenn, my son, young and crafty, I will also take a request from you, as long as it's reasonable.'

'I want my brother, Fennigus, to come with me,' I said. There was little to ponder. Why would I not want Fennigus at my side? I needed him, his sword, his comfort, and knowing that the two surviving sons of Biturix still stalked Danu's green land.

'No,' he said, casually, stretching and taking a drink. 'Fennigus is a fine lad. He makes us all proud. Not so much the day you attacked the Ashmore clan, but the both of you have been pardoned from our judgment. I was watching your drills today. He lorded over all, and I would fear facing him in combat. Why, I'd want him as my chariot driver, if we had the time to train him. And that's why he's going to be sacrificed tomorrow to Epona.'

When Ambicatos had told me that the most brilliant warrior will be hung tomorrow, I had already known Fennigus' neck would fill that empty noose.

'Unless you wish me to pardon him. That's all I can do. I'm already upsetting the law by allowing you and my daughter to leave. Any more and I'm afraid my position will be taken from me so fast that my successor will overturn my order, and the three of you will be barred from leaving altogether. Moreover, the less of you moving through the moors, the less likely you will be spotted. And Fennigus is a big target – would he even fit through the crevice?'

The answer was that he wouldn't. He was too tall, too broad and too muscular. Besides, when I think of it now, Fennigus would have never agreed to run away with me in the moors while the men he spent days training die against the Hillmen. He'd want to fight and die among his beloved friends.

'Please, druid, pardon my brother, and let him die against the Hillmen.'

'Of course. But now we will need to replace the sacrifice for him too.'

'You don't mean…' said Aine, her sobbing suddenly ceasing, a kind of growl lurking in her voice.

'It must be Rocatos.'

Shrieks erupted throughout the house, Aine flew across the room, and Ambicatos apprehended her. She rioted in his arms.

'You can't hang my son!' she screeched, repeating herself until Ambicatos put a hand over her mouth. Myrnna kept her head low and her shoulders bobbed. One of the guards poked in his head in awe of the commotion.

Ambicatos motioned for me to leave. I stood up as quickly as I could and left. As I did, Myrnna glared at me with a piercing gaze. She averted her eyes when I looked back.

I left unceremoniously for such an occasion. I fingered the grooves on the brooch on my chest. The whole ordeal fell on me. I returned to my tent, and drifted to sleep undisturbed. I awoke when the voice of Calli haunted me again.

For a price…

CHAPTER VI

The crowds poured into the grove at first light. Warriors with spears in their hands. Women with babes at their breasts. The elderly leaning on their canes. Children and dogs strewn about. Hundreds of us had come out on this breezy morning to witness the sacrifice.

An image of Cernunnos stood in the grove, a thick oak trunk, leafless but crowned in antlers. It stood amongst the thick oaks with their yellowed leaves. We gathered around the outer fence in throngs, waiting for the sacrifice to begin.

Cammios stood next to me with his arms crossed, and face expressionless.

'I like you, son,' he said.

I thanked him.

The crowd cramped around me. Fennigus and the boys stood by. They stank of beer.

'You're not very good,' Cammios said to me, and Fennigus eyed him. 'But you're dedicated, and that's what I like.'

A young man and woman entered the grove.

Rocatos was the warrior chosen as the finest warrior of the Ashaig clan. Son of the chief druid, he had been trained as a charioteer, and before fate had changed her mind, he would have had the honour of driving the chariot of his father tonight. He walked with his chin held high, his shoulders at ease. He was adorned in a golden torc, signifying his nobility, and wore a pure white cloak, along with a yellow tunic, green-yellow check trousers, a felt rusty-yellow hat; the proud fashion of our clan.

Claradestras, daughter of a druid on the council, walked at his side. Her hair flowed in the wind, so long that her golden locks dangled at her loins. A wreath of marigold and heather had been placed on her head. She wore a white dress, held by a bronze pin at her right shoulder. Her golden armrings matched her hair, and she wore white sandals. She looked like a wraith of white and gold walking in the realm of green. She wore a blindfold, since it was claimed by her father that she hosted three pupils in both of her eyes, a mark of a prophetess of power that should not be seen by mortals. I had never seen her eyes, and since the blindfold remained on after Epona took her sacrifice, I could never verify this.

Cammios left me.

The chief druid trailed by eight druids, came into the grove first, the lot of them an array of grey beards and white robes. Behind them came the six Vates, who had moustaches but no beards, with long hair, and were gowned in brilliant yellow robes. Then came the three Bards, not distinguishable from the other denizens of the hillfort save for their shaven faces, and the lyres that each carried.

Ambicatos approached Rocatos and Claradestras. He held a golden sickle in one hand, and a sprig of mistletoe in the other. Three other druids flanked him, one holding a chord, another a club, and the final a knife.

Ambicatos raised his hands. The sun hit the golden sickle.

Aine, watching from the side, burst into a wail. Another woman at her side joined her wail, and soon the wail petered into a long *ahhhhh*. Aine too wailed into an *ahhhhh*, and both women held the notes. Soon, the women roused to sing their cry-song, and soon the entirety of the womenfolk keened. They keened throughout the entire procession.

'Goddess of horses, mare of the rivers, patroness of riders – hear your children. Today our finest warrior and our purest maiden are to die for you. Today we bloody the grass in the great name of Epona. Today we ask that you grant us serenity in our peace, and bloodlust in our war. Today we will all die for you, Epona. We will kill our enemies and ourselves alike in your name. But take these two as a preliminary death, and let the vates know your signs!'

Ambicatos set down the sickle and mistletoe, and put a hand on the back of Rocatos to make him kneel. His son complied. Ambicatos lurched down and whispered something into his ear. Rocatos spoke back. No one heard what they said.

Stone-faced, Ambicatos removed the gold torc from his son's neck, and bashed it against a rock until he battered it into pieces. Gold chunks had been scattered all over the green grass. It looked like a broken sunbeam.

The chief druid took the cord in his hand, and twisted it around the neck of his son. He placed his foot on the upper back of his victim, and with a pause, he twisted each end of the cord. Cries and gasps murmured in the crowd as Rocatos grabbed at the cord around his neck. He squirmed and fought until he was blue in the face, and Ambicatos released the twist.

Before Rocatos could catch his breath, Ambicatos seized the club and smacked him across the back of the head with it. Rocatos fell backwards, crushing his ankles behind his body, and Ambicatos and the knife were upon him. Ambicatos had aimed for the heart, but missed, and his son wretched. Ambicatos then stabbed again, and his son gasped, and the third time he struck caused Rocatos to tremor, and in his death throes he flailed his arms for a moment and then splayed out, stiff.

The keening soared to great heights, and Aine's voice delved into another instrument, that of screaming. The chorus of keens quieted her scream, until her scream assimilated back into the keen, so low I could hear the birds chirping in the arbours of the bloodied grove.

The vates looked to one another, nodding.

'Epona has taken her warrior!' shouted one of the druids.

Ambicatos approached Claradestras, leaving his son gurgling ghastly. The girl trembled.

She was led by the druids to an oak tree, where a noose had been hung from a bough. The druids placed a stool under the noose. The maiden climbed up on it, with the help of Ambicatos holding her hand like she was crossing a rivulet.

Ambicatos placed a hand on the back of her head, dunked it, and looped the rope over her neck. She loosened her hair from the noose.

She exchanged words with her druid father. Two other druids with spears approached her, from the front and rear.

Ambicatos kicked the stool out from beneath her, and one spear impaled her through the chest and the other through the stomach. Her limp body dangled from the rope, a white silhouette against the great brown trunk of the oak tree, the spears sticking out of her like a hunted seal.

Gasps ruptured through the crowd, quieting the lament, but the women soon keened their fullest, rocking their bodies, clapping their hands, and their song sailed above the awe.

The keen quieted. Ambicatos shouted.

'Epona has taken her maiden!'

The vates muttered amongst themselves.

Ambicatos shouted again, and he waved his sickle in the air. 'Now let these deaths not sadden you, for they died for Epona. Let us not hold ourselves in sorrow for these deaths, for today, we join them! Let their deaths boil your blood! Let their deaths raise your spears! Let these deaths make your swords cry 'vengeance'!'

Ambicatos cast off his robe, and skyclad, he ran towards the track, the crowd parting for him.

'Honour Rocatos and Claradestras with your sweat, before you could avenge them with your iron!'

He then ran down the trackway.

The men were all shouting loud and trampling down the trackway. There were horses neighing as warriors leaped upon them, dogs bayed and snarled, the cattle and sheep and goats all trampled away from the tide of men that armed themselves and began to sharpen their iron. I followed Fennigus and his warband into the muddy trackway. As I entered the track, I passed Myrnna. She shot me a glance, her wet eyes squinting. The body of her brother, the warrior, along with the maiden, lay there for the Morrigan's children.

Dusk cast a red canopy over the hillfort. We had finished the festivities of the day early. We drilled in the way of the first day, throwing stones, racing, pulling ourselves up on boughs.

Fortune came to us in one way. The vates demanded that each beast that could not be ridden or sicced on the enemies was put to the knife. The gods received a portion of each reaping, as did the sidhe, the ancestors, and Vitallis, the founder of Dun Ashaig. We ate the last bit of food and drank the final drops of ale. We spent our last moments before nightfall dancing to the pipes and lyres of the bards.

Nightfall approached. The vates decreed that the warriors charge the Hillmen head-on, and we all began preparations for our final night on Taman.

First, the druids slaughtered a stallion in the red twilight. The druids funnelled its blood into a great cauldron, and Ambicatos bathed in its blood and gore while it cooked. He drank from the broth while sitting in the cauldron like a roast, and was stained red after he pulled himself from it. They crowned him king with a wreath of mistletoe, and gave him a bronze sceptre, gifted from the mound of a long dead ancestor. The nine druids entered the grove of Cernunnos, and emerged armed with spears and with golden-wire torcs around their necks.

The newly crowned king would lead the charge against the Hillmen. This custom was altogether strange to us, since we had no kings or lords save for when we went on our battle-wandering, but the vates knew the will of the gods.

All men were lined in rows in the grove, nude, and the slave girls were tasked with painting us all with woad from head to toe. Using beeswax, the servants spiked each man's hair, and curled their moustaches. Most men had been given one-handed spears and shields, though some were left with knives or clubs. I had Bodvoc' sword, in its scabbard, wrapped around my waist.

Fennigus and his men stood in the line awaiting their dressing. I stood next to my brother. I could not believe he had been chosen for the grisly sacrifice today, and I feared what he would say if he knew I had pardoned him. No one except for Ambicatos and his family knew I would leave that day, as far as I know. In truth, my dear Luceo, I was glad that they would not know I did not die with them that day.

'Hurry up, come on! We want to die tonight, not tomorrow,' said Vosenios to the slave girl painting his feet.

'Hey Brenn,' Fennigus said as the slave girl dressed him in woad.

'Yeah?'

'See you on the other side,' said Fennigus.

'You too,' I said. I meant to say more, and my dear Luceo, I wanted to tell Fennigus how proud I was of him, and how I wished I could be half as strong, courageous, and masculine as him before he died, but I said nothing. Then Fennigus snickered.

'Hey, do me a favour and jerk it a bit?' Fennigus said. The slave girl was painting his genitals and Fennigus let out some moans. Fennigus' band laughed, as did some other men in the ranks.

After the slave girls finished woading the last of the warriors, the druids divided the warriors by their battle prowess and experience. Fennigus nodded to me when they moved me to the last row of warriors.

'We will meet again soon!' said Fennigus, casually raising a backhand to me, and going back to chatting to Cractacus. Guilt spiked through me. Did

I really deserve to live when Fennigus died? Would Myrnna be better off protected by him than me?

Harrowing blares from shrieking bronze instruments quenched whatever guilt clouded my mind.

'Gangway!' the champions of king Ambicatos cried.

The trumpeters carried long, top-heavy, curved bronze trumpets that morphed into the gaping maws of beasts – boars, dragons, sea monsters, horses – called the carnyx. It spouted a rattling cry when blown into, more akin to the bleating of a goat than a horn, to irritate and intimidate their enemies. Nine trumpeters marched down the avenue, each playing a carnyx, boar-headed war trumpets that curved up, held high above the player's head.

The warriors divided to form a track, like a blue meadow of iron flowers, and a chariot thundered in the distance.

The carnyx resounded, and their players held their bronze instruments in salute, one-armed, as if they held spears. The thundering of the chariot pounded the ground. Pulled by two horses, both white as clouds, king Ambicatos rode through the sea of his warriors. All eyes averted to him, clad in nothing but horse blood and a bronze horned helmet. His charioteer whipped the horses into a frenzy.

King Ambicatos shouted 'Epona!'

Behind him rode more of the king's champions on horseback, eighteen proud men, severed heads riding their spears. The pounding of the hooves hit the chests of the warriors, and war cries were shouted. The carnyx bleated to signal the goddess of battle the Morrigan to lead the charge.

The warriors moved out in a blood-crazed jogtrot. The king rode through the palisade first, the stampede of his woad-covered entourage shivering the great wooden structure like a windswept tree. He stuck his spear up into the hanging skull of Vitallis, plugging his spearhead into its neck hole, raising the skull on his spear like its spine. Thus, Vitallis led the vanguard of the charge into the Hillmen.

Dog masters loosened eager dogs, while cries of 'Epona!' and 'Lugus!' and 'Camulus!' and 'Morrigan!' and 'Vitallis!' flew into the air, spewed by spasmed-faced warriors. Pommels beat against the backs of shields as they charged, unorderly, without strategy, their tactic to unleash an unbridled and unchained frenzy. They would break the nine-day siege by rush of flesh and iron.

King Ambicatos had other plans for me.

I nearly felt light in the feet and heavy in the hands as bloodlust swept me up to charge me into the fray. I had been painted in woad and my hair waxed in spikes, I was as armed and naked as my brethren that charged to their deaths. But my opportunity arose, as no one was looking, since I was the last in line. I shirked away from the line as it advanced down the trackway. I ran away.

On the other side of the hillfort, Myrnna waited to flee with me. A frantic commotion rose as I raced through the grove. After I emerged from the grove, I found myself in a sea of madness. Women wailed, children flew, bloodied bodies strewn there and about. A woman followed a child up the rampart, and when the two climbed to the stone-lined top, the woman shoved the child off, and flung herself after him. I will describe no more.

I spotted Myrnna, and Aine embraced her amidst the red madness.

'Leave!' cried Aine, tears streaming down her face.

Myrnna did not budge. I tossed two packs down the well. I slung the shield over my neck and grabbed Myrnna by the arm.

'Come on, down the well!'

Myrnna hesitated. I shook her and she shouted, 'I love you' to Aine, and went down the well.

I hauled myself into the shaft, and took one last look at the fort from the inside. It was garnished with bodies, viscera, and rivulets of blood. In the sacred grove where children once chased butterflies, now death chased them. May the Hillmen's blood upon my weapons never dry.

Before I descended the shaft, Aine nodded to me. I saw her fingering at her knife as I descended.

Then I heard a grunt and someone collapsed to the ground, followed by agony, nothing but dull echoes as I descended the well.

Myrnna fell into the cold well water as I climbed down after her.

'Let me go first and check how it looks outside,' I said.

Light emitted into the cavern through a crevice, where a boulder had been pushed to plug the entrance to the well. I peered outside, gingerly, praying to the gods that no Hillman was out there. I saw nothing but the darkening light of twilight, and heard nothing but the whistle of the wind.

I beckoned Myrnna to follow, and launched myself against the boulder and pushed it, shoving the boulder away enough for us to slip through, and the last light of twilight spilled into the cavern.

Pebbles cascaded down the well behind us, and a yelp echoed from above, followed by a splash. I rushed over to find a child face down in the water table. She floated lifeless. I propped her up, and her head hung limp. I looked up and saw dark figures climbing down.

'Someone's following us down! The Hillmen will notice if many are running out in the moors! Out now!'

I sat the dead girl upright on one side of the well, and we ran out. We ran along the hillside of the fort to the west back towards the forest. We passed the shaft of the arrow that had been shot days earlier into the earthen wall. I turned, and grumbled, seeing Myrnna trailing far behind.

A racket from the entrance erupted, and dozens of women and children raced in different directions across the heather.

'We're going to get spotted!' I yelled 'Come over here!'

My heart raced. Cold, hard Badb crept in my chest and cut my heart just as the briars crept around my legs and cut them, too. I bled and feared. Surely, the Hillmen would still have patrols? I didn't know. We raced toward the pine forest and I hoped none of them awaited us there.

I led Myrnna up a hill, and as we got to the top, I turned and, in the distance, at the entryway to the cavern, figures ran after the fleeing women and children of Dun Ashaig, snatching them up, corralling them with rope. Some of the women were struck by bullwhips.

Dragging Myrnna down with me, we fell on our bellies in the heather.

'Down the hill and to the pines – stay down – we don't want to get spotted!'

We wormed our way through the heather, snaking around rock outcrops, and crawling through murky bogs. Clouds of midges swarmed us. Myrnna kept cursing under her breath, and finally she stood up and swatted at them and I nearly screamed at her.

'What's worse: bug bites or the Hillmen?' I asked.

Scraped by briars, caked in mud, and bruised by stones, we carried on, silent.

The roar of the carnyx brayed over the moorlands. We neared a tentacle of the pine forest that reached out into the moor, and after some scouting, we positioned ourselves among the dark trees. We caught our breath. Obscured by the pine forest, I opened my pack and clothed myself with my green-yellow check trousers, my undertunic, my yellow overtunic, a rusty-yellow felt conical hat, Bodvoc's shoes, and my green cloak which I fastened with Aine's bronze brooch. I fingered the brooch and looked at Myrnna, who huddled against a stump.

We walked along a byway, ran down a slope into the valley. Through the fortress of trees, came the sounds of battle. We peered out through the pines, and from the far distance, just enough to hear the battle sounds, watched from the vantage point of the darkened forest.

The entrance to Dun Ashaig, the snaked trackway enclosed by earthen walls, was visible from here. On the moors, the innumerable Hillmen waited, armed and armoured and mobilizing to the entrance.

Ravens cawed above us, and flew out of the pines and across the heathery hills. The children of the Morrigan hungered.

The torrent of warriors from Dun Ashaig flooded down in a great wave into the countless bodies of Hillmen that hurried to dam the trackway. The Ashaiger clansmen crammed into the tight tunnel and pushed forward into the broad but dense defensive line of Hillmen.

A great shoving match ensued. Hillmen bowmen slung arrows into the crowd of woad-clad warriors, but the clansmen fired back with slings. Bodies crumpled on both sides.

After a collective shove, the barricade of wood-clad Hillmen broke. The dam was breached, and an unrelenting surge of stampeding horses crashed into the Hillman. The horses washed over the Hillmen, kicking and bucking and even biting, panicked by the havoc. The chariot of the king crashed into the line, and crushed hillmen under its wheels. Javelins whirled, spears struck, clubs swung, swords slashed, arrows pierced, shields battered to splinters. Snarling dogs sprang into the fray.

The Hillmen swarmed the clansmen.

I dared not avert my eyes. Myrnna trembled at my side.

'We need to get to the trackway while the Hillmen are still fighting,' I said.

I led the daughter of the short-reigning king through the pine forest, and up the other side of the valley. The moon emerged in the pale blue sky while the red sun still sank. The arbours of the spruces were just thick enough to cover the battle, and soon the frantic noise of horses whinnying, dogs barking, men shouting, and the rattling of weapons dulled.

By the time the forest waned, and we emerged on the moorland again, nightfall had befallen Skye. No sounds came from the war raging just beyond the hills. We ran down wild moorland to the trackway near the foothills of Slighan. We curved around one of Slighan's Hill-daughters, and from this view, we could see Dun Ashaig. We stopped and looked.

Far into the distance, in the dark of night, a glow emanated from Dun Ashaig. Nothing could be seen save for flames under billows of thick smoke. Embers fell into sheer darkness below the hillfort.

I grabbed Myrnna by the wrist, she pulled away.

'Don't touch me,' she said.

I had no response.

We went down the trackway, the backdrop of the flickering of fire and billows of smoke merging into the clouds signalled the end of Dun Ashaig and its clan.

For a price...

CHAPTER VII

The moonlight lit the trackway that snaked like a brown ribbon. To our west, boundless moorland, and to our east, the Slighan Hill.

I felt naked on the trackway in the full moon. In peacetime, we drove our cattle down from the mountains to it and to Dun Ashaig. Now during wartime, the Hillmen had trampled down it to Dun Ashaig. Hillmen patrols, Hillmen marauders, the victorious Hillmen parading down the trackway after sacking and burning our fort. Yet we had to stay on the trackway, since the moorland possesses treacherous footing. I touched the hilt of Bodvoc's – no, *my* sword. I was just one man, but I would take at least one more of them with me if it came to it. My oath called for it.

Was this invasion the price the hag promised me? Had my meeting with the hag of the hills led to the sack of my stead, the death of my family, and of my entire clan down to the last child?

To the west, Bodvoc and Lappie lying in their own blood in our house. To the northeast, Fennigus and the boys sprawling out on the battlefield, faces skyward. Then ahead of me, the white path that cut into the blackness, with Myrnna step and step.

We carried on. Heathery hills stretched grey, and the dark blue sky hung over the horizon. I recognized the loch with its linden tree on one end and the hanging tree on the other, and my farm lay just west of the trackway. Just west, now devoid of cattle, sheep, and slaves. Our house stood just like a shadow.

My heart pounded harkening back to when I found Bodvoc, Lappie and the slaves in the entrance. Now, I am sure they were rotting, all unburied, picked at by the Morrigan's children. Soon, too, the house would rot, and then fall from its foundation. The stone foundation would be pilfered for another structure by the next inhabitant of the land, and so too the byre, barn, fences, and shed. It would all rot and leave nothing but the middens, my land just a skeleton with no flesh to dress and no voice to tell the tale. The peat fire warming the chilly mornings, Lappie's wet tongue slurping me awake. Auneé's call for quail eggs and bread for breakfast, Bodvoc's collection of fox skins. The house, its warmth, its light, its thatched roof, its wattle-daub walls, its green and yellow paint, the brown woollen rug on the floor, Lugus' wheel nailed to the door and the big pinewood door itself, all its histories and stories before I had been born – all would die with me. I ought to build Bodvoc a mound and place Lappie at his feet, if the children of the Morrigan would be so merciful as to leave a morsel to bury. All of this rumbled within me, causing tremors like an old man's trembling hand, but I had to carry on down the trackway.

Fennigus ought to be buried in such a manner as well, as he died in that battle outside Dun Ashaig. Blade in hand, big white eyes, the warp-spasm about him, his boys flanking him, beautiful, handsome, brave men, all to their graves in the moorland. I must say, my dear Luceo, I had trouble keeping my form when mourning my brother's death that I had missed, but I must stay strong for Myrnna.

Soon the breeze brought us the dreadful smell of decay. The cawing of crows from the byre tomb of my cousins cut through the cold night air. From here, I could see shadows garnished in crows. I suppose Vasenus had taken another route, but my oath was my route and I trod its path.

Myrnna groaned, gagged, then vomited. The wind never ceased dragging the awful stench to us for some time, all the while the crows cawed throughout the night. Truly, the Morrigan blessed them with a great feast.

The wind stilled, and I began to sweat in blue streams of woad. Myrnna began to slow, I suggested that we rest, and wondered out loud where to sleep. We sat in the weeds off the trackway, and Myrnna insisted we did not need to sleep. She wrapped herself in her brown wool cloak and huddled against some bushes. We shared a flask of water until she cried out:

'Those idiots! Those idiots ran out of the cave like a hare from a hole, and they were all taken! The Hillmen took them all! Who knows what they do with them! Mother at least… mother at least is dead, so the Hillmen can't take her.'

She sat silently, and I watched the bright moon and the stars. I found the moon an ill omen from a dark god. We called the moon the eye of Balor, the old god of twilight and blights that Lugus had slain. Lugus caught his eye and cast it up on the night sky and now it lights my path.

Something suddenly caught my eye.

Down past the stream that the moon sheened white, the hag's mound stood. Its cairn-crown in disrepair, lopsided long-stones pointing haphazardly in every which direction that looked like blackthorns in the dark. Something was there, a fleeting thing. I said nothing to the quiet Myrnna.

After a spell, we started down the trackway. The cold wind swept down, Myrnna shivered, despite her cloak. I wrapped myself in my cloak. Shivering under our cloaks, we drew closer to the hag's cairn. Passing clouds darkened the moorland now, and the figure grew darker until the trackway dimmed. The moonshine breached the clouds and illuminated the figure, the lustre of the bright moon and stars revealing an old woman in a tattered red robe kicking her heels on top of the barrow.

We both stopped.

'What is she doing?' asked Myrnna.

'That's the hag of the hills! That's Calli!'

I did not know if I should run away or run her down with my sword. Badb just crept up through my chest. I shivered and I was thankful for the cold, so that Myrnna did not realize I was shivering from fear.

'What did you call her – Calli?'

'Calli, she's the hag of the hills!' I said, unable to say more.

'Cailleach, the queen of winter,' Myrnna said in disbelief.

The Cailleach was the old hag that stole summer from us and blighted us in autumn and then devoured autumn until it became winter. She darkens the world and casts it in white and eats all the leaves from the trees. She loves stones which are cold and hard so she makes the entire world cold and hard. On Beltane, Bride, goddess of the hearthfire, arrives to banish the Cailleach, until that frosty goddess returns the day after Samhain.

Did I really meet the Cailleach? My dear Luceo – did I really meet a goddess? Did I see a goddess with my own eyes? Did I break bread and eat stew and then make a deal with a goddess? What sort of ill has the Morrigan for me – I have become unlucky.

'What an omen!' said Myrnna. 'I don't like this! Oh, good Danu!'

I yearned to turn and flee. I never wanted to see the hag again. Her stretched, mummy-like face, those red daggers for teeth, her sidhe guests which I refused to look at. But we could not turn back, the Hillmen were there. The Hillmen could have been where we were going, too, but we didn't know that and it was our only chance to get to safety. Then we would find a boat and row to Dun Torrin or stay close to roadless lands and trek through the mountains and moors. But we had to pass the hag's cairn.

We pressed on.

I grabbed Myrnna by the wrist, and she put up a meek resistance, her soft white hand so cold and stiff, but she gave way and we started down the trackway again.

Come back… come back to the Slighan Hill!

Myrnna fell upon her knees. 'Danu, oh Danu!'

Danu, our mother goddess. Where is she now, with her warm bosom for us to clutch? Where was she now, when the hag caused us to shiver so cold?

'Cailleach… I heard it in my head – great Danu!' Myrnna cried.

'Ignore her! Ignore whatever she says to you!'

We pressed on, Myrnna behind me, as if walking against the wind bellowing a harsh gust. The figure had disappeared from the mound. There was nothing but wild moorland on either side of us, shadows of the red and black mountains off in the distance, the mound silent.

My meeting with the hag remained in my throat like a rogue piece of bread. I had a desire to tell Myrnna about it. She, too, heard the Cailleach's voice, just as I have since I had reached nine Samhains. I spoke as we passed the cairn.

'For ten years now, the hag has spoken to me, beckoning me to come to the Slighan hill,' I revealed to Myrnna.

'In desperation, of which I am not going to tell you,' I continued, 'I followed a wildcat that led me up into the Slighan Hills. There I found her, and her hut. I broke bread with her in there… I think she has something to do with the Hillmen.'

I gravely worried that I would be held accountable if I had told too many people the entire story. My people, as much as I love them, fear the sidhe, and the fact I had a voice in my head alone could get me killed. If I had told the common folk everything, they'd stake me to the bottom of a bog or nail me to a board and set it alight or simply toss me off a cliff and let me batter all the way down, and then piss on my body. I probably told her too much, but what would she say, and to whom? Myrnna had big, innocent eyes that allowed me to say all that I needed to say.

I wanted to tell her more. I wanted to tell her everything about my ordeal at the hut of the hag. She had almost been a druidess, and they discern some of the will of the gods, I thought, and she could have offered me some guidance.

I opened my mouth to speak but a cackle rattled in the air. It sounded like neither man nor woman, neither near nor far, but as if it were always there.

We turned to the cairn.

There the Cailleach, hag of the hills, danced madly. She had popped up like a phantom, red squirrel on her shoulder, red dog at her feet. Her cackle wrapped around my ears, a shrieking harridan's caw. I tried to scream but nothing came out. Then Myrnna screamed.

The cackling hag stood among the haphazard spike of cairn stones, arms akimbo, clicking her heels, grinning. Around her, a ring of weefolk donned in red, long, pointed caps, all spun together in a circle.

I disentangled myself from the mad show, as one does from the snare of many briars, by stiffening my knees and locking my eyes in the darkness of the long trackway. I grabbed Myrnna by her arm and yelled at her.

'Don't look! Run!'

We ran down the trackway as the clouds obscured the moon. The moorland became nothing but a shadow, nondescript, just rolling plains of dark. I stormed down, plunging into its murky depths, Myrnna behind me, the cackle of the hag and the clicking of her heels growing fainter but still present.

'The gods hate us,' Myrnna said, between breaths.

As if in response, the cackling resounded, and it delved into an indiscernible chatter. Calli's creaking voice over-ached it all.

Come back... come back to the Slighan Hill...

The Myrnna screamed again, her shrill scream like daggers in my ears. I felt faint, and yearned to turn back, and return to my house, curl up in a ball in my blanket and cry for Auneé to console me and then explain to me why the Hag of the Hills, the queen of winter, Cailleach, goddess of cold and geese and butter has haunted me, and what price I must pay to her.

The hag's voice itself silenced my pining.

You will return. I want you to return, dears...

Dance, dance with me...

We ran as fast as we could down the endarkened path, until Myrnna ran out of breath. She slumped up against a log on the trackway, knees to her chest. She was muddy now and looked not like the daughter of a druid, but a common peasant girl soiled from their daily toiling.

We caught our breath, and then I decided that I had owed her more of an explanation. 'I should have known. She introduced herself as Calli. How foolish am I?'

'Cailleach, queen of winter,' said Myrnna, 'doesn't your kind assemble an effigy of her, and toss it from farm to farm, and whoever harvests last gets stuck with her, and thus ill luck for the season? Then you all burn it in spring – when Bride, the spring queen returns?'

'My kind is of the warrior. We just farm due to happenstance.'

Myrnna said nothing. For her, it must matter little what kind I was, we were all warriors up on Dun Ashaig, and now our clan was gone. Yet I still owned land, and a sword, and my kind would always be of the warrior.

'I can't believe you actually met her! And now we can see her! Do you know how many druids claim they meet the Gods? I never believed any of them, and now I am not so sure.'

'I wish I never had,' I said, and now I sounded whiny, I think now, for all men ought to accept what the Morrigan spins for them. 'I was wandering on the Slighan Hill, and I was so thirsty. I sat and drank from a spring and she was then behind me. She invited me into her cottage. She fed me and then I could see the sidhe! Little men, like what we saw on the mound. A beautiful woman, a man much like a goat, and a cat with a man's grin, from ear to ear…'

'I was told never to speak to anyone about this, but I suppose it doesn't matter at all now,' Myrnna said. 'I also have *the sight*.'

The sight. It was often the subject of gossip among the clans. If someone had what they called *the sight* – they could see the sidhe, and often were able to retrieve knowledge from them. Weaving, healing, smithing – all skills supposed to have come to us by means of the sidhe. People with *the sight* – usually women but not always – were respected and feared. It was both a gift and a curse, really, for both good and bad could come from those who possessed it.

Gift or curse…

I must have *the sight* now. I don't know if I have always had it and Cailleach had blossomed it within me like a flower in spring, or if I had it fostered upon me, like an orphaned child. I did not know, and I wanted to know more.

'Tell me about it.'

'I've just seen them in glimpses – nothing like tonight – with the hag and her dancing weemen – it was terrifying! I've seen a white horse not quite right, not quite walking on the ground… the grass it grazes not quite disappearing. I've seen a handsome lad in the loch, a squirrel that looked too red, little men with big red eyes in the moors that frightened me so, but nothing ever like tonight, never… never a goddess! What did the hag say to you in her hut?'

I hesitated. I did not want to tell her everything. I did not want to tell her that my deal with the Cailleach may have cost her everything. We had to get to Dun Torrin, run by that scoundrel Fenn Beg Corm, himself a half unfriendly, moody outlander, and if he still lived and still had his fort then we could only hope his reaction would be half-way pleasant when we turned up there, poor and at his complete mercy. He'd probably demand the poor girl's maidenhood just for some food and shelter. He never liked our clan or Ambicatos but from what I had heard of him, he was very generous. This was, of course, if the Hillmen had not already overrun his dun. Then where shall we go? Hibernia? Alba? Gaul? Perhaps the Hillmen had already overrun all these places, and the entire world was overrun with them and we were doomed, and I had doomed all by accepting the hag's price?

Myrnna kept eying me, probably wondering why I said nothing, but then I looked beyond her and in the distant foothills, the shadows moved.

I rose to my feet and watched, hand crawling to the leather grip of my sword. Nothing came, though I knew that in the total darkness, even deer rove like monstrosities until they come into clear view. But in the now full moonlight, I witnessed shadows morphing, shadows going from one shadow into another, shadows taking shape. My sweaty fingers clenched the grip of my sword.

The shadows spurted forth a black blob. It bounded across the moorland, fast-paced, and the thud of its footsteps hit my chest.

Then I saw its size. It stood thrice as tall as any man. We flew down the trackway as fast as a quarried deer. I then turned and I regretted it, for I saw a shadow as tall as an oak and as wide as five bounding across the moonlit heathery hills right toward us.

The ground quaked underneath us. The shadow-giant pounded the ground with each of its long bounds. A ghastly grey thing with great girth, clad in nought but a loincloth, came hither, and he wielded a log as a club. I could not see above its naval, but its naval was at the end of a fat hanging belly. It stopped and we ran forward a few paces, and I turned again to see its face obscured by black shaggy hair, and it outstretched its arms and chased after us like a toddler in play.

'Badb – Macha – Fea!' I cried out, but instead of the three darkly faced ladies, Camulus lit me afire. We could not outrun this thing – its legs were too long. I stopped and pivoted, sword drawn, and faced the giant. It was my duty to defend Myrnna. Again, I will swear, my dear Luceo, whatever Brennus was, he was no coward.

Myrnna stood there overawed and she fell into the mud, and looked up, gawking.

Each thundering footfall beat against my chest. Camulus then numbed my pain.

'A giant!' Myrnna screamed. For a brief, odd moment, I recalled our clan stories about giants in the olden days who dwelled in our lands before our ancestors had vanquished them.

The giant stopped in front of me. The misshapen thing stood at least three times my height. I saw first his toenails, yellow-brown and curled in great tusks. He had thin legs, too thin for his flabby frame, the latter dominated by a bloated grey gut that hung over its tattered loincloth. I could barely see above its dirt-black kneecaps, and his bellybutton resembled a knot of worms. He looked down at me, and I was reminded of when I had been a small boy. He had a gaping maw of teeth, chipped and yellow, atop a weak chin. A stench permeated the air, emitting from the fungus-plagued, hairy flesh of the giant. He had large, red-pupiled keen eyes. His great belly hammered out when he let out a hideous laugh.

'Greetings, travellers!' said the giant, grinning like a father catching his son up to no good, 'I'm Ciuthach, and the queen has ordered me to take the two of you to her!'

I found no words.

'Got nothing to say? Put your sword down! That bitty little sword can't hurt me,' he said, and laughed again.

I did not sheath my sword.

There had been giants in the days of yore. They had hoisted up the big stones on the island, and in other stories big stones were said to have been giants cursed by the gods. They lived in our land until our ancestors came and drove them out to make room for us, for they were too stupid and savage and deserving of slaughter. Still, some giants lived in the mountains, some of the more superstitious said, or in distant lands, but we never saw them. Just as we never saw the hag or the sidhe or any of the other things of the night that haunt this trackway. It stood before me, gazing down with red eyes.

'What are you?' I asked in a hushed tone, dumbstruck by it all.

'A giant, what do you think I am?'

I had seen giants before, in the Slighan Hills, when the four figures carried the house of the hag. Those litter-bearers seemed unreal, different from this word, unlike this one.

'As I said, the queen wants you and the girl to come with me to her,' he said and giggled.

I said nothing, my fingers weak on the hilt of my sword. How could I ever protect her against this giant? I smelled piss, and did not know if it were I or Myrnna or the giant.

'And what a pretty little girl she is,' Ciuthach said, and laughed.

Myrnna scuttled away like a crab, scrambled to her feet, and raced down the trackway.

'You can run all you want, girl! But you will never outrun the hand of your queen!'

Myrnna ran off into the gloom. The giant did not pursue her, and I thought perhaps it was because I stood in his way, but it could have simply stepped over me. I knew I had to bind it here to me, to allow Myrnna ample time to run and hide.

I stood at the feet of the giant, barely above its knees, armed with a sword athwart a giant that had spawned from the shadows of the moors. Badb clawed Camulus away from my blood now.

A memory came to me. My father and I, in my seventh spring, were on the mainland to visit some cousins of ours. On the track, a bear plagued by mange lunged out of the brush. The bear came for us, it had just one eye and that eye was filled with rage that it unleashed on us with slavering jaws. My father had drawn a javelin and chucked it into the one good eye of the bear. The bear was then completely blind. We watched the bear lumber around aimlessly, wheezing.

For me, as just a boy, my father was godlike, and even now I always come across stories of him and his feats that I had never known before, and I still look upon him in wonder. I remember looking up at my father. He stood so silent, his mouth wrung, his eyes focused. He had eliminated the threat and now he pitied it. I had then asked him how he stayed so calm. When he answered, his voice rang through my years:

Nothing is unconquerable. Even our gods can die.

Those words were my courage. My brows furrowed and I gripped my sword tight and I thought myself a match for whatever the shadows spat out. The giant was no more undefeatable than the bear.

But this queen, who is this queen?

'Tell me, Ciuthach – who are you, and who is your queen?'

'The queen is the queen and I'm her servant,' he said. A tight-lipped response, but I sensed a slither of stupidity within his droll voice. I would trick him, but first I should learn about this queen.

'Tell me then, Ciuthach, for I am at your mercy – where did you come from?'

'Funny thing for you to ask me,' he said, and he patted me on the head. 'My ancestors were here long before yours. You killed them off and now we're back. Any complaints?' he asked.

'I won't complain, but just ask,' I said, 'I do not know what you are, but I know you had not existed until you showed yourself to me. Tell me, why can I see you now?'

'Why can you see me now?' he asked, grinning wide. 'Didn't Myrnna tell you? You have *the sight*! And now you can see us, and we can see you, and all those around you can see us, too, if you let them.'

At the feet of the giant, I had not been able to surmount all of what he said at that time. His words were like water pooling on soil, eventually seeping in after some time and reaching the roots. He was right – we had slain the giants in the olden days, according to our lore, and I did possess *the sight*.

'I see you because I have the sight, and that allows others to see you. If I had not the sight, then would you not exist?'

'I would exist. We, the sidhe, all exist, just you can't see us most of the time,' he said.

Good. Now I will trick him, perhaps to let me go. I had no plan, but thought to Lugus, the god of craftiness, to inspire me with his silvery tongue.

'Who is your queen?' I asked again.

'The queen is the queen,' he said, grinning.

'The queen is the queen, but not all are queens,' I said. Truth be told, Luceo, I had not known where this path would lead, and I feared a dead end, but I trudged on.

'Silly human,' he said, and his grotesque long hand shuffled my beeswaxed hair, 'what else is a queen?'

'The queen of bees,' I said.

Ciuthach laughed, a hearty, jolly laugh, and he looked down at me again, his bright big eyes amused. 'The queen is no bee.'

'Your queen is the queen bee!'

The giant furrowed his thick brows, his mood shifted like the winds, and his jowls flapped and he shot a gust from his flared nostrils.

'A dragon is no bee!'

A dragon?

'A dragon is a bee if it is your queen!'

'My queen is the mother of giants.'

I interrupted him.

'The queen of giant bees!'

'No!' Ciuthach tossed his club. It woofed through the air and I failed to see where it landed.

'The queen of giants is Slighan!!'

Queen of giants.

Slighan.

Come back to the Slighan Hill…

'You said she was a dragon!' I had to keep it up. He was flustered.

Ciuthach's eyes bulged as he laughed down at me so hard that my hair would have winded back had it not been moulded in beeswax.

I found the courage to look into his eyes, big white puddles, irises like red henges.

My father couldn't kill the bear easily. Bears have thick fur and blubber, and all one stab from a spear does is enrage the bear further. This giant, too, had thick blubber, and I imagined my sword would be nothing but a bee sting to him. But the giant has eyes, and like blinding the bear, I could blind him, if I could just get to his eyes.

'You're clever,' he said, 'the queen is going to like you.' He leaned down a little, his boulder-like fists akimbo.

Just lean down more…

Ciuthach flared his nostrils and puffed. 'Enough of your tricks. The queen wants you to come along now.'

'Does she think I am a bee?'

'I said no more tricks!' he cracked his knuckles, the sound like tree trunks snapping. Drool dripped down like a tipped-over bucket.

'I'm sorry, but what did you say?' I cupped an ear.

'I said no tricks! No– tricks!'

'What?'

'What are you, deaf?' he asked, clenching his fist at my face.

'What? I'm very sorry, gentle Ciuthach, but you are going to have to speak up. I am a bit deaf.'

Ciuthach leaned down toward me and came face to face. He eradicated the dull scent of milkweed and cow muck from the air, and his man-breasts jiggling near my head. When he opened his great, shark-like mouth, his breath almost caused me to vomit.

The oval, puddle-like left eye of the giant twitched as he repeated himself again, so loud that his deep voice beat against my ears.

'I… said…'

Twitching left eye. An omen. Then was my chance!

A thundering cry bellowed across the moorland. The giant wheeled back, and I hung from the hilt of my sword, the blade jammed into the left eye of the giant. My blue legs dangled against the belly of the beastly monstrosity that retched in agony.

Ciuthach's greasy hair flopped about, his other eye poured out a rivulet of tears. I grasped a clump of mattered hair and swung across the face of the giant, ripped the sword out and went to jam it into the other eye. I missed and jammed the air near his ear, and fell upon the ground, a torrent of blood from the giant pouring out and splattering my clothes in red. I had intended to impale the other eye, but Danu pulled me back to her bosom and now the half-blind giant looked down at me through both of his eyes, one tearing, one bleeding.

A roar echoed across the moorlands, so loud it must have rippled the nearby stream. I then ran, as fast as I could down the trackway. Ciuthach quaked greatly, his feet shook the ground, but he seemed rattled. I still had his hot blood smeared and dripping all over me.

'Slighan will have you!' he called out, 'come back to the Slighan Hill!'

I raced down the trackway, wishing for night to end, horrified at the prospect of another meeting with the unknown.

'Thank you, Lugus, the victory is for you, and the blood spilt in your name, and I will sacrifice to you greatly at Lughnasa.' He had granted me the silver tongue, to trick my enemy. I could not have blinded the giant without his wisdom.

And father! I drank deep from his wisdom that night. I could never have thought of blinding the giant, had I not seen father blind that bear. 'Thank you, glorious Biturix.'

I slowed my pace. The giant had not followed me. I had defeated it, in part, and secured my oath to Ambicatos. But where did Myrnna go? I looked all around and saw nothing but darkened fields of moorlands at either of my flanks. How could I find her? Did I dare yell her name, with Hillmen and who knows what else lurking about?

In the moonlight, I began my search. I would search all night, until dawn ate away the horrible blackness that spawned that monster.

'I will find her. I must find her. My oath depends on it,' I thought.

CHAPTER VIII

I scoured the moorlands all night for Myrnna. It was a daunting thing. The moorlands stretched vastly along both ends of the trackway, strewn in rock shelters and boulders, streams in deep gullies, and the long-robbed foundations of old buildings. I yelled for her despite the threat of Hillmen hearing me.

To make it all worse, I found nothing but death. The Hillmen had ravaged all. Before Beautiful Bride had reddened the sky to wake the world, I had found something that wrenched my heart. On the trackway, half-stuck in the mud, I came across two felled horses in great red pools. They were brown stallions, lean and muscular beasts that had been robbed of their trappings. The stench of blood sullied the air, and near them laid two naked warriors, no older than I, face down in the mud with wooden stakes driven through their backs, spiked to the ground. There were great splinters of wood and broken wheels, and I realized it had been a chariot.

I pulled the spikes out and wheezed at the viscera wrapped around the spikes. I righted the two warriors, and closed their eyes. They were beautiful, lean, and Lugus-like. I should have laid them near their horses, but I had to move on to find Myrnna.

All along the trackway, I entered and exited the crow-strewn farmsteads, and left with more hatred against the Hillmen, and still without Myrnna. Three men impaled on stakes, through their arses and out their mouths. An old man hacked to death. A torso stuffed into the belly of a rotting horse. A young boy brained against a wall of an abandoned home. Heads with cocks hanging from their mouths posted on a fence. A young fox gnawing on a severed hand. Roofs burned, horses slaughtered, sheep gone, foodstuffs plundered, no women or children in sight. Often, I ran into mere bones in a roundhouse; the Morrigan's children were hasty in their feast. The putrid stench and sight and even sound when the bodies farted was all over. I recognized some of them, if the Hillmen or the carrion eaters had not disfigured them too much. They were neighbours, friends, kinsmen. All dead, all nothing I can do. It exhausted me to search the farmsteads, and

I dreaded it, but the trackway was hardly better. I am sure the battlefield outside Dun Ashaig looked even worse. I decided, there and then, to kill all Hillmen I found until there was no more blood left to spill.

The songbirds filled the morning, and Belanus sheened the moorlands gold, the sky clear, while the Slighan Hill loomed. The trackway ended several paces before me, the moorlands rolled into greenland, hillocks and then a frown of pine forest. It was Torrin forest, a wall of pines where our chiefs should be hunting stags on shared land, and after it the coast, and then to Dun Torrin, the cliffside fort with its high ramparts and that brooding foreign king. I headed forest-bound and found the path that Cúchulainn once walked. I entered the pine forest with the canopy over my head and pine blanket under my feet, and found the byway. A squirrel flickered throughout the trees, frogs croaked from a mossy pond, and then I spotted men deep on the pathway, and they spotted me. Their shadows stopped, turned, and approached me.

I thought to run, perhaps, since I would be one against many, and I did not desire death yet, but then one must have entered a treeless spot, for his hair burned blazing fire. He was a redhead. Hillmen are not redheaded. The second one then followed shortly, and his hair too glowed, but gold. Hillmen are not blond. They aren't Hillmen!

They approached me from the left. Now, this may sound odd to so-called civilized men, but a man does not approach another man from the left. We will traverse through briars or down a deep gulch or even over a mountain if it meant approaching from the right, the only way to approach a man.

Unless you're looking for a fight.

The two of them weaved in and out of the pine trees and then hopped over a creek. They were both lads, stripped to the waist, lanky, with long hair. They wore check pants of white and yellow, cinched at the waist by string. From just their pants I could tell they were foreigners. They came closer and I now realized one carried a longspear leaned against his shoulder, and the other a shortspear and shield. The redhead stepped in a bog and stopped, but then the blond gave him a light shove, and that set the redhead marching through the bog and the blond followed, both lads coming toward me.

'Why on the left?' I asked when they came into earshot.

'You're on our road,' said the blond one behind his comrade. I understood what he said, and understood he spoke a tongue similar to mine. They were *Celts*, from where – Alba, Albion, Hibernia, Gaul, Iberia – I did not know.

'There's no road here,' I said, so naïve back then, but I fingered the hilt of my sword, and readied to unhook the shield from my neck.

'What's the word?' asked the redhead one.

'He doesn't know it,' said the blond. 'Look, he has his woad on.'

The redhead was taller and muscular and had a fish-mouth, always open, with a gap tooth, and a freckled face. Both had budding moustaches that had not quite filled out yet.

'If he doesn't know the word, then he has to pay the toll.'

'Tell me – have you seen a girl? A brunette.'

'Think we found her last night, chief,' a third voice said behind me, in another *Celtic* language I did not recognize.

I pivoted to see a short man behind me, armed with an iron dagger gleaming in the sun. He too was stripped to the waist, and he had baggy green trousers, and a yellow-brown check cloak wrapped around his shoulder. He possessed long grey ringlets of hair that danced at his shoulders, a thick grey moustache, and tawny, leathery skin. He had small blue eyes and he never looked me in the eyes when speaking. He seemed aloof, yet I suspected he wanted me to think that.

'You found her last night? Really?'

'Your sword – hand it over,' said the short man.

'Who are you people? Bandits?' I asked. I had heard of lawless men that prey on lone travellers in Alba, but never suspected them on Skye.

'I'm Antedios,' said the gap-toothed lad, his spear shaft in both of his hands and iron point aimed at me. 'That's Cattos.' He gestured to the shorter blond armed with a shortspear and shield. 'And that's Aldryd.' He gestured to the man behind me, dagger still poised. 'And you're on our road.'

'You're going to pay the toll,' Aldryd said.

Black Badb crawled in my chest as red Camulus tremored my sword-arm. I unhooked my shield and unsheathed my sword and did not know which way to face, for they had already surrounded me. 'You're foreigners! This is the commons – it's my clan's road!'

'This is no man's road now, chief,' Aldryd said. 'Except ours. Put the sword down. Rather, put it down at your feet. We'll let you live if you just drop it and leave. Real easy, chief.'

I refused to answer as Camulus raged in my heart. Where is Myrnna? By good Danu – has she been taken? Will she be sold into slavery? If I could get Myrnna back, then I would put my sword down. The thought of losing Bodvoc' sword hurt, but I had sworn an oath to Ambicatos to protect his daughter no matter what. The sword for my oath.

Cattos and Antedios fanned out on both of my flanks.

'Tell me – where is the girl! You'd better not have touched her – I am her protector!'

'You're her protector?' Aldryd asked. He rubbed his grey chin. 'Well, no dispute then if you're dead. Stick him! Go – lads – go!'

Badb entranced me, she bound me to the ground, I did not act as the three closed in on me. Then the corpse of my brother entered my mind. How many did he fell before he himself fell? Could Badb have ever bounded my father?

Nothing is unconquerable. Even our gods can die.

Those words burned in me as the longspear plunged toward my thigh. I slapped the blade with my shield and held the spear away from me. I charged at Antedios, the edge of my shield sliding down his shaft.

'I am Biturix's son!' I shouted at him. If I were going to die, Antedios will come with me. I sought revenge, not for myself, but for Myrnna. And death hemmed in on me, both Cattos from my right and Aldryd from down the bypath, my foemen readied to strike me down from three places.

I rushed Antedios, butted the spearshaft so that his arm leaned awkwardly away, and then I slashed at the unguarded man.

Antedios sprawled away from me, spear landing softly on the pine carpet below. A fourth man appeared. He had grabbed Antedios and tossed him away. His shout had halted Aldryd and Cattos, and the man stood arms waving, shaking his head, as Antedios collected himself from off the ground.

'You idiot! He almost gutted you!' he yelled at Antedios.

The man was tall, fat, sturdy, bald, skin-faced, and ruddy. My eyes were first drawn to a bronze torc wrapped around his neck, though he spoke *Celtic* with a thick, strange accent. He wore a red kilt and wooden sandals, and I had rarely seen such bright red-coloured clothes before on someone. He had deep scars over his chest and one across his face. With his shimmering torc and red garments, he was outfitted both legally and brutally.

'He said *Biturix*. I know that name. You're not killing him,' he said to his men. 'At ease.'

They all lowered their weapons, though Antedios kept a gape-mouth, gap-toothed, goofy grin on me. He breathed heavy and so did Cattos, both red-faced, ready for another round at a moment's notice.

Aldryd, on the other hand, looked nonplussed. He leaned against a tree and crossed his arms.

'Oh, calm down you two,' the newcomer said to the lads. 'And you, too,' he said to me.

I had not lowered my sword, and I could feel my shoulders hunched to my ears, and realized I stood on the balls of my feet.

'Put the sword down,' he said to me.

I refused.

'You said you're Biturix's boy?' he asked, hand to stubbled chin.

I nodded.

'You ever hear him mention the name Tratonius?'

'No.'

'Too bad, because that's me. Biturix was an old friend of mine. I knew he had sons, doesn't surprise me you almost ran poor Antedios here through!' he said and grinned to show he was missing at least half of his teeth. 'Come on, put the sword down, I wouldn't dishonour Biturix by betraying his son, that's what you're thinking, right?'

I lowered my sword. Tratonius stared at me, he had big grey eyes and a straight, long nose, and there was a hard kindness in his face. I sheathed my sword, and felt it secure in its sheath, away from the grubby hands of banditry.

'Now, what are you doing here?'

'This is the commons!' I shouted back at Tratonius, and he raised his palms in response to me. 'How dare you ask me that! You foreigners come here and threaten me on the path Cúchulainn took when he travelled from Hibernia to train in the Cuillins with Sgàthach? You demand my brother's sword on my ancestral home?'

Tratonius held out a hand, nodding.

'Who are you?' I asked.

'We're sellswords,' he answered.

'Who do you work for?'

He failed to answer.

'The brunette! Tell me, where is she?'

'Yeah, we have her, what of her?'

'You didn't… touch her, did you? How is she?'

'How is she?' Aldryd answered from behind me. 'Don't know, didn't try her yet.'

I wheeled around toward him, and before I could even think of grabbing for my sword, he had flicked his wrist to show me his drawn dagger.

'He's joking,' Tratonius said.

I was breathing heavily, and I could not fathom how any man could joke about such a horrible thing like that. I have seen men lose their lives for lesser slights, and I should have drawn my sword and slashed his thick, wrinkly throat, but that would have been suicide and thus a breach of my oath.

'No one's touched her,' Tratonius said. 'Her maidenhood is fine.'

'She's mine,' I said. 'Her father was the chief druid of Dun Ashaig.'

'She's not yours anymore. Her father's dead.'

'I swore an oath!' I cried out, and my eyes and his locked, and though his expression did not change, he seemed to frown with his eyes. Now Luceo, I came to know this man very well, as did you, and I would be right to say that I saw pity in the eyes of the old mercenary captain. I saw pity buried behind his scarred, tired face, right there on the path that Cúchulainn had walked a long time ago.

'You don't look much like your father,' he said, 'and I never saw him so desperate as I see you. Now come on, son, do you really think you'll get her back?' he asked.

'I'll do whatever I can to get her back,' I said, 'even if that means killing you.'

Tratonius grinned at that. 'There's your father!' and his face relaxed. 'But listen, son, her father is dead, so your oath is over.'

'That's wrong,' I said. 'He made me swear it knowing that he would die!'

'Told you it was easier to kill him,' Aldryd said, and leaned against the tree again.

'We'll ask Verc,' Tratonius said. 'Former druid, he knows this shit.'

I had a feeling that this Verc would not be on my side, but my hope brightened.

'Come and visit our camp,' Tratonius said. 'We'll settle this over some food, and maybe I can tell you a story or two about your father.'

I neither agreed nor disagreed, but Tratonius took my silence as agreement. He hit me lightly in the meat of my shoulder and walked down the byway.

'Good, I need a catamite for the night,' Aldryd said, and I did not say anything because I did not know what a catamite was. He, too, then walked off with Cattos.

A former druid, I thought. Auneé didn't like the druids too much, and she always warned me of their cunning nature. A druid will agree to your terms until he no longer cares to, and then he shall breach his word, citing some divine law the rest of us had not heard of, because only druids can discern the laws of the gods. I was still covered in blood that had fountained over me from the giant, and I imagined this Verc declaring my entry an ill-omen and discarding my argument as unfounded before he even heard it.

Antedios looked at me, spear slung over his shoulder, mouth drooped open. I looked back and we stared at each other for a bit, and then he spoke. 'Good work, you nearly got me.'

I nodded, we locked eyes for a moment and both grinned.

'Then let me ask you,' I asked him. 'Do you have a tub of water so I can clean this blood from me before I meet this former druid?'

'What blood?' he asked.

I looked down at my tunic and trousers and found them clean. I unsheathed my sword, Antedios jumped backward, and the sword shimmered unstained in the sun. I sheathed it.

He looked at me curiously, and then left, and the mercenaries disappeared into the green meld of pine forest. I hurried to catch up. I followed them out of the forest, questions and worries harrying my mind.

Antedios chatted to me about Verc and gave me some advice regarding him as we headed toward the mercenary camp. We had gone through the frown of pine forest and emerged on the coast. The smell of brine and the baying of seagulls signified a normal balmy early autumn day. Behind us, lay a span of moorland that was an excellent hunting ground but haunted by sidhe, and home to a clan that is probably dead and nameless by now. In front of us, a black rim of shingles where sea-eagles dump their shells to crack them open, and then the grey ocean. The mercenaries camped on the slither of grassland before the shingles, a series of white tents contrasted against the black shale rocks, like mould on rotten food. There were men strewn about, and even some women, a campfire in the centre, two pack mules grazing on the grasslands, some barrels, a wooden frame with hanging clothes, and the smell of cooking meat as we came down toward them. I noticed little else, for I was terrified of the prospect of the Hillmen finding us, but no one seemed concerned.

'There are Hillmen!' I blurted out, hopping across a stream. 'Don't you know what happened to my clan last night?'

Aldryd, who strode across the treacherous shingle spread as sure footed as a goat, turned to me and shrugged. 'We have a deal with them.'

A deal with them Hillmen? Just as I were about to ask him more, Tratonius began speaking to a tall man in a green tunic, and Tratonius pointed back at me. That must be Verc.

At the camp, Verc looked down his meaty nose at me. He had a hard face, a high hairline of grey-blond hair, and a thick, long moustache. He stood a head taller me. He was an old Gaul, a druid-turned-warrior, and Antedios told me that he hated the Romans and if I wanted to get on his good side, I would tell him I hated the Romans. I told him I hated the bastards, and he asked if I knew who the bastards were, and I didn't. That did not seem to matter, since it was as if he were a dog and sniffed me and smelled something he disliked.

'You're not the relative of the girl, so it means nothing.'

I stared up at him. He looked back down at me. Badb pounded in my chest, reminding me of my failure with each beat.

'You can do one thing for me, though,' he said, and squinted his eyes.

'What is it?' I asked.

Verc walked toward a tent and beckoned for me to come. I followed, looking around, getting strange looks from the other men, and glanced around for Myrnna. He opened the flap of the tent, stuck it into a wooden peg in the ground, and entered. I followed.

The interior of the tent was an orderly bed of skins and woollen blankets along with rugs and sacks stacked on one side. He picked up a wooden box and shoved it at me. I opened it and was met with a putrid stench.

'My shoes smell. They're also leaking. Fix that,' he said, and left the tent.

I looked down at the brown leather, pointed, stinky shoes in the box. I dropped the box and the shoes spilled out on the grass. I left the tent and looked for Myrnna.

Outside among the tents, one man around the campfire caught my attention. He was large, so tall and so fat, whale-like, with thin black hair in a tiny ponytail at the nape of his neck, big beefy hands whittling a chunk of wood with a long, broad dagger, and someone had just told a joke so he let out a great bellow and shivers ran down my spine. Though most of the men there intimidated me, this massive man intimidated me the most. It was as though he could gut a man with that knife as simply as he whittled with it.

I put him out of my mind and called out 'Myrnna!'

Some commotion came from one of the tents, and I looked around and the mercenaries now had noticed me. Tratonius walked toward me from the shingles, he had been speaking to a blond man with a fishing pole reeling in a fish. He unhooked the fish from his line and plopped it in a bucket and started toward me.

I ran over to the tent with the women's voices and ripped open the flap. I was met by a woman with striking long dark hair. She had a small, rounded forehead, a thin but long nose, full ruby lips, and a glowing smile. She had a beautiful face, though aged, with a dark mole on her delicate chin that gave her a lasting impression. Due to her beauty and posture, I had first thought she was some queen held captive by the mercenaries, until I saw her garments. She wore a simple wool dress that clung close to her lithe body, the trace of her nipples visible, and a leather collar around her lithe neck. She was a slave, and I thought it was a crime to see such a pretty and dignified woman in such an ugly and undignified way.

'Puer! Oh, puer!' She said to me, then she looked over my shoulder. 'Tell me, Tratonius, oh domine! Tell your most beloved slave Sabella what this handsome puer is doing here! Have you a guest that needs loving arms?'

'We have a guest here that needs to fix my shoes,' said Verc, whom I had not noticed behind me.

Behind the slave woman, Myrnna rested on a sheepskin bed, and she looked up at me with shining eyes.

I wanted to shove this slave out of the way, grab Myrnna and run away. Run away from these horrible mercenaries and their twisted laws and slavery.

'Come here, boy,' Tratonius said, and he grabbed me by the shoulder and beckoned me away from the tent. I moved and Sabella closed the flap.

We all sat down at the fire: Tratonius, Verc, myself, and the fisherman they called Marthelm. Marthelm must have been in his forties, and he had a knot of blond hair tied above his ear. He had a trimmed dark blond beard and fierce blue eyes that burned so hot in his head that they resembled the blue of flame. He dumped the fish, a ling, out of the bucket. It flopped about until he stunned it with a rock, then he chopped its head off, cut it from gill to tail and its guts spilled out, and began fileting it on a cutting board across his lap.

'I swore an oath,' I said, fingering the brooch that clenched my cloak together.

'Her father is dead, I told you,' Verc said. 'But if you insist, there may be a way we can sell her to you.'

'How?' I asked, fingering my sword in its sheath, catching a glimpse of its leathered handle. It hurt to think about departing from that sword, but if it meant purchasing Myrnna, then my oath must take precedent over my sword, though I had started to believe Bodvoc travelled with me as I wore his sword, and guided my sword-arm when I struck with it.

'You don't want to do it,' said the man filleting the fish. He looked up at me, and nodded. 'You should find another way,' he said in a thick accent that I could not pin down, but it sounded similar to Auneé's when she got upset.

'Let him make his own decision, Marthelmaz,' Verc said. 'He's a freeman, and a warrior, aren't you?' he turned to me. 'They painted you with woad and your hair is spiked, and you own a sword. You're a warrior.'

'I'm Biturix's son,' I said. 'We are descended from Lugus, and I demand that you take my oath seriously!'

'Biturix – I know the name. But you aren't your father and as far as I know, you have no clan any longer. You're a lonesome warrior and we aren't giving your girl back, unless you work for us.'

'You talk too much, Vercerterx,' Marthelm said.

'Then you tell him, if you are more efficient, Marthelmaz,' Verc said with a wave of the hand. A girl in a tattered, undyed dress passed him by, her dirty bare feet unsure on the ground. She had short-cropped blond hair and a leather collar, and she was clearly another slave girl. Verc caught eye of her rear, and he grabbed her by her little wrist and pulled her toward him. She sat in his lap, expressionless. We made eye contact, and she just stared through me. I shuddered at her dead-gaze.

'They want you to sell yourself into slavery,' Marthelm said.

Badb pounded in my chest. I'm a warrior, how could I even be a slave?

'Look, son,' Tratonius said, 'our hoisting slaves drowned on the way over here. Your islands are terribly stormbound, lucky to get here alive. We're real short on hands and we need people to sharpen our weapons, help stitch our clothes, carry our shit – tell you what, you work for, let's say, five years, and if we still have Myrnna then you can have her back.'

My woad ran down my forearms and calves in streamlets of blue sweat, and the beeswax melted down my forehead.

'Five years?' I asked, bewildered.

'Yes,' Verc said.

'Maybe we can do four years,' Tratonius said.

'No, five. The girl is a maiden,' Verc said.

'Come on, he's Biturix's boy. Four and a half.'

'You don't have to decide today,' Marthelm said, 'sleep on it. None of the men here can afford the girl. She is safe for now.'

'Don't be so sure. The Hibernian wants her, and he claims to have land over back home he's willing to trade,' Verc said.

Four and a half years of my life, working for them, as a slave. I could think of little worse. Yet my oath drove me to this path, the Morrigan, goddess of fate, cackled behind me. I was sure of it. When Cúchulainn stood dead on his legs against his enemies, she shapeshifted into a raven and perched on his shoulder, and mocked him, and now she mocks me here, seated humbly on a log at this campfire.

'And how do I know in four and a half years you shall both set me free and Myrnna will be mine?'

'My word,' Tratonius said. 'All a man has in this life is his word. Break the word, and you break yourself as a man. Come on, boy, I would never break my word, especially to the son of Biturix.'

'Four and a half years of labour for a maiden?' Verc said. 'What sort of crime have you bestowed upon us, Tratonius? What sort of deal have you made?'

'That's a long time,' Marthelm said. 'He may not survive.'

'I will live. I will live long enough to take Myrnna. You just wait.'

Verc scoffed and ruffled his moustache looking down at me. Tratonius put two fingers in his mouth and whistled. Sabella came out, crying *domine*. She probably had been eavesdropping since she carried with her a razor and a leather collar.

'Strip it all off,' Verc said.

'I'm keeping my belongings,' I said, fingering my baldric and running a finger over the leather grip of my sword. 'And my land.'

'Your land is owned by the Hillmen now, so that's a different dispute,' Tratonius said. 'And you can keep your things, but you can't have them on you.'

'Foolish,' Verc said, 'you're letting him keep his sword? A slave with a sword – what do you bring upon us, Tratonius?'

'I'm Biturix's son. I am a warrior, a descendant of Lugus.'

'It will be in your back first,' Verc said to Tratonius.

'He won't dare, because then we will just sell the girl and his oath will be forfeit. Now come on, son, you agreed to your slavery. Go along with it.'

They kept speaking but I lost their voices. My head spun. They spoke but I spoke over them, and there I recited my lineage from Lugus to Biturix and to myself. All proud warriors, god-blooded, men who braved the ocean and settled on Skye a long time ago, who drove the giants into the sea, just as I drove my sword into the giant's eye last night. I was a warrior, I carried a sword, I carried the blood of the gods, I carried my name. And now I was enslaved, through my own will. I reached the last name and that was my own, and Bodvoc's sword bade me unsheathe it and impale myself upon it to end such a dishonour. A dishonour I had brought upon my forefathers.

For a moment, I hated the chief druid. I hated him for ripping me from my destiny of dying at the side of my brother and our clan on the rolling moors of Dun Ashaig. To join my brothers and father and all my forefathers in Tír na nÓg, where only the bravest warriors sit among the olden heroes. Now I stand among these rotten mercenaries, for that's what they were, rotten, I could see it on their gaunt faces hidden behind deep scars, and now my thoughts subsided when one whistled and out came Sabella, and I caught Myrnna's big brown eyes behind her. Her eyes shined in the dim light of the tent, and we locked our gazes and then she shouted at me.

'You idiot!'

Sabella approached me as the three aged mercenaries surrounded me. The slave mistress motioned for me to raise my arms, and I did, and then she unhooked my baldric and removed my sheathed sword. The other two slave girls, blonds, pudgy-faced and snub-nosed *Germans*, lugged out an open wicker chest. Sabella placed my sword and belts in the chest, and off came my hat. I looked up at the overcast sky and watched the seagulls swirling above as she unhooked my brooch, and I pleaded for it, but she assured me it would be safe in the chest, and then she removed my cloak. Next came my tunic, my shoes, and then my trousers, my socks, and finally my undertunic. I was naked on the brine-breezed beach.

The German girls came. They had sponges and a bucket, and they scrubbed the woad off my body, Sabella instructing them to get every bit off it, and Sabella herself rinsed the beeswax out of my hair. I began to recite my lineage again throughout. Sabella motioned me to kneel and I refused.

'I will not kneel.'

'O Servi!' Sabella said, smiling at me and jiggling my dangling balls. My fist curled. She placed two hands on my shoulder, and her hazel eyes gleamed. 'Servi! Kneel or we will have to make you,' she said with a big toothy smile, and I wondered how such an old slave could have such a full set of white teeth.

I again refused, and she said something to the German girls in their language. Sabella walked behind me, and then a snap. I winced, and there stood Sabella behind me with a bullwhip. Blood rushed to my rear where the slave mistress had smarted me. I knelt, grumbling, and began reciting my lineage again.

I heard a snipping sound above me, and my hair trickled down my face and neck. Sabella had a pair of shears that snipped about my head, and by the time the Germans had finished washing my body, I had short-cropped hair, and then with a razor she shaved my head and face until both were as smooth as my knuckles. Then they led me toward the ocean, my bare feet rasped by the hard shingles and empty broken shells, and dipped me into the cold water. I came out and then Sabella wrapped a leather collar around my neck and handed me a loincloth and a pair of flimsy sandals. I was a slave, and I accepted my fate, holding in my heart that it was temporary, and that I'd be free in four and a half years with the Myrnna's maidenhood and my oath intact. They led me back to the three elders of the mercenary tribe. I trembled, I seethed, I bowed my head and said nothing.

'Your first order is to finish fixing my shoes,' said Verc, 'they are from Etruria, and I am fond of them.' He stroked his long grey moustache and pointed toward his tent. 'Go on, slave. Now.'

I followed his order, reciting my lineage under my breath, my oath in my mind, and hatred in my heart for the Hillmen.

For nine miserable days, I toiled on the beach tasked with tedious work. In the mornings, I fished and then prepared breakfast, and often had to go into the hinterlands with the German girls to fetch mushrooms, herbs, fruit, and berries for Verc, Cattos and Antedios, who refused to eat fish, but I did not mind for the air was fresh and the Slighan Hill obscured from my vision in the pine forest. After breakfast, a multitude of tasks affronted me. I had to clean, cook, wash clothes in the stream, sew patches on tents, sew patches on clothes, feed the mules, brush the mules, organize, repair, labour, all day and into the night. Then cook dinner and afterward Verc would order me to hold his wooden ale cup, and he would drink it and then sit it in my hand and all I had to drink was water.

All the while I worked closely with the slave girls. Sabella grew cross with me often, if I did not respond to orders quickly enough, she would yell 'age, servi!' and if I still did not comply, she would lash me with her bullwhip. One morning, I grew tired of her cruelty and raised a fist to strike her. She dropped to her knees and began to cry hot tears down her cheeks and she begged me, called me *domine* and handsome and sweet and offered me the wondrous pleasures of her flesh if I spared her my fist. When I spared her and turned around she snatched the whip from the ground and smarted me across the back so hard that I bled.

The German girls, Frowon and Mawaz, on the other hand, hardly responded to me at all. I knew the whip across their rears had broken them long ago. I still remember the look in Mawaz's eyes when Aldryd had pulled her on his lap, the look of a dumb, dead beast, and I had taken up this life of slavery to ensure my Myrnna never would bear those dead eyes.

At twilight and in the evenings, we trained to fight. We had wooden swords, and Verc mostly led the trainings, though Marthelm and the Greek, who called himself Aster, also instructed us.

'Teaching a slave to fight is stupid, perhaps,' Verc said to us one night. 'But he is still a man. If we ever need a spare arm, he will fight for us, and the better he is at fighting, the better off we are. Besides, he is a warrior, and warriors ought to fight.'

I enjoyed the time I spent training. It was mostly with Antedios and Cattos, who came from the Dobunni people of southern Britain, but occasionally, Cicarus, the Hibernian warrior came to fight with us. I disliked him, and he thought little of me, seeing me as nothing more than a servant and hardly worthy of his time. He bragged to me that he owned land and cattle. It was an irony, my dear Luceo, for my father's mother's side came from Hibernia, and my brothers carry Hibernian names and call some of our gods by Hibernian names, while the rest of our gods we call by Britannic names. Cicarus did not seem to recognize that at all, and I resented his disrespect.

Myrnna was treated well, for the most part. She did little work since Tratonius said that work would sully her beauty. The sun would burn her skin and wrinkle it, the harsh ground would harden her soft feet, and the toil of labour would slump her curved back and broaden her lithe body. She said little to me, and confided in only Mawaz. That vexed me. Myrnna did, however, assist Verc in the nightly sacrifice, where we burned some grains for the good Danu to ensure good luck for us.

These nine days, little of note happened, besides one day where I had been foraging in the forest with the German girls, and Aldryd, who had decided to go for a walk. We were collecting some wood blewits from an oak trunk, when I heard dozens of footsteps coming from the byway.

I ordered the girls to duck behind the trunk, and I did so as well. I glanced around for Aldryd, and did not see him. On the byway, at least two dozen dark-haired men carrying spears, shields, clubs, and axes marched. Their weapons were all hewn from grey flint and that in combination with their dark features signified them as Hillmen. Badb crawled through my chest until Camulus, Father of War, had struck me, and I seized a rock next to me and formed a plan to snap forth and strike one in the head, but I dropped the rock because that would be suicide. As much as I desired death to free me from my enslavement, and as glorious as that would have been, and as deep as red Camulus struck me, I could not bring myself to break my oath. I just remained hidden, and felt as rotten as the trunk at my knees, for I desired to venge myself upon the Hillmen. Then Aldryd shouted something from among the trees.

'Go on, get up, lad,' he said to me, not hidden at all. 'Remember? We have a deal with them.'

The Hillmen had spotted me. I could make out the features of the men now. One man, third down the line, looked familiar. It bewildered me, since he looked like this man from the Tarbert clan, a clan that lives deep down the river. I had traded a sheepskin for a beaver hide, and I remembered that because this Hillman had just snorted and spat as he did when we traded, as if he had disagreed with the trade but went through with it anyway. It couldn't have been him, and I suspected foulness from the hag, haunting me here, misshaping this man as a man of my memory.

The man passed and I lost that thought, and another thought sprang up. I jumped up on the log and shouted at them. They stopped and looked at me and I twisted my body, bent over and yanked down my trousers, and wiggled my dirty arse at them.

There were grumbles and I am sure at least one man readied his weapon, but their superior, who led from the back, yelled at them, and they moved on.

I turned to Aldryd, my head bowed like a guilty dog.

He laughed. 'That's right! Those guys are a bunch of dog shit, dog shit from a dog that ate some bad eggs. They're a bunch of shit with their shit stone weapons, don't they know iron is the master of all? You showed them your arse!'

My insult of the Hillmen had amused Aldryd so much that he convinced the others to permit me to take the night off from my duties, and he even shared his ale with me. I became his cupbearer, and he kept calling me catamite, a word I did not understand. But he allowed me to drink his ale, and drink I did, for I had not drunk in a long time and as we sat around the fire as twilight grew, I drank much.

CHAPTER IX

The evening of the ninth night was both my biggest regret and my biggest accomplishment. My most shameful and my most proud, and the night where I had been both killed and reborn.

The campfire cast a glow over us. We sat in its smoke and warmth. The work had been done for that day and when Aldryd asked if I could have no duties that night, an air of ease overcame everyone. They all drank more than usual, and all sat together in a big circle rather than clusters, and they were less harsh on the slave girls.

I still had no idea why we were bivouacked on the beach and how or why they had a deal with the Hillmen. Usually, that side of the sea-loch was crawling with fishing boats, but I saw no one except for the Hillmen that one time. The mercenaries didn't know the fate of the rest of Skye, and they knew nothing about their queen, Slighan, as the giant had called her. It all vexed me, and I stewed in my uneasiness, and just listened to the mercenaries.

They were drunk, and Aster the Greek, normally quiet, boasted of his adventures. He spoke of battles on the sea where so many men died that when they washed up on shore, they were more numerous than seashells. He named places like Macedon and Marsselus and Carthage and Numidia. Every time he would finish a story, the great big Umbrian Orca would shout with his booming voice, 'oh yeah?!' and then double whatever Aster claimed, whether it was men killed, women taken, or slaves captured. The others too, would seize the conversation, and speak of their slaughters, and worse, their oath-free lives, swearing fickle, day-bound oaths for nothing but riches. After the job was done, they would swear a new oath, sometimes even fighting against previous allies, jumping from one lord to the next like a pack of vultures devouring one body at a time. I could hardly follow their stories, full of names of people and places and nations I knew not, their stories so jumbled and contradictory and convoluted that all I got out of them was that they liked to fight, drink and fuck mostly, and that they all hated the Romans, whomever they were. After a few hours, I had grown to love the Romans just because the mercenaries hated them so much.

I sat in front of Aldryd, one cup in service to him, one cup to my lips, and both of my hands grew shakier. I drank a lot, and then Tratonius washed up onshore like a beached whale after bathing. I learned he was the adopted father of Antedios and Cattos, and the three had been off on a skerry, sunbathing in the day and then watching the sunset. It was a dumb idea, for lord Nodens, our god of the Ocean, sends his waves like his wayward hounds to drown men beneath their frothy fangs, but who listens to a slave?

Tratonius pulled his trousers up and tied them and started toward us. Sabella handed him a filled cup and he sat next to me.

'How are you holding up, lad?'

I nodded, not sure of what else to say.

'My boys like training with you. Your father ever teach you to fight?'

'Briefly. He was never around, and I was too small to train properly.'

'Well, you have his blood in you. You're going to be a great warrior someday. In four and a half years, I'll train you to be my charioteer.'

'Do you Umbrians have chariots down there?'

'Not for war, but for racing. But do you know how I got this torc?' he asked and patted the bronze torc around his neck. It was twisted wire that ended in bulbs on either side of the gap of his fat neck. It looked gold when the firelight hit it. Torcs to our people were the sacred oath between a lord and his men, and the gold the ultimate gift of Taman, and it meant that this man commanded men on Taman and only answered to the gods above.

'I killed a Dubonni chief, bastard of a fight,' he said, and toothily grinned at me.

'And I fucked his wife,' Aldryd said, and motioned for me to give me his drink.

'He had a chariot. Your father dared me to ride it – and would you know, I was a natural! I got myself a Briton charioteer – slave boy – about your age, died of dysentery – what a mess! Antedios is my charioteer now, but he's too tall. It's uncomfortable for him to crouch down in the car – you could be my charioteer. If you behave, that is.'

I thanked him, unsure of what to say. To be a charioteer for a lord was a great honour. I had little time to think about it because Aster and Cicarus were raising their voices.

'I have the head of an Amazon,' Cicarus said. 'I went deep into Scythia and then we fought against the Amazons, and I took the head of their queen!'

'Impossible,' Aster said. 'There is no such thing as Amazons.'

'Come on, Aster,' Cicarus said, 'I saw your Parthenon with my own eyes, and those blond women fighting your ancient warriors adorn its friezes!'

'That is just showing a myth, you ignorant Keltos,' he said and spat. *Keltos* was another name for what the southern men called us. *Gauls, Keltoi, Britons.* They had many names for us, and I did not care. Cicarus headed off toward his tent.

'I'll never forgive you Keltoi for attempting that sack on Delphi,' Aster said, and then he raised his voice. 'Maybe I should sack your tent and take that head you cherish so much!'

Cicarus returned cradling a wooden box against his chest. 'You're raving, old man. I'm far too young to have been at Delphi, but my grandfather was, and he brought a head back to Ulster! But I have seen the temple at Delphi, and I cannot say I would not mind sacking it and, oh – that sweet oracle! Hair like the night sea, eyes like Danu's brown bosom, skin like the purest fairy,' he said, and then looked at Myrnna.

Aster tutted. 'Worthless barbarian! If it were up to me, I'd sell you off to the Scythians since you like them so much. See if they will listen to your lies about Amazons!'

'Behold!' Cicarus said. He opened the lid of the box, and a faint scent of cedar emitted from within and underpinned the smoky air. He then cantered around the circle, and each man grimaced at the sight in the box. When he stood before me, he shouted 'Behold, slave! Behold the might of Cicarus of Ulster, slayer of the Amazon queen!'

His voice had ruffled me, and I looked down into the box and the cedar smell assaulted my nose. I coughed and peered down, and in the red-yellow light, a red-headed, blue-black skinned mummified face grimaced up at me. Cicarus shut the box.

'You know, slave,' Cicarus said. 'She speaks prophecies to me. Perhaps if you work hard enough, I'll ask her of what the Morrigan spins for you.'

'Bollocks,' Aldryd answered for me. 'But I'd be interested if her tongue still worked.'

Cicarus settled down and began to drink.

Aster picked up his lyre and began to string.

'Not that shit again,' Aldryd said. I had never heard of a man who disliked music, and I welcomed the soft plucking of the strings to the sound of boasting, belching and belligerency.

'He can't play for the life of him! A Greek who can't play music! He must be unique! Cut it out, you're music-deaf! I should cut your fingers off and then you can try and play!'

'I play it well, your ears just hear it wrong. You barbarians have inferior ears, you cannot hear the subtleties that we in Hellas can, and you never will, for you are bronze-souled.'

'Bollocks.'

'Your father would have loved this,' he said to me, laughing.

He informed us all that he had a story about an adventure he had with my father once. I wish I could have felt joy, since I long for stories about my father, but my status as a slave reminded me of my shame, and I could think of nothing but how I must put up with this for four and a half years. If I survived.

'You're going to make the four and a half years,' Tratonius said, 'and maybe if you behave well, we can figure something out to make it shorter.'

Tratonius then told us all a story about an outstandingly fat village wizard far up in the northern lands. They were sent there to retrieve a bone trinket, but he wouldn't part with it. My father had found out that the wizard had grown so fat because every day, he ate a great steak from a beast found frozen in the tundra. The wizard had grown so large that he could no longer walk, and he requested that my father and Tratonius go and fetch him some more of that steak. They had found that the creature, which they decided was a gargantuan mole with long shaggy fur and long teeth, had gone rotten, so they spent the night digging and eventually found another one. Thus, they fed the wizard the steak, and then the wizard complained of heart pains and died a few hours later. In his death throes, he rolled over on his belly and his great girth destroyed the trinket.

Night pinnacled. The waves crashed against the beachhead. Seagulls had rediscovered our camp, and Aldryd tossed breadcrumbs to them, encouraging them on. Aster toyed with his lyre. Marthelm and Verc duelled in a game of dice, and Orca led Sabella into his tent, and her moans disturbed me as I imagined the giant mounting her. It grew late and Tratonius continue with stories. Myrnna yawned off in the corner and started up to go to bed.

Aldryd pulled one of the slave girls, Mawaz, onto his lap. Somehow her eyes roved to me, those horrible daft eyes, her mouth gaped open. I wanted to pluck her miserable eyes out from her sockets, and then I turned to see Cicarus pull Myrnna on his lap. She gave a meek resistance, a hand on his chest, but blushed.

All the while the eyes of Mawaz burned in me. I could feel them on me, those dead, dark eyes, and I swear, my dear Luceo, it was as if the Morrigan herself had perched upon Aldryd's lap to mock me. It was as if she would sprout a voice within Cicarus' bodyless head of the Amazon, who would give me the prophecy of 'I will hump her!'

Myrnna had settled neatly into Cicarus' lap. No one seemed to be stopping him as one of his hands ran up her white leg, and the other grabbed her delicate shoulder. She squirmed, and then she made eye contact with me and her father's visage stared down my soul.

Cicarus noticed me. I must have looked angry, though I felt so numb, and he frowned at me, and then his face relaxed into a wide, toothy grin.

Thereupon red Camulus struck me hard. He incited me, sent hot blood rushing into my head and drumming my chest for war. All men know this feeling, Luceo, all men know when they see a woman that they had been courting, or that they desire, or that already belongs to them, and another man wrongs her. Every man understands Camulus firing arrows into his blood.

Cicarus looked up when I walked over, confused, and I shouted something at them that I barely remember what. No cups were raised to lips. The dice game ceased. Aster continued to play the lyre sheepishly. All eyes were on me and then I acted.

I seized Myrnna like a fox seizes a hare, my arms wrapped around her and the intensity and my drunkenness caused me to drop her, and she hit the grass in a thud.

'Don't you touch her!' I shouted at Cicarus, my finger in his face.

'Slave! Get your finger out of my face!'

'Don't you touch her!'

'I said, get your finger out of my face, slave!'

Cicarus grabbed my finger and wrenched it. I cringed, punched him in the jaw, and we both fell over the log he had been sitting on. My bare chest met his, his hot breath on my neck, his hair prickling against my face as we vied against each other. Someone grabbed me from behind, pried me off him, and shoved me back. I fell backwards and found the pithy bare body of Tratonius hunkering me down.

Despite the warmth of the fire heating my side next to me, I began to shiver. Something was in the air. All the men had crowded around us and I had been dragged to my feet. Cicarus had a red face, his fists balled, bouncing from foot to foot.

'You want to try that again?!' he shouted at me, his broad nostrils flared.

'How dare you sit that girl in your lap! You can't do that!'

'Said the slave! Come on, slave, try it again!'

If I could stand up to the giant, then I could stand up to this Hibernian. I raised my fists.

'That's a poor idea,' Marthelm said, but I hardly paid him mind.

'Whip him!' Verc shouted at Sabella. 'What are you waiting for, whore? Whip him! It's your job!'

I turned to face my fate but then Cicarus shouted out.

'Let me whip him! Someone needs to teach this slave to behave!'

'No, damnit! Settle down!' Tratonius said, raising both hands. 'No blood!'

'Is that it, Tratonius?' Cicarus asked, bouncing from one foot to the other still. He was topless, barefoot and had striped baggy brown-white pants on that fluttered as he hopped. 'You give years of your life to this company, and this is how I get treated? An outsider – a slave at that – can just hit me and then I can't hit him back?'

'The gods demand this sleight be settled by blood,' Verc said.

'Good, I'll gut the bastard!' Cicarus said and ran a thumb across his hairy gullet slowly.

Tratonius shook his head, red in the face, and shouted at them.

'Then fine – we'll settle this!' he said, then gasped for air. 'But no blood!'

He stood between us, palms aimed at us, and then in a near quiet voice he said: 'Sit down. Drink. Then we can settle it.'

'I'm not sitting down,' Cicarus said. 'I'm wild! I'm feeling it, oh Good Dagda, Pretty Mother Danu – I'm feeling the warp-spasm! It's crawling through my face like so many hatched spiders – come on, slave, face the hound of Ulster!'

For a moment, I believed him. He had a lean, muscular body, not a pinch of fat on him, corded and scarred. His dark hair flowed in the wind and his eye was twitching. The *warp-spasm*. That was what Cúchulainn, our demi-god hero, experienced in combat. His body hardened like bark, his movement became like the waves, his fury like fire. His face would contort and shift and look all askew– it horrified his enemies before he struck them down in one blow.

Nonsense. Cicarus was a man. I possessed *the sight*, and I saw none of that on him.

'Nine days ago to this night, I stood against a giant,' I said. 'So come on, puppy of Cullan!'

'That was also a poor idea,' Marthelm said.

Cicarus dashed at me. Tratonius blocked his path and Cicarus bounced from Tratonius' girth. Cicarus gathered his feet and started shadowboxing.

'Fine – fight with your bare hands – what do I care?! But no weapons – no blood – one round!' Tratonius said.

'Can I mediate?' Antedios asked, and I had not even seen the lad.

Tratonius turned around and grabbed him by both the shoulders as if to shout him down. 'Yes, you may,' he said.

I know Luceo, it was just a boxing match. Yet I knew that the stakes were higher than they appear. I was a slave, and to defeat a freeman would humiliate him, and elevate me. I would earn the respect of my superiors – and indeed, Myrnna's honour had been at stake there, also. I wanted to earn their respect, especially Myrnna's, and show them I was worthy of her father's oath. Besides, I didn't like that arrogant son of a bitch, and on that brine-breezed beachhead, I yearned to pummel him into a bloody crumb. Red Camulus had forced my hand, and now I shall honour him with victory.

The mercenaries formed a tightly packed ring around us. Antedios, serving as our mediator, had drawn a sloppy circle in the sand to designate the boundaries of our bout.

I had been drunk, very drunk, so drunk that the sidhe had clouded my mind. I bounced from one foot to the other, and shadowboxed, mimicking my foe. He was all riled up and ready and so was I.

'Ah – boxing! It reminds me of my time in the gymnasium,' Aster said. 'They should be nude – mediator! Why are they not nude?' he asked, but Antedios just shrugged.

'Here are the rules,' Antedios said to us. 'No one leaves the ring. No kicking. No biting. No grappling. No scratching. No hits to the groin. Just fists to the face and torso. First one to get knocked down for the count wins. Oh, and don't leave the ring. Got it? Fight!' He then put two fingers in his mouth and whistled, but nothing came out, just a squeak. Tratonius pushed him away and whistled hard, as if to recall a rogue horse.

Now Luceo, for a moment, I had a weird feeling. It was as if I had looked down at myself from the sky, shirtless in the moonlight, hyped and embattled by my own anger and ale. The mercenaries were all cheers and jeers. Cicarus bobbed up and down. Marthelm looked sombre, as if he observed his son about to make a terrible mistake. Myrnna stood silent.

I fell back into my sunburned body. I stood up to the giant. I can stand up to Cicarus.

'Watch his left jab,' Marthelm said.

I found myself on the ground, the ascendant stars nothing but sparks circling a blurry moon. I climbed to my feet.

The next moments were dreamlike, something far and distant like the blue-red that loomed over the Cuillins. I questioned if I were really duel-dancing in a flesh circle near the beach in a boxing match against that bellicose Hibernian. The crowd yelled at me. Some clapped. Even that old whore Sabella egged the fight on. I understood little.

I had never boxed before.

It was far too late, Cicarus struck me again. I fell on my back.

Antedios began to count. I somehow climbed to my feet in a stupor, and raised my fists and Cicarus' fist slid through my forearms, and floored me again. Antedios resumed his counting. I ended up on my knees, wobbled a bit, and I felt itchy. Then I heard a woman scream. It sounded like Myrnna. Or maybe a slave girl. I never did find out.

The low voice of Marthelm woke me up. I found resolve in that voice, in a way. He was fatherly, so was Tratonius, but Tratonius had hot blood, while Marthelm was both soft and hard, like bronze. The dancing flames behind Marthelm's head lit his light eyes, and he placed a hand on my shoulder.

'You're just fine,' he said to me.

The full moon had blanketed the beach in a lustre of white. I mistrusted full moons, for the sidhe lurk in the shadows more at night, or perhaps, we can see them easier due to the enhanced moonlight. See, even the tides now banged against the shingles.

'Poor servi!' Sabella cried, her long hard red nails scratching at my face. I pawed her away, and she retreated her hand, and Marthelm helped me up.

I drank water from a cup, and Sabella now rattled off all the duties I had to do tonight to make up for the ridiculous boxing match. Across the sward, Cicarus had been seated on that same spot on the log. I sat down across from him again, next to my box of things, and sipped water from a small earthenware cup. Sabella had disappeared and returned with the whip, and this caused my hand to tremble. Camulus' grip had not slipped from my heart, and then when Cicarus caught my eye, he grinned. The German girls passed by him lugging buckets of water, and Myrnna followed them. As she passed Cicarus, he slapped her arse, she jumped and the bucket fell and tumbled, some of the water hitting the fire and sizzling. Red Camulus had gripped me hard and shoved me. My box was open, and then I had Bodvoc's sword and charged toward Cicarus. I hopped over another log and through the smoke and there I had my sword poised to strike him down, never had I been so angry, never had I been so Camulus-struck, never had my bloodlust been so thirsty since I had beaten down that Hillman with a rock. I raised it to crash it down on him and he could do nothing but raise his forearms over his head and then someone grabbed my arm and tossed me down.

Someone stepped on my throat. I wheezed and the sword slipped out of my hands. I received a kick to the nose and blood rushed to it. I writhed in pain on the well-trodden grass, the sand grains engulfed my feet as I dug them into the ground.

Tratonius stood over me, holding my sword.

'You lost, damnit, get over it!'

I did not think he had seen the groping of the poor girl, but it did not matter now. I had been hauled up and now Tratonius, Verc, and Marthelm stood around me. Orca had Cicarus in a bearhug, and the Ulsterman rioted in his arms, shouting curses at me that I shall never repeat, and there was much commotion in the camp.

'What did I say about a slave with a sword?' Verc asked, and then stared me down.

'You've become a problem for us,' Marthelm said to me, and I could tell he was angry even though neither his face nor voice showed it, though his German accent sounded thicker now. 'While yes, Cicarus should not have touched her, you acted unjustly. You should not attack an unarmed man. That is dishonourable. There is shame upon you.'

It stung me to hear that, and that shame would carry with me forever. I would feel it when I awoke in the morning. It will disturb my rest, and it will cause each meal to taste less satisfying. There will be shame upon me and my line, and indeed, my grandchildren would carry the shame. I had acted in dishonour, and though impassioned as I was, it was no excuse. I could not look Marthelm in the eyes and my shoulders slouched.

'He needs to go,' Verc said. 'He attacks our friends unprovoked! How can a man sleep with this scoundrel around?'

'Yes, it is true,' Marthelm said. 'You must go, Brennus.'

'But Myrnna,' I said, and Verc interrupted me.

'She's ours, not yours.'

Where could I even go without Myrnna? How could I go? It did not matter. How could I get Myrnna back now if I must leave the mercenary company? I was free of my bonds but not free from my oath, and now both were broken. It couldn't be!

I turned to Tratonius, my mouth agape, tears in my eyes.

He showed me his palms. 'You forced my hands!' he shouted at me. 'I went through so much trouble for you – by the gods I did! I convinced the council to take you on as a slave and I was going to do my best to keep the girl from getting sold until you could purchase her – and this is what you do! This is what you do!

'Now – go on – get out of here!' he shouted so loudly that my ears hurt, and he stormed off. I caught sight of Myrnna, looking down at her feet.

'It's not that easy,' Verc said. 'You have to buy your freedom.'

'My land?' I asked.

'We don't want your land, that would be a dispute with the Hillmen,' he answered, 'everything you own. You have to hand it over, and then leave.'

'Leave me my sword,' I said, tears in my eyes. 'It was my brother's.'

'Shut up!' Verc snapped at me. 'Don't you dare whine.'

'But my brooch – it's my oath.'

'Shut up or I'll strike you down! Yes, that is what we should do, pull out your entrails and read them and let the gods decide what to do with you!'

'You are lucky, very few can attack friends of ours and survive the day,' Marthelm said, 'hand us over your things, and go.'

They sent me over to my box. I picked it up, and brought it to them. Verc dropped my sword into it. I unhooked my brooch, Aine's cloak dropped to the sand, I pulled off my tunic, untied my shoes, and slipped off my socks. I stuffed everything into the box, then placed it at their feet, and closed the lid. Verc leaned over and yanked my leather collar, I gagged as it choked me until it tore off. He pointed over my shoulder, over into the dark yonder.

'Now go on, go.'

I turned to leave, in just my trousers, lost in my thoughts, and in my shame, and it was too late before I heard the frantic footfalls that rushed behind me. A flurry of blows struck me in the back, but they did not really hurt, and there was a brown mass of curly hair wagging in front of a red face. It was Myrnna, and she screeched at me.

'You idiot! My father trusted you!'

She pawed me with open fists against my chest and shoulders, and a single hot tear flicked against my face as Sabella pulled her away from me.

'Oh puella! – servus is free now – let him go, there is work to do.'

I wandered away from the bivouac, a free man. Weaponless, without my cloak and brooch, and with broken oath, into the dark yonder. I wandered down the shingle beach and listened to the ducks quaking as they floated as little shadows near the coast. I listened to the calm of the waves against the beach to my right. I listened to the gentle breeze whistle through the wild moorland to my left. I wandered for hours until my bare feet hurt too much from the shingles, shells, and sand, and I sat on a cliff over the ocean and wondered how long it would take me for me to muster up the courage to fall over it. It was the only way to regain my honour.

I dozed, somehow, vaguely aware that I should not hide from my fate, and vaguely aware that I was on the Black Headland.

CHAPTER X

I woke up just after dawn. I had not slept long, and I hailed Belus, the sun god, just as I had every day. That is what Auneé had done, and Bodvoc as well, and indeed my father, and his father. I then stopped myself from completing the ritual, where I would sit and pray to them for a productive day, because I did not deserve to speak to my gods any longer. I was an oath breaker, and I should not be alive too much longer in my shame.

The wild moorlands with high hills were behind me, and in front of me, the endless ocean. A narrow path of shingle, shell and sand curved along the coast, and from the tuffs of wool in the heather, I could tell it was a sheep trail.

I heard some honking behind me. A flock of geese uprooted from some inland loch, and fluttered into the sky and then flew off across the sea. Then a voice chirped behind me.

'Geese, you know what that means, right?'

There behind me stood a man in a soiled white robe.

'I don't know what that means,' I said, and he approached me. 'What's does it mean?'

'I can't tell you that,' he said.

'Who are you?'

'Don't you recognize me?'

My blurry eyes failed to know him. The man wore a bleached white robe, though tarnished, and he carried a golden scythe pocked in green.

'Druid Cammios!'

I hardly knew him. He had a matted grey beard and greasy grey hair. His eyes looked tired, with heavy blue-red eyelids, and I could smell him from nine paces away.

'Who are you again?' he asked. He had commanded many men, and it was understandable if he had not recognized me, especially with my shaved head, and without my garments that designated my role.

'An oath breaker,' I said. 'And you must know that,' and then I realized that he had to have died during the siege of Dun Ashaig. I jumped up, Badb pounding in my chest. 'Are you a ghost?!' I cried out, afraid that he had been sent here from the Otherworld to kill me, even though death is what I desired, he scared me deeply, especially with his dirty clothes as if he had crawled out of his grave.

'No,' he said. 'But what did you say you are?'

'Oath breaker,' I said. 'But how did you survive the battle?'

'Did I?' he asked. 'There are fates worse than death.'

'Aye,' I said. 'Let death take me then.'

He said nothing for a while, and came closer, peering at me. He was shorter than I.

'Did you flee, too?'

'Flee? You deserted?'

He squinted, and a tear came down from his wrinkled eye. 'Do you know what they do to druids?'

'No.'

'They sew us up in the bellies of dead horses and suffocate us. Or they strap us to poles at high tide and let us drown. Or they sit us with stakes up our arses until the stakes impale us through the mouth. What do you think I did?'

'But how?' I asked, because last I had seen of the battlefield, the Hillmen outnumbered the Ashaigers at least twenty to one, and they had surrounded the narrow entryway of the hillfort.

'I escaped,' he said. 'But the rest of the druids – who knows? It was so cowardly of me. I should have fought.'

He began to weep, and then he began to blabber. He stopped making sense, or I could no longer understand him, and as shameful as I felt, I still hated him for doing what he did. No one could call themselves a man if he left that battlefield alive. And he looked at me, eyes squinted, a half-smirk on his face. He hated me, too, because he knew what I did.

'You deserted also,' he said.

'No, the chief druid ordered me to leave with his daughter.'

His eyes widened, and then he shook his head. 'The bastard, that was against our council. What did you do, then?'

'I lost her to mercenaries and broke my oath to him.'

His eyes squinted again. 'You know the fate of oath breakers, do you not?'

'Do you know the fate of deserters?' I asked him.

He straightened his back and his eyes bulged. 'I'm the druid. You cannot talk back to me,' he said.

'What are you going to do, kill me?'

'You want that,' he said. 'But you're going to kill me before you kill yourself.'

And we were silent. We just stared at each other. I could look him in the eyes, his tired old eyes.

'I'm ordering you to kill me,' he said. 'Toss me off this cliff.'

'No.'

'Are you hungry?' he asked.

'Yes.'

He walked off toward the high green hills, and I followed. Rockfall cluttered the hills, and I followed him up the steep ascent, often on all fours. The blue sky above us and the blue sea below, I knew that if I fell, I would likely die. I would at least break my legs if not my neck, and rot there. I cared little, because death is what I deserved.

We came to a rock shelter, nothing more than a gneiss overhang. All I could see from there was the blue sky and blue sea. Pebbles crumbled from its ceiling and I wondered if Cammios paid any mind that it may collapse and crush him. Inside, there was an extinguished campfire, and some flint tools, including a grey knife blade, a hammerstone, and a small scraper. I knew sometimes one can find such things in rock shelters, and Auneé told me these were the tools of the sidhe who inhabit these places. I would never have dared to use them, lest I invoked their wrath, but Cammios seemed carefree.

'I have grouse. He was lekking on a stone in the heather. I struck him with a stick. He should not have been lekking so late in the year. Do you know what that means?'

'No, tell me,' I said to him.

'No, I cannot,' he said.

He had already beheaded and de-feathered the grouse. He started the campfire and spit the grouse over the it, and roasted it whole. We said nothing as it cooked, and when it finished, he butchered it with the flint knife, and plopped a portion on a space of stone in front of my lap. I ate with my hands, still nervous about the prospect of damning my luck for using the sidhe's tools, even though I had damned ill-luck upon three generations of my descendants, if I ever had any.

'After we eat, you will push me off here,' he said with his mouth full.

'No,' I said, mouth also full, savouring the crisp roast of the grouse wing. 'Perhaps the sidhe shall push us both for using their tools.'

Now he looked at me again. He squinted, and shook his head. 'These are mine.'

'You knapped these?'

'No. I found them when my father sent me into the tomb. I found these, instead of finding a weapon. That's how I became a druid, it was a sign from the gods.'

Cammios swallowed and then stared at me. 'I said too much to you, I should push you now,' he said.

'Before you do, druid, tell me – did a god give the tools to you? Did the sidhe? An ancestor? All men say yes, but perhaps all men lie, and keep up the lie together out of fear of it not being true for them and no one else.'

'What did you get, then?' he asked me.

'I never went into the tomb,' I said.

He stopped eating. He now grabbed me by both of my shoulders and shook me.

'Do you know what that means?!'

I now grew nervous, we had been seated on unsteady seats and his shaking of me threatened both of us falling. I needed to die, yes, but it should be on my terms, I felt.

'Let me go, you utterly mad fool.'

'Mad?!' he shouted at me, and his voice echoed down the hill. 'I am not mad – listen to me, I am a druid! By the good Danu I am a druid! Please! You said you never went into the tomb – you never became a man!'

I now squinted my eyes at him, suspecting an insult.

'No, listen! It is not the end for you! It is too late for me, but not for you!'

'Then go on!'

'To become a man, you must receive something from them: the gods, sidhe, ancestors. You are not fully a member of the clan – your oaths are void, like a child. Think about it! If a child swears an oath to his mother to never go near the bog, because the bog-hag's going to grab him by his ankles and yank him down to drown, but then he just goes near it anyway because that's what stupid children do – was he an oath breaker? No! He's a child, and unable to swear such an oath! Listen to me, you fool – you redeemable fool – you are no oath breaker, for you never had an oath to break!'

'Then what could I do now?'

'I will help you,' he said, shaking me hard. 'I will help you redeem yourself! I am the druid and I am ordained by the gods to turn you into who you are!'

'Then help me, please, help me, Cammios!' I cried out to him, grabbing his arms. Pebbles tumbled down the cliff under my bare feet.

'Only if you kill me.'

'Help me first and then I will kill you!'

'Swear an oath,' he said, his eyes wide and desperate and wet. He had stopped shaking. Swear it to Osimus.'

'Why Osimus?' I asked.

'I cannot tell you – just swear it!'

'Then I swear to Osimus that I shall kill you if you help me!'

'Then let us go down now, it is so dangerous up here!' he said. 'Be careful! At twilight, I will make you into the man you are.'

I descended first, later regretting it, since I was younger and fitter than Cammios, and Cammios came down above me, and if he fell then we would both tumble down together. I recited my lineage to myself, from Lugus to Biturix, and Cammios agreed that he knew I had been a warrior, though I looked like a slave now.

As we descended, pebbles and chunks of earth fled down in our wake, and razorbills and oystercatchers flew to and fro, which distracted me.

'Do you know what razorbills and oystercatchers mean?' he asked.

'I don't know, tell me.'

'I cannot tell you, but watch it!'

I lost my footing, and I slid down, my arse skidding hard on the thinly covered rocky cliff. Pebbles and dirt flowed over my face and down my body and then Cammios rolled down. He rolled down and further down. He finally stopped himself on a knob of the cliff. I scuttled down to him, and though he sat there silent, I could tell he had not been badly injured, just full of scrapes and bruises.

'Do you know what this means?' he asked, recollecting himself from the ground.

I thought he meant the fall, but then he held up a glittering grey macehead. It was polished and had an empty socket where a handle would have been. It resembled something the Hillmen would carry.

'A gift from the sidhe,' he said, and when he turned to me, his eyes looked so glazed. 'It's a sign, and as thanks...'

He put the flat of his hand on the gneiss slab under him, spread his fingers and then smashed the macehead down upon them. He rolled over on his back, wheezing dryly. I worried he would roll off the knob and so grabbed him by the shoulders, and he started jabbering again.

'Penance!' he cried, and he brandished his mangled hand. He then started down the hill. How with crushed fingers, I don't know, but I followed him down.

'Wait here,' he said. 'I will return to you just before twilight to begin the ritual. Listen to me good, Brennus, listen to me good – you have a second chance now, but there is no chance for me. You will become the man your ancestors had created, and you will fulfil your promise and kill me. That I know.'

He headed eastward down the sheep trail with his mangled hand stuffed in his robe. Belus, the sun god, reddened the horizon. That revealed the start of the new day for my people.

I prayed to Belus. He sank further down the horizon. I had no thoughts and just sat there at twilight. Behind me, the green stony foothills obscured Slighan Hill, and in front of me, the shale beach of uneven slabs, the limpid ocean that shone red-yellow now. The brine-breeze flowed through me, it seemed. Peace had reached me. I was to become a new man, and shed off this husk of nothingness that I had been left with by my own foolish heart.

A jolly hum. A feminine voice hummed over the crashing waves. I should not have looked. I had ventured deep into the Black Headland, where boats are wont to wreck, where erring sheep never return, where the sidhe roam. Yet I looked.

There I saw her reclining on a shale slab. A young woman, no older than I, waist-deep in the ocean that breathed over her lower body. Wheat-coloured ringlets danced at her lithe back. She reposed there nude, her skin white as bleached bones, her body as desirable to me as a slavering dog desiring scraps. She combed her hair with a seashell.

'Come back to the Slighan Hill!' she said.

Badb! How could that be? That sentence knocked me out of my stupor. This was the sidhe! I climbed to my feet and turned to run, and her hair had turned green, as if strangled by seaweed. But then she sang again, extended an arm, that lovely, endearing hum, and her hair appeared golden again.

'What did you say?' I asked her.

She stood up, revealed her youthful body to me, her hips swaying as she walked across the rough shale like a bird on a rope. The sun had set the ocean alight behind her. I closed in on her, and she on me.

'You know what I said, Brennus,' she said, her voice playful. She had a sharp face, with a snub nose and a smile as endearing as her voice. She hummed again.

'Queen Slighan is waiting for you. Did you know she is now the queen of this island, Brenn? Our queen has returned!'

I shook my head. She hummed more and I found myself drawn to her.

'It's all thanks to you, sidhe-walker,' she said.

Once we came into close quarters, my worries had left me. I just stood there enthralled by this lusty girl, as salty droplets fell from her perky pink nipples.

'I am Negorm,' she said, and ran a tendril-like finger over my face.

'What are you?' I nearly sighed.

'Oh, what am I? Just a vessel for our queen,' she said and pointed over my shoulder. I turned and there the red hill of Slighan lit up the darkening sky. I shuddered, turned back and noticed that her hair was now green, seaweed green, or just seaweed and not hair at all.

'I'm here to persuade you. We know what you did to Ciuthach, the giant. But the queen is merciful, and understands you were just scared of my poor brother.'

Brother? What monstrous womb could squeeze through such differing forms? I thought, and then lost myself to the shadow of Slighan.

Slighan came forth and oppressed me, it crunched my spirit and begged to pull me to my knees. My bare knees hit the cold, wet shale. Negorm rubbed my bald head with both of her tendril-equipped hands. Humming, she pressed her crotch against my face, the soft hair bristling my lips, and she giggled.

She urged me up, and I climbed to my feet, and she put both of my hands on her cushy rear, wrapped her arms around my waist and hauled herself against me. I could do little to resist. Her skin felt oily; even scaly like a lizard. She slithered in my arms and this harrowed me, and truncated my desire for her.

'Your reward for freeing Slighan,' she said, her hips thrusting near mine, her hard nipples grinding against my bare chest, her lips brushing mine. Soon her tongue wrapped around my tongue, as if in a bind, and her lips tasted sour, and her tongue felt split, like a viper's. My heart began to race and I desired nothing more than to flee, and I would have swum across the ocean if it meant shirking both her and the Slighan hill. The latter I could feel almost more than the lusty sea-sidhe-thin. Negorm pulled me down onto, and she splayed out on all fours on the shale. I could do nothing but obey her spellbind.

'You're coming with me,' she said. 'We're going to meet queen Slighan down in the Ocean! Yes, indeed – there is much to see down there! Come, Auneé is there too! She's sitting on Bodvoc's lap! They're all down there.' She reached down and squeezed my pulsating boar tusk.

I had to resist. I knew the tales of the Black Headland. One tale told of a sidhe that lures men into the water, and promises them love and marriage and children, a gilded glorious life down in the depths. And they drown. They're called morgens. *Morgen... Negorm... of course! Badb! I cannot die before Cammios has made me a new man! But how could I resist this?*

Nothing is unconquerable. Even our gods can die.

I had one chance.

'I do,' I said. 'But let me take you from behind.'

Negorm's eyes widened to the suggestion. My dear Luceo, I don't know what I ran into that day on the shale beach in the Black Headland. I still do not truly understand my *sight*. Could I have seen her if the hag had not unlocked it? Could I truly have humped something such as this, which may very well be an illusion? Could it really drown me? I still do not know, and I do not think I will ever fully know, but at that moment it mattered not.

Before I took her, her eyes, as bright as they had been, looked as if they had turned to slits. I wrenched myself free, gripped a handful of seaweed-like hair, and smashed her face into the shale.

Her horrid face turned over her shoulder. Her mouth agape. Two fangs dripped venom from her scaly lips. Her eyes slitted up. I fell, drew away apace, and she lunged at me.

The sea-thing was upon me. Her arms hugged around my torso and she bowed her head to sink her fangs into my shoulder. I wriggled away, liquid dripped from her onto my shoulder and it stung. Her fangs dripped venom. They had sunk into my shoulder and I screamed and she gurgled as she sucked the blood from me.

I wrestled myself away, I fell backwards and scrambled to my feet and pulled up a piece of shale to pelt her with, and then came the rod. She recoiled at the blow. It was Cammios, he had a wooden rod and he smashed it over her head twice, then thrice. Negorm screeched.

'Begone, sea-slut!' he shouted at her. 'By Belenus, the light of this world, I banish this darkness! Begone!'

This checked Negorm, her eyes sank low, she slithered away across the rocks as if she had no bones in her body. She slinked into the ocean and never returned.

A veiny, cold hand fell on my shoulder, across the bloody wound.

I was breathing heavily with my eyes fixed upon the sea, and it now vexed me. I feared such a thing would return.

'Your last trial before becoming a man,' Cammios said. 'You resisted that morgen.'

I barely had, Luceo, and I've always wondered if it jinxed me.

Now Cammios stood before me, in the waning light, his robe scrubbed clean, his hair combed, his beard waxed, his face free of blemish. He seemed nonplussed by my attack from the morgen.

'She will do no harm to you,' he said, running a cold hand over the wound of two red holes on my shoulder. A smile flickered over his face.

'It's time for you to become the man that you will be.'

He led me away from the sea, and out of the shadow of the Slighan hill, toward the grasslands that bordered the shale beach to the red scrubby hills. We came upon a lonely stone that stood upon a stony knoll. It was broad and flat and it bent toward the sea. Cammios sat me down with my back toward it, and the bright sun blinded me. He instructed me to close my eyes.

'And don't you open them, until it is bright no longer.'

I sat there, the bright sun flaring my eyelids red. It began to hurt. I began to writhe while alone in my own thoughts. Bodvoc's dead body. Lappie drooling blood. The battlefield outside Dun Ashaig strewn with bodies of my kinsmen. That little boy brained against a rock. Aine's body thudding to the ground as we descended the well. Myrnna's dreadful eyes. Cicarus' bloody knuckles. The pile of my clothes and things on the beach. My ascent away from the mercenary camp, feeling as if the ghost of chief druid Ambicatos wept in the wake of my footprints. I hated it all, and I wished I could open my eyes and focus on something else, and then the hag herself began dancing in my mind, kicking her heels, that old crone dancing madly, her eyes red, her cackle ascendant, mocking me.

'You're alight,' he said, and then his rod tapped my head. 'Don't you open your eyes.'

They stayed closed. Hours passed. Soon the sun sank deeper, and the redness dulled, and the pain left. I began to wonder just what Cammios was doing. The old druid was mad. He had gone mad.

What could he possibly give to me? Become the man that I am? I am disgraced, dishonoured, and oath broken.

The sun must have set because my eyelids went black. Now there was faint light, and I thought of nothing. I became numb to it all, numbly resentful, and then just numb.

After a long time of nondescript thinking and sitting, Cammios thumped me on the head.

'Open your eyes.'

The full moon shone bright and had greyed the world. The sea looked grey, the moorlands grey, the sky alight with Danu, our goddess of all gods, whose breastmilk lights the sky from horizon to horizon.

'Belanus has blessed you with his fire,' he said, 'you have gone through your second trial. Now you must face the final trial, and you will become the man that you are. Go up that path yonder,' he said, and pointed to a sheep path through the scrub that led up a hill.

'What's up there?' I asked.

'The man that you will become,' he said. 'Go. Salvage your oath, if you dare.'

I started up the path, thinking little, the heather brash against my bare cold legs.

'And remember,' he said. 'When you come down, you're going to kill me.'

CHAPTER XI

There in the high moorlands, among the scrub and night croakers, I started up the hill. The stars shone so brightly, and the moon so silver, and the moorland opened around me. It was grey and there was nothing around, just the moors, and had I not felt so calm at this time, I would have feared more giants, or morgens from the sea, or the hag herself.

It will be but for a price...

I spat at that quote. She offered me the life I wanted for a price, yet I did not want this life. I wanted to cast it away, and I wanted a new life, and Cammios offered me that.

My eyes rose to the endless gulf above me, stars swimming in it like so many seagulls, and I turned to view the sea and spotted a sliver of red-yellow over the horizon, Belanus' last refuge. My feet caked in mud, I crested the hill and there I met my tomb.

The land sank down into an ovular shape around nine craggy outcrops on this breast-like rise. Three slabs of granite capped by a flat capstone formed the tomb. It slanted down into the depression, like descending stairs. Its entryway faced away from the moon and received no light from it. Its portal stood as pitch black as the sky.

The man that you will become...

To become that man, this man had to die. Luceo, we know that some men must die so that others may live. This is true in war, this is true in family, this was true for me. There could not have been both the man I was, and the one I would become. I pulled my trousers down and stepped out of them, and clad in the stars, I stepped into the tomb.

The tomb was dark, the hard dirt floor cold to my bare feet, the air musty. My head became light as I descended, and for a moment, I thought I had not stepped down into the tomb, but rather that the entirety of Taman had flipped, and I walked into the black sky. Moonlight poked through a tiny hole in its rear wall, and illuminated the chamber in faint blue light. I could see many bowls, cups and suchlike placed around the chamber. Some scrappy and rotting carpets laid out on the ground, and what looked like the skeletal remains of a sheep piled in one corner, and then the skeleton of a man laid in the centre. Supine, skeletal hands were folded over a bone handle of a sword sheathed in a mouldy wooden scabbard. I leaned over it and the stench of cedar oil assailed me, and I recalled Cicarus' so-called Amazon head.

The thoughts fell out of my mind, dissembled, as easy as the skeleton would, if I were to move it. I would kill Brennus. Brennus would die and with it all his disgraces, and with his death, I would receive an attempt to save my oath.

I leaned over the body again, its bleached bones illuminated by moonlight, and I stared into the blackness of its eyes. His head faced southwest, towards where the Otherworld was: westward, far west, wester than the most western druid islands, and far beyond the ocean. This man had made that journey, and yet his body remained in this lonely tomb.

A mouldy green cloak had snared the body, wrapped him up like a cocoon. His hair was still spiked in beeswax, and he had a long red moustache, thin and fragile.

Kneeling at his right side, for one never approaches a man on a journey on the left, I thought about him. I thought about what kind of man deserved such a burial. I spotted a skull under the crook of his arm. A dog to hunt with, in the Otherworld. His hands still gripped his sword. He had been a warrior. He must have been strong, manly, and kept his oaths. He died not a moment too soon or too late to command the land with his tomb.

I sat there naked, shivering from the air, unarmed, drenched in shame. I reached down to touch his hard, cold hand.

And you will emerge a man.

I knew what I must do. I do not know if my *sight* had instructed me, or the sidhe that inhabited the tomb, or if the warrior himself had guided my actions. I just knew, the same way I knew how to breathe, eat, and sleep, I knew I had to become who I am.

The bones trickled into the folds of the cloak as I unravelled the shawl from the skeleton. A glimmer of yellow-green on the blade of the sword flickered in the moonlight when the arms shifted. I removed the bony fingers from the bone handle. I felt the corroded bolts, and raised the sword into my hands. I ran my finger along the chipped handguard, squeezed the bulbous pommel, prodded the stubby quillons, and then ran my tongue down the cold, dinged bronze blade, pocked in verdigris.

My tongue bled. It was still sharp. It was a bronze sword, not an iron sword, and I nearly wept at its age.

Our ancestors cast bronze swords, and spears, axes, and tools like the adze, but we never used bronze except for jewellery such as my brooch. Bronze swords often turned up here and there, when we would wade into water to spearfish and step on one, or when we explored these old tombs. Sometimes, they turn up in fields piecemeal. If a warrior dies, then his sword must die as well.

While looking at the green blotches on the blade, I discovered a series of faint scratches. After a spell, I understood that the scratches formed what southern men call an inscription. Thus spoke the sword.

On the opposite end of the blade, a swirling pattern had been chiselled into the chappe. I pondered about it, and recognized it as the faint remains of a spiral, the symbol of the dead's spirit spiralling down into the Otherworld, and then emerging as his descendant.

The swordsmith had dedicated the sword to Green Cernunnos, and now he, the horned one, had possessed me. The world spun, and all became hazy and unclear. My body trembled as the moonlight went askew, and all the tomb appeared asymmetrical, as if a giant had lifted the tomb and broke it in two, and then when the daze faded from me, I found myself sitting on my legs with the sword across my lap, and I knew that Cernunnos had birthed a new man, and that man resided now in me through the sword.

'Hail Cernunnos!' I shouted out and my voice echoed in the tomb, as if it had been much greater in size. 'Hail Lugus!' I shouted again, to honour my ancestor. 'And hail the death of Brennus!'

I left the dead warrior naked now. The undershirt had become far too rotten, so I just fastened his tattered, cold, hard overtunic on my body. I pulled up the green-yellow check stiff trousers around my waist. I buckled the mildew-stricken leather belt around my hips, and hung the mouldy scabbard from it by its baldric. I clamped and snapped multiple feeble belts into place, each buckle forming spirals and knotted patterns of bronze. I hooked a goat-sack to my belt that possessed some unplanted wheat seeds. I put on his leather shoes, and tied the laces around my ankles. I donned the soiled cloak and cinched it across my chest with a corroded bronze brooch.

The yellow-green, fur-lined conical hat sat on my head and its pointed tip scraped the ceiling of the tomb. Everything was rather damp, sordid, but glorious.

The warrior had been laid out on the back of a wooden shield, like a bier. I peeled the shield from Taman, and the bones slid off. All sorts of denizens of the dark scattered in an array of silver, red, and black in the yellow stain on the ground.

The shieldface had been painted green, but only faint chips remained. Its wood was warped, its rawhide decayed, and its planks loose. I missed my Ashaiger shield, for this shield was far too large, and I remembered my father once said 'large shield, small balls,' but it had been gifted to me by Cernunnos, and the man I now am had used it, so I strapped it to my back by its frayed leather strap.

I stooped to reassemble the bones, and then something in a tiny hole revealed by the imprint of the shield caught my eye. Another figure rested in the funeral bed. I reached into the tiny hole and was awed at what sat in the palm of my hand.

It was a figurine, and I knew, perhaps by my *sight*, that it had been an image long forgotten. It possessed the body of a man, but it looked as if caught between the world of man and the world of beasts. Catlike, but far more regal than the typical Alban wildcat, fiercer, beastlier, and more manlike. Its muzzled, elegant face smirked in the way that only men can. It had such living eyes that seemed to follow mine while I turned it to examine it. The colour had been yellow-brown and I did not recognize the rock it had been carved from, but later I would learn that it was from the teeth of one of those giant moles Tratonius told me about.

My *sight* caused me to weep. I wept not out of sadness, but out of its beauty, and its age, for my *sight* had allowed me to feel how old it had been, and it was so old that I thought it had been from a time when men were not entirely men, but these cat-men.

I cradled it to my bosom, it was so precious to me. My ancestors left it here for me to find it. It marked the time that links me to them, and reminded me that I shall always carry my ancestors with me, even if their world has long been vanquished.

That figure never left me. I still carry it in my pouch, to this day, and I am determined that if I never have a son, then I ought to have my men destroy it if I were to fall in battle. It must end with me, if I have no worthy descendants.

I resettled the bones of the man I now was, in his original position. I kissed his cold forehead. I thanked him again at his knees. I had been reborn in the tomb, and I was birthed from its womb back into the bright moorlands.

The brine-breeze extinguished the musty smell from my nose. The trousers I had discarded before I left the tomb flapped, stuck on some heather. No, they were no longer mine. They were Brennus' trousers, and I was no longer him. I left them flapping there.

The wind petered out by dawn. The time had slipped by, passing like a hurried traveller in the night. I could not account for the time lost, but I thought perhaps it had been when Cernunnos armed me with his sword.

'Good riddance,' I said to the flapping trousers.

I emerged from the tomb a new man, bronze sword hung at my side, clad in a dead man's clothes. Then, in the rose-fingered dawn, I marched down the moorlands, back to the headland, toward the coast. I would follow the beach and head back to the bivouac, where I would confront the mercenaries. I must challenge the mercenaries to single combat, and I shall win back Myrnna and salvage my oath.

Perhaps I shall die, but then I will die as an oath-keeper, as a man of honour, and with all the manliness of Lugus passed on through the new soul in my body, and expressed through my sword.

By the time I reached the coast, Belanus had spangled the ocean in a gentle gold, and early morning seagulls scoured the shells brought in by the new tide. My feet crunched down the coast, and there I could see no trace of the bivouac, but a white ball rocking back and forth near the steep cliff overlooking the sea.

The waves crashed below at the shale beach. The gulls screeched in the air. The chilly morning wind carried salt. There I found Cammios jabbering, his robe soiled again and tattered at the hem as if he had been wrestling a badger. When I drew near, he lifted his head up, squirrel-like, and scrambled to his feet. He fell at my knees and hugged them and sobbed. There I pitied him. Cammios hugged me tight, until he sniffed me, and then looked up at me, and his eyes darted.

He stood up. We stood at an arm's length from one another, with the wind blowing his hair all over his face. He pulled his hair back behind his shoulder. He looked aghast.

'You've done it,' he said.

'I'm a new man now, and I thank you for your help.'

'No,' he said, and he pointed toward the wooden scabbard around my waist. 'Let me see it.'

I unsheathed the bronze sword. His eyes widened. I handed it to him.

'Bronze is Belanus,' he said. 'You walk in his light now. His light comes through your sword. His light emblazons your soul.'

We were silent for a while, and he spotted the inscription.

'It looks like writing,' I said.

'No,' he said. 'It is not writing. These are not letters. It is something else… it means that you are destined to avenge our clan. You will salvage your oath. Your name will live forevermore!'

He began to weep, and I did not know if madness had stricken him again, but his tears ran down the sword's blade.

'You have redeemed yourself,' he said, 'no… a new man. You are a new man now. You must choose a name for yourself, and that is the name that shall live on forever! Brennus is dead, long live Brennus!

'But as for me,' he said, and he shoved the sword back at me, and I grabbed it, and I just held it up toward the sun, thanking Belanus.

'Let me find peace now,' he said. 'It is time to fulfil your promise.'

He backed up toward the edge of the cliff.

'Kill me.'

I did nothing.

He grabbed a handful of my rotting tunic and pulled me toward him.

'Why must you die?' I asked.

He began to jabber again, his words nonsense, he spoke as men do after being stricken from sleep unexpectedly. He looked around, aimless, and backed up again, some pebbles crumbling down the cliff below. His eyes met mine and they came back, his jabbering ceased, and he smiled.

'We had an agreement. You swore to me that if I made you a man, you would kill me. Now do it.'

'Brennus swore to you, and I am no longer Brennus.'

He let go of my tunic, fell, and thudded against the ground. He began to kick his legs like a toddler. He cried and whined and even shouted and I left. I left him there, in all his misery. I did not understand why he would not just kill himself. I pitied him, and I should have killed him there, I owed him that at least. Luceo, truth be told, I got out of that oath too slyly.

I headed down the coast, back toward where the bivouac had been. Did Cammios tell me the truth? The inscription on the sword, did it really foretell that I will not only salvage my oath, but avenge my people, and bring glory to my name? I believed it would, Luceo, and I believed that I could defeat the mercenaries all with my newfound power, win Myrnna back, and take her to the refuge of Dun Torrin as I was forsworn to Ambicatos.

For a price...

CHAPTER XII

First light had come and gone, and the sun rose over the high moorlands. I followed the coastline, having left Cammios to his madness, and descended the shale beach. I passed where Cammios had sent the morgen slithering back into the sea, and I shuddered, and then I ran to get away from the Black Headland.

I had a plan. My plan had been to challenge the mercenaries to single combat. Tratonius would have disliked that idea, but I would evade him and goad the *Celts*. I'd call Antedios and Cattos cowards, insult Cicarus' mother, and tell Verc just how much of an awful druid he had to have been to be among this traveling scum in his twilight years. I would tickle their sense of honour, I would rouse them to anger, take their honour hostage, so that they could retrieve their honour should they face me in single combat. One by one, I would defeat them, until they were all dead or shirked from my sword, or I had died in honour defending my oath to Ambicatos.

It was an ill-formed plan, Luceo. I had little combat experience, I intended to challenge veterans, and there were many of them. But I believed I would win, for I believed Cammios' prophecy when he had read the inscription on my sword.

When the camp first came into view near the limpid sea-loch, I noticed no cooking fire. When I came closer, down the dry sheep-shit strewn grasslands, I found the camp deserted. Save for their mules tied to a post, the camp possessed no men. I found it odd, since they had left their belongings there. The mercenaries, Myrnna, and the slave girls were all gone. I spotted their tracks that led up into the moors, up a pass that went into the low mountains.

I followed their footsteps, and I could tell by their spacing that some had been hurried in the muddy track, and then it became scree and I emerged through the pass and crested the hill. There an expanse of red moorland sprawled out before me.

I unsheathed my sword because I had a feeling something went awry, and the regularity of the moorland had been broken by the presence of tall reeds around a loch. It cratered in the moorlands, sky-blue, and shimmered in the morning sun. A crane walked along its muddy banks. A chatter of birds passed by above, and frogs croaked unseen. I reminisced of the sombreness of the barren moorland. I had enjoyed hunting for pheasant in my youth in the moors, but now the hag had sullied my love for it. I disliked it, for I feared the sidhe, or another giant, or the hag herself.

Come back to the Slighan Hill…

The damnable voice had returned from the depths of my soul and rang inside of me. I had caught a glimpse of her grey crown poking up over the closer red hills. That thought left me when the faint sound of a lyre came from the other side of the loch. I heard, something splashing about, like a dog thrashing in the water after ducks, and I rounded the loch in haste toward its reedy side.

The reedbed receded when I neared a willow tree, and there I saw it from beyond the reeds.

'Badb – Macha – Fea!' my voice choked.

Multiple things dunked up and down in the water. There was a great commotion of multiple shouts. A blue-red mass surrounded by blurs, perhaps sacks, dunked in the water, and figures squiggled at the water surface. Once I understood, Badb struck me with horror and I nearly pissed myself.

Legs dangled. Heads bobbed. I first spotted Orca, that Umbrian bear of a man, and he went down in the water with a hard splash. Then came up Aldryd, curly grey hair matted to his face. Sabella hung aloft; some red-blue rope coiled around her stomach. Tratonius swung by, flying on a blue-red rope. Cattos fell in the water as Marthelm came up from it. All the sellswords and their slave girls were there, dunking in and out of the water like playful dolphins, shouting and screaming and writhing with tentacles coiled around them.

The tentacles came from a monster in the shallow loch. A fleshy, red-blue, newt-faced thing with vine-like appendages was drowning my former masters. A nude Myrnna rose out of the water, a tendril wrapped around her belly, her eyes black. Two other tentacles plucked the strings of a lyre above its bulbous head. It strummed a sweet tune.

You can salvage your oath, if you dare.

The words pounded in my chest. I unhooked my shield and cast off my garments, sword-in-mouth so I may swim, and then penetrated the reeds.

'Father Lugus!' I cried out.

Tendrils wrapped around my shoulders, crept down my arms and coiled around them. They felt slimy and soft and another pair wrapped around my ankles. The twitching appendages seemed countless. A fleshy hook grabbed my sword-arm, and I clenched my blade in my teeth.

I yanked back, screaming as a thick tentacle curled around my torso, and shut my arms to my sides. I struggled, shaking my body, wrenching myself out of there, with all my might, attempting to writhe myself from that slimy grasp.

The thing turned its hideous face toward me, its glowing black eyes sent Badb pawing up my chest. My feet dragged in the mudbank toward it. Two iron-black eyes, just like the eyes of Myrnna. Myrnna! This thing would drown her!

My scream was strained through the blade of my sword.

The black glowing eyes of the fiend flickered. The thing gargled like a frog, and its entire head hinged open in a sickening creak, like the lid of a chest. That revealed three sets of jagged teeth, a set of throats, and a slurping black worm-like tongue that flapped around like a lure.

The tentacles pumped harder around me and squeezed the air from me, and I almost lost my sword to the loch. My teeth held the sword steadfast like a dog to its bone, and I flexed my arms under the slimy tendrils and felt its strength waning beneath my wrath.

The tune from the lyre settled me. It sounded much louder than the dull splashes of the water. It soothed me, overriding how I jerked my body, and the thing dug into my legs and drove them into the mudbank, and the music became so sweet.

The tentacles vanished in the mist. Where an unspeakable fiend once sprouted from the water like a lily pad, a succulent womanly form stood.

It was Negorm. She ran a hand down her small, perky breasts, and across her supple stomach. She moaned and beckoned me with her other hand. The lyre strummed on.

It all soothed me. When I looked upon Negorm in the dewy loch, I looked upon love. It was as if we were newly married, and she waited for me to deflower her in a mesh of pure love and hungry lust.

No more tentacles wrapped around my chest. No hag cackled in my ears. No more threatening giants. No more mercenaries. No more mad druids. No more Hillmen. Just her, love, and sleep.

Negorm's mouth did not move when she spoke. Just behind her, a flicker of the wet dark hair of Myrnna, her tentacle-wrapped, naked body floated through the air and punctuated my foggy trance.

Come back to the Slighan Hill...

'No!'

Negorm faded.

The slimy tentacles wrapped tightly around my body. They constricted me, they squeezed me, they pushed the air from my lungs. Badb kicked me in the chest when I gazed upon the toad-headed thing, its gaping jaws unhinged, my feet dragging toward my death in its sloppy fish-lips. A relief came to me, that I would have died with honour, on my feet, and painfully. I would have been freed of my oath, for I had not committed suicide, and we all would have gone to our deaths together. Myself, Myrnna, and those wretched mercenaries.

Negorm came back to me then. The air quieted, and it was a blustery late summer morning. The birds chirped in the trees. She stepped out of the deep water, waist deep, droplets falling from her red nipples. She smiled, her red lips beckoning me, and I could feel her breath. Would death come to me so sweetly?

Nothing is unconquerable. Even our gods can die.

'Lonnbeimnech!' I cried out the epithet of Lugus. *Sword shouter.* I had shouted it so loud that the blade jittered in my teeth. I stared right into the glowing pit-black eyes of the monster.

'Father of Kings, Father of Cúchulainn, Allfather of Alba, fierce striker, long arm.'

I screamed, dry and long. I gave myself into the *warp-spasm* of Cúchulainn.

Spreading both of my arms like a perched eagle, the creature wailed a monstrous sound from its two hideous mouths as its tentacles loosened at my summoned power. I dropped the sword from my teeth, grabbed the hilt, and poised it skyward.

'Lugus!'

Even our gods can die. This will die!

Its head lulled back on its hinges, and a bumpy black tongue slurped its lips.

Tendrils crept back up my legs from the depths, like ivy, entangling me in its grasp. I could not get close to it.

Long arm!

That was it!

I cast my sword hard, point first. The flying sword impaled the grotesque head of the thing. It wailed a horrid cry, its jaw slapping shut like an unhinged chest, and the bodies of its victims plopped into the water. Some of its tentacles wiggled, others spasmed, and its wretched body cocked to the side, drooling black ink.

Aldryd popped up out of the water first, followed by Cattos. Soon, too, others emerged, some gasping for air, others in pain. The monster disappeared without a trace, and it left me awestruck. Then I remembered. Myrnna!

Myrnna dragged herself to the bank. She cooed the name of Bride, patroness and protector of women, and blessed herself with her a trembling, soggy hand. Nearby, Tratonius beat on the chest of a prone Orca, who then started coughing up water. Aster in turn beat on the chest of a prone Verc.

I could do nothing but aim my head skyward, and thanked Bride for looking after Myrnna. Surely, Myrnna owes Bride as much as I owed Lugus for guiding my hand that slew that loch monster.

There Myrnna sat, naked, clad in mud and pebbles, her dark hair matted to her face. I wished to grab her and hold her. She was my oath, and if I lived, I was forsworn to protect her. I stood silent, though, for I must be strong when others were weak, just like I was when Cammios kept falling into madness. I owed him, too, for I was a new man, the man I was meant to be, and the man that Myrnna needed.

Your oath may be salvageable.

'Brenn?' a voice asked from behind me.

Antedios stood there, breathing heavily, with a face in bewilderment.

'Did you save us?' he asked.

'Badb – Macha – Fea!' I shouted. 'I saved you!' I shouted so loudly so that the lot of them could hear it. I looked around and saw all of them. Tratonius. Cicarus. Orca. Verc. Aldryd. Cattos. Antedios. Marthelm. Aster. Sabella. They all looked half-drowned. I then lorded over them, confident because I knew what I had faced, a monstrosity brought forth by my *sight*, and I alone with *the sight* could face and defeat it. I stood there, they on their knees or slumped, I standing straight, and they all unarmed, and I armed with the bronze sword. Osimus, the god of inspiration, who now inspires me to speak my tale to you, Luceo, inspired me then with an idea that would satisfy my vengeance.

'Lugus and Bride and Osimus!' I shouted aloud, 'I am your son!'

'He saved us,' Tratonius said, marching over to me. He was shirtless, and his pithy, scarred body jiggled as he raised an arm and pointed seaward. 'Let's leave – who knows what will come out of that damn lake next – come on, all of you, get out of here!'

Everyone left in haste through the reedbed. Tratonius waited for everyone to move out, and then he gave me a look of impatience. I raised a finger to him.

I waded back through the loch to the spot where the monster had fallen dead, and I fished my bronze sword out of it. Streamlets of loch water slid off the blade. I shook it dry, and my eyes locked onto the swirl, and then to the inscription. It dawned upon me that Aster may know how to read it. I ought to ask him.

My precious sword, so dear to me already. In Lugus' name! I should bend it and send it to him as thanks. But I couldn't, and I still can't, and I do not know why.

Tratonius approached me while I collected my shield and the dead man's clothes. 'Just what was that thing?' he asked, then cast a look to the loch. 'Nevermind for now, move out, and tell me later.'

We all strode away from the loch and down the moorlands back toward the camp.

'I can't believe you killed that thing!' He said, his face red, his eyes wide.

'Aye. And you owe me your lives. And I will demand compensation.'

Tratonius flashed a gap-toothed grin at me, laughing, and struck me playfully in the meat of my shoulder. 'Of course you will!'

He walked past me and down to his comrades.

We trotted through the high moorlands, down to the lowland and back to the coast. The ocean had calmed, the seagulls quieted, and the mercenaries all waited in their camp for me to make my demand.

You can salvage your oath.

CHAPTER XIII

We found the two girl-slaves huddled in the scrub. Sabella brought them back to camp and comforted them with some honey, but they were worse off than ever. I wondered, perhaps, if they wished for the demise of their captors so that they would be free.

Sabella cooked us some mackerel for breakfast while Tratonius relayed the events to me. After I had left down the headland, they heard strange noises from the ocean, as if it belched and gurgled. In the morning, the four girls and half of the mercenaries went up to the loch to take a bath. They never returned, so the rest of the mercenaries, suspecting something afoot, all went up to the loch.

They did not find anyone in the loch except for a woman who played the lyre, with waist-length blond hair dipping into the water. They all told me that the woman sparked an urge in them, and bewitched them. That was all they remembered, except for glimpses of the toad-thing that possessed many tentacles. They were all caught in those numerous things like a slimy spiderweb. The song, however, never stopped playing delightfully.

The four girls, too, relayed their version of events. While they bathed in the loch, they heard the faint sound of a lyre, and they listened. It came from far away, yet so close. Soon a man emerged from the loch, knee-deep, near the weeping willow. He had flowing blond hair, a slender body, and he played the lyre, with his eyes closed.

'It was the most beautiful song,' Myrnna said. 'Even the bards of Ashaig could not have sung something so beautiful. I lost myself.' She lowered her head. 'It choked and strangled me. I could not move. I could not think. I just lost myself in my pain and blankness.'

We sat there for some time. Sabella finished cooking. Low tide had come, and the slaves collected shellfish from the mudflats in competition with the seagulls. We ate among the white ring of tents, the bonfire crackling and blazing, the sun already strong and burning my face. We just sat there, all of us silent, listening to the roar of the sea and the footfalls of the slave girls on the shelly mudflat.

Aster picked up the lyre at his feet, and strummed it. He stopped when Cattos and Antedios looked at him with open fish-mouths.

'We call it a siren where I'm from,' Aster said.

'It is a nacken,' Marthelm said.

'You're both wrong. It's a morgen,' Verc said.

'Yeah, right, we all call it something. But I never thought we'd ever see it,' Tratonius said.

'My grandpa saw a kelpie,' Cattos said, and Tratonius cuffed him on the head. 'Everyone's grandpa has seen something. Again, never thought I would see it. None of us did.'

We all fell silent again, and the brine-breeze blew over my cold bald head. I put a hand in my pouch and strummed the lion-man figure. I ought to grow my hair like its hair, so I shall never have a cold head again. They shaved my head and debased me and allowed that awful harlot to humiliate me in front of Myrnna, the gods, and the shade of my father. Now I sat among them again, after my banishment, their lives owed to me. I would never be their slave again.

I thought of the giant who threatened to kidnap Myrnna. The morgen, whom I had nearly humped, and had offered to take me to the hag. And the hag herself, the Cailleach, laughing at me from her hut in the Slighan Hills.

'The giants that you unleashed,' I quoted the morgen under my breath. I recalled the four gigantic shadows carrying away the hut of the Cailleach after I had accepted her gift. Just what had I unleashed upon this land?

Did *my sight* bring these beasts into this world? Possibly, but that was all Brennus' misdeed. I was no longer Brennus. The mercenaries were now mine, and soon I would claim my toll for saving their lives. Myrnna would be mine again. My oath had been saved through my sight. *Gift or curse, Cailleach!*

Aster stared at the lyre for a while. He fingered the strings lightly. He wrung the strings up off the bridge and smashed it down onto the grass, then he stomped on its body in a thud, and smote the instrument until it was nothing but a fragmented mess of wood and string.

'Finally, tired of that thing,' Aldryd said, and he fell silent again. They all did. I stood up, hesitated to say anything, and Tratonius waved at me.

'We owe you, don't we, son?' Tratonius asked.

Verc stared at me, his bushy moustache drooped over his lips. Then there was Cicarus, grinning, arms folded. They all owed me, and I would take it all from them.

I hesitated. I must admit, Luceo, I had cowered for a moment. Sure, these men all owed me their lives, the highest price, but they were still men. Mercenaries, hardened ones, and most of them not particularly fond of me. I was just a lad then, Luceo, and so bold I was, and foolish to think I could be their leader, when I had never led anything. But my time had come to rule at last, and before it floated away like the petal of a blown dandelion, I had to clutch it. I clutched them.

'That's right, you really do owe me,' I said, and I centred myself among them.

I looked different. The horror of the new day faded, and we all left the world of stupefying trances. They must have noticed my rotting clothes, the tattered, tawny, dirty clothes I wore, the tattered cloak, the wooden pommel hanging out of the warped wooden sheath. They must have caught flashes of the greened bronze blade when I rescued them from their black-eyed trance.

My shoulders relaxed. I stood straight. My people must be avenged. The Hillmen must be vanquished from Skye and all good Danu's green lands. The brooch of Aine must clasp my cloak to my chest again.

I unsheathed the sword that I had pried from bone-cold fingers. I had been looking at Verc and Cicarus, for I reckoned they disliked me the most. They both recoiled, but did not act further, though Cicarus had placed a hand on the leathered sheath of a sword at his waist, which I noticed was Bodvoc's. I kept my eyes locked on his swordhand, ready for him to draw it, wishing for him to draw it so I could cut him down.

Cicarus did not draw the sword fully. His bushy black eyebrows furrowed, he just stared at the tip of my bronze sword.

'Why do you have that sword?' I asked him.

'What's it to you?' he asked, hand on handle, with his other hand fumbling with the brooch of his wet cloak. That was the brooch Aine had given me, and my face went red, for that Hibernian bastard had taken my sword, my brooch, and my cloak.

Brennus' sword, Brennus' brooch, Brennus' cloak. Now I shall take it all back.

'You owe me your life,' I said.

'Aye,' he said. 'Name your price and get on with it.'

'Brennus' clothes,' I said, 'and his brooch, his sword, everything taken from Brennus before he was sent away from you.'

Cicarus nodded. 'Is that all?' he asked and must have found it a fool's price. I could have taken much more from him, but I desired nothing more from the Hibernian bastard, and figured he would leave us all now, and I would not need to worry about betrayal.

'Tell me how you bought it,' I said.

Tratonius answered. 'He traded some hacked up silver to the treasury for it. We're running low on funds. We're about to run out of food.'

'What of Myrnna?'

'She belongs to the treasury,' Tratonius said.

I had my answer, that she had not been sold yet.

'Who owns the treasury?'

'It's communal, but I decide,' Tratonius said.

'Why do you get to decide?'

'Because I'm the lord, but no one is sworn to me. I still wear the torc, though,' he said, and knocked his fist against the twisted bronze around his neck.

Now I had my answers. I knew what I must do to get Myrnna back. I knew what had to be done to salvage my oath.

'Tell me then before I make my demands,' I said, now talking to Tratonius.

'Put the sword away,' Tratonius said, and showed his palms.

'Tell me,' I said. 'Tell me now what you are doing here, why you came here, and what you are planning to do here. Tell me!'

Tratonius' eyed widened, and he grinned, and Cattos and Antedios at both his flanks began to stir on their log seats.

'Tell me, you greedy, no-oath, harlots!'

'What did you call me, you little shit?' Verc said and jumped up out of his seat. He put a hand on the handle of his sword, but Tratonius rushed and grabbed his sword-arm.

'Put the sword down!' Tratonius shouted, and then shouted at me, 'and don't you dare insult us! We're all half drowned and we all probably shit ourselves and –'

He grabbed his wooden plate of fried mackerel and tossed it down the strand. Seagulls swooped down after it. 'I haven't even had fucking breakfast yet!'

'Tell me!'

Tratonius, huffing, red-faced, slumped down back on the log. Verc sat back down, eyes on my sword, hand still on his sword handle. Cattos and Antedios spoke among themselves, and Aldryd had left to take a piss. The rest watched.

'We're here to work for the queen,' Tratonius said.

'The queen?' I asked, and remembered when the hag had spoken of the *queen* Slighan. A chill went down my spine.

'The queen of the Hillmen, Slighan.'

'By Badb's tits – they really have a queen?'

'Yeah, you heard right. We've been told to wait here for three weeks, and then we were to go and work for the queen. We have a truce, no leaving this camp for three weeks. The queen knows who moves about her island.'

'It is not her island,' I said. 'It is my island. This is my island. Do you hear me? My ancestors came here when the world was young. My forefathers rid this land of the giants and the hill people and all the other monsters. Now all three are back and I shall rid the land of them again. And now, listen to me, I will take my toll for your lives now.'

I aimed my sword at the seven men. Cattos. Antedios. Verc. Orca. Marthelm. Aster. Tratonius.

'You,' I pointed my sword at Aldryd, who was pissing on the mudflat. 'Come back here, now!'

He shook himself and returned, and sat down, arms crossed, nonplussed.

'You're not working for Slighan,' I said, and looked right at Verc. 'You're all not going to fight for her and her Hillmen. None of you. I swear by the mound of my father, Biturix, under the sky of Taranis, that I shall have Slighan's head.

'You are all my men now. Every one of you. You're fighting for me. We're going to fight against the Hillmen, if it kills us all. Now you must all swear an oath to me. I will release you after I have her head!'

All of the men were startled. They spoke among themselves, and my mind was in a whirl, I could not hear what they said.

'You're not serious,' Tratonius said.

'You're my men now,' I said. The sun caught my blade.

Someone laughed. I did not hear who. A vestige of my old self pulled at me to scream at him to reveal himself, but I kept calm. They would not laugh soon.

'Tratonius, you were under the service of my father,' I said.

'Indebted retainer. Thirty years ago,' he said, his head in his hands, and he drew them down and smeared the sweat down his bald head.

'You're all indebted retainers now, except Cicarus, who has paid me already. Not for life, but until the task is complete. Then you are free of your debt. What say you? Is this not the law of all men?'

We all looked at Verc, the former druid, who had a smile across his face and a hand on his chin.

'He can't be right. Come on, Verc – tell him he's wrong,' Antedios said.

'He's right. We owe him our life. But he is not as smart as he thinks he is. There will be a way out, and I will discover it,' Verc said.

'Until you do, then, you're my indebted retainer. We're going to Dun Torrin, and we're going to fight the queen of the Hillmen. We're going to fight against her hordes until all the Hillmen are gone from the island. Indeed, all the giants and morgens and other monsters. So sharpen your weapons.'

Cattos and Cicarus had been talking to each other, talking under me, without regard for my voice, and I finally yelled.

'Listen to me! All of you, now! The Hillmen took everything I had. They killed my brothers, my dog, my slaves, they took my cattle, and they took my sister-in-law. They burned our dun and butchered my people. They killed our warriors, they killed our druids, vates, bards, our King. They took our women and children. I will have revenge!'

My chest heaved, Camulus had burned greatly within it, and I took great strides among the centre of the mercenaries. My eyes even teared, but I did not cry.

I heard a sob. I looked over the shoulders of Cattos and Cicarus. There, Myrnna stood in the shade of one of the tall tents. She sobbed, a dry heave. She was in a dress that clung to her wet body, and she stared at me, and my tears vanished for I had to be strong for her.

'You're not going to do that,' Tratonius said.

I imagined splitting his bald head open like an apple with my sword.

'What says your code?' I shouted at him, and he winced. 'All of you! What does it say? I save your life, you owe me yours! It is the code of all men, wherever they are from? It is honour!'

'You're right,' Tratonius said. 'You're just not going to be able to do it.'

'Why not?' I asked.

'Think about it. You just don't have the combat experience.'

'I killed a man! Maybe two!'

Verc sneered. He sneered hard and then he too stood up and pointed a finger at me, despite my sword, far longer and sharper than his finger, being aimed at him.

'You're a whelp. How many men have you killed, Cattos?'

'Fifteen,' he said.

'And Antedios?'

'Fourteen,' Antedios said, 'Cattos is lying, though, I killed that Etruscan!'

'See?' Verc said. 'They're the same age as you. They've killed nearly thirty together. Imagine how many I have killed? Imagine how many have died at my sword, while you were just a babe, suckling, and I was killing, and when you drank milk from your mom's tit, I drank the blood from the skulls of my enemies. You are an idiot if you think you can lead us!'

'I stood up to a giant! And that morgen! I killed it, that monster in the loch, I slew it and I saved all of you and you will listen to me!'

'True,' Tratonius said. 'Your hands aren't clean, son. You're not afraid of a fight. I saw that when we were first introduced. You just don't have the leadership experience to lead men like us.'

'I don't care. You're all in debt to me. This is my decree. None of you can do anything about it!'

'Like Hades, we can't!' a voice boomed from behind.

Orca got up from his seat. He lumbered up, slowly, and brandished an iron dagger.

'I've had enough of you,' he said, and pointed a meaty, dirty finger at me. I checked. He stood over a head taller than me, and possessed massive brawny arms and wide shoulders. He was so big that I could probably fit inside his chest and belly, if I squeezed-in hard enough.

'I'm not going to get talked down upon by some brat that killed just one man! I challenge your debt by law of blood!'

It spread throughout the men. I stood under Orca, his black beard full of morsels of mackerel, his dark eyes ablaze. I nearly cowered, that iron dagger in his hefty hand could probably take my head off. I looked around and Tratonius shrugged.

'You want men's oaths? Then expect a challenge,' he said, and I wished he had not said that, because I saw fire rouse within the eyes of Verc, and the others must think the same. I had to defeat Orca, because if he won his freedom through blood, and if I even lived, I would have to fight the rest, and even if I somehow managed to defeat Orca, there was no guarantee I would defeat the others, especially after wounds or exhaustion.

Tratonius spoke again, 'but not to the death, we have enough of that already!'

'If they can avoid it,' Marthelm said.

'Then avoid it,' Tratonius said. 'Slash, don't stab.'

Orca's eyes looked tired, though fierce. He passed the dagger from hand to hand, squaring me up, approaching me slowly.

I could have backed down. There was a safe route, Luceo, and that was to back down from the fight and just demand Myrnna. That was all. Demand the girl and leave for Dun Torrin. But I had my plan. The plan had formed after I had birthed as the man with the bronze sword. I was destined to be a lord, Luceo. It was my blood. It was my heritage. I needed men, since all lords have men, and these were good, seasoned, proud men to have. I had to defeat Orca. If I lost that fight, then I would lose all the men, and my rebirth would have been for nothing.

'No shields, you can use that sword if you want,' Orca said. 'But it doesn't matter. Just bend over so I may shove it up your arse. How dare you demand oath-debt from me! I have killed men for less! Why, I will tell you… once I had been brought to Rome – in chains – for I was pillaging their caravans that dared pass into Umbrian mountains. I let them take me there, bound, naked, humiliated – but it was a ruse! I broke my own chains by just the strength of my sinew, and I slew the magistrate by bashing his stupid blond head in with my broken cuffs! I am no one's oath-man! I spit on your debt! Fight me, now, man-lover!'

'Aye,' I said. I poised the bronze sword at him. We stood two men's lengths away, and the mercenaries all formed a ring around us.

'He's more experienced than you,' Marthelm said. 'And bigger. But you're craftier.'

I wondered why Marthelm would offer me advice.

'Don't take him lightly,' I heard Verc say to Orca. 'Remember what he did to that monster in the loch!'

Orca's great hairy breast heaved. He was shirtless, and he was covered in a thick mat of black hair with white patterns much like an Orca, hence his nickname, I suppose. He kept one hand akimbo and his dagger hand at his breast, and he approached me. He blew snot out of his nose onto the ground as he neared.

I had to defeat him. There was no other option. I would lose my oath this time. Nothing would be salvageable. But how? He was much bigger than I, more experienced, and less inhibited. He slew men as easily as he farted. Badb crawled in my chest and threatened to cower me before him and plead with him to find another way.

Orca charged me. I parried his blow and our blades screeched and we danced them against each other. He drew his dagger back, then poised to strike. I raised to parry, but he had feinted and grabbed my sword-arm with his big meaty fist. My muscles contorted, I dug my feet into the ground, I groaned hard as Orca pried the bronze sword from my hands. He tossed the sword over the heads of the mercenaries and it clanged down somewhere far away.

I wheeled backwards away from him. 'Badb!' All that trouble to get a sword, such a powerful sword, and now I stand disarmed.

Orca grinned at me, his fat neck jiggling, waiting for me to surrender. I considered it, but the words of my father returned to me then.

Nothing is unconquerable. Even our gods can die.

That thought brought me back nine Samhains. Once while training, I charged my father with a blunt dagger, and my father smacked his palm against my clenched fist. The weapon flew out of my hand. My father had disarmed me with ease.

That did little to strike me with confidence. It was easy for my father to do that. He had grown up a warrior. He had lived as a warrior. He had died as a warrior. I struggled to even hold the sword correctly. How could I ever defeat Orca, especially when I had been disarmed?

No, that would have been what Brennus would have said. I am no longer Brennus. I am the new man now.

Nothing is unconquerable. Even our gods can die.

But you're craftier.

I hopped over to him, much in the manner of Cicarus, and Orca juggled his dagger from hand to hand. I raised my fist to punch Orca, who raised his knife in response. But I pulled my fist back, and ducked behind Orca and punched him hard in the lower back. Orca wheeled around and struck at me and I ducked and then elbowed him hard in his fat gut.

Orca wheezed. He raised his now glimmering dagger to strike. I saw my opportunity. I clapped both hands against his burly wrist, just as my father had done to me. The dagger launched out of his hand and landed in the grass. I grabbed it off the ground.

A meaty hand wrapped around my forearm. Orca moved slow, but he moved right, he was upon me and his great girth had closed the distance between us and now I had become disarmed again, for his grip was too hefty for me to move my arm. I pulled my fist back and struck at his face, but he just dug his head down into his shoulders and my knuckles checked against his big, hard, head. He began to wring me about, my feet off the ground, like a hare in the jaws of a dog.

I dug my heels into the ground and wrestled with him for the dagger with my other hand. Our bodies jammed together, trading saliva and sweat, his fat man-breasts and chest warm against mine.

But you're craftier.

The gods had blessed Orca with much pithiness. His barrel chest. His bulging belly. His sausage-fingers that wrapped around my forearm and wringed and wrenched. His short fat feet and his stubby little toes in his sandals.

Stubby little toes!

I stomped hard on the crowd of sandaled toes. Orca yelped and let go of my forearm. It had been a relief, as if I had been unbound. Orca stumbled back and composed himself just as I swiped the dagger at his chest.

His arm was butchered open. Blood sprouted and the flesh flapped like a tent caught in the wind. He cried dry and fell to his knees. He had raised his arm to defend his chest and I had cut it wide open from wrist to elbow. I leaned down and put the dagger to his double chin.

'Surrender!' I shouted at him, the black-bloodied knife bristling against his unshaven neck.

Orca could not even answer, his arm nothing but a flank-steak.

'Stop the bleeding!' someone yelled and shoved me out of the way. Sabella came running out with a leather sack.

'Brenn won!' someone shouted, perhaps Antedios.

'I am not Brennus!' I shouted back. 'I am the man with the bronze sword,' I said, and pointed to Mawaz. 'Bring me my sword!'

She complied, and now I had two weapons.

'Who is next?!'

I waited for the next opponent. No one stepped up to the challenge.

They watered his wound and stitched it up and he moaned all throughout it. He complained and even threatened to slap Sabella, who laughed at him, and told him to hit her hard, but he didn't. There was much blood all over the campsite. He had lost a lot, and I overheard Verc muttering that he hoped it would fester and he would die. Sabella finished stitching him and he drank water and demanded food, and Frowon brought him some fish. He gnawed at it like a dog.

'You got me good,' Orca said, licking the grease from his fingers.

'It was a good fight,' I said.

'It was! Now I have this ugly scar. I'll never hear the end of it. Another ugly scar. You're pretty and young, you know,' he reached out to touch my bare chest. 'I used to look just like you. I was pretty and young and energetic, now I'm fat and ugly and old,' he said, with a sigh. 'I'll never hear the end of it when I return to Umbria.'

I handed the dagger back to him, handle first. With a raised voice, I spoke.

'Since no one is going to challenge me, then,' I said, and Verc spoke up.

'Teutoles! Lad, we're still half drowned!'

'I've made my demands. And if you don't like it, we can get back into the pit.'

Verc said nothing. He was standing up, his arms crossed over his thin chest. He was a lithe man, with skinny shoulders and thin calves, but there was something wolflike about him that made me uneasy.

'Told you it was easier to kill him,' Aldryd said, sipping his ale. 'He's got balls. And now he has us by the balls. Bloody bog people on this island – can't expect them to give us a break.'

'You're mercenaries! Listen to me – what do you mercenaries want? You live on the road. You make widows. You sell women and children into slavery. You live for gold and glory and women.'

'I'm in it for more than just the gold, glory, and women. I'm after revenge. And you're all going to help me, but don't think you won't get anything out of it. The island teems with plunder, once we pillage the Hillmen. They took our women, our cattle, who knows – it is all for the taking.'

'Not too bad. So be it,' Aldryd said.

'But you're still not experienced enough to lead us,' Tratonius said.

'Then you will train me!'

'Who, me?' Tratonius asked.

'Yes, you. All of you. I want to learn to fight better, I want to learn how to speak your languages,' I said and looked at the Greek. 'I even want to learn how to read!'

No one answered. Cattos and Antedios just looked at me, eyes affixed to their spears. I knew they desired to challenge me, but neither of them stepped up to me. I had won their lives and now they owed me, was it worth a wound like Orca's? Was it worth their lives?

The tomb of my ancestor renewed me. Clad in his death clothes, armed with his cold sword, and blessed by his lingering ghost, I salvaged my oath. Myrnna, looking on from the side-lines, was mine again. I now had my men. I was lord, and I would wage war with my retinue, just like my father had. What I thought had been destined to remain an unobtainable dream, became the truth before my eyes. I fixed my eyes upon the clear blue sky, basking in Belanus' light, his chariot wheel spinning his glory upon me. I looked upon my men, my weapons, my mules, my horses, my tents, my slaves, and my girls. They were all mine, and I thanked Belenus, my father, and my ancestor, and I caressed the lion figurine in my pouch.

Now that I was a new man, I needed a new name for my men to swear on.

I unsheathed the bronze sword and approached Aster. He flinched, and climbed to his feet, but I held out an empty palm. I handed the sword to him handle first. He hesitated until he raised an eyebrow when I pointed to the inscription.

'You're a Greek. Is that Greek writing?'

He held the sword close to his brown eyes. 'Yes – where did you get this?'

'From the tomb of my ancestor,' I said. 'Is it a word?'

'Actually,' he said, running his dirty finger over each letter of the inscription. 'Iota, theta, and alpha – but another letter that appears twice. Digamma. We don't use it where I'm from.'

'What?'

'You wouldn't understand, you're a barbarian after all.'

'Then tell me what it says. Is it a word?'

'Nothing I know of,' he said, and handed it back to me. 'But it's pronounced *Widaw*.'

He drew me in close and I leaned over his shoulder. He had lean shoulders with a physique covered in moles, like rigged quartzite. He spoke *Celtic* with a heavy accent that I struggled to understand. 'Widaw, I think. See that? That's a letter, and it represents a sound,' he said, pointing to the inscription, 'that's the *wa* sound, then *uh* sound, and *da* sound, *ah* sound, and *wa* again. Widaw.'

'Is that the name of the sword?'

'It must be,' Marthelm said. Marthelm took my sword from Aster. He placed a finger under the edge of the blade and let it hang loose until it balanced on his finger. He nodded. He then stood up, and waved it, took a sidestep, and stabbed in the air. Verc took the sword from him, and did much the same as Marthelm.

'A fine sword for thrusting', Marthelm said, 'my sword is called Tiwaz,' he unsheathed his sword. It was long and flat without a blemish of rust on it, and had a polished antler handle. 'It was blessed by the god Tiwaz himself. I honour him with each strike. Yes, yes, your sword is called Vidav,' he said, mispronouncing the *wa* sound as people are wont to do.

'Vidav the bronze sword,' Aster said.

Verc lunged forward, stabbing the air, then gathered his feet together and lunged again, sword-point first. 'A fine stabbing sword indeed, Marthelm. A waste on a novice, and bronze is no match for iron,' he said without looking at me, then handed it off to Cattos, who too found the balance point. Cattos handed the sword back to me, and I held it in both of my hands. Its green-pocked bronze blade shimmered in the sunlight.

'Vidav,' I said. That word rang as the name of my ancestor. Now he empowered me through his weapon. I would honour him with each strike.

'Brennus is dead! I am Vidav! You will all swear an oath to me.'

The men all said nothing. I would get their oaths. I would release them only after I had the Hillmen queen's head, or death took me.

I thought back to when the new warriors had been sworn in on Dun Ashaig. They did every nine years, on Lughnasa. The druids oversee the ceremony, and circle around the naked warriors, clad in their white robes. The warriors each swear an oath to their lord, and fall to their knees, kiss his ring, and are hit with the flat of his sword. They did this one by one, and then they are clothed and given swordbelts by their lord. Their lord and his men all swear an oath to Lugus, god of oaths. The men swear to serve their lord with their lives, and the lord to always care for and love his men.

I am Vidav. I am a new man. Yet I was still partially the old Brennus. I would need an oath swearing ceremony, presided over by the druids. Yet it had to be different. I would not force nudity upon them, since I feared the foreigners would resent me for it. I would not have belts to give, but I would promise them cloaks, all matching colours for our retinue. I would also need a druid, and I knew where to find one.

'Hail Vidav!' I shouted and poised my sword skyward.

'Hail Vidav!' Antedios replied.

'Hail Vidav!' Cattos and Antedios both said in unison. I never asked if they were mocking me, Luceo. Regardless of their sincerity, it rejuvenated me. The miasma that overshadowed me, that pitiful disgrace when I left the mercenary camp and Myrnna to the mercy of the sellswords, had been cast away. The mistakes that had turned me wretched and forlorn had sunk away from me like the tentacles of the loch-thing after I had slain it.

'What say you?' I asked Cicarus. 'What are you still doing here, free man? Go home to Hibernia.'

'I will not leave yet. I don't want to leave my friends. Yes, you heard me, I don't want to leave my friends just yet. I promised Tratonius I'd stay until Beltane, and I mean that. So, you have my friends as your oath-men, fine, but I'll fight for you for spoils, I suppose. Just don't try to get me killed, I'm off to Ulster after Beltane, and I want to see my grandmother.'

His declaration of loyalty to his friends took me aback, and I could not object. I could use all the help I could get, though I feared he would take revenge upon me. I would have to post a man outside my tent each evening as I slept. It was a good idea, with the Hillmen about, to keep sentries anyway.

'So be it,' I said. 'But you provide for yourself. And you don't have access to our girls. And tell me, Tratonius, is the tent he sleeps in his?'

Tratonius shook his head no. He had been quiet, grumbling to himself or others.

'Then it's my tent now. And Myrnna. We're sleeping in there together. Now, let us eat breakfast. At twilight, when the sidhe are at their most powerful, we shall all swear an oath to Lugus.'

We ate breakfast. My slave girls had collected shellfish from the beach. Antedios, Cattos, and Verc all refused to eat the food. 'The sea is where you go when you die, and one should not eat from it.' Verc said. They ate some sausages instead, but we would need more food for them soon.

After we ate, I cornered Aster near his tent. He had been sweating and dragging a large empty red pot. 'Greek, you know much about things we don't here. Teach me everything.'

He looked surprised. He edged past me. 'Teach a barbarian? Your language is inferior,' he said, moving further away. 'You will never understand without knowing Greek.'

'Then teach me your language,' I said, and he went aghast.

'Teach a barbarian Greek? And what for?'

'So you may teach me your ways. You Greeks have much power, and you're skilled at war, and you have all sorts of expensive things we don't have. It must be the power of your tongue.'

'It's because the gods have blessed our land. We are the bravest,' he said, and held his head up high and smiled and flipped his long, curly black hair behind his shoulders. 'Do you know why the gods despise you? It's because you think you're brave. You put on a good, brave show, but once the battle starts you cower like women.'

'Then teach us not to cower like women.'

'I have taught these men not to, and I will teach you, too,' he said.

'You let him insult us with that trite?' Verc said, emerging from his tent. His shirt was off and he combed his long, grey moustache with a shell comb.

'You Greeks think you're brave, too, but you're not. You hide behind your armour like a child hides behind his mother's leg. A Greek can never beat a Gaul in a fair fight,' he said to Aster, and then to me, 'I will drill the men.'

They both looked at me.

'You're a *Celt*, as these Greeks call you,' Verc said to me. 'Don't let these foreigners insult us. Where is your pride?'

'You'll never get anywhere listening to Verc,' Aster said. 'Do you want the secrets of the world revealed to you, or wallow in excrement? Or, more importantly, do you want to win battles?'

The first dilemma had come to me at high noon, between the white tents flapping in the wind. I became aware of the grey ocean sapping at the shelly beach nearby, and of the gulls circling the islet on the horizon.

'Trite!' Verc shouted, his face red, and I shirked because I thought he may strike me. I remembered who I was, his leader, and stiffened myself, but he huffed and stomped one of his feet. 'Do you know why I've lived so long?' he said, and then puffed his chest out at me. 'With so few scars?'

I had no answer.

'Skill, boy, skill!' He shouted, and his big moustache ruffled. 'I lived so long by the skill of my hands that moved my blade and shield to protect me. I charge headlong into battle with nothing to protect me but my skills and what Great Danu has birthed me with. The Greek,' he said, and pointed to Aster. 'The Greek has lived just as long as I. The Greek wears armour, and when his skill fails him, his armour protects him. Where is the honour in that?'

Aster shrugged. 'The honour in that is to live longer to fight longer and protect what you love longer. What use are you if you are dead? Your wife will be raped, your children sold into slavery, your possessions all for the taking. Why waste your life?'

I was no use to Myrnna if I were dead. There was no dishonour in death protecting them, yet I yearned to live to finish my mission, to bring them to Dun Torrin.

'I will learn the ways of the Greek,' I said. 'They have many riches, and riches can only be won through war, so they must be right.'

Verc sneered at me, and turned away in a huff and went back to combing his moustache.

'Aster, you will teach me Greek, and then you will teach me everything that you know.'

The Greek shrugged. 'I'll try, but you barbarians have slow minds. It's too foggy and cold up here. Your minds are much slower as a result.'

'Verc, you were a druid,' I said to him, and he turned around.

He nodded.

'Then you will teach me astronomy, and how to discern the will of the gods.'

'No,' Verc said, and his gaze went down and he shook his head. 'No, I can't,' he said, without eye contact, and he returned to his tent and pulled the flaps closed.

'We'll go up to the hills now for your first lesson. But I don't have high hopes that you will retain anything,' Aster said, and left.

The sky yellowed. The seabirds flourished along the coast: seagulls, oystercatchers, razorbills. Seals reclined on the chain of broken islets, shiny black blobs on the bright horizon. Soon the deer in the forest behind us would be wandering about. Sundown came. The last day I walked Taman as Brennus had peaked and waned, and now I was to be reborn as Vidav.

I ordered the men to gear up. They all donned their war-outfits, the *Celts* in their bright coloured clothes, the four of them a piebald panoply of green, blue, yellow, and brown. They all spiked their hair in beeswax, and Verc stylized his long moustache. They armed themselves with their one-handed spears and their oblong shields that ran chin to toe.

Then came Orca, the great Umbrian in his red tunic. He wore a rusty bronze breastplate and his girth spilling over it, and he carried a long dagger at his hip, a one-hand spear, and no shield since he could not use his injured arm.

Marthelm then came with a fringed check blue-white cloak flowing behind him. He wore a light green tunic and brown hose and had a red belt with an emblazoned belt buckle of bright bronze. His blond-grey hair was capped in a conical brown hat that contrasted with his grey eyes, and his beard ruffled ferocious in the briny wind. He had his sword Tiwaz at his side in a blue wooden scabbard fitted with bronze, and carried a long lance, and a bright-yellow painted shield.

Then came Aster, so bright in the sinking sun. He wore a bronze breastplate over a red tunic, high leather boots that reached just under his knees, a bronze helmet with a wide visor, and a round shield, shaped and coloured like the sun. The Greek carried an iron sword, a *xiphos*, at his side, and in his hand, a one-handed iron spear. My eyes nearly teared at his beauty, and I knew I had made the right choice to have him drill my men. I yearned to learn his art of war.

Finally, Tratonius came. He wore a bronze chestplate chiselled like muscles of an athletic man, a blue-green fringed check cloak, a red tunic belted together by brown belts, bronze knee-high greaves, and a bronze helmet polished that it shone. The helmet had a spike where a black horsehair plume fluttered. He was equipped with a short iron sword, a set of javelins, and an oval shield painted with a blue boar that possessed a golden fringe. The torc clasped tightly around his thick neck. He possessed mismatched equipment, methinks, for nothing seemed in place, yet he still wore it all well, for I recognized him as a leader, even if he followed me now.

'You made us dress for war for your ceremony,' Verc said. 'It was a great effort. But tell us, boy, how do you expect to complete this without a druid?'

'There is a druid out yonder,' I said, and pointed toward the black headland. 'And he was the one who helped me become Vidav. We will seek him out now. If we can't find him or if he's dead, you can do it.'

We left with the sky darkening, and I led the men down the sheep trail along the coastline. Cicarus volunteered to watch the camp, so we left him with the slave girls. I brought Myrnna along, because I did not have the trust to leave her with anyone.

After we passed diving razorbills, we spotted a white blob on the edge of the cliff. It moved, and when we came closer, the blob spanned out on the ground. We drew nearer to it, and it was Cammios in his soiled robe. He stood up, and paced, oblivious to our presence and jabbering to himself. We climbed the hill to him, and the wind whipped us so hard that we had to shout. He teetered on the edge of the cliff and invited me to shove him off.

'Have you all come back?' He asked. Verc, Antedios, Cattos and Aldryd stood behind me. 'My men!' Cammios shouted at them. 'I command you to kill me!'

'These aren't your men,' I said to him.

'They aren't?' he said. His face was wind-whipped red, and his eyes teared. His drab hair and soiled robe juxtaposed against the golden sea behind him. How he had become so dirty overnight, I did not know. 'Then who are you?'

'I'm the man from the tomb. The man you saved.'

'I... I saved you?' he said, and his eyes became wetter, and he stopped pacing.

'Don't you remember?'

'You're dead!' he said, patting my rotting tunic. 'You're dead... in a way, yes.'

'No, I am alive,' I said. 'Come on, we have to complete the ceremony. I must be named.'

'Yes,' he said, and the tears flew down his face. His eyes calmed. His hand, clawing at my chest, stopped shaking. 'You must have a new name. It is sundown. Who are these men?'

'My warriors. They're all swearing an oath to me after I am named.'

'These aren't my men,' he said, and he laughed when he saw Marthelm, Tratonius, Aster and Orca. 'These are foreigners!' And he looked at the rest, 'more foreigners!' And at me, 'you're foreign, in a way now.'

I unsheathed my sword and his eyes drew to it. I pointed to the inscription.

'That's me. *Vidav*. That is what my name is now, and the name of my sword.'

'I will name you, and swear your men to you,' he said. 'If you kill me.'

He ran a finger down the blade. Blood dripped down into the brown moss below. He sucked his finger.

'Will you?'

I hesitated. He was a madman. The goddess Fea, of stark, screaming madness, had begun to grip ahold of him and wrench his sanity. Why should he suffer so? Besides, I had weaselled out of killing him before, even though I had promised him I would. I owed him death.

I nodded.

'Swear to me,' he said, and he grabbed me by the collar of my tunic, and pulled himself close. His breath smelled of fish.

'I know I am mad,' he said, as if he could hear my thoughts.

The druid forbade Myrnna to witness it, so she sat in the bushes with closed eyes and covered ears. Of the ceremony, the Cammios permitted me to say little. When it was over, I had a new name, eight men sworn to me, and Tratonius relinquished the twisted wire torc to my neck. Cammios died. I will say, my dear Luceo, I am happy that he died while Fea's wrath had left him as the moonlight lit his bright eyes. We left his corpse there, and I left Bodvoc's sword in the tomb of my ancestor.

CHAPTER XIV

We returned to camp, and I burned the clothes of my ancestor in the fire, to ashes, dressed myself in my old clothes that I had traded back from Cicarus for his freedom, and cinched the brooch on the cloak Aine had given to me. I sat down among my men at the fire. I ate, I drank, I was content.

That night, the men were quiet, but once they drank, they began to recount their stories and chat amongst themselves. Verc, Antedios, and Cattos complained they had little to eat, which was nonsense since the ocean had plenty to offer.

I retired in Cicarus' former tent, and brought Myrnna in with me. We had spoken little since I had rescued them from the loch-thing, but for the first time since before I had botched the cattle raid, I could rest. I had my men. I had my oath. Soon, I would have my revenge.

Lying next to Myrnna vexed me. Her soft white arm brushed mine. Her lithe body heaved slowly. I could not touch her, of course; I had sworn to keep her a maiden until married. This kept me up late. She even rolled over and leaned against me in her sleep, her soft curvaceous form against my shoulder, and I could not sleep at all.

Aster woke me up in the morning. He barged into my tent, and hectored me out, and I found myself dressing hastily for war. He drilled us, us being Cattos, Antedios, Cicarus, and Marthelm. That was how every day went for the next three weeks. We drilled in the mornings, taught mostly by Aster, but occasionally by Tratonius.

Each day, we trained until the late afternoon after much warcraft during the day, and then marched up the hills in the evening. There he educated me in the ways of the Greek, first in the language and its grammar, and from there math, philosophy, physics, history, poetry, music. He educated me daily until midnight. May the gods love him! He taught me so much, and I will forever remember that, and cherish the man. Though, he refused to teach me to write. 'You're too old,' he told me, and Verc once said that men who cannot write have better memories than those who can, so I never pressed it.

Some often spoke of those baleful men called Romans. Tratonius refused to speak about them, though I suspected he knew them well, for he wore some Roman equipment, and was said to have killed a German king when he warred for the Romans, and that is where he had gotten his helmet. The men roused the more they spoke and drank, and finally one evening, Marthelm spoke to me.

'Remember these words, Celt,' he said, and he leaned back, crossings his arms to show the deep scars across them that ran along them like black ink. 'We will not tolerate the Romans forever. Soon we Germans will break over the Alps like a river over a dike after a hard rain and at high tide. We will end the menace once and for all.'

'I drink to that!' Orca shouted, his words slurred, spit hit me in the eye. He leaned his great girth over me and banged his cup against Marthelm's and then mine, and we all drank. I thought from the way they described the Romans and their triumphs that they would not succumb so easily. I agreed with them to show solidarity with their plight, for I was their leader.

They told stories every night around the fire. It attracted us like crabs to dead fish, and we gorged on the stories. Often we stayed up so late that, while I was a young lad and so were some of my men, the older men suffered for it yet they trudged through the following day bemoaning their previous night, only to drink themselves silly again the next.

Their stories thrilled me beyond belief. Luceo, you were fortunate to ride with some of these men and hear their tales. I heard of great battles on mountain passes. I heard of giant animals called elephants that men ride and shoot arrows from and are so monstrous that they can kill a man by just stepping on him, yet it feared mice like mice fear hawks. I heard of Egyptians and their magic and great towers of stone. I heard of Jews, who deny all gods except for one, and that one demands their foreskins as a sacrifice. I heard of men that live so close to the sun that it burns their bodies black and fries their hair into grizzle. I heard of men in the far northern edge of the world who have become so used to the cold that they sleep naked in the snow, and beyond them, men with fur like wolves. Then there were the Amazons out in the east, who chopped their right breasts off so that they may fire their bows easier without their milk-givers in the way. They enslaved men and

bred the best men and women like lords breed horses. I heard tales of sea
monsters with tentacles that can wrap around the greatest of Greek ships. I
heard of Etruscans, Macedonians, Thracians, Nemidians and other people
that seemed so distant and dreamlike. Most of all, I heard the stories of my
father from Tratonius, and I lapped up the stories, the thirsty and grateful
dog that I was. I memorized them so I may tell them to my children.

Though sometimes, my mind drifted. I thought of how the truce we had
with the Hillmen would end soon, and that the men would want a new truce,
but I would not grant them that. I thought of Bodvoc rotting in my home, and
Fennigus and Ambicatos and all my clansmen all rotting in the moors outside
Dun Ashaig. I thought of Dun Torrin, where Myrnna may finally be safe.

Once, at midday, while we sat on a hillock, shirtless and sweaty in the high
noon sun, and bruised after a long day of training, Antedios and Cattos
complained that they had no more food left to eat.

'There's fish,' I said.

'We don't eat fish,' Cattos said.

'Then eat it anyway,' I said.

'We can't eat fish. It's against our laws.'

'And besides, who wants to eat fish? They're slimy and disgusting,'
Antedios said.

'Then we will hunt a seal,' I said. Some seals had been basking out in the
sheltered shore nearby.

'Not seals either,' Cattos said. 'They're just fish-dogs.'

I started down the beach to return to the camp and search for food. Just
on our camp's edge, I found two dogs chasing gulls and scavenging around
the shells. They were sleek, one grey, and one brown, short-haired with long,
pointed faces and floppy ears. They were without mange, and I knew them
to be hunting hounds from Albion. Only kings could have had such dogs as
companions. How they ended up on Skye, I never knew.

I walked toward the dogs and whistled to catch their attention, and they
ran toward me, kicking up sand and shells, and both lunged at me. Soon I
found myself on the ground with wet tongues slopping all over my face, and
I hugged them both and patted them on the head and they pranced around
me as I climbed to my feet. I found them to be a high omen from Nodens, god
of dogs, and I reckoned to sacrifice to him that night as thanks for his gift.

'You are my dogs now!'

I ran off toward the camp, where the billow of smoke smouldered into the sky. The slave girls had been cooking more ling, cockles, and mussels. The hounds chased after me, and soon both ran at my flanks, and then they ran in front of me and we reached the camp.

'We're hungry,' Verc said, as he kneeled to pat one hound, the grey one, on the head. The brown one was in Orca's lap, licking him on his bristly face. He laughed aloud and hugged the dog tightly until it whined.

'Why can't you just eat fish?' I asked.

'These bog people,' Aldryd said, slurping a raw cockle up. 'They won't eat anything from the sea. Fish. Shellfish. Seals. Birds. Nothing. Damned stupid, it is.'

'The sea is where one goes when they die. It is the gateway to Otherworld. Eating a fish may jinx you,' Verc said. 'Listen now, lad, I marched with Tratonius' sellswords for over a decade and he never complained that I didn't eat fish. You're the leader, so you have to feed your men, and what do you do when they don't eat fish?'

I said nothing.

'Hunt, boy, you hunt! No one owns this land now, so no one will challenge our right to hunt. We are lawful in this pursuit. You even have two hunting hounds, and it is that time of the year when the bucks are rutting. At twilight, we grab our spears and the hounds, and pray to Cernunnos that he blesses us with a buck.'

Verc was, of course, right. To hunt was the simplest solution. I had eleven bellies to fill, including us ten warriors, and we were always hungry. Just one buck would last a long time for all of us, but I still did not understand why these 'bog people' as Aldryd called them just could not eat fish.

Late that afternoon, we headed up into the hills. Verc, Cattos, Antedios, the German slave girls, and the two dogs. I allowed the men to name the dogs. Antedios named the sleek grey one Chaser since he liked to chase gulls, and Cattos named the brown one, with whitened age around his nuzzle, Groaner since he mumbled when he sat down or got up. 'We should have named him Orca – they're both grey around the face, and they both groan all the time,' Cattos said.

We passed through the shrubland moors, through the pass of black craggy mountains of Cullinan, and into the old pine forest.

The slave girls, guarded by Cattos, went off to forage, while Verc, Antedios, and I sent the hounds through the forest. We brought longspears with flame-shaped blades, and we'd hoped for the hounds to flush out a stag toward us. We searched the pine carpet for signs of our quarry, and found deer droppings and freshly broken shrubs, along with deep hoofprints. We followed them with the pine canopy above us. Slowly, steady, ready to earn our dinner. I had loved hunting ever since I was little and my father had taken me out into Alba to hunt whenever he came to visit, and now I hunted with longspears, hounds, and men sworn to me. We were even dressed in our war clothes while we stalked the forest for our prey. I thought my father would look proudly upon me for that.

The sun began to sink down below the grey ocean. The birds sang their song in the green beard above our heads. A squirrel chittered away with an acorn. The frogs croaked around streams that the hounds drank from. But we found no deer. Our hunger groaned, and Antedios began to whine, and we even ran into Cattos and the slave girls, who then joined us since their baskets were full, but we still needed the deer. I could not feed them on a few baskets full of berries. We needed a deer to sacrifice and to feast upon that would not only satisfy Verc, Cattos and Antedios, but bring all of us together. I intended to sacrifice to Nodens that night, and I had to fulfil that promise. Most of all, I had to be the one to track down the deer to prove myself to my men.

The night encroached, and the forest darkened. It was a clear night on a full moon again, so I did not fear trudging back down the moorland to camp, but I feared the sidhe.

Verc grumbled. 'You've been leading us astray. I knew it! You're still angry that we won't eat fish, is that it?'

Before I could speak, Verc raised his hand. 'Follow me, men! I will find us a stag. This boy, despite growing up on this island, does not know where to find quarry.'

'Look, over here!' Cattos said.

I found the two lads crouched in the brush just before a clearing, with a loch in the centre of it. A plump, grey figure laid lazily across its muddy bank.

'Is that a seal?' Antedios asked.

The three of us crept toward the clearing, trailed by the dogs and Verc. Both dogs sniffed. Groaner snarled.

'Heel!' I said in a hushed tone, and both dogs cowered, circled, and slumped to the ground in the pine needs. *By Danu's great red hair, how did a seal get so far inland?*

'What is a seal doing all the way up here? How'd he climb up that hill, through the forest – what's a seal doing so far away from the sea?' Cattos asked.

'Waiting for us,' Verc said. 'Yes, this must be a land seal – not a water seal. It should be fit for us to eat. Men, spears ready!'

'We have no land seals here,' I said.

'Nonsense. You just haven't seen one yet, what are you waiting for, lads?' he gestured toward the seal. 'Spears ready, spears forward,' and he put his fingers in his mouth to whistle for the hounds.

'Wait!' I said. 'I've hunted in this forest all of my life and I have never came across a land seal! I have never even heard of such a beast!'

'Don't doubt me, lad. Don't forget that I was a druid. If you're worried that it is sick, then you don't have to eat it.'

Something queer shone about the seal. It rolled on its side, and reclined in the shallows of the loch that lapped at its black flippers. For a fleeting moment, it looked nothing like a seal at all, but a man.

'Wait!' I said now. 'There's something different here!' I had little time to say more, for the men advanced with their spears.

'Forget it, Brenn,' said Verc. 'Or Vidav, or whatever you call yourself now. We owe you, but we aren't going to let you starve us.'

'It's Vidav!' I said through my teeth. 'And listen to me! Do you not forget the loch-thing?'

'That was an anomaly. It was a monster local to the loch. Trust me, I know, I was a druid, and you are a warrior, and I know these matters better than you.'

The seal had eyes far too manlike. The birdsong had ceased, it ceased so abruptly that I wondered if I'd ever hear them sing again.

'Don't kill that seal,' I said. 'Listen to me! I have the *sight*! How can you not see that?'

'As I said, you will not starve us. Lads, forward!' Verc ordered Antedios and Cattos, who paced gingerly over the brush toward the clearing, long-spears first.

Verc whistled hard. The two dogs were alerted. 'Sic!'

Chaser and Groaner bounded over the wall of brush and into the clearing, they split and both flanked the seal, their hackles up, and barking. Cattos and Antedios advanced.

I no longer saw a seal, but the tanned skin of a white-haired bearded man who reclined in the shallows in the same manner as a seal. He sat up.

Leaping over the brush wall, I ran in front of Cattos and Antedios and shouted 'No!'. I shouted so loud and hard that even the hounds stood still, skidding in the mud. The men halted.

They all must have seen him. They all just stood there gawking. Verc, Cattos, Antedios, the dogs.

He was an old man, frail, wrinkled, and skinny. His beard and hair were thin and white. He looked rather annoyed, indifferent to the embattled men that just threatened to skewer him with spears and sic the hounds on him.

'A selkie?' Verc asked, bewildered.

The old man yawned and looked up. His voice sounded weak and tired. He had large brown eyes, curious and deep like that of a seal's.

'I am not a selkie. I do not dress in a seal's skin. I was a seal,' he said. He stretched, as if stiff from a long afternoon nap, and faced my party. 'Why did you bother me?'

'They were going to kill you because we thought you were a seal! But I have the *sight*, and I saw that you were a man. Did you not see us? Our spears? Our hounds?'

'I saw you, but I was in no danger. I could have just turned into a fish. If you tried to fish me up from the loch, I would have just turned into a skeeter. If you tried to scoop me out, I would have just turned into a speck of dust and blown away with the wind.

'Oh yes, I have been many things. I have been the flower in a bride's hair, I have been a salmon in the jaws of a bear, I have been the heart of a man who dares, I have been a laugh from a maiden fair, and I have been the tension of a warrior's stare. I shift, I am Seonaidh, and I shift my shape like a god.'

We said nothing. What could we say? Even the hounds stood as still as the bronze statues of hounds I have seen in the southern realms. What could men ever think when faced with the wondrous? What have we even to add?

It satisfied me to see Verc silenced. Back then, when I was younger, I laughed later about it. I laughed because he tried to explain the loch-thing, and tried to comprehend my *sight*. I laugh no more, because I do not comprehend it, either.

'You can see into the Otherworld, my good lad,' Seonaidh said to me, 'your power is potent. Some are born with it, others receive it, but someone enhanced yours, yes? It can be a curse, a blessing, or maybe both. It all depends on how you swing that door. And when you can see it, others can, and when you cannot see it, others cannot. That is your gift or curse.

'Your men posed no danger to me, but you did try and intervene to spare my life. For that, I am grateful. I will do two things for you. I have the gift of foresight. I can help you, but not interfere. In three weeks, march down the strand, not the roads, not in boats over the ocean, not over the mountains. Head south. Do this no matter what your companions say. And the second thing I will do is, well, farewell!'

As the seal had vanished, and the old man had taken its place, now a marten had taken the place of Seonaidh. It glanced at us, then scampered off and disappeared into the gloom of the pine forest.

Before we could collect our words, a brushing in the bushes alerted us. There stood a magnificent buck with nine spikes from his antlers. It nosed around, then stopped to stare at us.

'That's not a shapeshifter, right?' Antedios asked.

'Red deer, as far as I can tell.'

Verc whistled and sicced the hounds. They split off into the forest, rounded and chased the deer right toward us. The deer pivoted and bounded away from the clearing, we all side-stepped and a flurry of spearheads sank into its body. We stabbed it many times until it sank to the ground.

I leaned over, careful not to get behind it, and placed a hand on its neck and stroked its fur as the life drained from its eyes. 'Thank you for the hunt, Nodens,' I said. Verc was leaning over me.

'And thank Seonaidh,' he said.

'Thank you, Seonaidh – two legs shall be tossed in the loch. One for Nodens and the other for Seonaidh. Men – tonight we feast!'

We lopped its forelegs off and tossed them into the loch where we had discovered Seonaidh as the seal. We carried the deer on a sturdy bough and out of the forest, finishing the hunt just before nightfall.

In three weeks, march down the strand, not the roads, not in boats over the ocean, not over the mountains. Head south. Do this no matter what your companions say.

We set out of the forest, down the moors, through the valley, and back toward the beach in the light of the full moon and the black gulf of night. Cattos and Antedios hauled our quarry, singing a rolling song about hunting, and the slave girls followed with baskets of berries. We had enough for a great feast, and I would hold the feast that night to celebrate my new name, our new companionship, and Nodens.

The stars lit the way, almost as much as the full moon. The great plough wheeled over the horizon, so stark that it checked me in the shrubs.

'Tell me, Verc, is that an omen?'

'Twenty years of my life,' Verc said.

'Pardon me?'

'Twenty years of my life, lad,' he said. He stopped walking, shook his head, and spat. Cattos, Antedios and the girls moved on and left us knee-deep in the heather.

'Twenty years of my life I spent at the druid's academy on Mona. Each day spent in darkness, face down on the floor, repeating what was said to me for nine hours a day. Twenty years and I was convinced the sidhe were beyond our comprehension, that there was no such thing as the *sight*, and that the gods lay beyond our reach.

'And then you, you, a warrior, and not even a reputable warrior, come along and you have the *sight*, and you prove once and for all that all we see on this world isn't all there is, that there is more to be seen, that our eyes cannot see far over the horizon. What use was my twenty years?

'Twenty years I spent learning how to decipher the will of the gods through their omens. The entrails of sacrificed animals. The flight of birds. And the stars. The stars, lad. On clear nights, I would head out to old Osimus' circle, and view the stars. I would memorize their movements and discuss their movements and their meanings with my fellow druids, and once I even travelled to Rome, and spoke with learned men down there. The stars were everything for me. It was the apex of all my knowledge. And most of all, I loved the stars. I loved to see them. Don't you get it, lad?'

I shook my head.

'By the gods, lad, I cannot see the stars anymore. My eyes are too blurry! What use was my twenty years of education – what use is a druid who cannot see the stars?

'Some men say that some down in the southern lands can fashion a device to alleviate this. But I'm too far away, and it's the will of the gods that I cannot see. And I fear, someday, I will go blind. So that is why, lad, I cannot tell you if what you see is an omen or not,' he said, and walked off toward the camp.

Down at the camp, the slave girls prepared the food. Orca had his big knife and butchered the deer with one hand while we all set up for the feast. The men had fashioned a long table from driftwood while we hunted. The deer roasted piecemeal on spits, and the fire curled up into the night, while Tratonius heard what had happened.

'March down the shore southward? Toward Dun Torrin? No, never.'

'That's what the sidhe said, we must listen to him,' Verc said. 'No matter how mad it sounds.'

'Mad? It sounds mad, do you say?' he said, and slapped his hands on the table. 'Don't you remember? They told us not to go down the shore, don't you know that? Treaty or no treaty, they told us not to, and we're supposed to go down after the treaty is over. Do you know what they will do to us?'

'We must trust in this sidhe,' Verc said. Tratonius left, and did not partake in the feast.

CHAPTER XV

The men slept that night with bellies full, drunk and content. The touch of ale had warmed them toward me, the stranger, the one with no battle experience. The one who was to lead them down the strand, where the Hillmen ordered them not to go, for which the penalty for disobeying was death. With all that in mind, and with the suspicion that my first march may be my final, I had one last desire.

I desired to go home.

It had been a while with the men, training in the daylight, learning in the moonlight, merrymaking with beer, stories and slave girls in the evenings, yet looming over all, I yearned for my revenge against the Hillmen. In this span of bliss, between peace and war, when we know we shall march toward chaos, I wanted a reprieve. I wanted to go home, and see my house, and give Bodvoc and Lappie and the slaves a proper burial.

Tratonius requested a rest day, so I granted it to him, and left Myrnna in the camp under the guard of Marthelm, who I felt I could trust the most, and started back down into the forest. I brought the *Celts*, so to say, Verc, Antedios, and Cattos, because I felt they were closest to me, and they could share my feeling when I reached my home, and understand my plight. Aldryd, too, was close enough, yet I felt he was bereft of loyalty, or clan, or place, as if he walked Danu's land just to kill and drink and whore.

We headed through the forest. We brought our arms and shields, for men should always be armed, because peaceful times can turn to war.

The dogs rushed through the heather, uprooting the songbirds from it. The moorlands passed us by, regular, unchanging, reddish and hostile. The trackway had been well-trodden by men's feet, and hooves of beasts. The sun beat down and we all reddened in it.

We headed down the valley, passing the black, loch-wreathed Cuillins where Cúchulainn trained with Sgàthach, goddess of Skye, still hot from his fury that no snow will ever stay cold upon their craggy peaks. We marched past these, and then came into the realm of the red hills, daughter of Slighan, and there the Slighan Hill loomed at the very spot where I had wounded the giant.

Come back to the Slighan Hill...

I pressed on, Badb clawing through my chest. I owed Bodvoc that burial, my dear Luceo. I did not want to go nearer to that hill, but I had to, and I hid my fear from my comrades.

Sheep grazed on a hillock, then they scattered when we neared. I thought them to be wild. The trackway had been cleaned up of bodies, by men's hands or carrion-eater beaks, I know not, but the broken wagons, the horse corpses, the gore and viscera were all gone.

We came upon the cairn, the hag's cairn, which Myrnna and I had seen the hag herself dancing upon in the moonlight. I slowed, and lagged, letting the lads walk in front, and went apace with Verc. I closed my eyes, and thought of Bodvoc's corpse, and thought of Lappie's lolled tongue, the loyal dead slaves, and I thought of all the dead Hillmen around them and how proud I was of them. I tripped in a hole and I caught my balance, opened my eyes, and we had passed the cairn.

'Aren't you forgetting something?' Verc asked me. I had no response.

'Your hat, lad,' he said. 'Don't you tip your hat at cairns when you pass them?

I locked eyes on the cairn's derelict capstones, and tipped my hat. Verc nodded, we left, and I took three paces.

Thank you, dear!

Badb struck me like a striking lynx, all claws and teeth, and she pulled me with her swift paws. Fear nearly overcame me, but I also feared to show such weakness to my men. My father would have been proud of me to see me so strong, so I pulled through until we left the presence of that horrid cairn.

We approached the border of my farm. More sheep were on a hillock in the distance, and some ducks waddled in the pond near the barn where Vasenus and all my cousins had laid dead. Smoke from the chimney signalled that the hearthfire was burning. The house's surroundings were well-kept, a new door had put on its hinge, and then that door swung open and then came the Hillmen.

Three Hillmen came out, and one whistled and shouted and more came, nine in total. They all had raven-black hair and wore brown tunics and brown-striped, green trousers. They came with stoneheaded axes, stoneheaded spears, and clubs. Slighan had cast a jagged shadow across my home, everything darkened despite the clear blue day, and her Hillman came to meet us at the trackway at the edge of my land.

Verc drew his sword, I drew mine, the Dobunni lads readied their spears. Both hounds began to snarl and Verc commanded them to heel, and they heeled and sat behind us with watchful eyes on the enemy, snarling deeply. We stood steady, four against nine.

While the Hillmen approached us, weapons ready, I checked my farm. There I saw pigs back in the pen, some young boys tending the barley field, and some goats grazing in the heather. This struck me as odd, and it was not until I spotted black-headed women lugging buckets from the stream that I realized that the Hillmen had repopulated the farm. My fields, my pens, my home, all taken by the Hillmen. My rage never burned so hard, Luceo, and I laughed because I would soon get to kill and die happy, knowing I would slaughter one of them at least for revenge, and I would die happy on the plot that reared me.

I stepped on my land.

'What are you doing here?' one asked, in clear *Celtic*, and I found it odd for a Hillmen to know *Celtic*.

'This is my land,' I shouted. 'My great grandfather built that house! My mother gave birth to me here! My brother died here! He died against you!'

The one who spoke, their leader I presumed, lowered his weapon, but they all advanced still. They stopped at spear's length, and I kept my shield guarding my left side and *Vidav* guarding my right. The iron boss of Verc's shield winked in the sun. He grinned, real wide, as eager for battle as a wildcat that spots a mouse, ready to pounce upon his prey.

'What, you just came to see your home?' He asked. He spoke Celtic so well, my dialect, yet the Slighan Hill looming and the tides of war rumbling, and the dogs snarling kept me from furthering that thought.

'This is my home, and you will leave it,' I said.

'We will not. But take a look at your home if you will, do it one last time, since you are *Celts*. We have orders from the queen to kill you.'

'We have a truce,' Verc said, and he calmed and lowered his weapons, as if calmed by a sympathetic touch. 'We're Tratonius' men.'

'We're Vidav's men now,' I said. 'I am Vidav, and tell your queen I will come for her head once the truce is over.'

The Hillmen all laughed. One scrawny boy even laughed at me. Oh, I would prove him wrong, Luceo.

'Vidav isn't a Celtic name,' the leader said. 'They have names like Ausciotes,' he said, and I recalled that name, a clansman from down the river. 'We have a truce, so what do you want?'

'What did you do with my brother?' I asked, through my teeth, my sword still drawn.

The Hillmen's leader had a long face with ruddy cheeks, and I could have sworn to the Three Fears I recognized him.

'The bones? Birds and dogs got to them first,' he said. 'We buried whatever was left in the midden.'

'I'm going there then,' I said.

'No, you're going to leave,' he said.

'This is my farm, and someday, I will make you all leave.'

That checked him. Both parties went silent, still, steady. Camulus tugged my sword-arm.

'Answer this truthfully and then you may,' the Hillmen's leader said.

'Answer what?'

'This question. Do you agree?'

'Yes,' I said, 'I am an honest man.'

'Good. Now the queen is looking for a brown-haired girl, a local girl. Her name is Myrnna. Do you know her?'

'Yes,' I said, and Verc gave me a look as if to quiet me, but I continued. 'She is under my protection. What's it to your queen?'

'What's it to you?' he responded. 'Go on, you can go to the midden. We're watching you, though.'

We walked around the Hillmen. I led my men and dogs through my old farm. It was a strange feeling, Luceo. So strange. I had lived there most of my life, and now I was just there to pay my respects. Such little time had passed, yet so much had changed, and everything felt different. It was as if the forest had changed from summer to winter without autumn betwixt. Strangers walked the pathways. Strange men tended the strange pigs. Strange children chased a puppy across the lawn. Strange women churned butter in my house, attended the hearth, and milled grain. I recognized nothing but at the same time, everything. There was nothing more to say. I felt that I had never been there even though I had walked where I walked from my earliest memories until that moment.

We reached the midden. It was half-turfed and strewn with shells. We found a recent disturbance and dug it up with our hands. I found many bones, bird-pecked and beast-gnawed, and then came upon the skull of Bodvoc. I could tell, because its jaw had been shattered by a spear. I held his skull in my hands, in the mucky midden. I ordered the men to continue to look to find the rest of him, but they found naught but half a dog skull. Lappie.

'Bodvoc… Lappie, I will mount your skulls to my horse, when I get a horse,' I said.

We righted the midden, not out of concern for the Hillmen, but it was my midden and I somehow took pride in its form. There was little more to see for me at my pasture, except that I vowed to retake it someday, and then the Hillmen came back. Four of them.

'Who said you can take skulls?' asked the Hillmen's leader.

I lowered the skulls to the ground, and red Camulus forced me to unsheathe my sword. Cattos and Antedios jumped at the sound, and the Hillmen brandished their weapons.

'What say you – you speak Celtic,' Verc said, 'what say you – you want to settle this like men?'

'We have nothing to prove,' the leader said.

'Do you?' Verc said, and he yanked his trousers down and his red balls popped out. 'Prove you have these!'

Cattos and Antedios howled with laughter while the Hillmen drew their weapons and I heeled the dogs. We stood in the shadow of my house. I remembered running into the arms of my returning father during the hailstorm just after my ninth Samhain. What would my father think if he could see my most hated enemies on my property now, truce or not?

'We have a truce, you madman,' the leader said. 'Calm down, all of you!'

'No one needs to get killed,' Verc said. 'Let's fight! Nothing to the head or face. No stabs! Come on, you cowards! You speak Celtic! Fight like one! One on one, four verses four, battle ends at the first cut!'

'To the first cut?'

'If we win, I get my skulls,' I said.

'And we will ask for nothing from you more than your humiliation when you lose,' the leader said. He held a flint dagger and a square wooden shield. Verc faced against the man with the two-handed ax, and Antedios and Cattos each faced against spearmen, black flint blades homing in on them.

The leader and I circled each other. I leaned forward, one foot forward and the other pointed right, knees bent, ready to spring, as Verc had taught me. The leader too came in the same stance, and then he pounced at me, his foot slamming the hard dirt ground and his dagger coming at me. I raised my shield, but he had feinted, the dagger skimmed across my belly hair, and then he slashed me across the shoulder. I had hopped back, and he stood heaving. I had been bested in moments.

The other fights raged. Verc and the axman vied for each other, while Antedios had been kept at bay by the reach of his opponent's spear. Cattos had closed the distance and struck his opponent in the thigh.

The leader licked the blood from his dagger. 'I'm going to crush those skulls and use them for pigfeed,' he said.

That alone nearly caused me to strike him. *Vidav* was still in my hand, near my knee, and I yearned to impale him and splatter blood upon the yellow paint of the house behind him. And then I realized who he was when he grinned and I spotted the pattern of his crooked teeth. He was familiar, yet distant. He was near, yet so far away. I knew him, yet I didn't. It was Ausciotes, a clansman. *He* was a Hillman!

'Traitor!' I cried. His eye twitched and he lunged at me, dagger first. I blocked with my shield. He sidestepped and then hit his shield against mine and pulled it away from my body, like ripping a baby from a mom's bosom, and struck at my breast.

Verc pinned his dagger-arm to the wall behind us. In an instant blood spattered across the yellow paint of my house. Ausciotes fell backward, armless, and Verc still had his severed arm pinned to the wall.

'Dishonour!' Verc yelled at him.

More Hillmen shouted and rushed us. A woman screeched. Antedios and Cattos raced over to us with the two hounds. Ausciotes looked grey.

Verc sprang in front, shield first. 'Run!'

I ran, the Hillmen rounded the house and others came from around the shed. The three we had duelled joined the fray and all charged at Verc. There I watched the master. He pivoted, blocked the ax from the axman, parried

an incoming spear from the spearman, shoved the axman back, stepped
forward and slashed the axman across the chest, and then held the next
incoming spear with the bottom edge of his shield. He pinned both spears
at once and rushed between them, slashed one foeman across the chest and
stabbed the other in the thigh. A Hillman with a club swung at Verc's back,
but Verc swung his shield behind himself and the club glanced off it, and
Verc spun around and sliced the fat part of his shoulder right off.

We rushed back over to Verc.

'I said run – all of you!'

'No! Come with us!' I shouted.

More Hillmen were upon us.

'I said run! All of you – run!'

'No!' I shouted back at him. 'Come with us!'

Verc glanced blows off his shield and sword-danced with the enemies,
now six, and none could land a blow on him. He would step around them,
which caused them to bunch up, and then in single combat slash or stab
them, then back off, allow them to regroup and then bunch them up again.
He used each one of them as a shield, and one by one, he injured them, and
if their injuries were not grievous, they would rejoin the fight. Cattos and
Antedios both at my flanks defended against incoming spearmen, and some
black-headed children began to throw rocks at us.

Chaser and Groaner launched themselves into the air and snapped at
the limbs of the Hillmen. Groaner pulled one down and Chaser had him by
the ankle and blood sprinkled all over like salt struck by a pickaxe. Antedios
stabbed a spearman through the leg and I rushed and blocked an incoming
spear from another, and Cattos lunged and impaled him through the chest. I
grabbed the attention of an axman who eyed Cattos while the lad attempted
to pull the sword from his foe's chest as he fell, and then Verc lobbed the
axman's head clean off.

Now even more Hillmen came.

They were upon us. They came down between the trees and the sheds
and around from the opposite end of the house, all armed with spears,
daggers, and axes, all stonebladed.

'Run! All of you!' I shouted. Verc refused to move, he had been in a
trance, much like the magic men I would meet later in life who roused

themselves into ecstasy with chants, drums, and herbs, Verc had roused himself into a battle-trance, with nothing but death in his eyes.

'That's an order, Verc!' I shouted at the top of my lungs and that took the trance from him. He gave me a look of despair, as if he wished to die where he stood, and retreated. Verc whistled at the dogs tearing into the whimpering Hillmen, and they heeled, bloody-snouted and loping ahead of us. We all ran down the trackway, sweating, heaving, our blades black with blood.

'And you see!' Verc shouted between breaths, 'that is why you train for single combat! Badb's tits with the Greeks!'

The Hillmen gave chase, and the children came to throw rocks. We raced down the trackway, the meld of the red moors on either side of us, the great shadow of Slighan looming over us.

We reached the hag's cairn, and there the hag checked us in the trackway. She stood there, a crag against our wave, grinning in her red robe.

'Badb – Macha – Fea!' I groaned and we slowed and stopped. The Hillmen did not cease their pursuing. Verc turned to them, and turned to the hag, his mouth agape.

'Cailleach!'

'That's what some call me, yes,' she said, her toothless grin not ceasing. Her body was twisted and her shoulders hunched. 'Looks like it's the end for you, dearies.'

Three dozen Hillmen came barrelling down the well beaten-trackway, kicking up mud, all armed, their black-blades dark in the shadow of Slighan. Verc fell to his knees, as did Antedios and Cattos, and even the hounds cowed and shuddered down to their bellies.

'On your knees, deary, like the rest,' she said.

My knees began to buckle. I began to shake. My heart locked harder than my knees.

I grasped the brooch at my chest, remembering my oath, my promise to protect Myrnna with my life. I could not do it if I were dead. If I were to die, I would be free of my oath. Yet I wished to die on my feet, facing my enemies, just like...

'Cúchulainn,' she finished my thought. 'You really think you are deserving of dying like Cúchulainn? Dear, you have grown arrogant! No, die on your knees, like the boy you are. Like the boy your father always knew you were. Like the boy Fennigus knows you are!'

My knees became so weak that they shook, and I began to lower. Badb found her way into my chest like a mole. I found the ground, and wondered what I had ever done to die this way, on my knees, and my brave comrades – most of all, Verc – succumbing to death on his knees like an executed coward. What more could I do? The Cailleach is a goddess, the hag of winter, the holder of all fertility.

My father. *Nothing is unconquerable. Even our gods can die.*

'I will let you live,' she said. 'For a price.'

'What price?' I asked, and it was as if time had all slowed, for the Hillmen should have been upon us by now.

'Kill him,' she said, and pointed to Verc. 'He desires death. So give him what he wants. Kill him!'

'No,' I said, and I meant it. I would rather die than kill Verc. Verc had saved me from Ausciotes. Verc was my comrade in arms, he had sworn an oath to fight for me, and a leader never kills his men.

'Then die with him,' she said.

'I will,' I replied.

She cackled. She cackled hard. I began to climb to my feet, and she ceased cackling. I climbed to my feet, and I held *Vidav* skyward, and then toward the Cuillins.

'Hail Cúchulainn,' I said, and I aimed my chest at my enemies, and I struggled against the weight of my own body. I locked eyes on the black craggy tops of the mountains named after Cúchulainn, and thought of him, and how fearless he was, and I knew I could never compare, but I thought myself worthy to at least mimic his valour.

Wings beat behind me. The heaviness lifted. Verc, Antedios, Cattos, and the dogs all scrambled to their feet. The Hillmen were far away now, so far they looked like ants rushing toward their anthill. A raven flew over our heads and a cackle resounded.

'Run,' I said to them, and we all ran down the trackway, passed the hag's cairn, passed the Cuillins. The Hillmen were out of sight and we prayed hard to Bride, protector of the Hebrides, that no more Hillmen would be on the trackway in front of us. We reached the forest and went through its byways and returned to the camp.

We had made it back. The hag's spell had been broken, and we escaped, and how the Hillmen had been so near and then so far when the spell faded, I do not know. How, my dear Luceo, we dispelled the hag's clutch, I do not know.

Before we returned to camp, as we ran down the hill toward the beach, Verc spoke to me.

'I cannot believe you were willing to die for me,' he said. Before I could say anything else, he continued. 'Too many men have died for me when I was a druid. Too many young men, all in their prime, sent to their graves while I lived. No more. I will never let any of you die for me again.'

We said nothing as we rushed to tell the others what had transpired. We had broken the truce with the Hillmen, and knew they'd take revenge.

CHAPTER XVI

By the time we reached camp, twilight had beckoned. Belenus waned, and Epona rose in her silvery chariot, silvering the roaring sea at high tide. We had left, harried by the hag, Bodvoc and Lappie's skulls uncovered on my farm, and the truce with the Hillmen broken. We gathered up everyone and told them what had happened.

'You broke the fucking truce!' Tratonius shouted, and he raised a stool over his head and smashed it upon the ground, and then he kicked a barrel, it busted and ale fountained out, and then he began to beat his hands against the sand on the ground. 'You broke the fucking truce!'

His ugliness spread among the men of the camp. They chattered among themselves, and Orca moaned some vulgarities until Groaner launched into his lap, and he cuddled the dog with his good arm.

'So fucking stupid!' Tratonius shouted. He was shirtless and sunburned and his big, scarred belly jiggled as he marched right up to me. 'Why did you even go there!?'

'The Hillmen were on my farm! That's my farm!'

'No! Don't you get it? The Hillmen own your farm,' he said, and his voice now calmed. 'They own your neighbour's farm. They own his neighbour's farm. They own every farm. While you were away, some Hillmen came to trade and we spoke with them. The Hillmen have conquered Skye, and they're going to begin launching attacks on the other islands. Nearly all of your druids have been handed over and executed. Every one of your barbarian kings has surrendered his sovereignty.'

I stood silent. Badb clawed in my chest. Nemain, goddess of frenzy, threatened to strike me to attack Tratonius, for the news filled with me with such battle-lust I wished to strike whatever was nearest to me.

'All but Dun Torrin have fallen.'

I grasped my brooch. I looked over at Myrnna, who held her own arms.

'Dun Torrin still stands?' I asked.

'It's besieged,' Tratonius said.

'Then we have to go and help them!' I shouted.

Tratonius interrupted me.

'No! How can you even suggest that? What do you think will happen if the nine of us go and attack thousands? It's suicide!'

'Seonaidh told me not to listen to you!' I shouted back at him.

'Seonaidh?'

'That's right,' Verc said, and stood next to me. 'That shapeshifter. He told us to march down the coast toward Dun Torrin, no matter what anyone said.'

Tratonius sneered, his eyes squinted, his face flushed and so did his reddened head. He sat down on the log nearest to him, and slapped his knees.

'You are joking. How do we even know we can trust him?'

'He gave us the deer,' I said.

'To Dis Pater with the deer!' Tratonius yelled. 'To Hades with it! We will eat fish and let the damned Gauls starve. Pay off the Hillmen.'

'Pay off?' I asked.

'You broke the truce. We'll pay the blood price and then form a new truce.'

'No,' I said, and I unsheathed my sword and Tratonius scrambled to his feet. His hand clawed toward the leather sheath at his side for his gladius, and I thought he was to draw it on me. Now Orca, Marthelm, and Aster all stood at his side, against Verc and I.

'We were told not to go down the coast by the Hillmen. It was part of the truce, yes?' Marthelm said. 'We must form a new truce, or they will simply kill us. We should do it now, before they send men to our camp to avenge their dead, yes?'

'That's right,' Tratonius said. 'Come on, son – yes, you have that power, but how do you know we could even trust it? Why, I ought to think that you're the reason for the evil we've faced so far, given your sight and all. I don't think you can trust that shapeshifter, not any more than you can trust the siren.'

'Told you it was easier to kill him,' Aldryd said, nonplussed. He sat with Mawaz in his lap, tickling her to make her wiggle around on him.

'Tratonius, my good friend,' Verc said, 'you must trust in Vidav! When the hag bewitched us, his power was able to break us free from it, and allowed us to escape. When we found that shapeshifter – who knows what would have happened, had he not seen its reality! My good friend, trust in what I say, I was a druid, and by the gods I cannot see well anymore, but I am not blind.'

'I must refuse,' Marthelm said. 'Gentle Verc – I am Vidav's councillor, as are you, my good friend Verc, and we disagree. Now Vidav gets to decide the vote since he's the leader, but Vidav ought to know that his men are going to be very displeased with this. Count them – who is with Verc, and who is with me?'

Orca, Aster, and Marthelm all did not budge from Tratonius. Cattos and Antedios then stood at either of my flanks.

'You, too?' Tratonius asked. 'My foster sons?'

'Verc's right, we would have been dead, I think,' Cattos said.

'Sorry, pappa,' Antedios said.

'Looks like we're tied then,' Tratonius said with a sigh. 'What say you, Aldryd?'

'Don't care, to the crows with the Hillmen,' he said.

'Cicarus?'

Cicarus, who had been sharpening a knife on a whetstone, did not look up while speaking. 'It's a stupid idea.'

'He's not my man,' I said.

'He's still with us,' Tratonius said.

'Then he can leave if he doesn't like it,' I said. 'Because we're following Seonaidh's advice.'

'And what was it, exactly?' Tratonius asked.

'Wait three weeks at the camp, and then head down the coast south, no matter what my companions say. That means we head out in three days.'

Tratonius laughed and shook his head and stood up. He grabbed a hold of Sabella's brown hand, kissed it, and pulled her toward his tent. 'The Hillmen will come in swarms and kill us here if we wait and do not pay them off. So good luck.'

Verc and Aster began to speak and it quickly delved into anger. They both spoke in Greek, and Verc seemed to speak it just as well as Aster, at least to my ears. For a few moments, I attempted to understand the conversation to practice, but they began to shout at each other and speak quickly, and the dilemma distracted me.

Tratonius was right. This would destroy our morale and turn at least half of the men against me. They were all sworn to me, but men could still break their oaths. A broken oath would damn him to a dishonourable life, yet it would still end mine if he happened to break his oath through my death.

I needed to placate them. I recalled to Dun Ashaig, when the druids all bickered among themselves over the besiegement, right up until Ambicatos' children had been bloodied in front of their very eyes.

Someone needed to be bloodied now.

Aster ranted. He ranted about *Keltoi*, about superstitions, and about the need to see an oracle. That much I gathered, and he ranted until he picked up his flute and sat perched on a driftwood trunk, wrapped himself in his cloak, and played the flute.

'Verc, maybe we should placate the gods?'

'In what way?' he asked, his face growing dark.

I told him what I witnessed upon Dun Ashaig. He gagged. He sat down, holding his stomach, as if he would vomit.

'That's just what the Greek would love to see us do,' he said. 'He thinks us Keltoi are savages and thinks we commit human sacrifices and other such atrocities. Tell me, what harm is it if a man we are to execute anyway is offered the gods? Either way, he is dead. What does it matter what words we say, unless to flatter a god in aiding us?'

'None of us here deserve execution,' I said. 'Perhaps we can abduct some Hillmen.'

'Not likely,' he said. 'It's risky. Seonaidh told us to stay here. I would think the Hillmen would come down after us. Perhaps Seonaidh protects us. But if we do not listen to him – wait three weeks, and then head down the coast, perhaps he will not protect us any longer.'

'Then we should sacrifice someone to him, to ensure he protects us.'

Verc went ashen. He looked outright disgusted, and he drew a knife. I flinched, as if he were to break his oath at the very thought of what I suggested.

'You better not be suggesting what I think you are'

'Not one of the men,' I said. 'One of the slave girls!'

Verc shook his head slowly, and then sheathed his knife. 'Very well. Sacrificing one of our slaves will show the gods we are committed to more than mere wealth. It will bring us all together, methinks. Besides, slaves aren't much better than beasts.'

'But which one?'

'Let me decide,' he said. 'I will watch them for signs. Bring them out to me when the moon is at its zenith, we shall conduct the ritual the night before we embark toward Dun Torrin.'

To that, I agreed. I retired to my tent. I thought of my farm, and how I must return there someday. I had left Bodvoc and Lappie's skulls there, exposed on the ground, but I had to retreat with my men to safety. That Hillman – once a Celt – defeated me, on my property, in the presence of the ghosts of my ancestors. And now the truce was broken, and half my men were against me.

I laid there upon a blanket, wrought with the weight of my burden. The hag. I had seen her again, and so did my comrades. How, and why, did she vanish, and how did the Hillmen end up so far away, when they were so close?

Myrnna came into the tent through the tight flap. She wore her heavy woollen cloak and she had her hands cupped in front of her. She smiled at me.

'I have some hazelnuts for you,' she said.

She kneeled next to me, and she poured the hazelnuts into my hands. I ate them, one by one, sitting up. She carried *Vidav* in its scabbard, having washed and shined it free of blemish. The tent was lit by the moon. Her hair looked so dark and skin so light, and when she removed her cloak, my eyes were drawn to her supple white shoulders. I realized why I had this burden now.

'We're going to Dun Torrin soon, aren't we?' Myrnna asked.

'Yes, in three days,' I said.

'Cattos and Antedios went and scouted,' she said. 'They say there are thousands of Hillmen on the coast.'

'So be it,' I said.

Myrnna sat down next to me, and put a hand on my shoulder.

'Brenn,' she said.

'Vidav,' I said.

'Vidav,' Myrnna said. 'How can we?'

Her face looked white.

'How can we hope to face thousands of them? And what about the truce? Please, do what is reasonable, pay them off, get another truce.'

'Didn't you see the hag?' I asked. 'Didn't you see the giant? Didn't you see the loch monster? I saw the hag again earlier today. We couldn't move and the Hillmen were going to kill us and then all a sudden she disappeared. I don't know what is going on, or what my power is, but that Seonaidh – the shapeshifter, as we call him. I have a feeling to follow what he says.'

Myrnna laughed short and hard. She mocked me with her laugher. 'A feeling? Is that what you base your leadership on?'

'Don't you mock me,' I said, and now I faced her. 'Don't you dare! I risked my life against that giant. I risked my life against that loch monster. I would never put you in danger if I didn't know what was best for me, for you, for all of us.'

Myrnna shrieked at me. 'Father would never want you to do this!'

She huffed and stormed out of the tent. I did not go after her. It was loud, loud enough for all the men to hear, and it would humiliate me to face them now. We had been demoralized enough.

I laid down alone and slept.

I gathered my fishing equipment in the early morning and met Marthelm in the dim light. We started toward the strand with our rods, buckets and a pouch of worms, when some barks from the heather in the hills startled us. There came much commotion when a black blur trampled into the camp harried by our dogs, with Cattos and Antedios chasing after them.

'Boar!' one of the lads cried.

The boar ran through the hard dirt of the camp. It smashed through pots and buckets and barrels and terrified the mules, who ran off to the limits of their tethers and brayed. The dogs cornered the boar into a cluster of tents, and the two dogs barked from its flanks, and then it charged Chaser. Chaser lunged out of the way and the boar ran through the campfire, kicking up ash in its wake and ploughing into a tent. The tent came crashing down, and out came naked Sabella, running away screaming while holding her tits with one arm.

Now all the mercenaries came out of their tents and armed themselves. Cicarus, Cattos, and Antedios pursued after the dogs with their longspears. Myrnna emerged out of our tent and I shouted at her to run out of the camp. She did. I grabbed a longspear from the weapon rack.

'Watch out!' Tratonius shouted and pulled Cattos out of the way of the charging boar. They both thudded to the ground.

'We're going to eat good tonight!' Antedios yelled as he leapt over his foster brother and father toward the boar, longspear in hands.

The hounds chased the boar to the junction between two tents, and then the boar charged Cicarus. Cicarus pivoted out of the way and went to stab the boar, but one of the dogs had gotten in between them and he pulled his spear back. The boar, silent and sturdy, now stood cornered by the two hounds. It began to grumbly low as I approached it, spear first. The two dogs flanked it, growling, with lips stretched over their fangs.

Badb pounded in my chest. One wrong move and the boar would gore me. It had wrecked our camp and threatened our lives. I must show the men that I am unafraid of this danger, and that we shall feast on its flesh tonight. There were worse ways to go, for we revere the boar. It is the symbol of bravery for us, and indeed this boar was brave, for he charged me headlong.

I stepped back, his jaws snapping at me. I stepped backwards, and it charged me. I aimed for its throat and stabbed, but hit its haunch. It squealed as I stabbed it again through the side, and backed up, and stabbed it again, and again until it fell to the ground and spun on its back. I ended its life through the neck, it quivered, and it died a glorious death of painful suffering.

'Fix the tent,' I said to the lads, after taking a deep breath.

'Why us?' Antedios asked.

'You brought the boar here,' I said. 'Didn't you lead it here?'

'Cicarus told us to,'

I looked over at Cicarus.

'A lord should be able to defeat a boar,' he said.

'Then I am that lord,' I said, and he said nothing. 'Sabella!'

She came trotting back, nude, with a pitiful attempt to cover herself. 'Oh, domine! You slew the beast!'

'I slew the beast,' I said, loud enough for all the mercenaries around me to hear them. 'Now, all of you – right this camp. We feast after sundown!'

The next three days passed. We fished in the morning, and trained and sparred with Verc instead of Aster.

'My feet are both my first offensive, and first defence,' Verc said. 'My shield is my weapon. My sword is my shield. Finally, my sword is my weapon.'

He then lunged at me, right foot first against my right side, shoved me back with his shield and slid his cold, sharp blade across my belly. A little blood dribbled down the shallow slash. He backed away.

'You're off balance. Look at my feet.'

I mirrored his pose, with my right leg forward, my left leg behind, my thumb on the underside of *Vidav*.

'I defeat my enemy not with my sword, but with their own feet. Footwork is my most valuable lesson to you. Listen to it well. You are not to train to win, but to train to be the best fighter.

Then you will win.'

During the nights, we all ate, drank, told stories, and the men enjoyed the slave girls. I refrained. I did not wish to touch any of the three whores. I thought them dirty and my father once told me *he who sticks his cock in fire gets burned*. I never understood what that meant until Tratonius explained it, and that scared me from the whores.

I will tell you, Luceo. I desired Myrnna. She had a true beauty to her, her milky skin contrasted to dark hair, her big, shiny brown eyes. Her tits and arse. If Myrnna had thrown herself at me, I would probably have broken my oath, and regretted it little. Alas, I could not touch her. I swore an oath to her father to wed her as a maiden. I knew not what that entailed, but to be safe and to upkeep my oath, I would not even kiss her, and felt guilty for seeing her naked in the morning, yet I could not bring myself to avert my gaze.

Those three days passed, and the Hillmen never came. We scouted and watched and waited. None. None attacked us at all. There were Hillmen by the thousands on the strand south of Dun Torrin, which was still under siege. And of Seonaidh, I did not know, Luceo, if he had been truthful, or if he had just been another dastard sidhe that would lead me astray. We must placate the gods, improve our morale, and enjoy our last night of peace before the day of war.

On the last night, I had my lessons from Aster in Greek grammar, philosophy, and warcraft, and at the edge of twilight I declared the feast.

We roasted the boar over the fire upon two firedogs. Myrnna and the slave girls had collected wild onions and herbs, and they made a stew.

Verc commanded Cattos and Antedios to spike their hair and twirl their budding moustaches with wax. They came out shirtless and painted in woad, bearing two carnyxes. They were long, polished bronze that looked dark in the waning light, horns longer than men that ended in snarling boar-heads. Verc walked between them, carrying the boars' head on a platter; it was decked in white flowers. The lads played their carnyxes with long and short toots of their horns. The music filled the camp and echoed throughout the moors, and all men ceased chatting and all attention turned to them, and we all stared, mesmerized by the music.

Tratonius looked nervous, undoubtedly worried that the war-trumpets would signal to the Hillmen that we meant war, and that they may attack us if they heard them. Yet he too became captivated by their serenade. The two lads played in sync, and it had been so loud, yet so soothing, that the music haunted the entire strand. Chaser and Groaner both fell to their bellies with their ears perked, and even the mules, tethered in the uplands, ceased their grazing.

Verc walked ahead of them. Cattos and Antedios played short bursts now, like a wounded boar, and then long groans when Verc placed the platter on the table. Sabella and the slave girls brought out an amphora of wine, and Myrnna placed a plate of wild forage around the platter. Verc, shirtless and painted like the Dobunni lads, held a knife in his hand, and he raised it to the sky and called out to Taranis, Teutoles and Esus, the triple sky god of thunder, lightning, and clouds, that the men down in Gaul worship. He beckoned me over.

I, dressed in full war gear, with my torc and sword and cloak, marched up to him, with a straightened back. He handed me the knife. I was to make the first cut of the best part of the meat. I was their lord, and their lord always gets the best part of the meat, even if he himself had not taken part in the hunt. This act was what had been conferred to us by our laws, and it was one I had to partake in, if I were ever to garner respect from both my kin and other *Celts*.

The cooked boar's aroma made my mouth water. When my knife sliced into its soft, tender thigh, all my pride came forward. If only my father could have seen me, there with men who knew me as Lord, with the oath-brooch at my chest, the lord's torc around my neck, and the honours of the first cut conferred upon me.

Someone's sun-burnt hand ripped the thigh of the boar off. There stood Cicarus, in his dark-green cloak and green-blue plaid trousers, with boar leg in hand. He bit into the meat, and chewed with his mouth open, grizzle sticking in his red beard. He chewed loudly and swallowed hard, and with bright eyes, he stared at me.

I winced. He was taller and more skilful and he challenged me. He had approached me from the left, and both he and I knew that was an act of aggression, and he had taken the best cut of the meat right from under me. He had beaten me once and now, Luceo, now he goaded me into a challenge that I could not back down from, so he may beat me again.

'Cicarus, just what do you do?' Verc asked. 'Why do you make war among friends?'

'Friends indeed,' he said between chews. 'What sort of friend would I be, if I let my friends march to their deaths on the morrow?' He beckoned to the men behind me. 'I challenge this madman that you call lord – I have taken the prime of the meat. Come and face me – and if you lose, then all of my friends are free from their oaths.'

He leapt upon the table, still holding the leg of boar, and he swallowed his last bit and shouted.

'What say you all?! Do you march to your deaths like fools tomorrow, because this man has a feeling, or shall you be free of your bondage?!' No one said anything, and he turned to me, 'what say you, so-called lord of the sellswords?'

I drew *Vidav*, the hiss from its scabbard soared over the roar of the fire behind me. Tratonius grabbed my arm. 'No blood,' he said.

There were many things I could have done, dear Luceo. I could have had my men kill him, for one. I had to accept his challenge, but I did not have to follow his request. The men were oath sworn to obey my commands. That would have been disastrous because they were all friends with him. Indeed, I did not know his true motive, but his plea for their lives resonated with the men who were in doubt of my plan. Killing him would have killed our waning morale.

I had to accept the challenge. He had been hurling javelins when I was still at my wet nurse's tit, but I trusted *Vidav* more than my fist. Tratonius had pleaded for no blood, and I should have listened to him for the sake of the morale of our men.

Cicarus knew I had no choice but to accept the challenge and play his game. He would choose boxing, indeed, because he had bested me in a boxing match that had ended in my humiliation. He would humiliate me again, in front of all my men, Myrnna, and the triple gods called to our camp on that night of feasting. He would leave me an abashed lord. I needed the men, they did not need me, and Cicarus had been so clever to expose that weakness.

'Shall we duel with swords, lordling?' he said with a grin. His cloak fluttered in the wind behind him and the bonfire danced wildly.

'I said no blood!' Tratonius shouted over us. I grimaced at the deepness in his voice, and would not challenge him on that.

'May I mediate?' Antedios asked.

'Yes, you may,' Tratonius said, clapping the lad on both shoulders.

Cicarus' grin grew wider, his snub nose rustled, and his eyes squinted. He knew I would not challenge him to another contest, such as drinking, or racing, or archery. The challenge he offered me had been martial and by martial means it must be resolved.

'Boxing,' I said. Cicarus laughed. He laughed hard, so hard, dear Luceo, that I swore right there to the Morrigan that he would never laugh again.

We unbuckled our belts, and placed them on the bench. Soon we were stripped to the waist, and the crowd gathered around us.

'Come on, lordling,' he said, his grin not ceasing.

'Over to the stream, then,' I said, thinking it a fitting place to fight.

'The stream?' he asked, and his grin faded. 'My good lordling, do you not remember the loch monster? That stream runs from the loch down the hill. Let's stay away from it.'

'Are you scared of it?'

'Come on, man,' he said, now crestfallen. 'You know what happened there.'

'Aye,' I said. 'When I saved all of your lives.'

'Or maybe you endangered us to begin with! I'm thirty years old. I have seen the world from Hibernia to Scythia, and never have I seen something like that before! No. That only showed up with you here and your sight!'

'Told you it would have been easier to just kill him,' Aldryd said, swirling his ale, away from the rest of us. I ignored him.

'You're afraid of water now, Cicarus? How will you wash yourself after I bloody you?' I asked.

'Don't give me that,' he said, now scowling.

'Coward,' I said. The words bit into him because his scowl deepened, his forehead wrinkled, and he wrung his hands.

I walked to the stream, and he followed, as did everyone else. I stood a step away from the stream in the gravel. I kneeled and washed my face with the water, and then cupped my hands and drank. I turned back to him. 'I see nothing in there, do you? Perhaps a kelpie – the white horse that drags us to our deaths?'

'Little lord,' he said, grinning again, and raising his fists. 'Cease talking and strike me, if you dare.'

I raised my fists and we circled. I stopped when his back faced the water.

'Be careful now, not too far back. You may slip in.'

'On with it, strike me!' He said, bouncing foot to foot.

'Do you remember its black eyes?' I asked. 'They looked like the Otherworld.'

'Quiet, by Mannanen, quiet, lordling!'

Lordling? I grew tired of hearing that insult.

'I saw into them,' I said. 'I saw the *Otherworld*. I saw you there, Cicarus.'

'Quiet!'

I quieted. Not from him, but because I heard something. Above the bluster of the men and the tinkling of the stream, I heard something. It was a croon, a hoarse voice, like from a twisted throat. It sang from the tents. And Luceo, I knew what it was. Badb! It was the head of the Amazon!

'Can you hear it, Cicarus? It's your head. She's singing – relax and listen.'

He stilled, he cupped an ear, and his face blanched. He heard it, too.

Eyes wide, he began to bounce again, approaching me with his lean fists raised.

'She's singing,' I said, 'can you hear the words? She tells me she's going to haunt you until you bury her, Cicarus. And when you're in the afterlife, her handmaidens are going to gnash your bones with their teeth.'

'Shut up, lordling! Shut up! It's all your tricks – I don't know what you have – sorcerer, if you are, perhaps this is all just an illusion? Why you, of all people, get to have this power? You're nothing but a lordling!'

I heard the last of that insult. I approached him now. I raised my fist to swing. 'A message from the Amazon queen: ill to your luck.'

Cicarus tripped. I dove in, shoulders forward, and punched him in the jaw. He staggered backwards, and I pummelled him now, both fists. The crowd roared as Cicarus fell to his rear and I smote him again and again and

again astride his shoulder, his body wobbled and fell backwards. Someone
pried me off him. Cicarus rolled into the stream and then shot out of it like
a wildcat out of water, onto his feet drunkenly, until Tratonius held him up,
arm around shoulder.

'Winner!' Antedios grabbed be by the wrist and pulled my arm into
the air.

'Now listen you,' I said to Cicarus, and pointed at him. 'You're welcome
to fight alongside us, but don't you dare ever challenge me again, or she'll
sing to you again, and you'll never rest!'

Cicarus said nothing. He just dizzied around, and Tratonius escorted
him back to the camp. 'We're all going to die,' Cicarus said, 'we're all going
to die, and I'll never get to see my grandma.'

We feasted. The men were sombre, and hardly were there any stories, just
grumbles and silent drinking. It was hardly the feast I had imagined after a
boar hunt, and before my first day of war, but I sat there, belly full of boar
and ale, with my men.

At the end of the feast, Aster approached me from the moorlands. He
was holding something in his hand, and the dim light obscured it. When he
came close, he held up my lion figurine, the other gift from my ancestor. I
reached down into my pouch and found it empty.

'It fell from your bag,' he said, and handed it to me. We returned to
camp, and in the bright fire, I showed it to him. He inspected for a while. By
the time he finished, Verc had taken Frowon away to his tent, while Sabella
and Mawaz cleaned up.

'Zeus Christus – I've never seen anything like this. Huh – I think it's
made of ivory.'

'What's ivory?' I asked.

'Tusks from an elephant', he said.

I had heard of elephants, gigantic shaggy beasts from very far to the
south.

'You found it below the corpse that you took the sword from?'

'I received both from my ancestor,' I said.

'What a strange thing, to find ivory so far from where elephants are.
And this indeed looks like a lion, huh. There are no lions here, are there?'

'No.'

'Yes, you can find some in my country, but they're rare. We hunt them.'

Marthelm motioned to take the figurine, and he held it in his hands. His grey eyes glimmered.

'I saw something like this, yes. When I was a boy, I crawled into a cave and there I found something that looked like this. I brought it home, and my grandfather was furious, and ordered me to go take it back, lest our luck be damned. I brought it back to the cave immediately and never went there again. It looked like this one, except longer. I'll never forget it.'

Orca ripped it from Marthelm's hands and handled it roughly in his meaty fingers. 'A lion-man,' he said.

'Lion man is *Leandros* in my tongue,' Aster said. 'Huh, so beneath the interred in the tomb?'

'In a little croft underneath.'

'Huh.' He received the lion figurine back. 'If the man whose things you took had this underneath him, perhaps that's what he was. This *Leandros.*' He placed it back into my palms.

'Then I am a Leandros also. That man was my ancestor. Perhaps we were first lions, until we walked upright, like this lion. We all became men, and that's why there are no more lions here. Yes, that's what I will do. I will be a Leandros, to honour him.'

'We're born from trees,' Marthelm said with conviction. 'But believe what gives you courage.'

'Vidav the Leandros, that is my title.'

'Huh,' Aster said, stroking his beard. 'I'm for a change myself. I don't feel Aster anymore. You know, Vidav, I too have been known by many names, and no one knows my birth name, and I will never tell anyone. Did you know that? Huh, I think I shall be Artaxes now.'

'Lion-men!' Antedios said. 'Let me be one, too, while I am in debt to you.' I nodded.

'And you, Cattos?' I asked him. He was crouched by a log and seemed to be shining something with his back to me.

'I'm busy,' he said. 'But all right.'

'Then we will become Leandros,' I said. 'And who else?'

No one responded except Tratonius.

'Can't,' he said and knocked his bald head. 'Can't grow a mane. Got some burns. But do what you want. Leandres, is that? That's plural, so you know,

Vidav. But also you should know that Aster here is now calling himself Artaxes – that means lion king. What a humble fellow he is! He is the lion king, while his lord just calls himself the lowly lion man. But Anatolius, Aster, Artaxes – or whomever he is this week, will never bow completely to a barbarian lord.'

Verc returned from his tent with Frowon, and now he lined up all three slaves among us. 'Come on, then, lion-man,' he said. 'It is time to pick the slave to die tonight.'

CHAPTER XVII

We spotted a small boat rowing toward us from the north along the coast. It carried three men, all dark-haired. They all were shirtless and in brown trousers and had dark beards. They docked at the jetty from where we fished and came to us. We met them, that is, myself, Tratonius, Marthelm and Verc, who were my council. Chaser and Groaner trailed us, and that was good, because lords have dogs. I donned my torc and met them there, in the glimmering sun. They were all unarmed. I noticed their leader wearing a headdress of eagle feathers, and he carried a wooden sceptre ringed in gold. He had gold arm rings around both of his upper arms, and a gold medallion hanging across the hair of his chest. They were Hillmen, and this was my first meeting with a Hillman emissary.

'We come to offer a truce,' their leader shouted in *Celtic*.

'At least hear what they have to say,' Tratonius said.

They came across the shale and we met them in the briny breeze. It was another clear day, and we were all sunburnt again.

'We have a message from queen Slighan herself.'

Queen Slighan? I thought back to what Cailleach had said, that her *queen* will return soon. Had I really released the queen? Badb crawled in my chest but I quenched her. I could not show insecurity in the face of the Hillmen.

'Who is this Slighan?' I asked.

'She is the Great Queen, the true ruler of Skye – even Sgàthach herself bows to queen Slighan – and the one who shall bring the light of quartz to the darkness of iron,' he said.

'That means they don't like metal,' Tratonius said. 'No iron or bonze, just stone weapons, right?'

'Yes,' replied the emissary. 'Iron and bronze are for brutes and cruel men; we are gifted stone by the queen. Your ancestors drove ours into the sea back in those days, because they used bronze. We hate it. We shall eradicate it from this world.'

Bronze. My sword was bronze. Luceo, at that moment, I knew that what I must do: slay this so-called queen Slighan with *Vidav*, the bronze of my ancestors.

'We've taken over Skye, and we have killed or forced to kowtow all those who wield iron and bronze that we have found. Only Dun Torrin holds out, and soon that will fall to us.'

'Dun Torrin won't fall,' I said. 'That Fenn Beg Corm is stubborn.'

'He's a dotard, and soon we will nail his guts to a tree and have him run laps around it,' he said.

Camulus now flared in me. He came to me without warning, a flickering fire. Truth be told, Luceo, I disliked Fenn Mag Corm. He was a foreign king from Alba, who carved out a petty kingdom on the south of the island because he had been banished from his realm. He brought with him his band of Eponians, those excellent riders that dye their hair black and wear them like horse's manes and dedicate every moment of each day of their lives to Epona. But I felt a kinship with that foreign king, because even though he was foreign, he was another branch of the same tree as I. I could tolerate him, but I had no tolerance for the Hillmen, the enemy of all *Celts*.

'Let us get to business,' the leader said. 'We are aware of your skirmish a few days ago. You've broken your truce, so the penalty will be steep.'

'I'll hear it then,' I said.

'We are aware that you have in your possession Ambicatos' daughter, Myrnna,' he said.

I had said back on my land that I had Myrnna with me. I remembered that Sego, Fennigus' lad, had said that the Hillmen asked Ambicatos for Myrnna, too. What did they want with her?

'Hand Myrnna over to us, and we will forget this besmirchment, and we will have a permanent truce. That and the offer for you to fight for us still stands.'

'Vidav would never give up his oath!' Verc said, crossing his arms in defiance against the Hillmen. I heard a hint of pride in his voice, and that caused me to puff out my chest.

Tratonius was quiet. I looked at him. He just looked back, forlorn, frowning.

'Well,' Tratonius said, 'what else will you request?'

'Myrnna only, or we go to war,' the leader replied. 'May I remind you that there are thousands of us and only a handful of you, and don't think you will be able to leave the island. We will hunt you down.'

'Then why don't you just come and take her?' I asked, and Tratonius groaned.

'We're giving you a chance. You see, the queen needs mercenaries still. Besides, she honours her truces. Hand over Myrnna or we will come and take her.'

'There must be some other way,' Tratonius said, before I could say anything. I wanted no truces with the Hillmen, and Seonaidh had advised us to march against them tomorrow, anyway. But I was curious about the Hillmen now, since Artaxes had taught me to learn about my enemy, so that I may war against them more effectively.

'Why does the queen need mercenaries? Especially ones that use iron?'

'It's temporary,' the leader said. 'The queen needs mercenaries to defeat Fenn Beg Corm, after which you will all be released.'

'And what does she want with Myrnna?'

'We're not telling you, but do know this, *Celt*, that we will have her, whether you hand her over or we kill you all and take her.'

Camulus pounded in my chest now. Badb shirked away and Camulus marched up and down my heart. I knew at that moment, Luceo, why men meet to speak of things of this nature unarmed, for I would have killed him then and there.

'He's not giving her up right now,' Tratonius said. 'Tell us a price to buy us some time to discuss this further.'

'Fine then,' the leader said, and I hardly heard his words as my mind wandered into the battlefield. 'A bushel of grain, nine pots of berries or herbs, three buckets of fish, and a slave girl. That will buy you a day.'

'Yes,' I said, 'then we'll give you just that. Pick them up on the beach in the morning.'

'Right, then,' he said, and nodded and the three of them left. Once they were out of earshot, I turned to my men.

'It's a start,' Tratonius said, 'but we're in a real bind here.'

'We're still marching down the beach tomorrow,' I said.

'By the gods, why, man? Why did you agree to their terms?'

'We'll give them just what they want, but they aren't going to like it.'

'You cannot mean that,' Tratonius said, his face went white.

'Yes!' Verc shouted. 'Tomorrow we sacrifice to Camulus!'

Tratonius stormed away toward the camp.

'I don't like it,' Marthelm said. 'But a sacrifice will show the gods that we are willing to give up something precious. Indeed, nothing more precious than a life, even a slave. Which one will you sacrifice?'

'Sabella has too much useful skills to lose. It must be one of the younger ones,' Verc said.

'Ah, yes, one of the Germans. Then let her die like a German. I will help you.'

'Good. We will conduct it together then. Now let us hold the feast. You will take the first pick of the meat, Vidav. Then you will truly be lordly!'

I will never tell you how Mawaz died, Luceo. It was grisly and unbecoming, and no one should hear it. I will allow that Sabella was involved, that repulsive thing she is, and I had wished it had been her so the world could have been less disgusting without her.

We burned the bushel of grain, smashed all nine pots full of berries, fruits and herbs against the rocks on the beach, we bashed the buckets and scattered its fish, and we left poor Mawaz spreadeagled on the shale. We sacrificed to Camulus, that blood-stained god, and thus the men stopped quarrelling with me.

The seagulls ate well that day. They whirled through the air and blanketed our sacrifice in white and grey. Then came the Hillmen. We watched them from afar, as they came ashore, and our gruesome sacrifice met them.

We decamped early that morning. The two mules were packed with our things. We poured libations to the sidhe that dwell near the camp as thanks for hosting us there, and we dressed for war. The *Celts* donned resin in their hair and waxed their moustaches. I would have joined them, as I had been groomed on Dun Ashaig, but I had been bald-headed and bald-faced when I had been enslaved, though I vowed to grow my hair and beard out now that I was a Lion-man. I wore my torc and my cloak. The dogs had been fitted with leather collars and wool smocks to protect their necks and chests. All the men were dressed for war.

In the centre of our former camp, among the streaming libations of wine that mixed with the foam of the ocean, Sabella led Myrnna to me. Myrnna had been dressed in her brown cloak, her tawny dress, and her jet necklace. She had ruby lips and blued eyelids painted by borrowing Sabella's make-up kit. She came bearing my sword in its leather-wrapped scabbard that Verc built for *Vidav*. Myrnna kneeled before me, unsheathed *Vidav*, and handed it to me. She then fitted me with my sword belt and scabbard, and I sheathed *Vidav* to my side. I thought we were ready for war, but then Verc cried from the west of the camp.

He came out of the rising sun, down from the hillock near the camp. The men surrounded me, all of them, even Cicarus, and they readied their weapons. Verc approached holding something, a bronze helmet fitted with two jagged bronze bullhorns. He stood before me and bowed.

'Camulus guides our path. He has chosen you. Accept his horns.'

He placed it on my head. It was heavy and strained my neck, but its power ordained me. I knew I was the war god now. It was an uneasy feeling, but felt right.

'Just remember,' he said to me, 'no matter what you call yourself – Leandros, if you must. Your father was a Celt. His father was a Celt. His father was a Celt. Lugus runs through your veins. Now you don the helmet of Camulus, and he leads us to war, as Celts.'

'Now, breakfast!' He shouted, and he, Antedios, and Cattos shouted together. 'After, Camulus! War!'

CHAPTER XVIII

Luceo, I wondered how those two mules could ever carry such heavy burdens. They were loaded with our tents and the rest of our things, including big pots and ashwood for spear shafts. They rarely complained, and when they did, it was because their hooves had not been trimmed or that there were loud noises nearby. We left them in a valley, where we hoped to retrieve them if we survived, and there we buried our wealth in a cave.

I carried a hefty burden, Luceo. It was the helmet of Camulus. It fit awkwardly on my head, its brash edges braised my flesh, and when the sun lit it afire, it made my head hot. I dared not take it off, Luceo, for I was the war god that day, and I could not complain when I led my men down the foe-strewn stand that was the way to Dun Torrin.

We ate well that morning. We ate venison, boar, flounder, berries, herbs, and fruit. The hounds had meaty bones to gnaw on, as did we all. Our day's god, too, had his share, and in this turbulent time, we had to placate him. We lit a great fire on the beach of our waste, and tossed whatever we would not carry or bury in it.

The men all donned their armour, yet I watched Artaxes in awe. Artaxes raised his shield, then he reached for his curved sword and fondled its handle. He donned his bronze helmet. He strapped on his bronze breastplate and bronze leg guards. He raised his spear to the sky. 'Ares, why do you force my hand? I am war, but I am just a man.'

Marthelm, after he observed the Greek, donned a bearskin cloak over his shoulders, which he called *Grandfather*, he adorned a strand with an amber bead around his neck which he called *Frau*, he raised his shield that had a red-white spiral painted on its face, which he called *Donor*, and sheathed his sword in a red-leather scabbard which he called *Tiwaz*. He finally took his spear, which he called *Father*.

'I see you admire them,' Verc said. 'And there is much to admire. They serve their gods well, and they are men! But don't be jealous of them. You are a Celt. We are the manliest of all, for we fight without any defence except the finesse of our hands. Do not forget that, even with all of this Leandros business.'

I nodded to him.

The men and I marched southward down the strand, leaving the poor lass spreadeagled on the shale. Myrnna, Sabella, and Frowon were all in the rear with one-armed Orca and the hounds guarding them.

The sky was cloudless, the breeze cool, and the ocean calm. Our feet shifted along the shale and scree on the slither of strand between sea and hillside. We were all donned in our war gear, bearing our weapons, and an eagle then came from the wall of hills and flew over our heads.

'Truly this is Camulus' day,' Verc said. He was hatless, but he had shaven the sides of his head, the haircut of the druid. I never knew why he had shaved his head in that manner.

'I hope you all ate well today,' Tratonius said.

'Boar and venison, how could it get any better?' I said. 'But why do you say that?'

'Boat,' he said.

A boat slipped away somewhere along the rugged coastline.

'Carnyxes!' Verc shouted. 'Play them, you idiots!'

Cattos and Antedios blew through the carnyxes. Their sound mourned over the strand. We kept apace, crossing streamlets that emptied into the sea from the hills. The coastline was jagged now and there in the distance was the silhouette of the peninsula where Dun Torrin lays. *We can see it, Myrnna, we can see it. We'll get you there.*

Then came the Hillmen. They charged down the cliffside path ahead. They flowed down like so many ants from anthills, flint-spears forward. They were far away but would be upon us.

'You'd better have eaten like kings!' Tratonius shouted. 'Arms! To arms!'

We all mobilized. Tratonius began to bark orders, and I hardly understood them as I fumbled, for he commanded the men that I should have been, yet I dared not speak up then, because he had more experience than I. Yet I had fought the Hillmen and he had not.

'Listen to me!' I shouted. 'I fought them before!'

'Listen to him then, by all the gods, by Dis Pater!' Tratonius shouted back.

'They gang up on you! They don't fight one on one. They are cowards! They use their numbers!'

Artaxes grabbed me by the shoulder and his lip snarled over his front teeth like a dog.

'Then put them at a disadvantage! You see that pass?'

There stood a crumble of boulders and shale all toppled over, three or four men high, that ran from the steep hillside to the shore of the beach. It looked like six men could stand abreast between it and the ocean.

'Plug it like a boat! Now! Shields out!'

We all rushed to the entry and plugged it like a leaky boat, a completed wall of jammed spears and shields. Cattos, Antedios, and I had all been left out, since there was no room, but then Cattos ran into the shallow ocean. Antedios tested the space next to Cattos, but his foot went too deep. He and I stood on standby, waiting to replace a plank that would fall from our bulwark.

The Hillmen poured down in a wave. There were dozens of them, all armed with stonebladed spears, stoneheaded axes, and flint daggers. They browned the red-green moorlands and blue sea and grey stone and then a sea of brown just crashed into the men in front of me.

I could never describe the sounds, Luceo. It all happened too fast to discern. There were shouts in front of and behind me, dogs barked, men grunted, spears and shields and swords all rang, scraped, thumped, cut. Men cried and shouted. I saw one Hillman impaled through the balls on Aldryd's spear, and Aldryd laughed so hard that his laugh carried over the tumultuous noise.

Another wave of Hillmen came down and pushed their comrades further into us. Antedios and I watched for bowmen among the Hillmen waiting above on the hill, but none came, and then more armed men ran down. Artaxes was either shouting orders or nonsense, for it was all in Greek and I could make out little, and then Tratonius started yelling in Celtic back and I found a moment in that battle to appreciate an Umbrian yelling in Celtic at a Greek.

Verc came out of the line, limping, an acerose flint-blade jammed into his side and broken at the shaft.

'Hold the fucking line!' Tratonius shouted.

I nearly knocked Antedios out of the way to jam myself betwixt Cattos and Marthelm, my leather shoes wet in the lapping ocean, shuffling through the shells. I had to prove myself to the men. I had to fight in battle. I had to seek vengeance upon the Hillmen.

A Hillman struck at me with his spear. I slapped the spear down with the edge of my shield. He ran forward, and I bashed him in the face with the shield. He stumbled back and Aldryd jammed his spear through his balls. Aldryd laughed again hard.

'I've taken four balls today!'

More Hillmen clamoured down the path and marshalled their battleline against us.

We vied with our spears and swords. I hunkered below my shield against a raging Hillman, whose eyes blazed and whose mouth gaped open like a striking snake. He shoved against me, they all shoved against us, some of them falling to our blades when they came close, but more Hillmen kept pressing on. They attempted to dislodge us from our position so that they could swarm us, and we refused.

'Hold it!' Artaxes shouted in Greek, and I thanked him later that he had taught me the basics, since I could understand so much now.

'Speak Celtic – you fucking idiot!' Tratonius shouted at him.

'I refuse – I will honour them!' Artaxes cried in Greek, and I did not understand what he had said then, but was told later.

The Hillmen piled against us, like so many men pushing down a tree. A brute of a Hillman came against me and shoved shield-first. I slashed at him but I could do no harm, because my arm had been pinned down by the weight that was against me. A great pressure pressed upon me. My feet slid backward, through the gravely sand, a slimy fish brushed against my calf.

'On count of three...' Artaxes' voice strained as he heaved against the enemy piling themselves to break the dam of sellswords.

'One.'

The Hillmen piled on even harder, even Hillmen on the high pathway were pushing down on the backs of their comrades.

'Two.'

The ocean wrapped around my ankles, I struggled to gain footing as I had stepped into a hole, and the Hillmen were splashing through and shoving us hard.

'Three!'

The Hillmen launched back in a grand collective shove. They had all been cramped together. Many lost their balance, some fell, others tripped, and there was general disarray among them.

'Murder them!' Tratonius shouted and his voice cracked. 'Murder them! Come on, murder them before they reform!'

Now iron was among the Hillmen, and blood mixed with sand.

We slaughtered them, Luceo. We slaughtered them there on the strand. We fought with the ferocity of cornered badgers, the stubbornness of hungry ravens, and the eagerness of unchained wolves. We hacked and stabbed and slashed and sliced by sword and spear and knife until our feet were wetter with blood than with seawater. The Hillmen panicked, heeled, and retreated, leaving their dead, dying, and wounded.

I approached a Hillman lying in the sand in a bloody crumple. I pointed *Vidav* at him. The Hillman looked back up at me, his eyes aglow, his face pallid, with the look of a man soon to be taken by death. His brown moustache twitched over his trembling lips.

Hatred overtook me, Luceo. I hated this invader, so unfortunate to fall within my grasp. I relished in slaughtering them and wished I could slaughter them all, and I would, one by one, starting with this one. They had killed my family, taken my land, sundered my homeland, enslaved women and children, and now dared to stand between Myrnna and Dun Torrin. He had to die, and I raised *Vidav* to strike his neck off his body.

'Come back to the Slighan Hill,' the dying Hillman said, not only in *Celtic* but even as an Ashaiger.

I began to sweat harder. Something had taunted me. I struck the foeman with my spear, and the life fell out of his eyes.

Dead Hillmen littered the area around us. Father War reaped his toll through me, for I commanded these men, and though I had not given them the orders, I had brought them here to conduct this slaughter. The whole ordeal happened so suddenly and with such brutality that it was like a passing breeze. The Hillmen army had attacked us and then they were defeated and now routed.

'Hail Camulus!' I cried out, raising my bloody sword skyward.

'Camulus!' Verc shouted. 'Hail Camulus!'

'Hail Athena!' Artaxes shouted.

'Mars, bloodstained Mars!' Tratonius shouted.

'Tiwaz – glory to his name!' Marthelm shouted.

The Hillmen routed. They left the jagged pass and soon none were to be seen except the dead, wounded and some stragglers, who were in retreat.

Camulus, Athena, Mars, Tiwaz – indeed. 'Kill them!' I shouted, my eyes on two Hill-foes that were attempting to escape but who were caught between two jagged boulders.

'Kill them, he said!' Aldryd said and soon his knife was upon them. He crouched down near a Hillmen who gripped his knee, yet Aldryd just slashed his throat, and then the bloody mercenary headed over to his next prey and reaped the throat from that one, and again and again, and I had never seen Aldyrd smile except for then and his smile was wide.

'Idiots! They could have been our ransom!' Tratonius said.

'Kill them,' Aldryd said. 'Kill them, big chief!' He said as he held the knife to a pleading Hillman's neck and pushed it in and then ripped it out.

I glanced over to Myrnna, who had her shoulders to her ears, and then I heard Artaxes. He was sobbing something in Greek and I looked at him. Without looking at me, but gazing down at the ocean, he spoke in *Celtic*.

'We don't deserve to live,' he said.

'What, man?' I asked.

'We don't deserve to live when Leonidas and his glorious three-hundred died in such a way.'

'Stop your babbling!' Tratonius said. 'We have to parley!'

'No,' Verc said, limping up to us. 'Seonaidh said to march down the strand. Down the strand we go!'

'It's our only chance,' Tratonius said.

'Our only chance of what?' Verc asked, limping up to him, the long bangs of the front of his head blowing in the wind. 'Our only chance of living? Why do you want to live so long, Tratonius? Have you not lived long enough? Have you regrets in your life?'

'It's suicide,' Tratonius said. 'There are too many of them. We will just be killed and that's it.'

'And what of it? Why should we, as men, seek to prolong our lives so long, when we can end them shortly in glory?'

'Then you go first, if you're so eager for glory.'

Verc started down the strand, and I followed him. After I caught up, I took position in front of him. The rest of the men followed me.

The shells shifted beneath our feet as we walked down the narrow strand between the sea and the hills, the black hot Cuillins in the distance, the red hill of Slighan somewhere nestled beyond. Gulls screeched over our heads and crows cawed from copses afar. Waves crashed against the skerries in the shallows. The land swept westward into the sea, and when we traversed the bend of broken boulders and scree, the wave-knocked, wind-harrowed cliffside fortress of Torrin appeared on the horizon.

There, around Dun Torrin, a swathe of black-headed Hillmen pocked the moors like a man moribund with plague. There were so many of them, a flint-armed horde – more men than I had ever seen.

'They're around the fort, but they haven't sent any more against us, but we can't see too well here,' Tratonius said. 'Send some scouts ahead.'

'Cattos – Antedios,' I said.

Tratonius placed a hand out to stop Antedios at his chest. 'Send Cicarus instead. He's shorter and more agile.'

Cicarus and Cattos ran off ahead of us. They headed to a jagged rock formation and they both hauled themselves up, and then they split-up. We continued down the beach, silent, and I looked back at Myrnna near pithy, hairy Orca, and she just gazed back at me with those big, shiny brown eyes.

'They should stay back,' Tratonius said.

'Stay back,' I said. 'Orca, be watchful of Myrnna!'

Cattos tumbled down from his perch, righted himself and rushed toward us. 'Hundreds of them!' he cried. 'Hundreds of Hillmen, marching down toward us!'

The men mumbled a bit, and I ordered them to march on.

'And Cicarus,' Cattos said between breaths. 'Cicarus ran!'

'Ran where?' I asked.

'When he saw the Hillmen, he just ran away! He said something but I didn't hear it.'

'The coward!' I shouted. 'You hear me, Cicarus?! You coward!'

'He owes you nothing,' Tratonius said.

'Let him go backward. We go onward,' Verc said.

'Madness!' Tratonius said. 'What is the purpose of this? What can we do against hundreds?'

'Seonaidh said,' I began, and Tratonius interrupted me.

'What is wrong, lad? Had Luna smote you with her kiss in the night?'

'We march,' Verc said, and he limped forward. I followed. The rest followed.

'Yeah, I get it,' Tratonius said. 'You Gauls are only afraid of when the sky falls down on you, or when the ground opens below you.'

Tratonius had been sarcastic, yet it straightened my spine.

'Who said that?' I asked.

'The Gauls that met Alexander,' he responded.

'Who was he?'

'The greatest king,' Artaxes said. 'So great that we are unfit to speak about him.'

'He met some Gauls. He asked what they feared the most. Surely, anyone would say Alexander. Who could not? He had conquered all worlds. The Gauls just responded that they were afraid of the sky falling and hitting them in the heads, or the ground opening up and swallowing them whole. Alexander's men had a good laugh, and he was grumpy for nine days.'

'Then that is all I fear,' I said.

'I know,' he said. 'You don't care when you die, whether tomorrow or the next year, as long as men speak of your deeds. That's what you Gauls say.'

'I've never heard that,' I said.

'Well now you have,' Tratonius said.

If all of us die today, and no bards witness our deaths, the sidhe will dance at our places of death and sing our deeds,' Verc said.

'I hope they are good at dancing, then,' Tratonius said.

We rounded the bend and on the long, narrow grassy plain between us and Dun Torrin, hundreds of Hillmen were gathered. They stood in clusters of twelve, and half of the clusters moved toward us. I could see nothing but a swathe of black heads and brown woollen tunics. Bowmen stood rank by rank, marching toward us, arrows nocked. Seagulls wheeled over our heads. The ocean crashed against the cliffside fortress of Dun Torrin, hazy in the distance, but visible. I looked back at Myrnna. She was almost to Dun Torrin. All that stood in my way were hundreds, perhaps a thousand, foemen.

'Forward,' I said.

'They'll shoot you,' Tratonius said.

'Have trust and faith in me,' Verc said. 'And fill your heart with courage.'

Verc and I stood abreast, and Marthelm followed so closely behind me that I could feel his breath on my neck.

'We are fearless – warriors, men, friends. Death and glory both draw near,' Verc said.

'Hubris,' Artaxes said.

'Befitting a lion-king,' Verc said.

'The gods will punish us,' Artaxes said.

'Then let them.'

We marched closer, edging toward the Hillmen. A tern flew down, its blue-white body squawking and it dove at us, swooping over our heads. We must have neared its nest, and now it was vexed. In those moments, I wondered why it could not understand that we were no threat to its eggs, and all the while it threatens us, a weasel could sneak into its nest and devour each of its young.

The Hillmen had spotted us long ago and their ranks advanced toward us, row by row, bowmen ready. Soon we would step into arrow range. I knew that. The tern flew away as I passed a glance over to the Slighan Hill. Then came the crows.

There was a storm of crows. Their squawking and cawing assailed me. They swirled around me, wings beating against my chest, their mouths gaped as they cawed. They whirlpooled around me, pecking at me. I raised my shield to my face and one perched upon my shield and squawked into my ear.

Come back to the Slighan Hill!

Hoarse and throaty crows cawed at me until I found myself crumbled over my leg. My shield thudded in the sand and *Vidav* clanged against it. The crows descended upon me and pecked and prodded with their hateful black beaks.

Badb herself flew among them, arresting me, imprisoning me to her wrath. I cowered on the ground, as still as bog water. Badb vanished when something else passed over me, something fleshy and red. I came out of it, and there I found myself crawling out from underneath Verc's shield.

He had been pelted in arrows. He sighed. He died on top of me.

Hot hands grabbed me. The whirlwind of crows had vanished and now Tratonius hauled me down the strand. I hobbled on my now bad ankle.

A wedge of Hillmen rushed us. They passed over the body of Verc and toward us. They outnumbered us nine to one methinks and they were armed with spears and maces and other flint weapons.

'They're going to fire again!' Someone shouted, I don't know who. The men all raced down into the confines of the rock outcrop jutting out of the hill, beyond the bend and out of sight of the Hillmen. I began to hobble back and then a scream, so shrill and loud and like a mother knows her babe, I knew my Myrnna.

The Hillmen had assaulted our rear. Orca dodged a blow from a mace and bound the foe's weapon with his sword-arm and worked the sword-edge through the leather thongs of his enemy's wooden hauberk. He stepped back and away and evaded another strike, the mountain of a man, still injured, finessed his way out. One Hillman shoved Sabella out of the way and another darted across the strand chased by Chaser and Groaner, and the last Hillman smote Myrnna across the face, and seized her as she fell, hoisting her onto his shoulders and darting up toward the inland slope.

I hobbled closer and closer, holding Verc's shield close to me, my spear in my clutch. Myrnna rioted on the Hillman's shoulders but she could not fall free. I whistled hard like Verc, and then came Groaner and Chaser and they loped across the beach, their snouts wet and red. They trailed the Hillman kidnapper until they came close. They forced the Hillman to turn around and retreat toward me, away from the slope, and then I prepared to take aim at the Hillman's legs with my spear. *Lugus, Long-armed, send me your aid, may I neither miss the Hillman nor strike Myrnna! Ambicatos, I will save your daughter!*

Groaner screeched. Another Hillman had impaled him through the neck with a flint-spear. Groaner wheeled on the ground, grounded by the spear. Chaser began to snarl and bark at his enemy and before the Hillman could dislodge the spear from the dog, Orca was upon him. Like some kind of bear, he charged, grimacing, his face so red I could see it bright from so far away. The Hillman finally yanked the spear out from the lifeless Groaner. Orca raised his sword and cleft the Hillman's head down to the jaw. Myrnna fell off the Hillman and she hit the ground, rolled up to her feet and rushed away. Chaser quarried the other Hillman toward me, his back to me, and I then raised the spear and tossed it. It went through the Hillman's back. Orca was still screaming and now wildly slashing and stabbing at the two other Hillmen and Chaser ran over to them.

'Here!' Tratonius cried. 'Come here!'

Myrnna fled toward him, and now I realized that the Hillmen would not shoot us if she were near us. They wanted her, for whatever reason, and by Camulus they would get her only if I lay as dead as Verc and Groaner. I hobbled to the men. We formed a circle with Myrnna in the middle.

'Wait for Sabella!' the slave mistress shouted, running toward the circle with Frowon trailing behind her. They joined Myrnna in the middle of us, and we all stood back-to-back, weapons drawn, with the Hillmen funnelling down the beach toward us.

'Orca!' Tratonius shouted, and he shouted again and soon we were all shouting at Orca as if he had been stricken deaf. He had been hacking at the Hillman who slew poor Groaner. The two Hillmen were dead and he and Chaser came back wet with blood. They joined the circle and Chaser stood next to me, hackles up, growling. Orca breathed so heavily and had been crying. I never thought I'd see such a brutal man cry.

There we stood, all seven of us in a ring, with Myrnna and the slave girls in the centre of us. The Hillmen now came, dozens upon dozens of them, from both sides of us. They were all armed with melee weapons, mostly flint daggers with blocky wooden shields, flint-tipped spears and polished stone maces and axes. They all had black hair, black as their flint, all black as bog oak, and their bodies adorned in wooden hauberks as brown as the sand below our feet. Soon we were surrounded by them, and Sabella handed Myrnna a flint-bladed knife.

'It's a better fate,' she said to Myrnna.

The Hillmen assembled all around us, readying their spears. We all stood there in a circle, awaiting our fate at the hands of the Hillmen. The Hillmen walked over Verc, his lifeless body half covered in sand, and I realized how honoured I had been for him to give his life for me, and to carry his shield before I met a similar fate. We would all die there, with Dun Torrin in the distance, shrouded in mist.

'Of all men to die like that! Such cowards the Hillmen are!' Cattos said, his voice cracking, and he swallowed a sob.

'Do not honour him by mourning, honour him by killing,' Marthelm said.

I unsheathed *Vidav* from my hip, my wrist skyward, my thumb on the blade just like Verc had taught me. I'll honour him by killing in his stance.

One Hillman shouted in front of us, and another behind us, and both sides crashed into us in successive waves. They pincered us, pressuring from each side, us just a shell of which to be pried open. I remember it well, Luceo. Their drab, dark clothes, their sandaled feet shuffling through the sand, kicking it up and dusting us, their black flint-tipped spears jabbing at us.

Tratonius had ordered us to spread out for room to fight and we defended ourselves.

A spear came at me and I slapped it away with the edge of Verc's shield. I jabbed my sword at a foeman, a lanky man with a soot-stained face, and he held down my sword with his as another spearman jabbed right at me. I blocked with the shield, and now another spear came at my exposed body. I cringed, bracing myself for the strike, but Aldryd slammed the spear away with his own. Tratonius took a step forward, poised to strike one Hillman with his spear, but pivoted and jammed it into the exposed thigh of another Hillman. I blocked again, and again, the spears pounding my shield like a hammer on an anvil. Chaser lunged into the fray, his jaw wrapping around the arm of a spearman. They tumbled over and Artaxes jammed the fallen Hillman in the belly with his spear, and blood spurted over Chaser's face. Orca whistled and Chaser fell back to our circle. An axman eyed me and swung at me, but I blocked with Verc's shield. The enemy lurched forward but slipped in blood and fell and then another spear was upon him. 'Hold them here!' Tratonius shouted. 'See your feet? Don't move past them!'

They pressed on. We held them. Spears assailed the air around me, I blocked and ducked and jumped back away from them. I hopped in and out of the footprints in the sand that Tratonius commanded I do not pass. The swathe of brown and black parted and four Hillmen charged into us, all waving flint axes. I buckled behind the shield and struck one in the thigh with *Vidav*. Tratonius shield-bashed one and then was hit in the shoulder with the ax. He yelled and struck again, smashing the Hillman in his jaw with his spear. The Hillman staggered around, blood and splinters of bone where his face had been, and fell over. The other Hillmen shoved into us, they shouted and I thought I heard them shouting in Celtic but then the weapons beat against my shield, and I hunkered behind it until Tratonius yelled at me.

'Vidav, attack them!' He yelled. 'Don't just use the shield as a wall, use it as a weapon!'

I shield-bashed the nearest Hillmen. He sprawled backwards and landed in the sand with a crunch. Another Hillman wielding a stone mace swung it at me. I raised the shield and pain shot from my hand to elbow, right down to the bone. I faltered in my stance realizing that the shield had been split right down the middle.

'What did I tell you?!' Tratonius yelled at me, as he parried blows from a spear with his sword.

The Hillman swung at me, I caught his hand with my nearly ruined shield, remembering what Verc had done, and pivoted and slashed his head clean off with *Vidav*. The head rolled and one Hillman tripped on it, when he looked down at what he saw he screamed and then others began to flee, and then before my eyes, the Hillmen retreated. We survived, and the hundreds of them had been checked by the few.

'They're hesitating,' Tratonius said, and laughed. 'They're hesitating! You're hesitating, you cowards! Remember that! Remember that every night you go to bed – with your bone-dry wives – that seven men scared hundreds!'

'Can we beat them?' Antedios asked.

Tratonius looked as if he would shout at Antedios, but then just shook his head and laughed.

'No, but it's a good death.'

'Then we can honour our gods of the dead,' Cattos said.

Two loud, long notes from the carnyxes soared across the beach. I savoured the sounds. I remembered the old myth where the dead men ride down to the Underworld, where they are dipped into the cauldron of rebirth by Great Dadga, and then return to this world at the sound of the carnyx to live again. I died when I killed Brennus, and now I live again, in this world anew, as Vidav, commanding a tiny group of men that stood against hundreds. The carnyxes heralded both my life and my death.

The Hillmen chattered among themselves, their chatter incessant to me as I would rather hear the ocean roar, the wind whisper, and the gulls cry than them in my last moments. Before I wondered if they could understand us, for the ones that possessed shields beat their weapons against them in unison, shattering whatever tranquillity their momentary quietness allowed, and one of them blew a horn. They charged at us again.

We held them off. We defended. We blocked and parried. We struck with our swords and spears when the opportunity arose. We counterattacked them when they attacked us. Only three of the Hillmen laid dead around us, but when they backed off, and by the gods, Luceo, they backed off, we left dozens wounded and the lot of them spooked that seven had held hundreds back.

I tasted sweat, I tasted blood, and the last Hillman I killed that day tasted my sword for I cleft him from eye to chin and his eye popped out and he stepped on it and fell over into his two comrades, who proceeded to shove him away only to be met by a spear from Tratonius through the thigh, while Aldryd stabbed the other in the chest. The Hillmen kept coming now, there must have been hundreds of them surrounding us entirely, engulfing us in a sea of black and brown against a grey sky and sea. Aldryd, next to me, grinned as he danced out of range of the foe-blades, danced back in, and stabbed the enemy, whittling them down like one whittles a sharp stick.

Then came the singing, oh Luceo! We thought we would die that day, and there sang Artaxes: 'Ares, you force my hand. I war for you, but I am just a man.'

He repeated that verse throughout, and I thought I ought to hear something Celtic before I died.

'The carnyxes, men!' I shouted at Cattos and Antedios. They dropped their spears and shields and raised the carnyxes from the ground and blew into them in hard spats, their spitting beast faces screeching out toward the Hillmen.

Now Orca and Tratonius sang something in their language. Tratonius was off-key but Orca sang beautifully, so unbecoming of the man. Soon Marthelm sang, too, in German. It was a discorded song, and it overawed me, as the carnyxes shot down the beach and carried the groans of the Otherworld to our enemies.

'Your sword has drunk much blood,' Aldryd said to me. 'It was fun to kill with you.'

I nodded to him.

'Do you resent me?' I asked Tratonius, my heart sinking.

'No,' he said. 'I knew it would end like this. I spent too much of my life sword-selling. It's not so bad to die now, here with the son of Biturix.'

That was all I needed to hear, Luceo. I thought of my father, at my flank. If only he could have seen me, in Camulus' horns, in a kingly torc, with Verc's damaged shield, bronze brooch at my chest. I was covered in bronze, gold, and iron. Men stood at my side, my men, my comrades ready to kill and die for me. I even had a dog, a hunting dog. A dog had died bravely in defence of my oath. A man – a warrior – a friend, had died to save my life. The hardest part of my father's death is that I could never tell him these things on Taman, and each day I walk and regret that, but perhaps when we meet in Otherworld, I will tell him of this day.

I imagined him at my side, and Bodvoc, at my other side, and Fennigus behind me, and Verc, and King Ambicatos, with their manly hearts ablaze watching me meet my painful end. Lappie and Groaner stood at my flanks. *I have become war, I am Camulus!*

The Hillmen charged. They hemmed us in from all sides now, a wall of shields, spears, and swords against a sea of flint. Flint-bladed spears decked in bright coloured feathers struck over my head, around my shoulders, between my legs, and clanged against Verc's shield. A Hillman struck at me with a flint dagger, so I swung my sword inward, toward my ankle, just as Verc had taught me. I parried with the blade of my sword and then twisted my wrist to slash him across the leg. He backed off, and more came. Then came more spears, more axes, more maces, more swords, more Hillmen.

Soon hundreds surrounded us. We braced against them. Tratonius swung his shield around his pithy body, blocking blows and delivering his own through his spear which clanged against the wooden hauberk of a warrior. Aldryd ducked and skidded and danced against them, stabbing and marring them. Cattos and Antedios had dropped their war-trumpets and struck with their spears. Orca belted verses in Oscan while he slashed the throat of a Hillman, whose head wobbled and creaked and fell backwards as blood shot up from the sand. Chaser tore at the neck of another dead Hillman. Marthelm's spear crushed the jaw of another Hillman who had just struck at me. Artaxes, his bronze form shimmering brighter than the sea next to us, tossed a javelin and it struck what looked to be a chief – marked by his red face – paint right through his collar.

Myrnna stared at me. I knew she did. I could not meet her eyes, her big warm brown eyes – too busy I was in my warcraft. I parried a spear and blocked a blade and chopped the arm off a Hillman who had charged me and then Tratonius struck another through his belly and his viscera poured out like a cascade causing him to slip in it. Aldyrd shoved his spear into the groin of a man and shouted about how many balls he had gotten. It was eight. We injured, we slew, we forced them to heel, but they kept coming. They all backed off again, the ground left in ruts and turmoil and the sand caked with blood.

I turned to Myrnna now. Our eyes met.

'I'll kill her, Domine,' Sabella said, and my gut wrenched. She was too eager. She wrapped her arm around Myrnna's shoulder and put the black blade to her throat. Myrnna just stared at me with big dry brown eyes.

The old whore was right. I should have Myrnna killed. She would ideally kill herself; but it was better for someone else to, I had to have the certainly that Myrnna was dead rather than taken alive by the Hillmen. Her father would have wanted that, and it would be for the best.

I shook my head. 'Not yet,' I said, and my knees buckled. What if Sabella could not kill her quick enough? What if the Hillmen killed us, broke through our line, and apprehended her? And then what shall happen to her? Rape? Sell her off as a slave? They wanted her. They cared enough about her to not shoot us, to sacrifice their own lives in retrieving her, to delay in killing us and let us humiliate them on the beach, skirmish by skirmish. If Sabella does not kill her, will my oath be a failure?

'Be merry,' Tratonius said. 'We're not long for this world. Enjoy your last moments, son. Let our enemies always remember the terror we've struck in them.'

'I am not afraid of anything except the sky falling down on my head, and the ground opening up under me,' I said.

And then they came again. Another horn. This time they charged their frontline with their backlines all shoving the frontline forward, to knock us out of position, to flatten our circle. Soon Hillmen were upon me again, many, shoving forward against my shield. I jabbed and cut at them with my sword, but my sword-arm had been rendered immobile by my own shield. I could not get a good cut, and my feet began to shove back, the sand building up behind my heels. It built up so high it threatened to trip me, and I took a step back. My comrades had all been pushed back, too, the big wooden shields of the Hillmen pressed against us, forcing us further back and toward each other.

Myrnna met my eyes again, and Sabella mouthed 'Now, Domine?'

'Now,' I said.

She didn't hear me.

Hoofbeats from dozens of horses raced down toward us. The pressure from the Hillmen lessened and released and Tratonius shouted.

'Stab them!'

We stabbed at them, they blocked, parried, some were wounded, the rest fled, and a great many of them began to rout. I turned to see before my eyes what was destined to remain out of my reach, my Myrnna released from Sabella's grip. The Hillmen beyond our circle parted and then came a horde of three dozen riders. They rode down from the steep slope that led down from the moorlands to the beach. They were all painted in woad and had sprouts of black hair, long and slender like the manes of their nimble horses. Their vanguard of them had long slashing swords with long shields, the rest equipped with spears. *The Eponian riders!* They crashed hard into the main body of the Hillmen.

The Hillmen scattered out of the way, at least the ones that could avoid the charge. The crash hurled bodies of Hillmen through the air, others lay trampled, those at the flanks were cut down by the long swords of the riders. The Hillmen fled so fast, out of our reach, and the riders regrouped and charged again. This time they ran past us and straight on into the fleeing Hillmen, barrelling into their rear. Hillmen fled in every direction now, down the narrow strand where they bunched up, and the Eponians began slaughtering them where they had little room to move. Other Hillmen dropped their arms and fled up the escarpment to the moorlands. Some even tried to swim away, and I know they drowned, because of the undertow.

Ten Hillmen attempted to pass us, three men's length away, to get to the slope from where the Hillmen had come down.

'Murder them!' Tratonius shouted.

'Come on,' I yelled at Myrnna who trailed behind us. 'Stick behind me!' She trotted toward us, too far away, and we all headed toward the fleeing Hillmen.

Someone drew a bowstring behind us. Another. Many. I looked and there stood five Hillmen up on top of the escarpment, nocked bows aimed right at us.

One fell on the ground, his bow and arrow fell and they both clanged against a rock. Then the other tumbled with a sigh down the escarpment. The next sighed and fell on his back, and the two who remained fled. Then Cicarus appeared on top of the knuckle of the hill, bloody dagger in hand.

'Murder them now, you dogs!'

Chaser charged in first, leaping up, the Hillmen lifted his shield arm as if to smash the dog away, but Chaser grabbed him by the shield-arm. Artaxes tossed a javelin right through the throat of another, he fell on his back and gurgled. Orca approached the Hillman wrestling against Chaser and sheared his shoulder off with his sword. Cicarus jumped backwards to dodge a blow from a Hillman's mace, jumped back in and stabbed him in the belly. The other two managed to flee, and Orca recalled Chaser.

'Forget them!' Tratonius shouted. 'Support the calvary! Murder them all!' We all began to race down toward the Eponian riders. 'And you, stay with us!' He shouted at Myrnna.

'Cicarus, I thought you abandoned us!' I shouted at him.

'I'd never abandon my friends. I saw the riders – was our only chance. We owe them – no time for talk, man!'

We all raced down the beach. Aldryd slit one, two, three throats of wounded or dying Hillmen on the way, quick as a snake, and even Orca jammed his sword into the back of a Hillman crawling toward the ocean in a trail of blood. The tide then washed over him. We raced beyond Verc's body, now just a lump in the sand.

'You're with me, brother,' I said as I rushed by. *No time to mourn, my friend. It is time for Camulus to reap his great harvest.*

Blood. Sand. Seawater. I don't know how to describe it otherwise, Luceo. We were the weasel among the eggs. Never had the shore drank so much blood, that the ocean must have risen by two men's lengths when the pools of blood all funnelled into it at high tide. High tide had come in, and we were all ankle deep in the ocean when we met the Eponian riders.

After the Hillmen regrouped, they formed, and then surrounded the riders, attempting to eliminate them one by one. We arrived there and rescued two of them by charging into the lot of them and sticking them with our spears, yet their numbers were too much for us.

The Hillmen reformed and changed their strategy. Now they surrounded the Eponian riders, sticking the horses with their spears like hunting deer or boar. One horse whinnied and fell. Another sensed the danger surrounding it, six Hillmen, and it kicked wildly. A Hillman sprawled backwards and skidded in the sand past me, his neck flimsy. Two riders shouted to each other, then they barrelled through the surrounding Hillmen and reformed. They slashed with their long swords to and fro, left and right, over and under all the while the Hillmen struck with their spears. A rider fell off his horse, pelted in arrows, and his horse spurred through the lot of the Hillmen until it tripped and crashed on its master.

The Hillmen wedged through the riders, cutting them off from each other. We finally reached them, and a party of Hillmen all armed with spears broke off and came at us. They drove two riders toward us. The horse of the rider closest to me took a stab in the neck and screamed with eyes big and white. We backed off and Hillmen came between us and the rider, and separated half of us from the other half.

The enemies rushed in around us. I sidestepped from a spear thrust, bashed the shaft with the edge of my shield, and held it as Aldryd jammed the spear into his belly, then pulled it back, and his guts fell out like stew meat. Artaxes tossed a javelin and it impaled a Hillman who had been warring against a dismounted rider, and the rider, a youth with his black sprout of hair matted to his face, hewed the arm off a Hillman and then rushed toward his comrade, mobbed by six Hillmen.

Now came the enemies we called the shining ones. We called them that, Luceo, because they came decked in golden armrings, necklaces, and brooches. They shined bright against the grey sea, the brown sand, and their dark-clad and haired allies. They had iron swords and oblong shields just as we did, despite their ilk hating iron. Their hair was as black as a Hillman's, but they wore white-blue striped tunics. They hemmed in on us.

The lot of us lined up against the shining ones, our line divided by the horseman being mobbed by Hillmen. Swords sang for me, Luceo. A sword struck at my shoulder. I raised my shield to block, and another swooped at my lower leg when I raised my shield. I bent my wrist to the right and caught the blade with *Vidav*, and slashed open the thigh of my attacker. There were at least ten of these shining ones, and I knew with them, blood would fall like a hard rain.

I could hear Tratonius yelling over it all, and Aldryd, Artaxes, Marthelm, Cattos and I slashed and hacked and dodged against the iron song of the shining ones. One rider who fought beside us then spurred his horse and flew headlong into three more Hillmen who had just charged us, knocking them over and trampling them.

The sea spray soaked us. The tide had come in ankle-deep now. Kelp wrapped around my ankles as we evaded or jumped over fallen corpses. The riders had regrouped themselves, and charged again against the Hillmen. The Hillmen scattered but reformed and by the time we had gotten there, the Eponians were rushing around, slashing their swords to and fro, their horses bucking and kicking. All the while the fortress of Dun Torrin became starker, like a dream fully realized. *We're there, Myrnna... almost.*

Now the blood fell. It fell hard, Luceo. Everything had happened so fast that I can scarcely remember it. Some of it is so clear, Luceo. Orca cleft the skull of a Hillman in two and I remember the brains oozed out. A Hillman stepped in horseshit, pulled his foot out, now shoeless, stepped onto a flint blade, cried out and then Chaser lunged upon him. They fell and Antedios poked his eye out with his spear all the while with Chaser gnawing at his gullet. Artaxes shouted in Greek, or cried in Greek, or just spoke to himself in Greek while his *xiphos* drank blood. A flint dagger came for him, and he bent his head down and his helmet absorbed the blow, but it left a crease in the helmet. He never got over it.

That much I remember, Luceo. I do not remember how many men I killed. Cicarus and Cattos would argue that they killed the most, but I doubt either of them kept track. I saw nothing but red. I thought nothing but red. And red is what I got.

Now we came closer, the Hillmen drew back but some began to scramble up the slope and flee.

The killing continued until I did not know if we were ankle deep in their blood or tide. Soon a tumult erupted out of the Eponian riders. From their high perches they spotted victory, for the forces of Dun Torrin swarmed our foes on the rear flank. Now we pincered them. Now we had them. Now we just killed and killed again.

How glorious it was, Luceo! My sword sang for them now. It sang a hymn to the blood it drank, since it had drunk so much, that had it been ale, my sword could not swing straight. How I wrought vengeance upon them! I thought of Bodvoc and Fennigus and Lappie and Vasenus and king Ambicatos and all the corpses of the women and children of Dun Ashaig and then I thought of the poor boy that had his brains bashed out on the road and then the owner of Chaser and Groaner... poor Groaner! And Verc's sand-buried body came into my mind as then we no longer fought the enemy, but rather slaughtered the ones unfortunate enough not to flee from us. We had come so far on the beach, that when an Eponian rider shifted out of my view, there stood Dun Torrin. I could see its stone walls, and knew why I fought so hard.

A chariot thundered on the strand. The Hillmen, many on their knees or dropping their weapons, all parted. Two white horses pulled a gilded chariot stood upon by a gilded man, shirtless but black-skinned. A cape of golden thread fluttered behind him, so regal that I felt smaller in its presence. He possessed long grey hair, a long grey moustache, and a gold torc around his dark neck. It was Fenn Beg Corm, and he looked so dark since his skin was stained in figures of animals and plants and the patterns of the cosmos. He carried a shield much like Verc's, and a spear. A severed head with a dangling tongue rode the spearhead. Dozens of black-stained men with red cloaks and armed with spears and swords followed him.

The Eponian riders all lined up and they raised their spears toward him. They shouted 'King!' 'Hail the king!' – 'Hail the king!' – Hail the king!'

I gawked at them. He had not been a king last I heard. They must have coronated him during the siege. Then I saw a golden, bejewelled crown upon his head.

'Hail Camulus!' I shouted.

Some men shouted, others shuffled, and riders backed away their horses. So much happened so fast, Luceo, that I lost myself. The Hillmen were parted, one side against the steep slope, and the other against the swelling ocean. We had won. Andrasta, goddess of victory, had delivered. I looked at my men. They were all heaving, blood-stained, some had cuts or bruises but nothing more. Tratonius. Marthelm. Antedios. Cattos. Orca. Artaxes. Aldryd. Cicarus. They all had their weapons ready, their eyes staring, smeared in blood. Their muscled bodies heaved. Even Chaser panted.

A Hillman, his jaw ajar, blood spilling from his shoulder, climbed up. He raised himself to his knees. Aldryd kicked him over, then held his boot on his head under the water. The short little mercenary laughed as the Hillman grabbed a hold of his ankle. Bubbles came up out of the water, and then no more.

Someone grabbed my shoulder. Myrnna. I wrapped my arm around her waist because she looked pallid. 'Why did he do that?' she asked. I had no answer.

Two of the shining ones came out from the bend. One limped, and the other was the one I had slashed through the thigh. They approached us unarmed, palms toward us, and then fell to their knees in front of me. The one I had slashed wrapped his arms around my knees.

'Spare us, please, man,' one said to me and I understood it. He had black hair, but I could tell it had been dyed, since I saw a smidge of blackness at his roots. He was around thirty Samhains, and had icy blue eyes, short limbs, a stocky body. His gold all glimmered, even his gold earrings danced in the light. His voice sounded so familiar.

'Why do you sound like you're from Skye?' I asked him.

'I am, lord,' he said.

The feeling that overcame me was indescribable, Luceo. Rage boiled in me, pure red Camulus, the helmet inverted from my head to my soul and I raised *Vidav*. He drew back and raised his hands.

'You're telling me you're a traitor?' I asked.

'Lord – we had no choice! It was join them or – Brennus?'

A farmer from the Ashmore clan. I knew him. We met him and his family at Dun Ashaig once. He had become a Hillman. This thought swirled in me until Camulus took hold of me, and I jammed *Vidav* deep into his throat. There was no finesse or precision. I put my foot on his chest and pulled *Vidav* out and he fell backwards into the water. The other scrambled to his feet but I hopped over his dying comrade and grabbed him around the arm. I bashed my shield into his face. He staggered backwards against the escarpment. I grabbed him by the hair.

'Traitor!' I screamed in his face.

'I'm sorry, Brenn,' he began to say. I peered down at him. He had the same bright eyes as that Ashmore clansman. I knew him once, too.

'Is that really you, Brenn?' he asked. 'It's me, Aihaun! Mercy, Brenn, mercy!'

I raised *Vidav* to stab his brilliant eyes out of their unworthy sockets. Someone grabbed me from behind, and so reddened was I, that I turned to strike and saw Marthelm.

'No, don't stop him!' Aldryd said, he was holding his gut laughing.

'He's had enough,' Marthelm said and released me.

Tratonius looked at me, lip trembling. 'You remembered your training today,' he said. 'You broke off your line and saved my life. You remembered to use your shield like a weapon, just as I taught you. I am proud,' he said. I never told him, but it had been Verc who trained me to do that, and not him.

'But I did not train you to kill surrendering men,' he said.

'They're traitors,' I said, and refused to look at Tratonius while I spoke. I just looked down at the dead traitor at my feet. 'Don't you get it? They killed my brothers. They looted my farm. They took my cattle. They slaughtered my entire clan. They invaded my island! They deserve to die. And now some join them? They'll all die! Aihaun, you die now!'

Myrnna vomited. It was all over her pretty white face and down her brown dress and dripping into the sea in droplets. She looked pale.

'Forget mercy, then. That's ransom money,' Tratonius said. 'You don't just kill them. Hostages are of so much use for us. Don't get so angry!'

'Loot their gold,' I said. 'There's your money.'

'Already am,' Aldyrd said. 'Come on, let's loot them.'

'If the king lets you,' Tratonius said.

Warmth ran down my legs. I had pissed myself. Then someone stuck a dagger in my thigh. Aihaun stared up at me, his blue eyes caught the sun, he bit his lip so hard that blood oozed from it as blood oozed from my thigh. He stabbed me again, and I wheeled back into the water, now knee-deep. Cattos pulled me up and Aihaun gagged as Aldyrd slashed him across the throat. I righted myself and now the remaining seven shining ones all sprang up and were upon us.

Cattos stood over me as two foemen came with their iron swords and struck at him. He blocked with his shield and parried another blow with his spear-shaft. Chaser came bounding through the water, splashing up everything, and he swam and grabbed the leg of a foeman who struck at Tratonius. Marthelm and another shining one were grappling against the escarpment over the dying Aihaun. A sword swung at me. I had dropped Verc's shield, and I raised *Vidav* to parry, but Cattos dove back, splashing water over me as he did, took another jump forward and slashed the shining one across the stomach, his guts spilling out into the ocean. Rising waves lapped at a dead steed behind me. All the meanwhile the Eponian riders sat on their horses in a line, watching us.

Tratonius parried and blocked, spun around and spun his shield to his back and three or more iron swords banged against it. Seafoam sprayed over all of us as the waves crashed against the rocks where more Hillmen and one Eponian and his horse lay battered in the rising water.

'Poke him – poke him – poke him!' Tratonius cried at Antedios who stood there slack-jawed, not moving. He gazed up. I gazed up also.

There upon Antedios' spear stood a bird-woman thing. Lanky, scaled long-heels, a black feather cloak fluttering in the wind from her bandy skinny neck. She had a grin, a hag's face, wrinkled, with black hair merging into her black cloak.

'Badb!' I cried out, falling backwards into the water. She danced on the tip of Antedios' spear on her black talons.

If Antedios could see her, then could the others? He stood frozen, the terror of Badb there upon his weapon. I cannot let her terror spread through my men. The shining one that battled against Tratonius, spear verses spear, poking and prodding at one another, glancing off shields, stepping in the knee-deep in rising water, paid no mind to Badb, even though she stood in his vision.

Badb looked off due northeast and I knew that was toward the Slighan hill. I could feel Slighan's shadow creeping over us. I could not let my men succumb to her.

'The day belongs to Camulus!' I shouted.

I broke off from the line, hopped over a dead horse and slashed at the back of a shining one. He whipped around before the hit could strike, and *Vidav* bit into his ribs. He groaned and I pulled *Vidav* out, and then stabbed at the other shining one, who blocked my attack. I slashed again but this time down into his groin. He cried and Antedios poked a lot now. He poked again, and again, and again, but he missed one blow and struck the rock wall behind an enemy, and his spearhead broke off his spear, so he drew a knife and poked that enemy to death. Tratonius dispatched another with a spear through the chest. Marthelm and his foe were entangled, their shields both blocking each other's weapons. Marthelm winced hard when his foeman slashed him across the back, but Marthelm had reached behind his enemy, pulled out a knife from a sheath, and stabbed and stabbed and stabbed until his enemy slumped limply against the escarpment.

We all looked around, eager to find more foemen, but we found none.

'Hero of the day!' Tratonius shouted at me. 'Well, hero of the afternoon!'

I crept my hand down to my three bloody wounds. My thigh, my side, my hip. I felt little pain then, but the ecstasy of battle had numbed it, I knew that. I sheathed *Vidav* and leaned on Cattos, who helped me walk now toward the line of crestfallen riders. Beyond them came many men afoot, pulling wounded Eponian riders and their horses away from the battlefield.

But my men all stood. Battered and tired Tratonius. Resourceful and loyal Cattos. Eager and sidhe-seeing Antedios. Glorious and sentimental Artaxes. Heartful and wounded Orca. Formidable and precise Aldryd. Sturdy and wise Marthelm. Even cunning Cicarus had come back, and fought with us. Bloody-snouted Chaser. Myrnna, the poor thing, my oath sound and safe along with her. Sabella and Frowon too, the good nurses that they were. All of us stood in victory together, and Verc and Groaner had paid the toll for our glory.

'Vidav?' Antedios asked me as I limped along with the aid of Cattos. 'What – what did I see on my spear?'

'Badb, the battle-hag, man,' I said.

'Can you explain why?'

'He's injured, man,' Cattos said. 'Leave him alone.'

We limped along, the helmet of Camulus askew on my head, Badb crept away from my chest and I thought of nothing but sweet Dun Torrin ahead, clear in the blue day.

'I'll never forget your help,' I said to Cattos.

'What I did was nothing, Vidav. Verc died for you.'

I turned my head to peer down the strand, where the tide now covered nearly all traces of battle.

Verc's body laid beyond the bend.

'Get his body before the ocean does – Aldryd, Artaxes, Antedios.'

'Groaner!' Orca said. 'We have to get Groaner, that brave little shit!'

'And we are to collect the mules before someone else does. And we must go back for our things,' Tratonius said.

'And then we feast in Vercerterx's honour,' Marthelm said.

'Your back, oh, your back!' Sabella ran over to him. Marthelm leaned back to show her. He had a deep, long gash. His face was pale and he heaved, and slurped his words.

'It's nothing, I am German,' he said. 'The other guy has a worse back.'

'And Domine!' she cried, and ran over to me. 'Domine! You're wounded, too!'

'It's nothing, I am a Celt,' I said, and wondered if the Germans called us Celt or Gauls.

'It wasn't nothing,' another voice said. I looked ahead of us. An older Eponian rider spoke to me. He had streaks of grey in his black beard. His body, like boiled leather, was sunburned and bloody. He had yellow, brown and green plaid trousers, a red cloak bordered with green herringbone fabric, and his horse was handsome and calm. He still held his blackened iron sword in hand.

'Galadrest, senior of the Eponian riders, first commander of king Fenn Beg Corm and servant of the goddess Epona,' he introduced himself. 'We lost many good men and good horses. More will die later. We intervened on your behalf.'

'Why didn't you help us in that last fight? Why did you just stand there and gawk?' Tratonius asked.

'They were not Hillmen,' Galadrest said. 'They were what you foreigners would call Celts, and they deserved a Celtic fight. And besides, what were you doing on the beach?

'Winning your war,' Tratonius said.

'This could have been worse,' Galadrest said. 'We won the battle thanks to the intervention of our king.'

'You didn't have to save us,' Tratonius said. 'Why did you?'

'This man there asked us to,' he motioned to Cicarus. 'We could not in good faith watch you get slaughtered, but you will have to compensate us.'

'And what will that compensation be?' Tratonius asked.

Galadrest's horse snorted as he raised the reins of the horse away from us. 'The king will decide that.'

'Then tell your king,' I began to say, but Galadrest interrupted me.

'And just who is the lord here? I see a man in a torc, but he has yet to speak until now.'

'Who am I?' I asked as Galadrest glared down at me.

'Tell him I said that I am the one who outsmarted the Hillmen, I am the leader of the mad march, the giant-bane, the slayer of the morgen, the druid's lost sanity, the one who dons the dead man's clothes, the wielder of the bronze sword, the friend of the seal shifter, the protector of Myrnna, the Leandros of the Leandres, the lion-descended, the brothers of battle-slain Bodvoc and Fennigus, the son of Biturix the great smith, the hag's fool, the cunning, the trickster, the avenger, the battle-hag enthralled, the singer of Lugus Longarm, the champion of men and hounds, the sidhe-ready, the enemy of Slighan, the oath bearer – the *Celtic* lord Vidav of the sellswords!'

I fainted, and collapsed into the ocean.

They carried me to dry ground. I remember the standing stone there on the beach in the boggy ground, we passed by it and I tipped my helmet to it, in my dizziness. Folks said the stone sang tales of old to those that could hear, and that perhaps it would sing the tale of the mad march down the beach, where many men had died and their bodies were carried out to sea like splintered wood from a battered boat.

Sabella beckoned Myrnna over, and they stitched me up with bronze needles and spiderweb. I hardly remember the stitching, because beyond the girls, twenty-seven naked Hillmen sat on their knees at the edge of the cliff, facing seaward. Behind them, one of Fenn Beg Corm's Eponians for each Hillman, holding swords in one hand, and the black hair of the Hillmen in the other. Fenn Beg Corm himself stood upon his gilded chariot, his white horses nervous, two wolfhounds at his side, and he shouted.

'Camulus!'

Twenty-seven headless Hillmen fell into the sea. Fenn Beg Corm's twenty-seven came back with dangling Hillmen heads. Cheering erupted and the throngs of Fenn Beg Corm's army began battering their shields with their weapons. The Eponian Riders all spurred their horses into a canter, and they trotted around the gruesome display. Cries of 'Camulus' and 'Morrigan' and 'Epona' ripped through the air. Beyond them lay the grey ocean, littered with floating corpses.

Myrnna turned away and vomited again.

They stitched up Marthelm next, who sat next to me.

'Your first battle wounds?' he asked.

I nodded.

'May you have worse next time!' he said, and he laughed. I only heard him laugh that one time.

Off in the distance, in the shadow of Cuillins and through a gentle glen, Aldryd, Artaxes and Antedios started back toward us. I looked back at Dun Torrin, its coastline rampart so inviting. Smoke billowed from the chimneys of the thatched roofs of the houses that stood within its ramparts. Women and children poured from it toward the army that stood between us and the fort, and there a discord of joy erupted. Some of them bore flowers and sprinkled them all over the sweating, bloody warriors. Others began recovering the corpses of the Eponians.

All the while Fenn Beg Corm's men piled the things of the Hillmen into a heap. They tossed first a few wooden hauberks and their bone pins, leather straps, and antler toggles. Next came horn and wood and antler handles of flint knives. They chucked woollen cloaks and leather boots and belts. The beach glittered in stone as the king's men piled flint and bloodstone and jasper and chert and quartz weapons of grey, black, green, red, white, blue-red up on the growing mound. Next, they took eagle feathers from headdresses, wool and leather shoes, wooden shields, and even the iron swords of the shining ones, and heaped them on, too. Then came a flutter of things, the king's men threw tunics and furs and hides of white and green and gold and brown onto the pile. They dropped gold earrings, gold rings, gold bracelets, and gold armrings which cascaded down the pile like streams from a mountain. Women smashed pots into sherds. The children came back from the strand with wooden mallets, stone maces, stone axes, stone knives, stone spears, stone-dead Hillmen limbs. They piled it all up until it resembled a mound of stony wooden golden flesh, and then they all surrounded it. Piece by piece, they chucked everything into the ocean. The mound grew smaller until nothing was left but flakes of stone and scraps of leather and this too, they collected by scraping it off the trodden ground with their hands and tossing it in. The ocean drank everything. Now the men over at the edge of the escarpment shouted 'Nodens', the god of the sea, since we had bloodied his domain throughout the afternoon.

Cattos helped me up and walk until I shooed him away. I shambled toward Myrnna, who looked at me with her big wet eyes. I grabbed her sweaty hand with my dirty, bloody, trembling hand. I lifted her into my arms, her arms wrapped around my torc-wrapped neck, my helmet slipped from askew to certain, and we looked onward toward Dun Torrin. Now the throngs that stood in our way washed away into Nodens, and joyous merrymakers danced in the blood-soaked sand and on the escarpment as the battle of the day had been won.

Aldryd, Artaxes and Antedios returned with Verc on his shield, and Groaner at his side. They laid his protective bier down, and pulled Verc's plaid yellow-green cloak over them both as a pall.

I set Myrnna down. I limped over toward the dead man and dog, and fell upon my knees. I could not believe this man, this warrior, this friend, had died for me. My men crowded around us, silent. Chaser sniffed around the dead, and slumped next to their bodies. Sabella let out a sob, whether from sadness or out of obligation, I did not know.

'That was a good death,' Marthelm said, as he stood behind me. 'He sacrificed himself for you, now sacrifice for him.'

'Verc, I will not enter Dun Torrin until you have been sent off to your ancestors,' I said.

CHAPTER XIX

We had retrieved mules and dug up our treasure, though we left a portion in the cave for the sidhe that dwelled there. What we left, and where it is now, I could never tell anyone, Luceo.

We piled many things into that little boat. We piled Verc's three javelins, five pots of grains and herbs, a bucket of butter, a Roman amphora full of wine, some leather skins of mead, some sea eagle feathers, a carpet, the last steak of venison, a conch shell, and quartz stones. Each of these had a purpose, which I will not speak of. It is between us and the gods, and not for the ears of so-called civilized folk.

The slaves had cleaned Verc's body, combed his hair and moustache, and righted his equipment on him. He lay on his shield, with his shoes on the wrong feet, and covered in his cloak. We placed his hunting spear at his side, and his sword in his hand, and I put his thumb on the flat of his blade as he fought with it. Groaner, brushed and cleaned, was placed at his feet, curled up in the way dogs sleep. They laid there in the boat, in the gentle breeze, as it drizzled on us. We would send him off now, due west, toward the setting sun, to his final journey. The sea is where we go when we die.

We all stood in our war gear, now cleaned and shined. We had eaten all of the boar and venison until our stomachs hurt, drunk ourselves dizzy, and poured ale into the sand and in the ocean around the floating coffin. Standing in silence, we held our spears aloft, the eight of us with our heads and blades skyward.

Sabella began to sob, and soon so did Frowon, and they delved into a keen. They keened louder and stronger until Chaser joined in and howled along with them. The rest of us stood there, silent, until the waves ebbed against the boat nine times.

Euchain, a local druid, had been requested to help us send Verc off. He came with an entourage of spear-armed men. In his white gilded robe and gnarled, mistletoe-wrapped staff, he lit three braziers. There was a carnyx on a red blanket at his feet.

'Donn, Donn, Donn,' he chanted the name of the god of the dead.

He sprinkled milk around the braziers as the smoke thickened around us. The keen lowered.

'For the spirits of our ancestors.'

The wind caught the smoke and it rose around us. He walked down the avenue we warriors had created, and rested a hand on Verc's leg. 'Warrior's end. Verc sleeps now, a dog at his feet. He journeys now to the Otherworld, where his ancestors await him.'

Euchain handed Tratonius a cup of wine and then distributed seven more for each of us.

First Tratonius poured his in the ocean. 'For my brother-in-arms, drink. I was wrong to doubt you. Sleep well.'

Next came Cattos. 'You were so proud of me when I killed my first man. It was as if my father was proud. I hope I will always make you proud.' He poured it, and sobbed. 'I will miss you so much, Verc.'

Antedios approached. 'What a warrior – and what a dog. I will think of both of you daily.' He poured it, and I spied a tear running down his face.

Next Artaxes came. 'Congratulations, old friend. You've made a Greek jealous of your valour.' He poured half his cup into the ocean, and then drank the rest. 'And for Dionysus.'

Now came Cicarus. 'Half a cup for the dog, half a cup for the man, both brave and valiant!' He poured his.

Now came Aldryd. 'Well, you caused us to waste some good wine. If I ever get to the Otherworld, you owe me!' He took a sip and poured the rest.

Then came Marthelm. 'Rarely do I awe at a mortal man, but today I am humbled by your fearlessness. I hope to face my death half as manly as you have. Wherever you are, drink with us, and toss a bone to the dog.' He swirled the cup and poured it.

Finally came Orca, haughty and laughing. He had the cup of wine in the crook of his arm, and he had his hair in a tight plait and brandished a dagger in the other.

'For my best friend!' he said and chopped off the plait and tossed it into the boat. His face was wet, and he turned to me. 'I'm not crying for the man. I would never cry for a man. But I'm crying for the dog.' He turned from me and poured his libation.

I then spoke. 'Here lies Vercerterx, a warrior from the Boii that died in the heat of battle defending his lord from a storm of arrows. He inspires us to be brave and manly ourselves because bravery, strength and manliness are what keep the sky from collapsing and the ground from crumbling. Verc held the sky and ground for me. Now too lies Groaner, a dog who died defending Myrnna from her kidnappers. We hope to someday drink with Verc again, and pet Groaner again in the Otherworld. Until then, we drink to their shades.'

Euchain pressed on the stern, and the hull scraped through the shelly sand and sent the boat adrift. 'The gods love the brave. They will find Verc worthy of them. Now, lads,' he said to us, 'in what manner has his heart been tried? Show us!'

The druid lifted the carynx at his feet and blew into it, it hooted, and then Artaxes played his flute while seated on a rock. A flurry of iron cut through the smoke. It startled me, and I reached for *Vidav* until I had seen who were fighting. Cattos and Antedios went blow for blow with swords, their shields forward. They both leaned forward, sword-hand at-waist, palms skyward, blade foe-ward, in the style of Verc. They danced their blades against one another, war-dancing away, parrying, blocking. They startled Chaser up from his bereavement with a flurry of blows, blocks and parries, the sound of wood on iron and iron on iron and wood on wood was so tumultuous that it sent seagulls shrieking up into the air. All the while the smoke wrapped around them, making them appear as shades as they slowed their pace. They both held their swords out, and their blades touched blade to blade. Artaxes increased his tempo when Cattos snapped forward, and when Antedios swung his sword to meet Cattos', Cattos slammed his shield into Antedios' hand and struck at his shoulder. Antedios blocked and then they were both chest to chest, and both slashed at each other's backs. Cattos had been hit first and choked a yelp, fell backwards, and rose to his feet. I could see a welt across Cattos' back, and Artaxes ceased playing.

Antedios stood slack-jawed, Cattos turned around, and Antedios cried and shoved his sword in the air and danced around. Then he drew his hand across Cattos' back and smeared the blood across his face. 'That was for Verc!'

'Hail Camulus!' Euchain cried. The men all shouted and cheered and clapped. I heard the names of the gods Ares, Camulus, and Tiwaz, and wondered if they all were the same god, or brothers or cousins, or friends, or even rivals.

'A Roman hug, so that's how it ends. Verc would be embarrassed, he taught them hard to avoid that,' Tratonius said with a laugh.

'Leave it to those idiots to do something so unskilled,' Aldryd said. 'But one's bleeding all right.'

I turned to watch the boat drifting off to sea. I could hardly see anything through the smoke except the silhouette of the boat passing on through the gold water of the setting sun. Chaser laid at my feet and I pet him.

'Donn, take Vercerterx into your arms,' Euchain said, and left with his bodyguard of spear-armed Torrinians.

We all stood in silence again for a while. The man had died defending me. I wondered if my men would have a funeral like this for me when I die. Did I deserve such? Verc died for me, so he must have thought I was worthy of him. The men must think I am worthy of them now, too. I thought it funny the things I thought about, for I thought about my father then, and wished he could have been there to witness this. Was it selfish of me? Yes, since I thought that I wanted my father to witness the funeral of a man who had died for his son, and to see the ritual performed by the men that call his son 'lord'. But our minds race when we send off the dead. I just thought only Verc as the boat floated away across the ocean, and over the golden horizon. Westward, ever so west, drift westerly, and sleep.

I felt a hand on my back. I turned to see Tratonius.

'I think it's time to go,' he said.

'I know, I just wanted to see the boat go over the horizon.'

'Right, but it's time to go. We feast tonight.'

Tratonius turned to leave, stopped himself and then put a hand on my shoulder again.

'You did well out there, especially for someone with such little experience. You saved me, Brenn, Vidav. Your father would have been proud.'

I had no words except thanks, for my thanks had been so profound that I had difficulty expressing it.

'But you still need more training.'

'Then train me,' I said.

'I will. First thing tomorrow.'

We all left, and as I did, I realized Chaser had not been with us. I thought perhaps he had been mourning at the beach, and I instead found him there snarling. He snarled toward nothing in the distance. I looked, and beyond my band, deep across the moors and near the mountains, four night-shaded giants carried the hut of the hag on their shoulders. They walked eastward. Badb crawled back up through my chest, and then my eyes were drawn to the mountains. The overcast sky had cleared and now I could see the grey-headed red hill of Slighan poking up over the horizon. Soaring wingbeats scoured the moors, and only I heard them, since the men walked away without noticing it.

'Badb – Macha – Fea! Grim goddess, why am I tormented?'

'Come back… come back to the Slighan Hill!' a voice responded.

I dashed toward my men, and whistled for Chaser. He loped behind us. We headed for Dun Torrin.

CHAPTER XX

Skulls. Skulls on the ramparts, skulls on stakes, skulls on the stone walls, skulls in piles in front of the entrance to Dun Torrin. A raven had perched itself on one skull, and it bowed to peck at the eye socket, and after each peck, the skull thumped against the wooden rampart behind it. We drew near, but it kept pecking, indifferent to us.

'Must be an omen,' Marthelm said.

Dun Torrin sat at the edge of the sea, over the cliff where the waves crashed down. It was circled by high wooden ramparts over a stone foundation, and those walls protected a wide sward. A two-story roundhouse lay in the centre, painted red and blue. It was the hall of king Fenn Beg Corm. Dozens of tents were scattered around the sward, where now many busybodies hustled to and fro, nursing the injured. Warriors were gathered in clusters and many men stood ahorse near the sacred paddock, where a standing stone in the shape of a woman stood among the dozens of beloved horses of the Eponians. The horses grazed. Do they feel the battle-fury that we do? Do they shake for hours after? Do they recall the blood and gore and death and details? I don't know, Luceo, but I think they do.

The walls were garnished in the skulls of the dead, and the wind beat hard on them and rattled the skulls. More ravens, crows, magpies and even seagulls pocked the skulls, sneaking in nibbles and waiting for nightfall so that they could feast undisturbed.

I walked donned in Camulus' helmet. Some of the warriors, sat on benches and drinking water, turned their eyes to me. Most were too busy, but those that idled gazed at me. Myrnna walked at my side, her necklace of jet pearls clattering, her arm wrapped around mine, though she walked as if in a daze. My men walked behind us, as did Chaser, followed by the slave girls pulling the mules, our things hoarded upon them.

We approached king Fenn Beg Corm's hall. The guards there demanded we disarm as per the custom of all kings' halls, so we disarmed ourselves.

With me, I took Myrnna and Chaser, then Marthelm, Tratonius, and Artaxes, my council now.

Inside, nine men lined the red wall of the roundhouse, all shirtless, Eponians with their black manes perfectly combed. Sunlight spilled in through the door behind me, and the men appeared as shades along the hall, silent, unarmed but prepared to restrain us if necessary.

At the other end, beyond the sizzling hearth, stood nine figures in white. I thought them to be Fenn Beg Corm's wives, for I knew he had been banished from his homeland because of his polygamy, something forbidden for us all. As we neared them, they startled a bit, since some were twelve Samhains old and probably feared sweating, limping, bloody, smelly men that barged right into Fenn Beg Corm's hall. The ears of two wolfhounds alerted to our presence, and one hound stood and snarled.

Fenn Beg Corm came from Alba, around the coast of the Cat People. Through marriage, he had claim over Dun Torrin, and when he claimed it, the Torrinians did not oppose him. He had arrived with his band of Eponians, and many young men from Skye and elsewhere in the Hebrides travelled to this fort to become an Eponian, though very few are ever accepted into the order. I never had the desire to be an Eponian, at least not one that serves such a rotten king. Each winter, he and his men go and raid the mainland, and often gifted our druids so few complained about him, but he taxed his people heavily and thus was unwanted by the farmers. His impious marriages earned the ire of the druids of our island, and we suspect he has his men steal our lambs and blame the thefts on wolves and eagles. Worst of all, he was a foreigner, and he had no business lording over even a petty kingdom on my island. Yet all of this was antebellum talk, for now, the war had solidified his rule because he remained, as far as I knew then, the last sovereign of the island. The Hillmen ruled all the rest, but Fenn Beg Corm resisted them successfully and earned the grace of Lady Andrasta, goddess of victory. And I knew this had been in part thanks to me, and my mad march down the strand.

The now-king of the Torrinians and Eponians of Dun Torrin was a wiry old man, saggy but sinewy. He had a long face and nose, bright blue eyes under black-grey hair, and wore a gold-embroidered cloak over a blue tunic, and red-blue check baggy trousers. He held a gneiss stone sceptre across his lap, and he drank from a silver cup, probably Greek wine. Most daunting of all, his skin was black, black from ink that stained all over him. He had spirals and leaves of oak, elm, and ash, and animals like wolves, boars, swans, and patterns of stars. He had been nearly covered in it, like fungus on a rotting tree trunk, and I reckoned it would take hours to count all the images inked all over his body. The gold contrasted harshly against the black; even his shoes were gold-trimmed.

'King Fenn Beg Corm,' I said. I removed my helmet and handed it to Myrnna since all must take what is on their head off indoors, and now king Beg Corm stood and approached me.

'Who is this?' he asked, and he had a gravelly, low voice.

'I am Vidav, son of Biturix – I was the lord present on the beach.'

'Biturix? I don't like him,' he said.

'He died a while ago,' I said, since I did not know what else to say.

'He was arrogant,' the king said, and came close to me. 'And thought himself lucky.' He smelled of ginger, for some reason, and he walked around me, eying me as if appraising me. 'He often put himself into danger, and often he would come out of it unscathed. Therefore, he grew even more arrogant. He thought he was invincible. He lived for a good time, but I am sure he died foolishly. He had what the Greeks call hubris, and the Gods punish men for that. Their punishment may take long, perhaps years, perhaps the Gods will punish the man's children – but punish they do.'

'We owe our lives to the Eponians,' I said, and I could nearly feel Tratonius ready to snap on me for showing my weak position.

'And you owe us the victory,' Tratonius said.

Fenn Beg Corm halted, about-faced, and walked sunwise around Tratonius.

'Owe you the victory?' he said in a mumble. 'It was pure luck. You should all be dead. No one should have survived that.'

'But we have,' Tratonius said. 'Our assault distracted them, they sent a hundred men to deal with a handful, then we defeated them time and time again. We won the battle because of that, luck or not.'

'It was foolish, and full of hubris, and the Gods will punish you,' Fenn Beg Corm said. 'I disavow your part, because I want none of that divine wrath you bring forth.'

'You can't do that,' Tratonius said. 'We won the battle, and the Hillmen heeled.'

'I admit that,' Fenn Beg Corm said. 'But I didn't like Biturix,' he said, and walked counter-sunwise around me. Then he glanced at Myrnna and eyed her.

'The druid Ambicatos' daughter? Have you brought her for my collection?'

I looked beyond the king and there stood his nine wives, from twelve to twenty in age, it seemed. What was remarkable to me was that each girl had different coloured hair. Strawberry blond, wheat blond, dark blond, light brown, black, red, copper, auburn, honey-blond – just no brunette.

'A good omen,' he said. 'Ten wives are enough for one man. Is she married?'

'No, king,' I said.

'I'll tell you what then, Biturix's son,' he said, and walked sunwise around me now, 'I will invite you and your men to the feast tonight, but after that, I want you out of Dun Torrin, and I'll tell you what then, I want you off Skye. I don't want you anywhere near me with your ill-luck, and the jinx that will come forth from your hubris.'

I baulked. I gulped and he halted and eyed me hard. He knew I had nothing to say now.

'Just wait!' Tratonius said. 'You will feast for the victory, but you won't accept how it was won?'

'Yes, that is it,' Fenn Beg Corm said and walked sunwise around Tratonius, and I noticed how hunched his back was when he walked. 'The Goddess granted us victory, but I don't want Biturix's son here. He thinks he's lucky.'

'But king, I am sworn to fight the Hillmen! I want nothing more than to war against them. Let me fight with you. Skye is my homeland, and I will fight for my homeland. I will die for my homeland,' I said, and my voice cracked.

'I want you out of here,' he said, and now I saw red. My fists balled, and I thought to end him right then and there and rid Skye of the first foreign usurper, one of many now.

But I did nothing. That was suicide. His men would kill me, or his son would kill me for blood-vengeance. And I could not commit suicide, not as long as I was oath sworn to protect Myrnna.

'Unless you wed Myrnna to me,' he said.

Myrnna gasped. She looked at me, but I did not look back.

'She must agree to be wed,' I said.

'I don't agree!' Myrnna said.

'Nonsense,' Beg Corm said. The old king stood chest to chest with Myrnna, eying her up and down. He grabbed her by the shoulder and nudged her. She turned around, confused on why he demanded that, and his eyes averted downwards. He nodded.

I looked beyond him, the old kings' wives all staring back at us. I imagined the king's flabby, leathery body crushing one of those petite girls, her squirming under him as he drools on her pouty red lips, and her shudders from disgust as he wipes his cock off on her leg.

'I will have this woman, she is fertile, with her wide hips, and will bear me an excellent son.'

'I cannot wed her to you, Ambicatos forbade it, and I must respect his wishes.'

'He's dead,' he said. 'And so is Biturix. You live, Biturix's son, but you will not live on Skye. I demand that you wed Myrnna to me, and then you may dwell here in Dun Torrin, and war against the Hillmen with us, since that is what you want. You will not do that for free, no. I will not have free lords roaming my island, damning our luck. That is folly for me. You will wed her to me, as my tenth and final wife.'

Myrnna and I locked eyes. Her eyes looked so dark in the dim light, and I wondered why the Hillmen wanted her. I wondered why they had sent an envoy to demand her, according to that young, now dead lad Sego, and why they refused to shoot us with arrows out of fear of hitting Myrnna, and would endanger themselves to slog with us in the melee. I wondered why she had such dark hair and eyes when both her parents had fair hair and eyes, and as I looked into her eyes, I saw them getting shiny, and the shinier they got the more her pink lips trembled and the more she stroked her own hair.

I said nothing for so long that Fenn Beg Corm walked around me again, counter-sunwise.

'If you won't wed her to me, then give me your oath.'

I looked back at Tratonius, Marthelm and Artaxes.

'Biturix's son cannot make his own decisions? He must have his elders decide for him?' Fenn Beg Corm asked.

Tratonius raised his eyebrow at me. He meant to say something, but Marthelm placed a hand on his shoulder.

Two worlds pulled me, Luceo. I would either swear an oath to Fenn Beg Corm or I would flee Skye. Oaths are sacred to our people. You cannot break an oath, to do so would simply damn oneself. An oathbreaker is an untrustworthy man, and who is he, then? All man has on Taman is his word. Once he breaks it, misery follows, and his ancestors shun him in the next world. To swear an oath to Fenn Beg Corm meant that I was his man for life. I would still command these mercenaries since they were oath sworn to me, but I then must act under this foreign king, his life before mine, until he dies, or I.

On the other hand, I could leave Skye. I could leave and travel in my father's footsteps. I could travel to Scythia and fight among them there and find gold and women and glory. I could visit my father's grave, and then kill myself on it, for I had forsaken my people on Skye. I left Bodvoc's skull exposed on the ground. Hillmen occupy my farmstead. Our men have been slaughtered, our women raped, our children sold into slavery. If, somehow, the clans of Skye ever retook this island, I would not share in the glory or the vengeance. I would be rootless, away from everything, off to wander and never find my way again.

To wed Myrnna to Fenn Beg Corm remained unacceptable.

'Think about it if you must, but you have until tomorrow night. I will only give you refuge for tonight.'

Fenn Beg Corm headed back over to his throne, a wicker chair decked in the skulls of his enemies, three from each armrest. He sat down and mulled and waved us away.

Marthelm and Artaxes had been whispering, and Artaxes argued that we ought to demand more time, and a longer stay for partaking in the battle, but we all found it hopeless and left.

Sabella greeted us outside. 'Domine!' She shouted, and she ran over to me, wrapped her arms around me and kissed me on the lips. Her large, squishy breasts pressed against my sweaty chest, and I baulked a bit.

'Shall you have a hero's welcome tonight?' she asked.

I brushed her aside, and Myrnna scowled at me. Her eyes were wet, though she seemed to hold back her tears.

'Take care of the girl, we must go speak now,' Tratonius said to Sabella.

'What does pretty puella need?' She asked, and crept over to Myrnna. She came up behind her and massaged her shoulders, but Myrnna stiffened, mouth open. 'Does the poor baby need some comfort?' She asked, and slapped the plait away from Myrnna's neck and kissed it. Myrnna squirmed.

We headed out of Dun Torrin to the coast. In the distance, Eponians patrolled the area. There was a great heap of wood off near the leeside of Dun Torrin, where men began to assemble a great man of wicker. Naked captured Hillmen, in the dozens, were hoarded in a nearby ditch, ropes wrapped around their wrists. Two smaller young dogs, black and white mutts, snipped and barked at a young, naked Hillman tied to a tree. Still, great throngs of warriors, stripped naked, shades in the silhouette of the setting sun, danced in a great clearance of the moors. They flipped and cartwheeled and rolled as pipers and lyre-strummers and drummers played wildly.

We stopped at a clearing, and I put my back to the Slighan Hill. I shuddered, and the men noticed me shudder, and they thought it had been due to this dilemma that Fenn Beg Corm had forced on me, yet it had not been that. Something had crept within me, a little voice, screeching inside. I nearly heard its words, but then they spoke.

'Just marry the girl off, she's a hassle for us anyway,' Artaxes said.

'He's not going to do that, so don't bother,' Tratonius said.

'No, let's talk about it. What's with the girl, Vidav? What do you know that we don't?'

'The Hillmen want her, and so did the giant, and they even sent an envoy for her father to hand her over. But her father is dead, and I don't know where that giant is and I hope I do not see it again,' I said.

'She saved us. We all would have been dead if not for her. They would have just shot us, but they wouldn't shoot us when she was with us. She's important to someone important,' Tratonius said.

'Hubris. We had pure hubris today. That barbarian king is right. We were lucky. I think that the girl brings ill luck. We will be hounded for her as long as she is with us. It will be detrimental. Let us get rid of her by wedding her to that barbarian king, and then she can be his problem,' Artaxes said.

'He's not going to do that,' Tratonius said.

I grew tired of Tratonius speaking for me, so I spoke.

'I swore an oath to Ambicatos, her father, that I would only wed her to someone she agreed to wed. She won't wed Fenn Beg Corm, and that is it.'

'I didn't know you swore an oath to do that,' Artaxes said. 'I thought it was more of a promise. Huh, I think this is a poor deal, what did you get out of this besides a brooch?'

I fingered the brooch that latched the cloak to my chest. Marthelm must have seen my face, and he spoke.

'This task that he was given is very important to him. So, let us not speak about it. Vidav, I think you should swear an oath to him. We came here to fight for the Hillmen, now we fight against the Hillmen. Fenn Beg Corm will offer us many riches from plunder. You will be his oathsman, but you will be on your homeland, fighting for it.'

'Vidav,' Tratonius said, and put a hand on my shoulder. 'You will not like what I am about to say. I watched you these last few weeks. You were nothing but a stupid boy when we first met, too idealistic. You threatened us and you even tried to box Cicarus, you were prideful and that was your downfall. You were our slave, and then you won your freedom and we banished you. Do you not remember that? Then you came back, a changed man – new name – new sword, and you saved us. You led us, despite our advice against it, down to our certain deaths. But we survived, we survived and humiliated the Hillmen. They will recover, but they will forever remember that humiliation that we inflicted upon them. But it was luck that we did so. You know better by now. You've learned now. You should learn that there will be no luck next time. I've seen what the Hillmen are capable of, Vidav. There are thousands of them, and thousands more come each day. There is no stopping them. This is the way Skye is going – to become entirely queen Slighan's domain. Sure, Fenn Beg Corm will hold out, probably all winter, perhaps even for years – or he will end up nothing but a mere client to the queen. But that is the end, the Hillmen are the future of this island. You should know that. Did you know that, in my country, a warlord crossed the Alps with his elephants? He will ravage the country, and there will be no more, or at least, it will be different after he is through. It is the same here. You will never have your farm back. You will never have your old life back. You will never have Skye back. Let us leave it.'

I had no words. I just stared at Tratonius. Something crawled through my chest, not Badb, for this did not scare me, but was just a feeling of looming defeat.

'And furthermore, it would be the best for Myrnna to take her far away from the Hillmen, since they have an interest in her.'

And then the whisper.

I'll give you the life you want, for a price.

Goosebumps prickled over my flesh, my hair stood up on end, my knees buckled, and I turned to the Slighan Hill. Thereupon it, a gigantic shadow, thrice the size of the peak of the mountain itself, with a great wingspan that would blot out the sun had it been high enough in the sky. A flying, massive, long-necked shadow of a creature. I fell to my knees and gripped the grass between my fingers, I held my head down and I screamed into the dirt.

Marthelm helped me to my feet. Now all three of them looked at me, and all three frowned. How could I ever tell them that my breakdown was due to that flying monster on the Slighan Hill, and not Tratonius' words? I could not justify myself, and I wished for nothing but enough time to pass to forget about this humiliation.

'Where would we go?' I asked.

'Back to my country. There will be great plunder.'

'You will join the foreign warlord?'

'Foreigners rule my land anyway, so I owe loyalty to no one.'

'How long will it take to get there?'

'Months, I'd say,' he said. 'But we should get as far south as possible before winter. To the dogs with another winter away from the Mediterranean.'

Bodvoc. I thought of Bodvoc's skull, left exposed on the ground of my farm. What did the

Hillmen do with it? Hang it from a rope? Crush it under their feet? Use it as a ball? Where were my cattle? Were they meat by now? Sold? Grazing somewhere else? What of Auneé? Where was she? Chattel? The wife of some Hillman warlord? Sold off? Dead? What of the corpses of my clansmen on the fields of Dun Ashaig? Carrion for the crows? Fennigus and his lads deserved to be sent off just like the great Verc. I yearned for revenge. But could I venge myself against the Hillmen, knowing what Tratonius said, that it is hopeless? Is that suicide?

'You don't have to make your decision now, you have some time,' Marthelm said.

'He has until tomorrow evening,' Tratonius said. 'I say you should leave, Marthelm says you should stay, what say you, Artaxes?'

'I said it already. I believe he should wed the girl to Fenn Beg Corm. We can get more out of Fenn Beg Corm for her. We can get more slaves, some gold – horses. He really likes her,' he said and turned to me. 'Speak to a druid if you are worried about your oath.'

We left, and then headed back toward Dun Torrin. We came to a copse of dying trees on the trackway, typical of my windswept, rainswept, stormbound island. Galadrest, horsed, watched over two shirtless men who stood over two naked Hillmen tied to a stump.

One of Galadrest's men took hold of the shirtless man on the left, an older man, his black hair matted over his eyes. He stretched the captive's arm out so the back of his hand lay over the stump, stretched his fingers, and then the other Eponian slammed a stone adze hard onto his fingers. The Hillman screamed so loud that Galadrest's horse snorted and threatened to buck, but he pulled on the reins.

'What was your name?' Galadrest asked loud.

'Krannus of the Ashmore clan!'

I must have looked aghast because Tratonius raised an eyebrow at me.

'And why did you serve the Hillmen?'

'They told me I had to or I'd die!'

Galadrest shouted 'Hit!' and the flat of the adze crashed down again on the fingers of the traitor. This time he screeched and whined like a girl, thumping his arse up and down and his legs curled toward his chest. He whimpered, and then the Eponians laughed, except Galadrest.

'And you?' Galadrest asked the other.

'Senghen! You know me, Galadrest!'

'Hit!' Galadrest shouted. A thump and Senghen whinnied like a horse.

'Why did you join the Hillmen?'

'They told me to serve or die, I had no choice!'

'It was better for you to die,' Galadrest said. 'How many of your clan joined?'

'Most, if not all of them.'

'Hit!'

Another thump and another scream.

We approached and stood next to Galadrest.

'How many traitors are there?' I asked.

Galadrest looked down at me from his horse, his eyes ablaze, and he turned back to them and commanded 'Strike – both!' The adze went down again, the men both screamed, and fingers fell upon the grass.

'A lot,' he said. 'Haven't you heard? Most of these so-called Hillmen are traitors. I'm rooting them out, so that they may pay the penalty, and their memories be forgotten forever.'

'Most of the Hillmen?' I asked, looking at the two men, wheeling against the stump. I knew Krannus, he was from a neighbouring clan and he often came to Dun Ashaig to trade. Now he sat there, missing fingers, miserable, scurrying against the stump.

'The traitors will suffer more than the others. There are others, too. Some of them haven't dyed their hair, the bastards. They're from all over. But most of the Hillmen seem to be traitors. The Hillmen force men to join them or, forgive me if I vomit, some even join them willingly. Either way, they are traitors or cowards, and they will suffer before they die. Hit!'

Two thumps and just one screech, Senghen had bit his lip so hard that blood rushed from his mouth. He choked and tears fell from his eyes.

'How could they?' I asked.

'Are you daft, lad? They're cowards and then they turn traitor. That is who the Hillmen are. They turn traitor and they give up all their ways. They become Hillmen, they don't use iron or bronze or metals at all, just stone weapons. They worship their queen like a goddess. Then she sics these pathetic wretches on us and we will defeat and kill them all. The only way they pose a threat to us is in their numbers, which grow because this world is apparently full of cowards and traitors. We defeat them whenever we meet them in equal numbers, all except the shining ones. And those are the worst. Slighan's elite men, good duelling lads, so loyal and fervorous for Slighan that she allows them, and them only, to use iron.'

I remembered now when we battled the shining ones. They duelled us as we duelled them, man versus man, iron versus iron, heart versus heart. Then I remembered when I found the traitor against the escarpment, Aihaun. How did he become a shining one, in that chaotic battle? If he survived it, could Fennigus have?

Pride struck me, I stood straight, looking at those wretches against the slumps, and smiled at them. I knew Fennigus and his lads would never turn traitor against us, and neither would I. I knew now that I could never abandon Skye, my homeland, no matter if it meant swearing an oath to that foreign, rotten king, and no matter if all the world turned into Hillmen and I stood against them all, alone. If the whole world stood against me, I would fight them and kill as many of them before they all killed me. I made my decision.

We left for Dun Torrin, where I would tell Fenn Beg Corm that I would swear an oath to him.

CHAPTER XXI

Blood spilled over the bier. A horse whinnied and fell. The king hacked at its head, again, again, again. The beast trembled and settled. Three white-bearded druids in blood-stained white robes crowded around it, butchering it where it stood.

The druids shouted 'Epona!'

Throngs of men, women, children, slaves, and dogs all crowded around the bier. The slaves collected the horse's blood in buckets. They ferried the buckets over to a cauldron, hot over the fire, and poured the blood in. Soon the slaves added vegetables and herbs, then came the druids with haunches of butchered horse meat to toss into the cauldron.

'Epona!'

Now came the riders, Eponians on their horses, scores of them all riding in a circle around the inner walls of Dun Torrin. They each held their spears outward with one hand and with the head of a Hillman in the other. The trampling of the horses created a tumult and then came Fenn Beg Corm, arriving at Dun Torrin upon his chariot. He sped right toward us, and the crowd parted. The chariot had been gilded, and the king himself bore a bronze horned helmet, the same helmet as the one that Verc had used to crown me as Camulus. His nine wives, all dressed in white, sent flowers fluttering in their husband's wake, the white petals landing all over the sward and in the brown ruts of the chariot's tires.

Now came jugglers, firebreathers, painted clowns, an animal handler with a whip whipping a young bear in the rear causing the beast to lurch to its hind legs and dance. There were whores with bare saffron painted breasts, wolfhounds trotting with swords in their mouths, pipers, drummers, trumpeters.

Then came the carnyxes that bellowed over all as the Fenn Beg Corm, danced from one rail on his chariot to the other, stepping forward and backwards, lunging onto one horse and grabbing its hinds and then flipping over to the other horse. The chariot raced past us as he flipped again to the other horse, and then stood with one leg on each horse, and unsheathed his sword.

While still in motion, his lean, scruffy charioteer tossed a severed Hillman head, its dry haunch of a neck still flapping with tendons and loose skin. The king caught it, and then flung it into the air ahead of himself. When the chariot came near the falling head, he impaled it right through its neck with his sword. He brandished the head toward the crowd. The Hillman had been a shining one, for gold dangled from his grey ears.

The crowd erupted into a roar. Cries of 'Epona!', 'Andrasta!', 'Morrigan!', 'Nodens!', and 'Camulus!' came forth, and then Fenn Beg Corm and his Eponians all assembled in a great throng, the king in the centre and fifty riders on each of his flanks. Then came the performers and they all crowded to the left and ride, and then at once everyone took a bow, except Fenn Beg Corm who raised the head even higher. The crowd began shouting 'King Beg Corm!' until others joined in a chant and soon nearly all chanted.

The druids came and hushed us all, and they rolled out the wicker man on a cart hauled by oxen. It was the size of five men, a wicker frame wrought like a man with a straw head. Its framework bulged and there were two sheep in its feet, bleating, and upon them a cram of men. I could not count, but all of them were naked, black-headed and beaten. Their bare skins were full of bruises, welts, and long slashes. Some were bleeding and others looked dead already, while more pleaded, some in *Celtic*.

The druids commanded the slaves to roll the wicker man to the centre of the fort. Then the slaves piled straw at its feet. The slaves scurried off as a flame-bearing druid illuminated red in the low light by his torch tossed it onto the straw. The flames spread and the men in the wicker shouted in discord. I could hardly hear them over the sizzling and the smell of skin turned sour. A great puff of smoke engulfed it all and when the wind picked up, the wicker man came crashing down, and after a while, all that was left of it all were charred husks.

Tratonius leaned into me. 'You Gauls love your spectacles.'

'What is a Gaul?' I asked him, because the Eponians wore their hair differently and possessed different garments than us.

'You,' he said. 'You ones with your check pants, and your hair up in spikes. You all live up north, some of you in the vineyards in Italia, others like you all the way on the stormy edge of the world. You all fancy lopping off heads, and you're similar in tongue and gods. And you believe the only fear you face is if the sky falls down on your head or the ground opens up under you.

'And this spectacle is Gaulish, very Gaulish. It befits such a fight as the one we had yesterday.'

I reached down into my pouch and touched the lion-man figurine, my ancestor. I then thought back to Verc on his boat, sailing back home to Gaul. If Nodens carried his body back home, his clansmen would recognize him as their own, since he wore their colours in his death. What colours do I wear? If I died far from home, would anyone recognize me if I were not in my clan colours?

I gazed upon the Eponians and their king, in their colours of blue, red, and green, check-patterned trousers and their long red capes.

My men stood piebald, multiple colours, multiple types of weapons and armour, a mixture of traditions from far-reaching lands. I hesitated. The old mercenaries would never yield to my demands for them to change costume or pick up Celtic weaponry. They have not even become Leandres. But the Leandres would, and so would I. I looked upon the Eponians, foreigners in my land, retaining their sacred rites, their dress, their ways. I then turned to my Leandres, Cattos, Antedios and Artaxes.

'We are to wear my clan's colours from now on. The green and the yellow. These are our colours.'

'A Hellene in Celtic colours,' Artaxes said. 'What an oddity.'

'We will still be Leandres,' I said, 'but we will wear clan Ashaiger colours. We will be Celts, and we will fight like Verc, and we will honour him and the Ashaigers.'

Now the slaves placed the benches around the sward and set the tables. Then we feasted on horse.

The sour smell of burnt skin never relinquished at the feast. The wind carried it and ensured we would all be reminded that we feast at night because at day death nearly dragged us all down to the Otherworld. After, we feasted on horse and drank ale with our feet propped on the backs of dogs, wetting lips and filling our bellies at twilight. Our table had all my men, with Myrnna seated next to me. She neither said nor ate anything.

We sat there for a while, myself dressed in my own clothes, and we discussed manners of dye for Artaxes and the lads so that they may wear Ashaiger colours. We needed saffron and woad, which was expensive, but we had gold and silver to trade, and perchance, plunder from the Hillmen in the impending raiding season.

After some time, Antedios and Cattos returned with Chaser. They had been out hunting, and Chaser came first with a pheasant in his mouth, the bird limp. Sabella and Frowon gathered it up, plucked its feathers and roasted it over one of the many campfires in the vicinity.

We sat for a spell, and I listened to the men speak. Today they spoke of the battle, and they recounted their triumphs and near pitfalls. We all drank to Verc again, and finally I asked Tratonius about what had been on my mind for so long.

In Italia, the Celts fight for the warlord. Why?'

'Because the Romans invaded their lands, and they want revenge,' he said with a slur, he had been drinking quite a bit. 'Took their crops. Took their gold, silver, iron. Humped their women. Probably humped the men, too.'

'Why did the Romans do that?' I asked.

'Why does anyone raid anything? There isn't enough space for all of us, so someone has to suffer.'

'And who should suffer?'

'The other guy,' he said, and laughed. 'Now come on, it's been years since the warlord invaded. I haven't heard who won yet. Maybe they're still warring. Maybe it will be over before daybreak. But there's much plunder in Rome. Much plunder. And we need a new Sabella, this one is getting old.'

'And the Celts in Italia – or your people – why did they not defeat the Romans?'

'Because that's the way it goes,' Tratonius said. 'I've seen it. Once it starts going, there is little to stop it. You can stand athwart a river and yell halt, but will it? It will wash over you, crash you into its bed and knock you silly until you drown. You could try to swim against it, but the current is always stronger than you. When it rushes, it rushes, and there is nothing you can do but float with it. You can swim with the current, and accept it. That's what the Umbri did. That's what the Cisalpine Gauls did. Now that's what the warlord is doing to the Romans. And that's what the Hillmen will do to you.'

I mulled over what he said for a while. I drank from my cup, barely listening to my men speaking of their stories. The king's son, Talorc, a broad-chested, broad-shouldered but baby-faced man of about my age sat at our table. He wished to speak with me, because he had heard of an

Ashaiger with a bronze sword and it caught his interest, but he ended up in a conversation with Artaxes who spoke too much about his own exploits. I looked at Talorc's inked-black body, attempting to make out the patterns that would send me a sign. No such sign came.

Perhaps it would be best to leave Skye. Tratonius may have been right. How could I stand against the grey tide of flint? It would topple me, crush me, drive me down. What was there left to fight for on Skye? For Fenn Beg Corm, another foreigner? The Ashaiger clan had been annihilated, and all the other clans have fallen.

'And what if Rome is already plundered by the time we get there?' I asked.

'We go to Greece,' he said.

'And what if Greece is already plundered?' and now Artaxes looked at me.

'Greece isn't one city, but many. Did I not teach you that?'

'And if all the cities of Greece are plundered?'

'Egypt,' Tratonius said. 'Anatolia. Persia. India. Sinai, perhaps something beyond. There will always be plunder for men like us.'

I ceased drinking my ale. 'I am not like you,' I said, my eyes low. 'I am for my own people, not just for plunder.'

'Not just,' Tratonius said with a toothy grin. 'That's right. Not just. We were all once not just, now we are just.'

At daybreak, we all rose to wash the blood, grime, and muck off our bodies. Fenn Beg Corm declared that we shall all wash in the sidhe pools, the wee pools of blue and green deep in the valley of the Cuillins.

The crisp morning air greeted us in the valley, where the crickets still chirped in the heather off the pathway to the pools. The pools themselves were part of a watercourse that cascaded down into a series of wee little waterfalls. Cattos, Antedios and I jumped in in succession. I submerged and then broke surface, wheezing. The water was freezing; I gasped but dared not remove myself from it, since Antedios and Cattos did not either.

I gasped again, and I wished to leave. I swam toward the rocky shore without thought, and then my head fell below the water again. One of the lads had dunked me!

Back to the surface, and they both laughed.

'What, too cold for you, lord Vidav?' Cattos asked. 'I've been in colder water!'

Before I could react, Antedios jumped on my back. The lad's legs were over my shoulders, and he attempted to grab a hold of the little hair I had on my head.

'Your hair is too short, I can't hold on!'

Then came Cattos, who climbed up on us, and I began to wobble and then Antedios slipped and the three of us chopped down into the water. I came back up, gasping again, and I wiped my eyes to find Frowon standing over us, motioning toward me.

'Lord,' she said, she had a shy smile and looked a bit red. 'Myrnna wants to see you. She's just over in the next pool,' she said in her best *Celtic*.

I hauled myself up onto the rocky ledge, pulled my trousers up and they stuck to my wet legs. I scrambled up the slope and headed to the further pool. There the pool had three waterfalls that gently washed into them, and in the middle of the turquoise starburst, Myrnna stood shoulder-deep in the water. Her hair had been loose and it hung in black wet locks behind her. Her skin contrasted so milky white against her dark hair and the bright floor of the pool. My eyes edged down toward her breasts, her hard, pink nipples visible below the surface, but then I caught her big, shiny, brown eyes.

'Thank you for coming,' she said as I edged closer to the bank of the pool. I hopped over a stream and stood at the ledge, then headed down the rocky path, and stood just a few arm's lengths away from Myrnna in the pool.

'Are you happy to have a bath?' she asked. I nodded, then her face went grim.

'Tell me, please, what is your decision?' she asked.

'I'm going to stay and fight,' I said.

'Why?'

'Why?' I asked, unsure what she meant.

'Why must you fight?' she asked.

'The Hillmen aren't defeated yet,' I said. 'They must be driven from Skye.'

'They won't be,' she said, nearly a whisper.

'As long as I live, they will,' I said.

'Beg Corm was right,' she said. 'It was luck that we survived that march! I was so scared, I was so scared! They had me, that poor dog saved me… oh…' She said, her hands clenched to her sternum. 'And you saved me.'

'I swore an oath to your father that I would,' I said, and I gulped, and looked up at the grey sky, wondering if Ambicatos would acknowledge that act.

'He really liked you,' she said, looking down at the water. 'He must have been so proud of you.'

I kept gazing up at the sky, the clouds swirling over the saffron horizon.

'He wanted what was best for me, and that was to be protected by you. He also must be happy that you refused to wed me to Fenn Beg Corm. But now you've gotten me to Dun Torrin, we are safe, and from here, we should leave.'

'Leave?'

'I… I don't want to be here,' she said, 'I'm tired of it all. The war, the battles, the skulls… the Hillmen, who tried to kidnap me… the sidhe that come out at night, the hag… I'm tired of it all. And then Sabella… I hate her, I really hate her! And Fenn Beg Corm's disgusting, nasty, horrible gaze!' She sighed. 'It's tiresome.

'I want my old life back. I want to leave here. I want to go somewhere else,' she swam toward me. 'We can leave. You're a lord now. You have gold. You can take the gold and buy some land and cattle somewhere, somewhere far away from here and the war and Beg Corm, somewhere far away where we can live peacefully with our cows. That is what I want, Brenn, that is what I want, I want to be away from here and to just live quietly.'

'But the Hillmen killed your father,' I said, and that came out as a groan, 'they burned Dun Ashaig. Do you not remember, when the women were strangling their children upon the hillfort? Do you not remember your mother, Myrnna?'

'Don't you dare tell me what my parents would have wanted! They would have wanted you to obey my wishes!'

'I swore revenge,' I said.

'And how many did you kill?' she asked, her voice cracking. 'How many more need to die before your vengeance is over?'

'All,' I said, and I laughed, and her mouth dropped agape. 'It will not be over until I have the so-called queen's head.'

'Why, Brenn?' she asked, shaking her head. 'It's what my father would have wanted.'

I ceased laughing. We stared at each other. I had nothing to say now. She knew her father better than I, far better, but I never swore to quit fighting.

'I can't,' I said. 'I can't just leave. I can't just give up. The gods will decide who is the master of Skye, and if they decide against us, then I would rather die with my brethren than live somewhere foreign.'

'But why, Brenn?' she said, and now she eased up out of the water. I watched the jiggling of her breasts covered in goosepimples, her nipples hard. She had been shivering and her arms wrapped feebly around her body. Streamlets came down from her netherhair. Her body was so white against the grey stones and red swathe of heather behind her. She waded toward me.

'My father told you that the man we agree on, you and I, is to wed me,' she said.

She came so close. She grabbed my hand. Her eyes erred to my groin which showed my feelings. Red, she looked away, but keeping my hand, motioned to me join her in the cold water.

'We can have a life together,' she said. Her hands reached to the rope of my trousers and untied the knot, and they slipped away. She glanced down, reddened deep, looked away, and I entered the cold water with her. She held my hands, her cold skin so soft, and I felt them rumbling against mine.

'We can leave this blood-stained land. You can rid us of those awful mercenaries – I hate them! Keep Frowon as a houseslave. Release the rest, but take the gold and suchlike and the mules, buy us land, buy us some slaves and cattle. We could be happy there. Someplace far away. You can have your old life back... you could be Brenn again,' she said, and her lip trembled. She was shivering and she drew closer to me, and soon her body was pressed against mine, and Luceo, never more had I been so tempted to break my oath.

I could hardly speak. I was so nervous that my knees shook. Not Badb, but Bride fluttered in my chest, and Cernunnos drove my lust.

'You can be Brenn again,' she said as her hot breath whisked against my face. 'You could wed me.'

She wrapped her arms around my neck and leaned in close. Her wet breasts squeaked against my chest. Her sopping hair braised my shoulders. She leaned in further and kissed me on the cheek, with the edge of her lips touching mine. She held it here, and I felt her breathing against me.

She swallowed. She looked at me, her eyes shining, and then she cried. She wrapped herself against me and cried, on my shoulder, her hot tears against my cold flesh. She kept crying and sobbing until her head bobbed against me.

After a spell, she pulled back, and holding my hand, just stared at me.

'I would love to wed you,' I said, and she kept staring. 'But we must stay in Dun Torrin,' I said.

She said nothing for a while. She waded away from me, then she picked up her sponge and soap and leaned against the rocks.

'Oh Brenn,' she said, and I knew she knew that it irked me that she called me that. 'Will you really swear an oath to that old king?'

'If I must,' I said, watching her breasts jiggle as she scrubbed them with the sponge.

She then turned around, and leaned forward, gripping a boulder with one arm and washing her back with the other. She extended her back and looked over her shoulder, grinning at me. 'What shall you decide? Brenn, I really don't want to stay here.'

She approached me, and biting her lower lip, wrapped a hand around my manhood. She giggled, looking up at me, as I breathed heavily, with an overwhelming desire to take her. I closed my eyes and turned my head and tried to pull away, but she tugged back on my manhood. 'Don't you want to wed me?'

'I will not leave Skye!'

Her mouth agape, she pulled away, waded back over to the rocks and picked up a cobble and chucked it. She did it again, and again and soon she began beating the sponge against the berg. 'I want out of here!' She cried.

Sabella and Frowon peeked their heads over the edge of the cliff and peered down on us in the pool. They came down and Myrnna called Frowon over to bathe her, and Frowon did so.

'Why hello, Domine,' Sabella said, licking her lips, and tickled my manhood. I pulled away from her but Myrnna huffed and shook her head.

I returned to the other pool. I bathed, found my clothes, and prepared myself to submit to king Fenn Beg Corm. I was to be his oathman, his attack dog, his warrior. And I would have my revenge against Slighan and her Hillmen.

CHAPTER XXII

Myrnna dressed me in my tent. She fastened my belt around me. She fingered my brooch, ran her yellow nail along the clip and fastened my cloak over my collar. Then she retrieved my *Vidav* from the chest and kneeled before me as she handed it and bowed her head. I secured *Vidav* in its scabbard. Myrnna stood up, and looked at me with wet eyes, then turned away. I took her hand and we left the tent.

My men were all suited up, too, the seven of them in their finest clothes, weapons, and armour. We approached the hall of Fenn Beg Corm. His guards came. We disarmed and entered the musty hall.

Fenn Beg Corm sat on his seat, stripped to the waist, petting each hand on the heads of his wolfhounds. I held Myrnna's hand and she held back tight. Fenn Beg Corm raised his upper lip at the sight of my men.

His face relaxed. He stood up, walked over to me, and pointed down.

'On your knees,' he said.

I complied. He neared and I could smell him. He was sweaty and stinky, but both his odour and the smell of flowers adorned him.

He wrapped his arm around my head and pulled my face into his chest. His hairy breast prickled my nose. His skin felt hard and leathery, and he wrapped his arms around my head. My lips touched his soft, pink nipple. I leaned my head away, but he pulled me back into him. I fell to my knees and tried to rise, tried to straighten my knees so I could pull away, but he just drew me in closer, my nose banging against his hard flesh, and he now commanded me.

'Suckle me, child.'

I sucked his nipple. I suckled it like a babe, and my eyes teared and I sucked, and he held me close to his breast. It tasted awful, it made sickening noises, and Tratonius looked askance. Someone laughed, probably Aldryd.

Kneeling, face against his old breast, lips wrapped around his nipple, sucking and sucking. I trembled, and then, after I stewed in my humiliation long enough, thinking of my ancestors, my family, and my Gods all witnessing this, he released me. I fell back onto the cold dirt floor, stood up, and wiped the spittle from my lips.

'Now leave,' the king said, and sat back on his throne.

I turned away, not looking my men in the eyes. Myrnna said something and I ignored her. I walked outside the fort walls, rounded them toward the coast, and sat down on a block of stone and gazed out at the rolling grey ocean. It was drizzling, though the sun still shone, and the breeze was chilly. I sat there for a long time, until Marthelm came over. He grabbed me by the shoulder.

'I am humiliated, what would my father say?' I asked him.

'There is no shame in doing what you must do to avenge your people.'

'He made me suck his nipple, I felt like a baby.'

Marthelm laughed. This was just the second time I heard him laugh.

'You even laugh at me,' I said.

'It is funny,' he said, 'but forget it, yes? Now we will fight against the Hillmen, and you will have your revenge, yes?'

A horn sounded. We both perked up and looked toward the trackway that led from the glen to the fort. Three dark figures came on foot, and we headed toward them. They were three Hillmen, the one in the centre holding a wreath of flowers, and the other two showing their palms. They were met by Eponians ahorse at the gate, and the Hillmen entered.

Hours later, we found out that peace had been obtained. The Hillmen sued for peace and promised to deliver ten cartloads of grain, ten cattle, and ten sacks of iron ore to king Fenn Beg Corm. We soon learned that the Hillmen had been defeated in the north of Skye, whose clans rebelled and launched an attack on the weakened Hillmen as soon as the so-called queen Slighan diverted more men to Dun Torrin. The Hillmen reached peace with the northern clans also, though Slighan still retained most of Skye. Fenn Beg Corm announced another feast, and this one in the honour of the Cailleach, and at the behest of the Hillmen.

I could never enjoy that, Luceo. I just brooded, ate little, and resented Fenn Beg Corm. I resented that he had my oath. I resented that he lusted for Myrnna. I resented that he made peace with the Hillmen. Now, what am I oathbound to? Shall we raid the northerners? Shall we make excursions into Rùm or Eigg and hump the sheep there? Shall we journey to Eire to war for the kings of Connacht or Ulster? Shall we sail west, to Kilda, or further west, where the druids say there is land with white bears and men who can't drink milk? I said nothing. My men drank, gambled, and whored. Myrnna said nothing either, or we avoided each other's eyes. Most of all, I resented eating in the name of the Cailleach, who gave me my gift or curse. I slept, or rather, just lay there in my tent, eyes raised to the whiteness of the full moon.

The next day, I decided to return home again to bury Bodvoc. The Dobunni lads, Marthelm, and Chaser formed the party, and I headed homeward.

CHAPTER XXIII

My farm looked so dark from where we stood. We walked toward it, through the puddles and slog of the trackway. It had been raining all night and our feet were caked in mud. There were fresh hoof tracks on the trackway; an Eponian patrol or hunting party. They could not have been Hillmen, since Hillmen hate horses, just like they hate iron, bronze, and druids.

The roofs of the house had been rethatched. The byre, where my cousins had died, had been demolished and a new one raised. There were cattle in the fields again, although not mine, since they were all yearlings, but they should have belonged to me if they grazed on my pasture.

The farm looked peopled, as did all the farms in the area. The smell of peat from the hearthfire rose from the house. There were men, women, and children all working. Women ground grain. Sheep, goats, and cattle were tended to in the fields. Hogs and ducks were fed. Dogs barked as we approached along the trackway. There were men knapping flint, and the chips and flakes of flint littered the entryway to my farm as we walked right onto it.

I had no fear of the Hillmen. We had peace, and I was here not to war but to bury my dead brother's skull.

What stood on the path struck me. It struck me harder, harder than being Badb-stricken, fiercer than being Camulus-stricken, and more enchanting than being Osimus-stricken. There was a shining one on the pathway, the stone-lined path that led to the entrance of my house. I said nothing because I could find no words, no thoughts, and only a prayer to whatever god listened to whisk me away from this evil.

'Brenn, is that you?' the shining one asked. He was shirtless, tall, with dyed-black hair, a budding moustache, brown-striped, green trousers – which I was told were the colours of Slighan – and an iron sword at his side in a scabbard. The shining ones were permitted to use iron, while the Hillmen shun iron, hate iron, spite iron. Now this shining one, iron-armed, spoke to me, and I felt enthralled by his voice.

'You're alive,' he said. 'Really?'

I stood in contrast to him. I had my green cloak, yellow tunic, green-yellow check trousers, felt rusty-yellow hat, and *Vidav* strapped to my side in the scabbard Verc made for me. My hair and beard were still short, though fuzzy now, and it would have been difficult for anyone to recognize me that knew me before Dun Ashaig fell. Now I hardly knew, yet knew deeply so, the one who stood before me.

'Why are you here?' He asked.

'To bury Bodvoc,' I said.

'Isn't he already buried?'

'Not his skull, last I was here.'

We came closer, and then he put a hand on my face.

'Good to see you.'

'Good to see you too, Fennigus.'

'I'll help you deal with his skull.'

I had nothing else to say. I just walked over to the midden where Bodvoc's body had been tossed. My men waited at the road, and then more shining ones came on the hill and watched us. Bodvoc's skull hung propped on a post in the centre of the midden. We took it down and placed it on a small wicker mat, picked up shovels, and then got to work. Hoofbeats sounded the Eponian riders. They sat horsed and watched us from the road, and their leader dismounted and approached us.

Fennigus and I got to work on the midden. I turned my head to the Eponian approaching, and found him to be Talorc. Talorc was not an Eponian. Being the prince, he was above them. He rode with them, though, and now he approached us looking confused.

'What are you doing, Vidav?' he asked me.

'Vidav?' Fennigus asked me.

'I'm no longer Brennus,' I said. I handed the shovel to Talorc and grabbed the grip of my sword. I unsheathed *Vidav* and the shining ones on the hill alerted, but relaxed when I flipped it over and handed it to Fennigus. Fennigus took it, balanced the blade on his finger, then turned away from me and waved it around.

'A bronze sword,' he said.

'*Vidav* is the name of the sword, and my name now,' I said.

Fennigus handed me back the sword. 'I liked Brenn better.'

'Cammios named me,' I said. I sheathed *Vidav*.

'What? Cammios?' Fennigus asked.

'Yes, Cammios.'

'Did he tell you what he did?' Fennigus asked, his face reddening.

'No.'

'Back at the battle, he made a deal with the Hillmen to hand his warriors over to them. They let him go in return – they usually execute druids, you know. My boys and I all became oathbound to the queen of the Hillmen thanks to him,' he said, as he turned to the midden and dug into it hard.

Cammios, you wretched bastard. I hope it hurt.

'He's dead now.'

'We're under her oath until Samhain.'

'And I under Fenn Beg Corm,' I said.

We dug into the midden, and soon it began shrinking, and the spoil pile on the other side of the trackway rose. Talorc sat down and watched us, undoubtfully to tattle to his father what I had been up to.

The midden had been dug down completely. There was pottery in there, shells, old animal bones, peat and who knows what else, and plenty of human bones, and what I thought were dog bones. They were all strewn, and we piled them all up. There were three skulls, probably the slaves, and half the skull of Lappie.

'So, we should build a mound, right near the road, so all that pass know a brave man died there,' I said.

'No,' Fennigus said, 'his skull should be mounted on my horse, so that my enemies know that a brave man's shade protects me.'

'Why should it be your horse? I found him.'

'Your horse is dead.'

'I will get another.'

'Then you could have him for half the year, and I the other half.'

'But what about the mound?' Talorc asked.

'Yeah, what about the mound? He should be buried like dad is, with Lappie and the slaves in his grave,' I said.

'No, it is not our custom to build burial mounds,' Fennigus said.

'Said the Hillman,' Talorc said.

'Take that back!' Fennigus said in a low voice, lip raised. 'We are not Hillmen! Hillmen don't use iron weapons. We are different!'

Fennigus looked gruffly at me. 'Who is this annoying little midge that sits here and bites my ear?'

'The son of Fenn Beg Corm,' I said.

'And why is he here? To watch you, like a child? Leave us,' he said.

'I am the prince of Dun Torrin – Vidav, is this the queen's puppy?'

Fennigus dropped the shovel. 'Off with you, you runty little princeling.'

'Answer, Vidav,' Talorc said. 'Is he the queen's puppy?'

'Just who is this queen – why does she have the same name as the Slighan Hill?' I asked.

'She was born on Slighan peak, to a giantess,' Fennigus said, and then Talorc spoke.

'Vidav – is he the queen's puppy?'

'Looks like it,' I said, and before I could say and *I am Fenn Beg Corm's puppy*, Fennigus drew his sword. Talorc rose to his feet, and showed his palms.

'I'm unarmed,' he said, 'and it was Vidav who called you the queen's puppy, not me.'

Fennigus looked at me, he did not sheath his sword, but he lowered it.

'Should the Hillmen have your brother's skull, Vidav?' Talorc asked.

'Stay out of this!' Fennigus yelled at him.

And now, Luceo, I erred. I erred badly, but I do not regret it, because the skull of Bodvoc does not belong to the Hillmen.

'You're a Hillman,' I said, and I snatched the skull from the ground. 'And I'm taking it, Fennigus.'

He sneered. 'No, you're not.'

'I am.'

'No.'

'Yes.'

I turned to walk away, and Fennigus dropped his sword and grabbed the skull. He tried to yank it out of my hand, and I dug my fingers into poor old Bodvoc's eye sockets. I dug my feet into the ground and pulled against Fennigus with all I could, and Fennigus pulled back, hard, and harder, and then he grinned and let go. I plummeted backward, the skull flying out of my hands. I thudded to the ground and the skull crashed upon a boulder, and shattered the nose bones. Both Fennigus and I said nothing.

'He broke your brother's skull!' Talorc said.

'You!' Fennigus snatched the sword from the ground and rushed Talorc. Talorc raised his palms to Fennigus, but Fennigus raised his sword. Talorc fled. He fled down the trackway, vaulted over the fence, all the while shouting for his men who had gone to idle somewhere. They came back now, at-arms, and now Fennigus whistled for his boys.

My eyes drew back to the skull of Bodvoc, cracked, face broken, and now Fennigus and the boys and Talorc and his men posed for battle. They clashed there on the pasture.

I escaped. I crossed the trackway and into the moorlands, and met my men there as the clamour of battle erupted behind me. I spun around, hand on my hilt, and there nine shining ones sword-danced against nine Eponians. The gold of the shining ones sparkled in the grey day as they manoeuvred against the long shields and long bright swords of the Eponians.

There, the now black-haired Fennigus dodged, and parried, and thrust, and pivoted against an Eponian with wild black hair. My brother and his foe snapped into combat, went blow for blow, and snapped back unscathed, then again. Fennigus' sweat glistened in the sun under his glowing gold, his iron sword singing through the air. I found myself short of breath as I gazed upon his duel.

'They can fight this themselves,' Marthelm said. 'They didn't help us against the shining ones.'

'It's too bad,' I said. 'It's been too long since I've fought.'

What a lie, Luceo. I sighed and smiled, and we all walked down the trackway, away from the fight.

My home melded into the redness of the moors as we headed down the trackway, Dun Torrin bound. The last I saw of my home was the smoke from the hearthfire billowing into the sky. An Eponian rider raced past us. I left Fennigus there, fighting at my home. I did not worry for him, because I knew he'd win that fight. He was Biturix's son, after all.

In the high afternoon, we arrived at Dun Torrin. Much commotion had budded, with warriors gathered in clusters, and Fenn Beg Corm standing on a dais flanked by his druids. We learned that peace with the Hillmen had ended. The war began again.

At nightfall, I waited for the last embers of the fire to flicker out outside our tents. Everyone had gone to sleep except the sentries that now guarded Dun Torrin by torchlight, Marthelm and I, and even Chaser, who slept under my feet.

'It's late,' Marthelm said, 'go to bed. The Hillmen may attack at daybreak.'

'I can't sleep.'

'You must sleep.'

'But I can't.'

'You were hoping that peace would last until Samhain, when your brother would have been relieved of his oath, yes?'

'That damn Talorc,' I said. 'Just who does he think he is, starting up a fight like that? I should have shooed him away as soon as I realized what he was doing.'

'Do not dwell on the backward, just forward, like our march down the strand.'

I sighed and it grew darker around, I reached into my pouch and fingered the ivory lion-man, a visage of my ancestor.

'I don't want to fight him,' I said.

'It does not matter what you want, it matters what the spinsters have spun for us.'

'The spinsters spin me wrong. He'd beat me, anyway. He is a much better fighter.'

'Then you will train, so you would give him a good fight.'

The last ember died. It was all dark now, save for the torchlights gliding outside the walls of the fort, and in the distant hills.

'If I have to fight him, then I want to make him proud.'

Marthelm stood up, and put a hand on my shoulder.

'Fight proud, for one of you will die first, and when you meet the other in the afterlife, you can then look each other in the eyes.'

He left.

I sat in in the dark silence for a spell. I knew now that I would have to fight Fennigus.

For a price...

Come back to the Slighan Hill!

EPILOGUE

My voice wanes now, my dearest Luceo! Now the fire blazes bright, the smoke is so dense that it clogs our throats, and the food so savoury that our mouths water when we think of it. We have a good life, my man. I am hoarse like a frog.

We've gone for a long ride. I don't have much more to say tonight, I feel myself right to settle down into my bed and sleep like the frog I sound like.

'It was a long tale, my lord. Get some rest. Tomorrow Osimus will light the fire again, and you will tell me of the war before Samhain, and the events that led me to you.'

'Yes, indeed! It is so cold outside, we have little to do but to speak, unless we are assaulted tomorrow. We have full bellies, warm feet, and women in our beds. How can we possibly convince the men to go lift some cattle in the snow?'

'But tell me, Luceo. I've poured everything to you, overflowed, like a drunken wine-pourer. What shall you leave out?'

'A lot, my lord. Some things are best left out, and some things are best put in. It's the will of the gods what the bards record, and not the work of man. Besides, it all ought to rhyme.'

'You bards weave strange tales.'

'Lord, your posterity will thank me for it!'

If you liked Hag of the Hills, please let me know by leaving a review.

AFTERWORD

This work is what I term heroic prehistoric fantasy fiction. Prehistoric does not mean cavemen, stone tools, and primitiveness, but simply that people did not write their history down themselves. They instead had oral traditions, and we know much about them from archaeological research. Moreover, others – namely the Romans and Greeks – wrote about them.

As an archaeologist, it is imperative that I stress that this is a work of fiction. I have taken great artistic liberty with many aspects of the Iron Age of Britain, as well as contemporary Europe and its myriad cultures and peoples. The book deals specifically with cultures most people would term *Celts*. It must be said that the people we could call Celts were not a monolithic culture, but a plethora of different cultures, with differing mores, beliefs, two separate languages (P and Q Celtic), and so forth. Nevertheless, some common threads do unite what we could call the *Celts* from linguistic to material culture. Someone attuned to various scholarly debates about the *Celts* will undoubtfully have picked up that the characters themselves often recognize these nuances.

That being said, I do appreciate and yearn for historical accuracy in period fiction. I find it a shame that so few depictions of the past, particularly peoples such as Celts or Vikings in media hardly understand the people or periods they are portraying. It ought to change, because it is better to strive for historical accuracy while taking artistic liberties. Stories about the past will become richer when they are enriched by historical sources, from archaeological, textual, folkloric, linguistic, anthropological, and so forth. The incredible amount of research put forth by academics, past and present, should not be neglected by fiction writers. Nonfiction is often conducted with love, and most researchers love the people and the past they dedicate their lives to studying, and fiction writers can only better their stories with that love.

In retrospect, I believe that I have done an adequate job in depicting many aspects of the world of 200 B.C. as accurately as possible while still employing artistic liberties. Most of all, I was unafraid to attempt to portray the past as how I interpreted someone living in 200 B.C. would have experienced it, that is, often alien and uncomfortable to a reader in the 21st century. It however must be reiterated that much of what we know about the past, especially the distant past, is open to interpretation, and neither I nor anyone else can ever claim complete and utter historical accuracy, no matter how ideal the interpretation.

This book focuses on Celtic mythology. As Professor J.R.R. Tolkien wrote: "[Celtic myths] have bright colour, but are like a broken stained-glass window reassembled without design. They are in fact mad."

Those familiar with Celtic mythology will understand that I mixed deities and the spellings of deities from different Celtic languages, figures, and concepts from a blend of Irish mythology, Welsh mythology, Gallo-Roman, and Romano-British attestations, and later folklore from England, Wales, Man, Ireland, and especially Scotland. This was intentional, and I refer to the great professor to sum up the reasons for this.

APPENDIX

This book contains some references to words that may not be apparent or known to the average reader. I have composed a short guide here:

AMAZONS – legendary warrior women from Greek myth, often depicted on classical Greek art, such as the bas-reliefs of the Parthenon. Said to inhabit the northern part of the Black Sea. Referred to in Celtic myths.

BARDS – first attested by Roman sources, a bard is a common word in the modern English language. In the context of this book, these are historians and record keepers. They are also poetry-crafters and are able to praise or besmirch others with their rhymes.

DRUIDS – first attested to in Roman sources, and continuing to be attested in Irish (medieval) myth, this is a complicated term for an even more complicated aspect of Iron Age Britain, often hotly debated by scholars. In short, druids were likely a priestly ruling class, that may have been engaged in more than just religious rituals, but lawyers, judges, generals, rulers, physicians, and other professions all rolled into one. A *druidess* is a woman druid, attested to in Irish myth.

VATES – these were a priestly profession mentioned by Roman sources that interpret the signs of the gods, such as the flight-paths of birds, or what the entrails suggest of an animal after sacrifice.

PERSONAL NAMES

CELTIC NAMES – a good portion of the names here come from Greek or Roman attestations. The casual reader of Roman history would have heard of at least one, Brennus. The enjoyer of Celtic Iron Age coins will notice that a great deal of the names of the Celts are from inscriptions of the coins, probably minted by chiefs or petty kings whose namesakes are on the coins. These names are identifiably Celtic, but were written in either classical Latin or ancient Greek. I am aware of the fact that some of these names are in the genitive or vocative cases – and I have chosen to consider them as nicknames.

LATIN OR ITALIC NAMES – these were chosen from a variety of available written sources.

GERMAN NAMES – the majority of these names are from reconstructions of the Proto-Germanic language that the Germanic peoples would have been speaking at the time.

GREEK NAMES – names of Greeks were chosen through a variety of available written sources.

HISTORICAL FIGURES

The historical figures listed below are mentioned in the story, but not included as characters.

ALEXANDER – ALEXANDER THE GREAT (356 B.C. – 10/11 June 323 BC). Emperor.

BRENNUS (circa 4th century B.C.) – the Gaul who pillaged Rome in 387 BC.

BRENNUS (circa 3rd century B.C.) – the Gaul who pillaged Greece in 278 BC.

HANNIBAL BARCA (247 B.C. – 183 – 181 B.C.) – Carthaginian ruler who invaded Italy in the Second Punic War (218 – 201 B.C.) Referred to as *the warlord*.

LEONIDAS I (? - 480 B.C.) – King of Sparta.

Other peoples in the ancient world are referenced directly or indirectly: Anatolians; Britons; Boii; Cat (from modern Caithness, Scotland); Carthaginians; Chinese (Sinai); Dobunni; Etruscans; Egyptians; Ethiopians; Finns; Gauls; Germans; Greeks (including Athenians & Spartans); Indians; Irish (Hibernians); Jews; Macedonians; Nemidians; Persians; Phoenicians; Romans; Scandinavians; Scythians; Thracians; Ulstermen; Umbrians.

SUBSCRIBE TO MY NEWSLETTER

Receive the first chapter of the second book in
THE BRONZE SWORD CYCLES duology
if you sign up with your e-mail address!

Exclusive content and author updates!

SCAN THE QR CODE BELOW &
ENTER E-MAIL ADDRESS TO SUBSCRIBE

www.oldworldheroism.com

Printed in Great Britain
by Amazon

21141936R00164